TAKING DOWN THE DEEP STATE

SUMMER HEAT II

NATALIE TRIUMPHS

HOUSE OF INDIGO

PROLOGUE

The excitement of the enormous crowd was almost uncontrollable as eager fans, curious observers, civil rights activists, reporters and some onlookers with nefarious motives waited for the plane to approach. Under DHS's and TSA's current procedures, the public was not allowed to greet the passengers as they walked off the plane. People inside the terminal were texting those outside with updates from the arrival monitor.

The ages of those eagerly awaiting the arrival ranged from newborns to people in their nineties, united in their quest to end the torture and halt the death count of America's teens.

The exhilaration was over a group of five American teens who were returning to the US to testify before the United Nations General Assembly about the torture and killing of young Americans in what had become nicknamed Gulag Camps, Gulag Schools and Gulag Programs. These were privately-run billion-dollar behavior modification operations that were largely unregulated.

The anticipated teens, known as the Wilderness Five, had made a major impact when they exposed the corruption of these American Gulags and of the parents, who had knowingly sent their own children off to be tortured or fixed, as the camps called it.

"There it is," a man with binoculars yelled. All the news stations turned their cameras in the direction to which he pointed as an aircraft approached the spiral of landing planes.

"He's right," a cameraman with a telephoto lens acknowledged. "It's got the Latin American Express Airline colors on the side."

The crowd cheered. Teens, adolescents and little kids jumped up and down, hollering with wild delight, believing this group of activist teenagers would change the way they and all of America's youth were treated.

Some of the excited teens and children watching the arrival started a chant: "Two, four, six, eight, who do we appreciate" but that's as far as the chant got as a loud explosion shook the crowd into silence and the plane they had been watching burst into flames and dust in midair.

"Oh, no!" observers in the crowd cried out. Parents tried to pull their little kids away as thousands of observers burst into tears.

"What happened, Mommy?" was a question echoed by several of the younger observers. Some of the teenagers watching screamed, "Down with the government!"

Some words that caught my attention were from the man with the binoculars, who pointed at the sky, yelling, "It was a missile! I saw a missile hit it!"

Santana put his arm around me as he, Bruce and Alonzo pulled me, Abigail and Emily back towards the parking area. Emily was actively sobbing. I, myself, had tears streaming down my face. Santana tried to wipe them away. Abigail looked like she was ready to go into combat.

"We've got to get out of here," Alonzo said. We were wearing Yankee t-shirts, caps and sunglasses, looking like tourists as we made our way to the car that had been rented by the Cuban Embassy. I kept thinking about the people aboard the plane: the pilot, the crew and the passengers. If the explosion had been a few seconds later, the planes in the spiral, also, would have been hit by debris, and there might have been even more deaths.

Guilt swept through me. We had escaped by switching flights in the post-check-in area of the airport in Georgia while our decoys and unsuspecting passengers died in our place. We had expected trouble when we got off the plane in New York, but not this. There was no doubt in my mind the explosion was meant for us.

"We came here to save lives and we've brought death," I lamented.

"They brought death," Alonzo countered. "You are not responsible for their actions."

"My daddy's body count continues to rise," Abigail angrily retorted.

"You don't know it's him," Bruce told her.

She glared at him.

"You're his daughter. He wouldn't kill his own daughter."

She continued glaring.

"You've got a new family now," I said, dampening her shoulder with my teary face as I hugged her. "We all do."

CHAPTER 1

The United Nations facility was between First Avenue and the FDR, near the East River in Midtown Manhattan. We entered through the underground parking structure, uncertain of how we would be received. We were accompanied by Ambassador Ricardo Sanchez, who had been newly appointed over the summer, and Alonzo Martina, my mom's new boyfriend and a prominent criminal defense attorney in Cuba. Alonzo quickly rushed ahead to the Office for The Coordination of Humanitarian Affairs to let them know of our presence and the need for secrecy.

Closing his eyes, shaking his head and with downturned lips, Ambassador Sanchez said, "My assistant was on that plane."

"I'm so sorry," I replied.

"It's not any of your faults. There are some very dark forces around that do not want you to speak today," he said.

"Alejandro!" Emily cried. "I've got to let him know I'm alive." Emily, who was fourteen and the youngest of our group, had found her first romance in Cuba with Alejandro. He had wanted to join us but his parents vetoed the idea. Now, I was glad he'd stayed behind.

"Alonzo's nephew? That kid won't believe any stories of our

deaths, and he'll see you soon enough when your testimony is broadcast," Ricardo told her.

We passed through the basement as people stood around watching television screens, showing the legacy news: ABC, CNN, CBS, NBC, BBC, Fox and others. All were listing us as dead, along with other unnamed passengers. This was nothing new. After escaping the American teen Gulag Camp, contractors tied to the U.S. Government thought they had succeeded in killing us multiple times before the Cuban Government granted us asylum.

As we entered the elevator, Ambassador Sanchez turned to us. "They think they got you. Are you sure you want to speak? You might be safer keeping out of sight until whoever did this is caught."

"We came here to testify," I said. My companions nodded.

"You think we will wait until they catch the whole US Deep State?" Abigail responded with a ready-to-kill look in her eyes. "They tried to kill us, and we are going to fight back, let the world know what they have done, make them pay for what they have done. They don't get to blow up our plane."

"Them's fight'n words," Santana said. "And I support that."
Bruce nodded.

I looked at Emily. She had been through so much. "Are you sure you want to go before the General Assembly? Or would you like to stay safe, behind the scenes, while we deliver your speech?"

"I'm not going to be left out. I was there as my friends died. Abigail's right. They don't get to do this."

We met up with Alonzo at the Office for The Coordination of Humanitarian Affairs. He moved us into the inner office and informed me, "I've contacted your mother to let her know you are all right. She's busy helping Rosa with the natural gas situation at her farm after last week's storm. "

"Is it going to damage her crops?" I asked.

"The government will be exercising care. The resources belong to everyone, but the food supply is also important. So, they are making sure to keep the organic produce organic."

"The kids are determined to tell their story. We need to get extra security for the hearing," Ambassador Sanchez said.

"I know. I tried to talk them out of speaking on the way to New York. These teens are unstoppable and far too brave for their own good."

"We know what the other teens are still going through in those camps and schools. We got out and we owe it to those who are still prisoners," Santana insisted, looking at me and almost taking the words out of my mouth.

After we had changed from our travel clothes into more formal speaking attire and returned to the inner office, Alonzo nodded approvingly. A call came through for Ambassador Sanchez. He picked it up and said, "Send them in." He turned to us. "You have some visitors."

The door opened, and Shannon and Jimmy came in. I ran over and hugged them. "I've missed you two." Shannon was my best friend before going to the camp. Jimmy was her boyfriend.

"We weren't going to miss your speeches, not for a million dollars."

"Well—maybe for a million dollars," Jimmy countered. Shannon punched his arm playfully. "Okay, two million."

"You came to New York, just to see us?" I asked.

"Actually, Jimmy was accepted into Columbia, but my mom was more eager to let me come to see you than to hang out with Jimmy in Manhattan."

"Congratulations," I said.

"You knew I had been accepted here," Jimmy reminded me. "I was thinking of Berkeley, but they missed their chance to accept me."

"Berkeley's hard to get into," I said. "But Columbia. Obama went there."

"Don't remind me. Mr. One into Seven Wars is not a great example to follow."

"It could be worse. I think new Presidents try to beat the previous war-creation records."

"Tiffany wanted to be here, but her parents were afraid for all our safety." Tiffany had been my other close friend from high school. "You can count on her watching your speech online."

"We need to go to the floor, now," Ambassador Sanchez advised.

"We'll be watching," Shannon said. She and Jimmy gave me another hug.

I looked at Emily. Her eyes were a little cloudy. "What's wrong? Second thoughts?"

"No. I just wish Alejandro could see me."

"They're broadcasting this in Cuba. Even another of your Deep State's fire and hail storms couldn't keep him from watching," Alonzo assured her. "I bet he and your new mom Rosa are anxiously awaiting your return."

She smiled and looked down at her outfit. "He said this was his favorite of my dresses. Do I look okay?"

There was something heartwarming about watching Emily's first love. Alejandro had helped save our lives in Cuba and never stopped believing in us—even after we had lied about our identities and wound up in a Cuban prison. His aunt Rosa had given all of us a temporary home on her Cuban farm and had adopted Emily, whose birth parents had had their daughter kidnapped to the Gulag camp, from which we had barely escaped with our lives.

"You look beautiful. You always do." I gave her a hug.

"Hey, something important, really important, before we go in," Santana said. He placed his hands on my shoulders with a serious look and then leaned in and kissed me.

"I could get into this," Bruce stated as he embraced Abigail.

I had to recenter myself and remember where I was as Santana released me. I looked at Emily and gave her a hug. "We'll be home soon enough and I'm sure you'll get one the moment you step off the plane."

"Did you guys go to a Gulag Camp or a dating center?" Jimmy teased.

Shannon playfully slapped his shoulder.

There were one hundred and ninety-three nations represented in the General Assembly. It did not have the power of the Security Council, but it did represent international opinion.

Most of those present had heard of us. As we listened to the English translation of his words, the Secretary-General, who was from Portugal, signaled for us to come onto the stage.

"I'd like to introduce five very courageous young Americans who survived many human rights abuses and attempts on their lives: Abigail Kreskin, Summer Tanner, Santana Barilla, Bruce Jenkens and Emily Hattan."

We walked onto the stage to a standing ovation from representatives of nations around the world.

To our disappointment but not surprise, the newly appointed American Ambassador to the United Nations, Mickey Comet rose and objected.

"How did she get appointed?" Abigail whispered.

"The last one wasn't Deep State enough," I quietly replied. "The intelligence community is working its way into controlling everything."

"These teens are Americans. They do not have the permission of their custodians to speak, and the U.S. does not authorize their appearance." Comet's words were met with loud boos that seemed to come from every corner.

The Cuban Ambassador rose. "All five have been adopted by Cuban families because their American custodial parents sent them off to be tortured in conditions that violate the Geneva Conventions. The Government of Cuba is sponsoring their speeches. Which other nations will join us in sponsoring these teens?"

Representatives from what looked like more than one hundred and ninety nations rose.

"The matter is settled," the Secretary-General declared.

Emily went first. "My name is Emily Hattan. I am fourteen years old. My parents thought I would be a more proper girl if I went to a wilderness camp. The school counselor sold it as a great educational experience. But I didn't want to go. So they had me kidnapped in the middle of the night. I was cable-tied. I struggled and was hit hard.

"When I got to the camp, I was stripped, hogtied and put into isolation. Because I didn't express joy over the treatment, I was whipped. The whipping left welts on my back that didn't go away. One of the nicer people in the camp was a guy named Jason. He tried to help my friend Summer and was subjected to shock treatments and died from them. Another nice boy, Jamie, was hung. One of the girls in my tent was gang-raped and bled to death. Other kids died horribly. We found the bodies of little kids who had died in what we called the little kids camp. Young kids were forced to have sex.

"I got out alive. I was lucky. After I escaped, a wonderful woman adopted me. I was told I did not have to speak, but I wanted to. It's not about us. We got out. It's about the teens who are still in these camps. They need your help."

The members of the Assembly stood in a long-standing ovation that seemed to go on and on. Then someone started shouting, "Emily!" and others echoed her name. The support and shouts lasted for more than ten minutes. I went over to Emily and hugged her. She was like the little sister I never had but always wanted. "They love you," I whispered to her. Nobody else could hear me because of the thunderous applause.

Next, Abigail spoke. Her hair had grown back in. It was short but very green. I was hoping that she would avoid discussions of wanting to Menendez her dad and stick to what we had discussed. Of course, Abigail was always someone to do whatever she chose, and nobody could change that. That's what I loved about her.

"My father is the Secretary of Defense of the United States. He didn't send me there blindly. He had visited the camp before he sent me there. There are parents who should never have children. He was one of them. Children should have the right to refuse torture. I was attacked by guard dogs because I tried to escape. And that was just some of the torture. There was a law on the books in the state where I was held, but nobody was enforcing it. Nobody is monitoring these camps. Though my camp had the children of a lot of leaders, we were not the exception when it came to torture. We were the rule. Everyone here has to decide for themselves whether they will pay lip service to opposing torture or whether you will actively work to stop the abuses in the American teen Gulag camps and to arrest and prosecute everyone who runs these camps and everyone who has sent children to these camps."

"Bravo" and "Yea" echoed through the thunderous applause that was even louder than Emily's. Emily and I hugged Abigail. "Good job," I told her.

"I held back," Abigail whispered. "If I told them what I really thought about the camp administrators and my dad—"

"I know. You did good. I think the leaders, here, are ready to arrest and prosecute your dad. The world already doesn't like his war policies."

"The sooner, the better," Abigail replied.

Bruce looked nervous. He gave Abigail a hug before stepping up to the mike.

"Go get 'em, tiger," she encouraged him.

"My name is Bruce Jenkens. My parents are scientists. They are supposed to be smart. When the counselor at school told them going to a behavior modification school would help me get into M.I.T., they listened. I even listened. I was sent to a Gulag school and then a camp. Like Emily, I decided against the agenda and was also tortured in both programs. No learning takes place in the American Gulag schools or camps. I was hog-tied, beaten, forced to engage in violent fights, like my friend Santana, and subjected to other inhuman conditions. Some of us were goaded into hanging ourselves. Quite a number of teens have died that way. In addition to the beatings, starvation and dehydration, we were also subjected to mind-games where they tried to use drugs and programing to get us to hurt others. We were ordered to do bodily harm to others and we were microchipped. What we went through is reminiscent of the mind-control experiments the U.S. Government has acknowledged its MK Ultra did in the Twentieth Century. Kids are not an experiment, and they should not be programmed to become violent."

A sound of shock went through the audience, followed by another standing ovation.

Next Santana spoke. "My name is Santana Barillo. My father is Congressman Barillo from California. I was a bit rebellious, but there are better ways to treat rebelliousness than with torture. When I was a kid, I looked up to my dad." He looked at me and then back at the audience. "What kind of a father sends their child off to be tortured? I was locked in a box, naked, beaten with chains, choked, forced to engage in violent fights and ordered to keep beating up the other kid once he was down on the ground and unable to continue fighting.

"As horrible as it was, I was also lucky. At that camp, I met Summer Tanner, the love of my life and they almost killed her. Even if I could forgive them for what they did to me, I could never forgive them for the torture Summer underwent. She is the most courageous person I have ever known."

This wasn't fair. Santana had me in tears. Everyone was interrupting his speech with applause. I wiped the tears, hoping to stay composed.

"Summer and I would have perished together in that camp, along with Abigail, Emily and Bruce if not for Paul, the son of camp director Evan Saunders, who helped us get out before he died trying to rescue others. Though Paul didn't make it, I will always remember his courage and be grateful to him for saving the person that matters most in my life."

He held out his arms. I moved into them, and he gave me a hug and then a kiss that weakened my knees, making it hard to stand, right in front of everyone. Only his strong grip prevented me from collapsing to the floor.

Not until Santana released me, did I hear the applause. As I turned towards the audience, I saw that everyone was standing and cheering, some shedding tears, themselves. The whole thing left me speechless. I was supposed to speak next, but I could barely think, let alone speak.

I stepped up to the microphone. "I—I. It's hard for me to speak after that. And usually, I'm not speechless." I heard a laugh. "Santana is amazing. All my friends who came here with me are amazing. Emily was thirteen when she had to endure that torture. Abigail is so brave and strong. She and Emily are my sisters. Bruce is so wise. Without these friends and other friends who came here to see me today, I wouldn't be standing here before you. I, too, was kidnapped. I was tased, beaten, cable-tied, handcuffed, water-boarded, stripped, left naked in a dark box for days and tied to a tree in the sun with no clothes to protect me from burning. I saw kids killed. Jason tried to save me. As Emily said, he died by electrocution."

I listened as the audience started shouting my name and applauding my speech. Looking down, I could see tears in the eyes of even more of the delegates.

I continued. "Sonja Jackson was my friend too. She was gang-raped. They let her bleed to death. As Santana said, Paul died trying to save lives. He got us the evidence you saw in that footage that was released. So many died, and I don't know if their deaths will make a difference. Are you willing to act? To let their lives count for something? Or did they all die in vain? It's up to you."

The full Assembly—all except the American Ambassador— stood up, again, and applauded us. Five, ten, twenty minutes and they still stood.

We went down the steps and sat next to Ambassador Sanchez and Alonzo in the audience.

"Great job," Alonzo congratulated us.

"You have them in the palms of your hands," Ambassador Sanchez said, looking at the continuing applause.

We listened to the rest through translators. The Secretary-General stated, "What we have heard today represents numerous violations of the Universal Declaration of Human Rights and of United Nations Convention on the Rights of the Child. I would like it to be moved that we find the United States in violation of these rights and call for an accounting of all children in these behavior modification programs and an end to the existence of such programs."

"I so move," the South African Ambassador's translation came as he stood.

"I second," was translated from the Spanish Ambassador.

"Wait," shouted, Mickey Comet. "Before you vote on this, I wish to speak."

"You will be given an opportunity to speak in opposition," the Secretary-General's translation said.

Delegate after delegate spoke with clarity on the need to protect, not torture, children and on the unconscionable cruelty authorized by the United States in allowing such camps and schools to exist.

Mickey Comet took the floor. "I have just had word that a grand jury has just indicted these Cuban Five for violations of the Espionage

Act of 1917. They turned over information vital to America to various news media and to the Cuban Government, evaded law enforcement, vicariously caused the deaths of numerous citizens and caused irreparable damage to the Angeles National Forest."

CHAPTER 2

I tried to hold Abigail down, but she pushed up out of my arms, crying out, "Who are the terrorists? Your government tried to have us killed because we knew too much. We didn't go to Cuba for vacation. We went there so we wouldn't die at your hands."

"We don't want to hear your conspiracy theories," Mickey replied.

I turned to Alonzo. "Will they arrest us the moment we try to leave the building?"

"They may try. Here you have immunity. They will try to attack it because you are Americans, but it should hold. You also have immunity in our embassy's car but the U.S. has trouble respecting immunity. We'll figure something out."

"Even if we survive long enough to leave, we'll never be able to come back to the States unless the charges are lifted," Bruce pointed out.

"Conspiracy theories?" Santana shouted. "Were Afghanistan, Iraq, Libya, Syria, Yemen and the rest of America's wars conspiracy theories or did our government choose to attack them, like it chose to attack us?"

There was chatter in different languages all over the room. The Secretary General called for the clamber to settle down.

Next up was the ambassador from Venezuela. He was speaking in Spanish. Even without my earphones, I recognized two names, "Edward Snowden" and "Julian Assange." I put back on the headphones. His next words translated were, "The United States Government has repeatedly committed human rights violations, from wars to torture to water-boarding and instead of taking accountability for their actions, they have sought to arrest those who dare to tell the truth. Unlike every other nation in the Western Hemisphere, the United States utilizes the death penalty. There is a reason the United States is the only member that is not a party to the Convention on the Rights of the Child. This situation must be monitored, and we must adopt a resolution telling the United States to end this torture at once. I, for one, believe that the United States must join the rest of the world in supporting human rights for children and in ending the abuses of these camps. These young witnesses must be protected."

The applause was loud and long. Representative after representative stood and offered asylum to us. The support was amazing.

The Saudi ambassador stood up and echoed Mickey's words, adding, "We cannot support lawlessness anywhere or we cannot expect the United Nations, to stand up against it anywhere. We must throw out this resolution and support the right of the United States to take back these American criminals and lock them up."

That was greeted with more boos.

"That from the ambassador for a country that beheads women for disobeying their husbands," Bruce commented.

The Secretary-General called for a vote and the motion passed almost unanimously, with only four nations opposing it.

As we left the Assembly floor, numerous ambassadors told us they were certain their governments would give us asylum. Among these were the ambassadors from Venezuela, Bolivia, Russia, Spain, Slovakia, Portugal, Italy, Iran, China and Nicaragua. We thanked them.

Back in the Office for The Coordination of Humanitarian Affairs, we asked Ambassador Ricardo Sanchez, "So we're protected in traveling from here?"

"You are classified as expert members of a diplomatic mission, right now. You have the kind of diplomatic immunity that envoys have at this point."

"We should arrange to get out of town as quickly as possible," Santana suggested.

The Secretary-General entered, and we all stood up. His English was a little broken but surprisingly good.

"Thank you for your assistance," Alonzo said in English.

"My pleasure. I am very worried about the safety of these young ones. I have word the Americans are going to try to breach their immunity, claiming they have faux positions and are under American jurisdiction."

"Wonderful," Santana uttered under his breath.

"That's my daddy for you," Abigail grimaced. "They wouldn't be doing this without his consent."

"You are probably correct," the Secretary-General said. "You are safe here, but the longer you stay, the harder it will be to evade the Americans."

"We could use some assistance with decoys," Alonzo requested.

"I was going to offer. I don't support deception, but I must take every precaution to ensure your immunity is protected."

A second later, Shannon and Jimmy ran into the office. "This is crazy! You are heroes!" Shannon exclaimed.

"So is Edward Snowden," I pointed out.

"But, unlike him, you weren't NSA. They forced you into the camp. The diary and pictures were taken by Paul."

"And apparently, getting out doesn't mean we're free."

"We will do our best to protect you and to convince your country to hold back on their threat against your freedom," the Secretary-General assured us.

"Thank you," I replied. "You are very kind."

"Muy Gracias," Santana added.

"It's nice to see a leader who is sane," Abigail said. "Wish we had one in the USA."

"I can see why you deserve this position," Bruce told the Secretary-General.

Shannon turned to him, "The Americans won't stop with seeking arrests. They kept trying to kill my friends after they left the camp."

"We think we have this handled," he replied.

"It will be okay," I tried to reassure Shannon, though I wasn't convinced.

"If you need anything," Shannon said. "Jimmy and I will be here for you."

"You know that," Jimmy assured me. "Good seeing you guys again," he turned to the others. "We'll be there if you need us."

The Tunisian delegation assisted us, dressing us up in their garbs and arranging for us to leave as part of their delegation. I was surprised at their comprehension of English. They had a private plane at the airport. We wore our travel clothes underneath. One group of look-alikes for us left with Ambassador Sanchez in the clothes we had worn before the General Assembly. A set of second decoys left in more casual clothes in a separate vehicle, and a third decoy group went with the Russian delegation. Unless the place was bugged, they had no way of knowing there were even decoys.

As we exited the building and got into the Tunisian limo, we heard shots from somewhere on the street. It was starting to remind us of back in Cuba when they were gunning for us. As the limo doors closed and we took off, a feeling of doom breezed through me, but I dismissed it.

JFK Airport was on Long Island in Queens. We planned to take the Queens Midtown Tunnel in crossing the East River.

As we approached the tunnel, we could hear a massive explosion as everything we could see appeared to be shaking and debris filled the sky.

I looked at my friends. They stiffened but stayed composed. I knew I had to stay strong too. I touched Emily's hand, which was trembling, though she seemed to be hiding her feelings. Santana put his arm around me.

The Ambassador murmured what I thought was Tunisian for "My God."

Our limo turned and went onto FDR Drive, a highway that wrapped around the eastern side of Manhattan. We traveled back, past the United Nations Building, towards the Ed Koch Queensborough Bridge.

The thunderous sound of a second explosion sent chills through my body. It looked like the buildings on the island were swaying, and I silently worried that they would fall on us. Traffic stopped.

This was followed by a third and then a fourth explosion. It was difficult to see with all the debris and dust falling from the sky. The Tunisian Ambassador received a call. He shook his head and informed us, "Queen Midtown Tunnel, Ed Koch Bridge, and two smaller bridges, gone. People are being warned to stay away from tunnels and bridges."

"Do you think the Cuban delegation got across on the Brooklyn Bridge?" I asked. We had all been taking different routes to JFK International. I didn't need to be told the explosions had something to do with us.

"It's not down yet."

More explosions, debris, dust and images of rocking skyscrapers hit the city and I feared that we would be taken out next. Santana put his arms around me. I reached around and held him tight. We'd go together.

Emily, who was sitting next to me, looked terrified. Santana seemed to catch my thoughts. Santana knelt down on the floor in front of her and we both held her in our arms.

"Alejandro," she cried, maybe wondering if she would never see him again.

"We'll survive this," Santana assured her and me. "We always do."

"Bellehi awadi hatha?" the Ambassador asked into the phone. He looked worried when he turned towards us. "Brooklyn Bridge. Gone."

CHAPTER 3

Both shock and sadness hit me. The Brooklyn Bridge. I had only been over it once as a child and now there was no Brooklyn Bridge. That thought went through my mind, overshadowing what I didn't want to think or feel.

"The Cuban delegation. Were they near the bridge when it went, and what about other people traveling over it?" I finally asked. "And the other decoy limos. Are they safe?"

"We don't know," he told us. "Manhattan Bridge, also gone."

I closed my eyes. Ambassador Sanchez and Alonzo were in a car heading over the Brooklyn Bridge. I knew there would have been other vehicles and also pedestrians. I started praying that somehow the whole Cuban delegation, and all the others were safe. As we were stopped in traffic, I kept hearing explosion after explosion. More and more clouds of debris filled the air, making it harder to see.

Our driver managed to exit and turn towards the Tunisian representative offices on Beckman Place. Two more explosions could be felt and seen. The road was blocked.

Another call came. After conversing with the caller, the Ambassador informed us, "Explosions on FDR. Traffic blocked, both directions."

"It's going to be alright," Santana assured me and Emily.

But I knew it wouldn't. The thought of people being injured or worse, most likely because of our being in New York, sent a feeling of sharp needles throughout my system. I feared I might throw up. I had to hold it in. I had to keep appearing to be strong for my friends, especially for Emily. I looked at Abigail. Bruce was holding her tightly.

"We aren't going to be able to make it back to either our representative offices or to the United Nations with FDR and city streets impassable between here and either location," the Ambassador went on. People were running around in the street.

"If someone is gunning for us, we're sitting ducks in the car," Bruce pointed out.

"If you get out, the Americans will try to arrest you for your Espionage Act," the Ambassador informed us.

The driver turned down 57th Street towards Carnegie Hall. "We're trying to get out through New Jersey. Routes out of east side have been hit. West side is possible. They are letting limited traffic over George Washington Bridge and through Lincoln Tunnel. It's our best chance of getting out of Manhattan," the Ambassador explained.

Continuing on, we heard more explosions. I worried that the whole island would go at any minute. I remembered back to Cuba when unmarked planes killed all too many people in an effort to silence us. All those lives, they mattered just as much as mine, but I didn't know how to stop the carnage and I didn't want my friends killed.

We approached the Spanish Consulate as Santana asked, "Didn't they offer us asylum?"

We discussed whether to stop or continue and decided that the best bet would be to get out of the city as quickly as possible.

"Wise choice," the Ambassador confirmed as we saw a line of troopers arriving outside the front of the Spanish consulate.

"We don't know what else they have planned, but if it does have something to do with us, we need to be out of here before they kill anyone else," Bruce said. "The sooner we are gone, the fewer people they will injure or—" He looked at Abigail, who was visibly shaking in his arms. "Injure badly."

"My Dad. He's utterly okay with killing everyone in the entire city just to get me."

"All our parents are going along with this," Santana remarked. I don't think any of us doubted that all this destruction was aimed at us.

With people running through the street, panicking, not knowing where the next explosion would happen, it was a slow, long drive. People ran past the car and banged on the windows. Behind us and in front of us, there was honking. Being from California, I wasn't used to a fraction of the honking that seemed to be acceptable in New York City. We slowly crawled past Fifth Avenue.

"Any word, yet, about whether the Cuban and Russian envoys made it out?" I asked. "And what about the other decoys?"

"Everything is too much in chaos," the Ambassador said. "If we can't make it out, we have part of a floor reserved at Midtown Hilton. It will have effect of diplomatic immunity while we are there."

We moved slowly towards Sixth and then everything stopped. "Traffic is blocked. We aren't going to be able to get out this way," the driver said. There were people in the street, blocking all traffic movement.

The car turned towards the Hilton, in the general direction of Times Square. We passed the Argentinian Consulate. I couldn't recall whether they had offered us anything. The street past Fifty-Third also seemed blocked. The car turned right on Fifty-third, pulled to the side entrance of the Hilton and drove into the parking area.

"We have suites of rooms here. We can stay until things clear," the Ambassador assured us.

As we stopped and exited the vehicle, he instructed, "Keep heads down and walk in middle of our group." We did just that.

It turned out that others from the Tunisian delegation were already at the hotel, waiting on the bottom floor for us. They escorted us up to our block of rooms, and we were given a suite for the five of us.

As we entered, and looked through the window, we could see that everything was in chaos on the street below. Terrified New Yorkers were rushing in all directions, seemingly looking for safe places to hide from the next blasts. I wondered if the next one would take out the hotel. I suspected my friends were similarly concerned.

New York, like other American cities, had a large homeless population and I could only imagine how frightened they were—especially families with little babies. We learned that the South African Embassy had rooms on the floor above ours. That was reassuring as they had been another of the countries to offer us assistance.

We turned on the TV. Bridges on the east and southeast sides had been blown out. So had the tunnels. Explosions had taken place near the United Nations as well.

Raquel Madcow was speaking. *"We don't know who is responsible, but a group that has been attributed with terrorist attacks was speaking at the United Nations today. Five suspects are being sought in connection with the barbarous thuggery experienced in New York today."*

"They're blaming us!" Abigail exclaimed. "Daddy, you bastard. I know you were part of nine-eleven!"

"We have alibis," I pointed out.

"On nine-eleven, Bin Laden was in an American military hospital in Europe. He had an alibi too. And they still bombed Afghanistan as if he were there," Abigail reminded us.

"But they killed him three times, or was it four?" I tried to recall, while attempting to lighten things.

"This is more than a minor problem. There is a lot of facial recognition in this hotel. I realize we were covered and kept our heads down but it's just a matter of time before they find us," Bruce warned.

"In addition to massive destruction in Manhattan and the bridges and tunnels, they are believed to have blown up an airplane over Queens earlier today. There is a city-wide search for the terrorists."

"Now we're terrorists, that's cute," Abigail said.

I could see Santana was having as much trouble as I was getting up a sense of humor.

"They are going to kill us, aren't they?" Emily asked.

"No," I and Santana simultaneously jumped in to calm her.

I thought about the public that had been eagerly awaiting us. Now they were being bombarded with repeated coverage about what monsters we were. Once again, the mainstream media was creating its own form of brainwashing.

Former eight-term Democratic Congressman Dennis Kucinich was interviewed on CNN. *"It is unlikely that a group of kids could have committed the acts in question. They were at the United Nations and were with other diplomats from the time they entered the country to the time they left."*

"He's the one person who really deserves to be President," I said.

"How do you explain the explosion on the plane they escaped?" Madcow asked.

"That explosion may have been meant for them. There is no evidence they were tied to the explosion."

Unable to shake the courageous former leader, the station cut to a commercial break. When it returned to broadcasting, Kucinich wasn't there.

Ina, the daughter of the Tunisian ambassador came to our suite. "I brought my computer. I thought we might see what is being posted on Fakebook."

She had taped over the camera on her laptop, apparently knowing that computers can spy on us without our consent or knowledge. Before she turned it on, Bruce asked, "Which version of Windows is this?" I knew he was concerned about the spying programs that had been installed on Windows in recent years.

"Seven. I've permanently disabled the microphone and camera."

"Smart girl. Best for us to be silent when the laptop's on, anyway."

On Fakebook, she went to Diego Morinda's page. Diego was an honest newsman who had worked for various popular news organizations. He had accurately exposed the atrocities of the wilderness camps and of the attempts on our lives after leaving the camp. His page was no longer available. Censorship. Ina searched his home site and found a video.

Diego started to talk about oddities with the explosions. Suddenly, the site went down. We went back to Fakebook and looked at other information presented there. There were links to various mainstream American news outlets, declaring us terrorists and calling any contrary reports terrorist-sympathizing and disinformation.

All the mainstream news shows had us creating the explosions. We hadn't even had a trial and we were credited with blowing up multiple bridges and tunnels. Where were we supposed to have gotten the explosives?

Emily started shaking. She was clearly terrified. Another fear struck me. If they thought Tunisia was harboring terrorists, our helpers from Tunisia might, themselves, be in danger.

After the computer was turned off, I spoke to Ina. "You know we had nothing to do with those explosions, but we don't want to put your family and friends at risk if they are looking for us."

"My father said that he would protect you. They cannot harm you if you stay with us."

"They think we are terrorists."

"Maybe they will find the real bombers."

Her father came in to speak with us. "I know you are scared. We are witnesses you had nothing to do with those explosions."

"The media isn't interested in the truth. They are busy creating a false narrative. And usually, these false flags end with dead counter-witnesses who can't talk."

"Let's see what happens tonight. Maybe things will look different tomorrow morning. We have been given responsibility for protecting five brave teenagers. That's what we will do," he said.

On the news, there were discussions of what should be done when we were found. Several Congressmen from both parties stated that, as terrorists who might endanger more lives, law enforcement would be justified in shooting us on sight. Somehow, this was no surprise as members of Congress had been talking that way for years about Edward Snowden and Julian Assange, whose only crimes were telling the American people what Americans needed to know about our government.

None of the stations mentioned the information we had presented to the United Nations nor the reception we had gotten from all the countries—other than the United States, Israel, Saudi Arabia and the U.K, all four of which wanted us in chains. The explosions overtook any message we had tried to present.

"Look, it's your state's lead Senator," Bruce observed. "Raquel Madhouse is interviewing him."

Madcow asked, "Do you think it's acceptable to take extraordinary measures with respect to teenagers? Is shooting them on sight acceptable?"

Senator Shifty responded, "We cannot take any options off the table when it comes to protecting the public. When you are fighting terrorism, sometimes you have to take steps that are uncomfortable."

"Killing us is uncomfortable?" I reacted. "You've known me my whole life, and you feel that killing me is uncomfortable?"

"The man is a senile looney," Santana said.

"Let's hope that someday he is the subject of extraordinary police measures," Abigail retorted.

"Didn't he vote for the PATRIOT Act, the wars, all of them, for the Wall Street bailouts and for the NDAA, over and over again?" Santana asked. "He's the real terrorist who has sacrificed American lives."

Madcow touched her hand to her ear, which clearly had some kind of earphone in it. *"This just in. The five teens tried to board a plane to Cuba at JFK. They eluded capture and are believed to be in Queens."*

"The Ambassador's car must have gotten across the bridge safely," I hoped. But the elephant in the room was that everyone in that car was still in danger. When it was discovered we weren't in the Cuban Ambassador's car, they might search the consulates and hotels of any country siding with us.

"This is ridiculous," Bruce scoffed. "There is no way a logical person would think we could blow up all those bridges and tunnels."

"They convinced people that Paddock got all those guns up to his room through a monitored service elevator and shot all those people in Vegas, something that was physically impossible. Whatever the media says, the masses believe," Santana pointed out.

"Do you think there should be additional sanctions or perhaps military intervention on Cuba?" Madcow asked.

"It's something we need to look into. Clearly, Cuba is supporting and even encouraging terrorist activities in the United States," the Senator replied.

"Do you expect the United States to take emergency action?"

"A session has been called for later today. But the President does not need to wait for us to act."

"Mom and Rosa are in Cuba!" I exclaimed. "Something has to be done."

"And Alejandro!" Emily freaked.

"Nobody is going to listen to us," Bruce said.

"Do you think this relates to the latest natural gas discovery in Cuba?" I queried.

"That fits. Look at Afghanistan, Iraq, Libya, Syria and so forth," Santana reminded us.

"Shifty has never met a war he didn't love. He probably dreams of dead children every night," I remarked.

"Maybe he's a necrophiliac," Abigail fumed.

"I wonder if Russia and other countries will come to the defense of Cuba," Bruce pondered.

"I used to watch Raquel. She is awful. She's almost encouraging them to kill us." Emily lamented.

"She gets paid millions per broadcast. She's Wall Street," I said. "She even libeled Bernie when he was running against Killary."

"So, what are we going to do?" Emily asked.

"We are in Queens from what they say. If we prove that we are not in the Cuban Embassy's car, maybe they will back off from war with Cuba," I postulated.

"You think we should get out of here?" Abigail asked. "I'm ready to find my dad and drag him before the cameras. This is exactly the sort of thing he's likely to have orchestrated."

"The Tunisian Ambassador won't want us to go," Emily said, more calmly. But I could tell from the quaver in her voice and her somber expression that she was still worried about Alejandro and Rosa.

"When they find out we are not with the Cubans, the trail might eventually lead here. Everyone tied to us is safer with us gone," I asserted. "Our leaders regularly drone bomb foreign countries with impunity and then lie about everything. We're endangering everyone by being here."

"Bruce and I could go out and make it look like our group is else-where," Santana suggested.

"Not without me," I reacted, insistently.

"Or me," Abigail declared, with a touch of anger in her eyes.

"Where else can we go?" Emily asked.

"They'll assume we're all together. Emily, perhaps you could stay here with them, and the rest of us could draw the perpetrators away," I suggested.

"Where you go, I go," Emily demanded.

"Suppose we do leave the Hilton. They have cameras in the elevators. They could do facial recognition," Bruce pointed out. "And there are cameras all over the city. The clerks may notice us."

"We could cover our faces with something the clerks will see as traditional clothing. I am more concerned about cameras outside the hotel," I said.

"We could go to a television station," Emily suggested.

"The ones that are calling for our execution?" Bruce asked.

"We need to act fast if we are to save both the Cubans and the Tunisians," I pointed out.

"What about all those Ambassadors who were on our side?" Emily asked.

"My dad is good at blackmailing people and foreign governments. I'm sure the news, elsewhere, is less biased, but those other countries may not have a choice."

"How do you think those bridges were blown up?" Bruce asked.

"Preset explosives?" Santana queried.

"You think HAARP might be involved?" I asked, guessing Bruce was wondering about that himself, given that his dad was one of HAARP's chief engineers.

"I don't know. It's possible. Whatever happened, we were framed, and somebody did the framing," Bruce replied.

"And that someone was able to blow up bridges in a city that had some of the strongest surveillance systems in the world," I pointed out.

"We may not know who, but I am betting this is a false flag activity," Santana said.

"When you look at false flags, you look at who benefits," I noted.

"Those who want to invade Cuba," Emily surmised. "The natural gas."

"The military industrial complex. They will get an additional budget to fight this sort of thing. Barriers to their use of military equipment in cities will be waived," Santana said.

"Security firms. Adelman and Chertoff made a fortune off Vegas.

We're lucky the Tunisian diplomats weren't subjected to their scanners when entering the hotel," I pointed out.

"They probably will be in the future," Santana warned.

We heard a knock at the door. I opened it, hoping there were no surprises. It was Ina's brother, Medhi. "Are you alright?"

"So far. We are concerned that we may have brought danger to your family," I said.

"Don't be." He went over to Emily. "I'm glad you and your friends are here. You are welcome to go back home with us."

Emily smiled. "Can't. They are threatening war with Cuba. They could attack your country, next."

He looked taken aback. "I saw on TV about Cuba. But if they are accusing Cuba, they can't then say that we were responsible."

"We don't want them to attack anybody," I said. "But if we try to go public, we don't want them to connect us with your country."

"You aren't thinking of leaving?" he asked.

"If we stay, we will only bring harm to your country," I said.

"Think of your father and sister. Please, don't say anything until we're gone," Santana implored him.

"You aren't going to say 'goodbye'?"

"It's best if we just go," I said. "Please give us some time so we don't cause anyone any trouble."

"Can Emily stay?"

"I need to go with my friends. Please, understand, and let us go," she said.

"I'll help, but wait just a few minutes,"

We had brought considerable American currency with us that we hoped would help us survive. We arranged outer outfits to look like Saris. Even the boys made it look like they were girls. There would be fewer questions about women covering their faces. Our casual clothes were underneath.

We were about to take off when Medhi returned with a couple of laundry carts and his sister. Looking at the carts, Ina explained, "For the elevators."

They both gave us hugs. Ina tried to persuade us to stay, but we all knew we couldn't. We thanked them for their courage and kindness as we got into the carts and they covered us with sheets.

Downstairs, Medhi pushed us into the laundry room and we exited wearing our coverings. We were out from the protection of the Tunisians. Our own government was ignoring whatever immunity we'd hoped we'd have. If we were caught, we were dead.

CHAPTER 4

We headed towards Times Square and shed our over-clothes in the bathroom of a popular eatery. We pulled up our hoods and used markers for mustaches—even me, Abigail and Emily.

"We have choices," Bruce said. "We aren't too far from the Venezuelan Consulate. The French and Russian Consulates are the other way, walking along Central Park."

"Venezuela has the best government," Santana noted. "But they are already under fire from the Americans. If we are going to go for a Consulate, the French or Russian would be safer."

Reversing directions and traveling towards the park, as we passed Carnegie Hall, Emily said, "I was hoping to sing there one day."

"Then I'm sure you will," I told her. "You've got the voice for it."

The crowds were still frantic outside, with fights erupting and people rushing around as if they were about to be bombed themselves. We went into a drug store. People were watching a TV screen where reporters were talking about the search through Queens for the teenaged terrorists.

"Good thing they are looking in Queens." Santana breathed a sigh of relief.

"I hope everyone in the Cuban car is okay," I worried.

"They aren't us," he whispered. "They'll be better off than we would be if they catch us."

"They aren't announcing any search for the Cuban diplomats or any arrests," Bruce pointed out. "If they think we ran at the airport in Queens, they could have let the Cuban delegation leave the country."

"Let's hope so," I said.

As we approached the park, we saw police in riot gear in front of various buildings. "I wonder if they will be watching for anyone approaching the consulates," I cautioned.

"Those officers might just be helping the elites keep the homeless out. We're in Queens, remember?" Santana quipped.

We made our way through the park. The homeless population was astounding. There were so many of them. I wished I could do something to help. "I wonder how they survive in the winter," I pondered.

"They freeze," Santana angrily declared.

"People can be really cold," Abigail said. "I was in Boston in the winter, and when I asked about the homeless outside, people kept spouting some mantra about, 'They want to be out in the cold. We offer them shelter and they just run outside.' It was like a programmed response as if they were quoting each other, almost word for word."

"That's probably from the TV, all the media brainwashing," I pointed out.

"And any independent news is being censored as 'fake news,' although it's more accurate than the MSM propaganda."

"Raquel Madcow is the highest-paid newswoman in America, and all she spouts out are lies and hate," Abigail stated.

"That's for sure," I agreed. I turned to Emily, who was shaking. "Are you okay?"

"I'm scared."

"We all are," I told her. I put my arm around her.

The carriages seemed to have been put up for the evening—maybe, because of the crowds. We walked past the zoo towards the Carousel. Every now and then we saw police officers rousing up the homeless who were trying to rest in the park.

"Where are they supposed to go?" I asked. "Mars?"

"If my daddy had his way, he'd nuke them tomorrow," Abigail grumbled.

An old woman walked by pushing a full cart of perhaps her life's belongings. She looked as if she could barely stand. Bruce offered to help her. Emily started to push the woman's cart for her. The woman was very thin, and I suspected she hadn't eaten in some time.

"Thank you. You are very kind."

"De nada," Santana replied, trying to take over the cart pushing. Emily shook her head, waved him off and continued pushing. It looked like a heavy cart for Emily, but she was determined.

"It is something. My name is Genevieve," the woman said.

"I'm James," Santana answered. "My friends are Toby, Elissa, Charlene and Jackie."

"What's with the mustaches on you girls?"

"We came from a costume party," I fibbed.

"Which is Elissa?" The woman asked.

I started to raise my hand, but Abigail beat me to it. "I'm Elissa. Where are you going?"

"I was hoping to make it over to the Met, the Metropolitan Museum."

"We can walk there with you," Abigail said.

"What a sweet girl. And who is this lovely lady pushing my cart?"

"Jackie," Emily replied. That left Charlene for me.

"You are such nice kids. What brings you to Central Park?" There was something about her style of speech and voice that reminded me of someone who had fallen from a more affluent life.

"We're on a tour of colleges," Santana lied. "We're looking at both NYU and Columbia."

"I went to Columbia," Genevieve said. "Got my PhD there."

"That's wonderful." I smiled at her. "What did you major in?"

"Physics," she said. "I was an engineer for Beklet until I was laid off."

"I'm sure there are a lot more altruistic organizations," I commented.

"I agree. After Beklet, I found out, I had been blacklisted."

"Why?"

"We were working on a project in connection with the Darkwave corporation and I accidentally opened a confidential file about Darkwave's soundwave technology."

"What kind of soundwave technology?" Bruce inquired.

"They were trying to use the tech to influence thinking but also to see whether they could use it to create explosions."

"Like high pitches and crystal?" Emily asked.

"It was focused on heavy substances like concrete, buildings, and cities."

"Is it similar to the technology used by HAARP?" I inquired.

"Much more extensive than HAARP."

"HAARP can theoretically create earthquakes, hurricanes. droughts and the equivalent of nuclear bombs," I noted.

"If Darkwave finishes their project, earthquakes and nuclear explosions will be minor in comparison." Her style of speaking was very casual as if she were simply reporting her findings to a co-worker.

"Remember those weird noises we heard when they were doing that experiment in camp?" I asked. "I wonder if Darkwave was one of the contractors they worked with."

"Do you remember any of the people you worked with at Darkwave? Perhaps an Evan Saunders?" Santana asked.

"I remember a guy named Jenkens. He was also with HAARP."

"Howard Jenkens?" Bruce followed up.

"Yes. That was his name."

Santana looked up. Bruce narrowed his eyes and shook his head. I looked over at Abigail who had put her hands on her hips.

"So, HAARP and Darkwave are connected," Bruce muttered.

She laughed. "It's all connected, honey."

"Maybe what we stumbled onto is more serious than the camps themselves," I pondered.

"Camps? As in camping?"

Changing the subject, I asked, "Have you been camping?"

"That's all I've done since I lost my home."

"I'm sorry," I said. "What happened?"

"When I couldn't get a job, I couldn't keep up the mortgage. My kids took me in for a little while, but they had their own lives, and an old lady isn't something that kids should have to deal with."

"I'm sure they didn't feel that way," I said.

She started to cry.

I wondered what kind of children she had that would let her live like this without helping out. Emily let go of the cart and hugged Genevieve.

"I didn't think they would feel that way, but they were right. I was a burden."

"That's terrible," Santana said. I could see he was holding back anger. I was angry, too.

"Someone ought to kick their asses." Abigail looked ready for action.

"If we had a home here, you could stay with us," Emily said.

"You must be a brilliant woman to have worked with Beklet, Darkwave and HAARP," Bruce acknowledged. "This is not how people should be treated."

"A throwaway," she said.

"What?" Bruce asked.

"In our society, people who no longer serve a purpose are considered throwaways. That's what I am."

"No, you aren't!" I strongly disagreed. "You are a very sweet lady, and it's tragic, how you were treated."

"If you wouldn't mind, I'd like to learn more about Darkwave's technology," Bruce interjected.

I had prided myself on science and math, but as I listened to the technical conversation between Genevieve and Bruce that followed, I saw that it was clearly above my knowledge level.

I had previously seen movies about brainwashing happening subliminally on TV and radio, but Darkwave's project went to a new level and turned movie plots into reality. Among other things, I learned from the conversation that Darkwave was also using microwave technology, which was suspected of being a cause of various California fires sometime back. Houses had burned, but not the trees around them. Then, there was the mind-washing and the potential for elimination of whole cities.

As we walked, Genevieve said that she had wanted to go into the Met but was afraid that they would not allow her to take her cart inside and she didn't want to lose her stuff. We found a place that had large storage lockers, big enough for her cart. We helped her put her cart in one and gave her the key.

With our guys, hooking arms with her, we walked to the Met. Santana gave her a hundred-dollar bill.

"I'll bring you the change."

"Keep it. It was wonderful meeting you, Genevieve," he said.

"Please wait, everyone," she said. She ran up to the window and came back with six tickets. "Please come in with me. My daughter has a painting in there. If you come in, I'll show it to you."

I felt sad for Genevieve. Clearly, she loved her children, and they had thrown her away like yesterday's trash, the same way society throws away some of the nicest people, particularly older women. I thought of cultures that respected the elderly. In America, people just waited for the elderly to die off. Then the next generation moved up and eventually died off without anyone caring. There had to be a better way.

We were still wearing hooded shirts with NYC marked on the front and trying to look touristy. As we entered with a crowd, we looked down as we held out our tickets and rushed through. They would probably not be looking for us at the Met, particularly since they thought we were in Queens.

Walking through the Great Hall, I was struck by its enormity and by how many rooms there would be to see if we chose to check out the whole museum. I had been much younger when my dad had dropped me off at the museum door with his secretary. She rushed me around, but I didn't pay attention to the exhibits back then. I had felt like a discard, just as Genevieve now felt.

We moved through the Greek, Roman and Egyptian sections, and my favorite, the section with all the full knight outfits. Finally, Genevieve grabbed me and pulled me towards a painting on special exhibit at the museum. It was a painting of the Hudson, very detailed and with precise brush strokes. Genevieve gushed over the painting, while I found myself very angry at a daughter who had had so much love and thrown it away. We continued on, in some cases, retracing our steps, hoping not to be noticed.

We were standing in front of a painting of George Washington Crossing the Delaware when a little girl pointed at us. "Mommy, that's them. They're the teens we thought were on that plane." She had seen through our minimal disguises.

CHAPTER 5

"Excuse me, Genevieve," I said. "We have to go."

"I don't understand."

"Neither do we," Abigail replied.

"I wish we could stay," Emily said.

"I hope we can talk again," Bruce quickly told her.

Santana gave Genevieve a hug as we heard the girl get louder, "Mommy, mommy, I know it's them!"

As her mom turned to look, we moved quickly towards the front of the museum and rushed out the exit but not fast enough to avoid the girl catching extra attention.

"We might be safe—unless the wrong person hears her," Bruce said.

"I saw a guard coming her way when she was creating the ruckus," I said. "Sweet little girl, though."

"What now?" Abigail asked.

There were no riot police close to the Met, but they could be seen outside the French Consulate as we approached it. "Let's try continuing on to the Russian Consulate," Santana suggested.

But when we got close to the Russian Consulate, we saw another line of officers we would have had to cross to get inside.

"Obviously, they aren't convinced we're in Queens. It's like they are waiting for us," Bruce noted.

We went back into Central Park towards the northeast. We found a spot in the North Woods section where we decided to rest, taking turns watching for the police. "You do realize there are cameras all over this park, don't you?" Bruce asked.

"Unless they got our pictures from the Metro, they may not realize how we are dressed," Santana said.

"Don't forget the facial recognition tech, complete with eye scans," Bruce reminded him.

"If they are checking facial ID on everyone who entered, that's a full-time job," Santana replied.

"Not for a computer," Bruce pointed out.

Abigail and I glanced around to see if we could locate anywhere we could rest and found a spot that looked hidden and unoccupied. Bruce, Abigail and Emily rested while Santana and I watched.

"I should have known better. I thought we were doing something good in coming to New York," Santana sighed.

"We all insisted on coming," I responded. "We expected problems, but not this. They aren't even going to look at anything we said. The news is going to suppress all our words. And the public will believe only what it is told, as it always does. They are well programmed."

"Hey, the fact that we're still alive and well after everything Evan and his cronies tried to throw at us tells me that our enemies don't have a chance against the Wilderness Five." He pumped up his arm in the air.

"Thank you. Sometimes it's hard to hold my optimism together. I'm scared, just like Emily."

"Remember all those old movies where things look hopeless, but love helps the main characters through." Santana put his arm around me. "We've been through torture, false imprisonment, numerous attempts on our lives, earthquakes, lightning and hail storms, and none of that could slow us down or stop me from loving you."

I smiled. "Or me from loving you. And to think when I met you, I thought you were a jerk."

"I was. But it was a show so Claudio and Marco would let me hang out with you. Remember the gooseberries?"

"They were the best thing about that camp, other than you and the friends I made." I sat, leaning against Santana, reveling in the feel of his arm around me. "Do you think we'll ever have a chance to just relax and enjoy each other for more than a couple of months?"

"It will happen."

"What if the U.S. declares war on Cuba? It will be our fault. I'm the one who was eager to come here."

"We all were. If we hadn't come here, they would have found another excuse," he replied.

"The President is being pushed into being pro-war. The Democrats and Republicans both cheer him on when he bombs people and criticize him when he doesn't. They'll be delighted if he attacks Cuba."

"We could disavow Cuba, or it could disavow us," he proposed.

"It could issue a statement that, when it finds us, it will turn us over to be sacrificed to the American Gods of War," I added, agreeing.

"Mars might like that, but then we would have to find another home."

"When there are fewer armed cops around the Russian Consulate, maybe Putin really will give us asylum. They are the only country with enough manpower to stand up to the US of A," I noted.

"And it does seem to be the country for American lovers. Lindsay Mills joined Edward Snowden there." He put on a reassuring smile.

"They are definitely better prepared for World War III than we are. Our chances of survival would certainly be better there."

"We'd have to learn Russian."

"Zdrastvuyte."

"See. You are already on your way to being a comrade."

I laughed. Santana smiled and then looked more intently. He leaned in, and his lips pressed against mine. It still felt as magical as the first time, more so, more intense, warmer. It was as if the rest of the world slipped away, no explosions, no pursuits, just bliss. New York didn't exist and all felt so right. All I knew was that, if we stayed like this for the rest of my life, I'd be happy.

"I love you so much," he murmured when our lips parted.

"Love seems like such a weak word for what I feel," I said.

He smiled. "We are wearing those rings Alonzo got us in case—" In our plans for coming to America, we were going to pretend to be married and get emancipated, like Damen, if our fathers tried to grab us.

Damen was a boy in California who had been raped by his dad, who had been granted full custody of the kid by a corrupt family court judge.

He ran away from home and when he turned sixteen he had a paper marriage to a very nice girl who wanted to help, got emancipated and then got the marriage annulled so he could live with his mom, his protective parent.

"My mom said 'no sex.'"

"But that's not how you feel?"

"No. But I want it to last forever. I just don't know if we'll live longer than tonight."

"I must be doing something wrong if I'm casting doubts on our future."

"Hard to be optimistic when the news media, the government and people we trusted growing up are okay with killing us."

"In the end, we're the ones who are going to win," he assured me.

"Once they declare the perpetrator of a false flag, they never turn back and undeclare it, no matter how much people doubt. Oswald, Sirhan Sirhan, Osama bin Ladin, Adam Lanza, Steven Paddock. If you ask the average person who was behind Las Vegas, they won't say Michael Chertoff and Asher Adelman. They'll say Stephen Paddock."

"Then, this will be the first. Because we deserve our forever."

"What's that?" I whispered.

Voices were echoing, loud, right behind us, coming from the other direction. We stayed very still, hoping our approachers didn't spot any of us.

There were multiple male speakers. Santana and I stayed hidden.

"Jerry didn't know what he was hit with."

"Tomorrow he is going to have such a headache."

"Did you see Professor Harris's wife? She is so hot."

"Don't let him hear you say that."

"Maybe, you can mix one of your solutions up for him so she and I can have some—what?" he reacted as I heard a clunk from where our friends were sleeping. It sounded as if he had fallen over one of our friends.

CHAPTER 6

"Hey, I'm sorry, man. I didn't see you. Why don't you get a room?" the fallen guy asked, having landed right beside our friends.

Santana and I watched, ready to jump out from behind our bush if they needed a rescue as Bruce, Abigail, and Emily looked a little stunned.

"A threesome. Why can't I be so lucky," the fallen guy continued.

I noticed that Abigail's and Emily's mustaches had worn off. Mine probably had, too.

"Really, I'm sorry."

"He's not sorry. He does this all the time. It's how he meets all his new friends," a second guy countered, moving through the bushes towards our friends and sitting down. The three looked a little older than us, maybe college-aged. A tell-tale was that they were wearing Columbia jackets.

"But watch out," a third guy warned, joining his friends on the ground. "He's got a zap machine that will knock you out." He pointed at the drunken guy.

"A zaaap maaachiiine," the first guy said. "I'm calling it a mo-mo-mlecular so-oma gen'rator."

"I helped him build it," the second guy bragged.

"Yeet, aren't you the kids who spoke at the United Nations?" the third guy asked, looking at our friends on the ground and then up at us where we were now standing on the other side of the Columbia guys.

"You are," the second guy said. "I belong to the National Youth Rights Association. I took my friends to the U.N. to hear you speak."

I could tell my comrades were thinking of a response. I wasn't sure how to react. We had been found out.

"You were gre-r-r-aat," the first one said with somewhat slurry words.

"He's drunk," the second guy commented. "Don't listen to him. Listen to me. You were great."

"Um, thank you," Bruce replied.

"Your dad works for HAARP, right?" the second guy asked. "We've been doing research into using radio waves to blow things up."

"But we're nice," the third guy added. "We're not going to send our kids to a Gulag camp. Not that we—" He pointed to his friends, "Would have kids together. But some day, if Professor Harris's wife is willing." His friends laughed.

"Thank you for your support," Bruce breathed a sigh of relief. "We seem to be in a bit of a bind."

"I heard. That bitch with her 'Espionage Act of 1917.' She looks like she was born in 1917," the third added.

Santana smiled.

"It's worse," Bruce said. "While we were en route out of town, someone blew up the bridges and tunnels towards JFK and they are blaming us."

"That's ridiculous. If you had blown them up, I'm sure you would have crossed them first. Or did you teleport yourselves back?" the second guy asked.

"We've been partying all day and hadn't heard that news," the third guy said. "They are always jumping to conclusions."

"They are ready to kill us if they find us," Bruce told them.

"Nooot good," the first guy slurred as his body and eyelids started drooping. "By the way, I'm Joooey. This is Boob and that's Daarren," he said pointing to his second and then third friend.

"Bruce."

"Abigail."

"What a beauuuty," Joey said.

"She's taken," Bruce advised.

"Emily." She stood up and walked over to me and Santana.

"You're hot, too," Bob said, reaching out his hand. Emily smiled and reached hers out to him.

"She's fourteen," Santana threw in.

The guy backed off.

Reaching out his hand, my guy said, "I'm Santana, and this is my girlfriend."

"Summer," I extended my hand.

"That's weird. You guys are wearing wedding rings," Bob observed.

"That's in case our custodial parents try to take us back. The idea was to pretend we were married so we could get emancipated," I confessed.

Santana looked at me cautiously, as if he thought I had said too much.

"They seem cool," I told him, hoping I was correct.

"What are you guys going to do? You can't hang out in the park forever," Bob said.

"We were going to go to the Russian Consulate, but it's surrounded by New York's finest," Santana remarked.

"Let me get this straight," Darren said. "You came here to testify about the mistreatment of teenagers, and someone set you up for blowing up bridges and tunnels, and the public actually believes it?"

"Seems that way," Santana replied.

"They'll believe anything," Bob said. "That's insane. Even my dog wouldn't believe that."

"You don't have a dog," Darren corrected him.

"If I did."

"On the news, they were talking about whether it was acceptable to kill us." Abigail grimaced.

Bob took a deep breath and looked upward. Darren put his hands on his hips. They looked thoughtful, and then Darren spoke. "We've got to do something. This could happen to any of us who go up against the 'Estab.'"

"Yeah, particularly you, Joey." Bob remarked, turning to his intoxicated friend.

"Police shoot first and ask questions later. Things may clear up in a few days, but by then these cats will be dead," Darren pointed out.

Joey looked down as if in thought and then back at his friends. He seemed to be coming out of his drunken state. "Got it." He shook his head around as if trying to clear his mind. "My roo-roommate bailed. Notified me that he's splanning si-swtich to Berkeley, but waiting until next month to ficially request a refund—case he doesn't like Berkeley. Bob, how bout you stay with me an we put the girls in your room an the two guys split up between my room an D's?" He turned to us. "They have private rooms."

"We got doctor's notes saying roommates give us headaches. Under the ADA, they had to give us private rooms for the same rate," Bob explained.

"Then, it's a 'yes,'" Joey said, raising his hands as if expecting a chorus from his companions.

His friends slowly nodded. "At least until this all clears up," Bob said.

"They will need to sign in tonight," Darren noted.

"I'll sign my brother Bruce, is it?" Bob offered.

Bruce nodded to Joey's comment.

Bob continued. "In and I'll tell them my sisters also came to check out my room. Joey, you come in ten minutes later and pretend that Santana is your half-brother."

"They need to sign out," Darren pointed out.

"Darren," Joey said. "You can flirt with the guard, if it's a girl, or complain about something in the hall, if it's a guy, while Bob and I go to the door and loudly close it. When he asks what that was, we'll sign them out, saying we forgot. At least, they'll be safe for tonight."

"We've got a problem. We can't use our IDs or they will know who we are," I said.

"That's right," Darren agreed. "Guests need ID cards."

"Columbia was rated the most secure university in the world, which is why-i-i a sign of intelli—genius is knowing how to break in," Joey remarked, still slightly under.

I was dubious, but we thanked them and tried to stay positive as we walked with them towards John Jay Hall, which was at the corner of 114th and Amsterdam. Joey walked wobbly at first and then straightened up as if he was regaining more of his sobriety.

As we reached W 110th Street and Ninth Avenue, we heard the command, "Stop," followed by gunshots.

CHAPTER 7

All three of our friends whipped out their cell phones and ran towards the shots. That was something I didn't normally see.

Three officers were firing their guns wildly down an alley. Joey discreetly pulled a small box out from under his sweatshirt, aimed it at the first officer and pressed a button. The officer collapsed. Joey did likewise for the others. They fell as well.

"What is that?" Bruce asked, as Joey discreetly put it away.

He opened up the box. It contained a small tube connected to some coils. The tube was positioned against an opening in the box.

"It's my version of a neutralizer, except instead of removing memory, it sends out electro-magnetic waves on a pulse that interferes with the flow of the nervous system, slowing everything down to the point where consciousness is lost. It's fast, and the government says electro-magnetic radiation doesn't harm people." His speech suggested to me the gunshots had taken him out of his stupor.

"Like I believe that," Darren said.

We went into the alley where an African American was hiding out between a couple of trash containers. "I can't believe I'm still alive," the guy said, looking himself over.

"I can't believe it either," I said. "Usually the police overkill." I looked at the bins and the walls, riddled with bullet holes. "I guess they figure if they shoot everything in sight, they'll hit their target. They were after you?"

"They're always after me."

"Good luck," Santana said.

"We're lucky half the city wasn't among the police's casualties," Abigail commented, looking at all the bullet holes.

"I hate to rush you," Bruce said. "But more will be around soon."

We all moved into a door next to the alley that turned out to be the back door to the kitchen in a little café. A worker inside looked at us but didn't say anything.

"Pleased to meet you," Joey told the guy from the alley, as he ushered us all out through the front.

"I'm Charlie," the target told us. "Charles, as in Ray."

"Hi, Charlie, as in Ray," Joey said. The rest of echoed the "Hi, Charlie."

"Don't know why they were shooting at me. I was walking home and suddenly, poof."

"You're Black," Darren said. "They don't need an excuse to shoot us, brother."

"In California, the police simply shoot people if they are Black, Hispanic, Muslim, female or marching against war," Santana remarked.

"Anyone who does the right thing is unfairly targeted," Darren noted. "It's the New World Order."

"Time for the guillotines," Abigail declared.

Several of us laughed. Bruce smiled at her comment and put his arms around her.

"Ah," you guys have all the pretty girls who aren't fourteen," Joey complained to Santana and Bruce.

We walked back to 114[4h] Street and then said our goodbyes to Charles, who went towards Fifth Avenue as we continued towards Amsterdam.

"I'd really like to discuss your invention with you," Bruce said to Joey.

"That's right. You were raised by scientists. HAARP, right?"

"Yeah," Bruce replied.

"I think he'd rather trade his parents for the Manson gang," Abigail said.

"Manson's dead," Santana commented.

"That's a step up." I laughed.

Abigail threw out her hands as if I had taken the words out of her mouth.

Bob looked at Darren. "It might take a while, but what if we move them in as furniture or in clothing bags?"

"I don't have clothing bags that big," Darren said.

"I have at least one clothing bag large enough for a girl and a couple of mattress cover bags. In the mattress bags, we can bring in two at a time," Joey offered.

His friends looked at him.

"My parents were afraid my mattresses would contain lice and so they made me bring them. I thought it was silly. Now, I'm thinking, right on."

They left us nearby and returned with the bags. Bruce and Santana were the first in. The students wrapped blankets around our guys and then had them climb inside a mattress cover and carried them through the door. I noticed that the boys were lying very still in their new one-piece outfit.

Emily and Abigail were next. I was to be last in a clothing bag. Joey and Darren did the carrying in case there were surprise inspections later. We didn't want Bob's room searched. It was decided the five of us would stay there until we were certain everything was clear. Bob would stay in Joey's room.

"You guys are carrying a lot of luggage up. I need to inspect," the security officer said, as I was being carried in the bag over Joey's shoulder. "And your mattresses were lumpy."

"We have rights to privacy," I could hear Darren say. "And we like them that way."

"Look, my mom cleaned out the closet and insisted I take all my clothing. I just want to go to bed," Joey added, loudly yawning.

"I want your badge number," Darren said. "I'm going to report you. Everyone on this campus has been cleared. That's why we were admitted. That's why the university trusted us to come here and get dorm rooms. Classes just started a week ago, and we've got too tough of a load to have all our clothing inspected."

I didn't hear much more as Joey was moving past with me while Darren continued to argue with security. Soon thereafter, we were in Bob's room. Joey took the bag and covers to his room and then rejoined us.

Darren came in a few minutes later. Joey hi-fived him as he entered. "That was cool man."

We heard footsteps somewhere outside. Bob opened the door a crack and looked out. "Security is in the hall," he said, quickly closing the door.

CHAPTER 8

I was more than a little nervous. We heard the approaching footsteps walk past Bob's room and keep going towards the end of the hall. Bob peeked out again. "They are going for Darren's room," Bob whispered as he closed his door again.

"What's the problem?" Joey asked. "They're looking in Darren's room. None of them are there."

Bob looked out again. "Another security guard is going for your room, Joey," he said. "The jerks."

"Will they question you when the full bags aren't there?" Bruce asked.

"We unpacked fast." Joey smiled. "But one thing for sure, you guys are safer in here until we get you valid student ID cards."

"ID cards?"

"I can arrange that tomorrow morning," Bob told us. "As part of my studies, I have access to the lab where they make them."

"Great," I responded, admiringly.

After security left, Bob showed us around the third floor. There were private one-use bathrooms and so we didn't have to worry about being watched taken showers. The view was nice. "This is really thoughtful of you," I thanked them. "You sure you can't get into trouble?"

"Nah. But we do need to come up with a plan until things blow over," Bob responded.

"My concern is all the facial recognition tech, including retinal scans, they are now using," Bruce related.

"They're overburdened with that. We'll figure it out," Bob assured him.

Bruce hung out with Joey and discussed the technology of the concussion weapon Joey had created. Santana hung out with Darren, talking about civil rights. Abigail, Emily and I made use of the single use bathrooms to take showers. Darren had given us some of his clean clothes to change into.

Darren was in pre-med. His cousin was working in a lab where contact lenses were made. He promised to secure some for us in the morning. Bob took some less than clear pictures of us for our ID cards and photoshopped them to change the eye-color on mine, Abigail's and Bruce's to brown and on Emily's and Santana's to green. Abigail was wearing a school cap, with most of her hair under it, but Bob had photoshopped it to make what was visible of her hair appear blonde. Joey knew a wig shop where he would be picking up a wig for Abigail in the morning.

Bob loaned me a small computer so I could look at the Internet information about us. Abigail and Emily took the bed and I bundled up on the floor. Bruce and Bob slept in Joey's room and Santana stayed with Darren.

The news wasn't saying how we were supposed to have set off the explosives, but they had found us guilty. In Queens, the police had set up a dragnet in their search for us. There was no mention of Ambassador Sanchez or others who had been in his limo. That meant everyone in the Cuban vehicle was hopefully safe or as safe as they could be, given that our government was gearing up for war with their country. We weren't even Cubans, but somehow they were attributing the events to both us and the Cuban Government.

I looked up Ryan Cristian and Jimmy Dore. Both were questioning the official narrative. That much was good. I knew they were heavily censored. But between them, they had more than a million viewers.

Russia had told the U.S. that if they went to war with Cuba, they would have Russia to contend with. Russia and China had flown some of their military planes to Cuba and offered assistance. Washington was angry and threatening the two super-powers. It appeared that, if Congress acted and declared war on Cuba, the result would be World War III.

The usual leaders, Gramcracker, Shemberg, Whitehut, Shifty, McConehead, Pegrossy and others were demanding the U.S. militarily take on Cuba and all its allies. To my chagrin, the Democrats were more hot for war than the Republicans over the events in New York, while the GOP was simply gung-ho on blowing up the world on any excuse on behalf of one imperialistic country in the Middle East.

The events that took place to hide our U.N. speeches could bring about the end of the world. My heart almost burst thinking about how, if we had kept silent and stayed in Cuba, we would not have placed so many lives in danger.

I thought back to the book, *The Hundredth Monkey*. I had picked it up in a used bookstore. It spoke about how if either the U.S. or Russia used even a small fraction of their nuclear arsenal, the effect on the planet would be to cause the death of all the inhabitants. The ones who didn't die instantly would go blind and would be crawling around in the dark until they did.

But what did our leaders care? They had underground cities. I had had a free pass to one. Sure, a thinking person would realize that our leaders would have to come up sometime and that it wouldn't be safe to come up for hundreds of thousands of years. But when had our leaders ever shown any foresight and intelligence with respect to cataclysmic events?

In searching the web, I found something more interesting. My hero Dennis Kucinich had attributed the events to Deep State. He pointed out that it was absurd to believe that five kids who had come back to testify before the United Nations about Deep State type events had time to plant explosives on the bridges and tunnels or to take down the FDR.

From out of the country, Cynthia McKinney chimed in, talking about how we had undoubtedly been framed and they needed to look at who benefited from the destruction. Apparently, there was a security firm that had been trying to put more advanced security monitors on the bridges that would x-ray cars and their inhabitants, down through their underwear. Cynthia pointed out that those were dangerous and that certain Deep State figures would make a lot of money off them. Also, apparently, some major insurance policies had recently been taken out on the bridges and tunnels.

The worst part was pictures of the hospitals filling up with victims. Like in Vegas, wheelbarrows and stolen trucks were used to drive and cart people to the hospitals. *Where did they wind up with so many wheelbarrows in New York City?* It wasn't like it was a farming community.

One girl had been hit so hard on one side of her head by a piece of concrete it went through and exited from the other side of her skull. After being hit with the concrete, she had helped rescue her sister and others who were injured and had made calls for help. One guy had had a sharp metal piece of a vehicle cutting through his femoral artery. Despite his injury, he manned one of the wheelbarrows, taking others to the hospital. I wasn't a nurse or a doctor, but I totally did not believe those injuries.

I turned to something called *Truthstream*. Due to the loss of net neutrality, it was way slower than most of the MSM sites. Apparently, there had been some kind of terrorism drill going on at the time of our visit. FEMA had put out an advance ad recruiting victims for an attack on bridges and tunnels in New York City to take place the same day as our UN visit. As I was watching the video, the site went down, and so I couldn't see any more. Nobody else was talking about the drills.

There was a claim that the death toll had reached seven hundred. I had nothing to do with the attack, but I felt some kind of survivor's remorse. I also knew that there would be people ready to lynch me and my friends for what we hadn't done.

When they killed Osama bin Ladin the third or was it the fourth time he died, there was no trial. They just killed him. The number of Senators and newsmen from both parties now lining up behind the "shoot on sight" was increasing by leaps and bounds. We were lucky that not everyone believed the MSM.

The next morning, Bob kept his word. He managed to get into the school computer and create whole profiles around new identities for us. Bruce was now Joey's roommate, Tony Milan, who, instead of leaving for Berkeley, had decided to stay at Columbia. He was a majoring in physics and minoring in chemistry. I was a girl named Sally Stallings from Florida who was majoring in photography. Emily was Linette Larette, a music major with a dance minor. Abigail was Carlie Marsden, a sociology major. Santana was Carlos Laluz and was majoring in political science.

Darren came through with boxes of disposable contacts and explained how to put them in. He had informed his cousin they were needed for educational purposes. His cousin rigged up phony sales receipts. Santana had given Darren money to cover the cost. For Abigail, they had obtained a long blonde wig to cover up her green hair.

When we all met up in the library at lunchtime. Joey summarized what they had seen online. "There were five drills going on yesterday, like on nine-eleven. They involved bridges falling, and tunnels collapsing and the FDR being blasted. The hospitals had planned to be filled with fake patients, who had signed up for the drills, The nurses were to treat the fake patients as real under the drill. I checked one of the Rent a Mourner sites and they are paying for fake mourners for the dead."

"But some people were hurt, weren't they?" I asked.

"Probably, but it's impossible to know how many. Certainly not the girl with the concrete going through her head or the guy with the torn apart femoral artery and the wheelbarrow. But online, they pull anything put up by anyone questioning the injuries, including the video doubting the guy running around with a shredded femoral artery, strong and capable of rescuing others," Joey said.

"The latest is they think they have found you in a brownstone in Queens and are planning an assault. According to the news, they are sending in a robot," Darren informed us.

"But people could die in their attack on the brownstone," I fretted. "There were three decoy cars, and we think the Cuban delegation may have made it across to Queens. At least we hope they did."

Joey pulled out his computer. "We might be able to do some postings to try to save the brownstone residents, but if you come forward, they'll kill you."

"I'll come forward," I said. "Nobody else, just me. I'm not going to let anyone die in my place."

"If you come forward, so will I," said Santana.

"I'm in," Abigail said.

"Four," Bruce joined in.

"Five," Emily declared.

"No, Emily," I said. "We can pretend that something happened to you. Please, let us do this without you."

"No," she insisted.

"We'll go with you," Joey said. "We can demand rights."

We walked to the exit in the Butler Library. There was a loud gathering with speeches in the South Field, East.

"What they did is a violation of all laws. Charges need to be brought, and they need to be brought to justice." It sounded like the speaker was talking about us.

"I'm going to the front. It might be a good time to introduce myself and proclaim our innocence." I looked into Santana's eyes. "I need you to protect everyone."

"You can't do that," Santana countered.

"I don't want any innocent people killed."

"This is a mob. Everyone here is angry," Joey contended. "You don't know what they'll do."

"I'll do it," Santana said.

"We all will," Abigail declared.

"No. Just me, please. We don't all have to be in danger," I insisted.

"The two of us are together. Always," Santana reminded me of our earlier promises.

"Three," Abigail clarified.

"Four," Emily said.

"Five," Bruce joined in.

We walked towards the front. This could be the end of us if the police came out shooting or if the crowd turned us over to them.

CHAPTER 9

The anger in the crowd grew. "Are we going to settle for this?" the speaker asked. "We could be victims next time. You, your brothers, your sisters. This could happen to any of us. And of course, we are targets. Look at what is happening. They are blindly killing without conscience."

We had made it to the front. Someone was doing access control at the side of the make-shift stage. "We've got to get up there," I said.

"You'll have to wait," the student monitoring the steps said.

The speaker continued. "The killer robot, who took out the Wilderness Five, must be dismantled and those who sent it in must be arrested and locked away forever, even if that means we lock away every officer in New York City."

I turned to my companions and whispered. "They think they killed us?"

"Looks that way," Santana breathed a sigh of relief.

I turned to someone in the crowd. "What happened?"

"They sent in a killer robot and it blew up the brownstone they were in. There may have been others in the building."

"My God!" I responded. I thought about the Cuban delegation. I hoped they were not in the building. I hoped nobody was in it when it went down.

"We are going to file a demand that the NYPD dismantle their killer robots and arrest the officers, including the police chief, who sent them in," the speaker announced.

I stood there shaking. My friends looked as stunned as I did. "Are they still talking about going to war with Cuba?" I inquired.

"The Russian, Spanish and Chinese fleets have formed a protective barrier around the island. This is big. It's the first time world powers have taken such a strong united stand against American imperialism."

Santana reached out, took me in his arms and held me.

"People died," I whispered. "How can we live with that?"

"We didn't do it. Somebody else caused the problem, and the police acted illegally."

"They didn't care that the people they killed might have been innocent." I started crying.

"Our government has been killing the innocent for years. This is just more of the same."

"It's not fair!" I started wailing. Suddenly I remembered my contacts. I didn't want them to wash out of my eyes. I did this trick of pulling on the inside of my eye area and wiping my eyes, but the tears wouldn't stop. Santana guided me out of the crowd.

I heard Abigail yelling along with the crowd. "3,2,1,0; NYPD's got to go!" And "Police, police, what do you say? How many kids did you kill today?"

Santana went with me into the lounge of the girls' bathroom in the Butler Library. I pulled out the contacts and wiped my eyes. The tears kept coming. In a minute I would have been on the floor, sobbing if not for Santana holding me up. "What are we going to do?"

"There's nothing we can do. I guess we need to give up on our old lives. Now, we've got new lives at Columbia for as long as they last."

"They won't last for long."

"We'll see. We've got a good crew with us." I heard a knock on the bathroom door.

Darren stuck his head in. "I was going to ask if Sally was okay, but I see she isn't."

"I don't know if my friends were killed or if others died because of—"

"It's not your fault. I've had friends killed by officers, and everyone always feels guilty, saying, 'It should have been me.' It would have been much worse if you had been there."

"Sum—or rather—Sally is very tender-hearted, but—" Santana turned back to me, "It's not any of our faults. We all would have stopped what happened if we could have. Sally, you probably would have sacrificed your life if you had had that option."

"You're a hero, Sally. What happened is tragic. I hope your friends weren't there," Darren said.

I nodded, continuing to cry. I kept working to dry my eyes. Finally, I put back in my contacts and went out to join the others.

As we walked out into the field, professors came out to speak against the use of robotic killers and executions without trials. Several speakers spoke about the threat of war and the insanity of imperialism. There were even speakers touting the importance of our mission in speaking against the camps before the United Nations. The news media may not care about the mistreatment of kids in the camps and might have ignored the whole thing, but Columbia's students and profs had picked up on it. Our message had gotten out.

As I walked through the crowd, arms grabbed me. "You're here!" It was Jimmy. "Shannon will be so thrilled." He turned and called, "Shannon!"

I shushed him and indicated I wanted him to whisper. "Don't let on who we are."

"Of course not."

Santana tapped him on the shoulder. The two hugged.

The next thing I heard was "Oh my God!"

Shannon hugged me.

"Let's go talk somewhere," Santana suggested.

The four of us walked towards the library and sat in the grass away from the crowd. We told them about how we had Columbia IDs and were hanging out until we figured out a plan.

"My parents insisted I go home, and I told them 'No way,'" Shannon said. "I was so worried about you."

"Where are you staying?" I asked.

"At the Midtown Hilton," Shannon said. "It's the largest hotel in town."

"We were there, yesterday, briefly," I said. "I hope the Cubans are okay. There were three decoy cars."

"We can pray. They had to have known the risks, but hopefully they are safe," Shannon consoled me.

"They were—they *are*—so kind." I started to tear, again. *They have to be alive*, I told myself.

"Don't worry. We'll just keep thinking positive thoughts."

"Maybe I can break into the residence system and arrange some private rooms for you," Jimmy offered.

"The more that is done along that line, the easier it will be to get caught," I replied.

Bob came over and we introduced Bob to Jimmy. The two seemed to hit it off. Things were starting to look up in some ways. I still couldn't get over the guilt of someone having maybe been hurt because of us.

By the end of the day, Shannon and I were sharing a room in John Jay, Abigail and Emily were in their own room, Bruce was rooming with Joey and Santana was rooming with Darren.

As we were eating in John Jay's first-floor dining hall, I told my friends, "I need to find a way to let my mom know I'm alive and well. I figure they will probably monitor any communication to her."

"I've taken care of it," Jimmy said. "I sent her a message telling her the packages she ordered were back-ordered but would arrive safely in due time. I signed it J and S. It was Shannon's suggestion."

"Thank you. I haven't heard anything about whether people were killed in the brownstone."

"They claim they killed you. They don't like trials or questions," Jimmy pointed out. "Remember when they supposedly killed bin Laden in Pakistan. They disposed of the body, or said they did, right away. The entire group of S.E.A.L.S. later died in a helicopter accident.

No witnesses to say it didn't happen. Of course, the people who lived on the street where it supposedly happened claimed it didn't happen. I think unless you come forward, you are safe."

"And nobody will remember what we said about the camps."

"You took on the military industrial complex and the CIA. They don't want anyone to remember any of that. Besides, a lot of students here are discussing what you said. They can't shut us up-not all of us, anyway," Bob pointed out.

"I've got some possible good news," Joey said. "I've been checking about those so-called injuries from the explosions. They were banning families from the hospital, like in Vegas, a sign that they were engaging in drills, not the real thing. A couple of the students said they blocked the bridges and the tunnels before the explosions. However, the FDR was pretty crowded. We don't know if any of those injuries were real."

"What about your parents?" I asked Shannon. "How long until they insist you return?"

"I told them it wasn't safe for me to travel and that I was going to audit classes here. I asked them to email me scans of my schoolwork assignments from California."

"And they are going to?"

"They aren't happy about it. But in view of what happened with the bridges, I was able to convince them that I'm safer staying put."

"Have you been in contact with Tiffany?"

"Yeah. I couldn't tell her any details about you, but I told her to keep the faith with a strong hint that it was more than just faith. I think she got the message. She's jealous that she can't be here."

"She's lucky. I wonder what they have planned next."

"If they think you're—you know—maybe nothing."

I knew the "you know" was in place of dead. "What about the war talk?" I asked.

"The Cuban Government issued a statement that they had nothing to do with the events of yesterday and that they are mourning the loss of the brave teens who died in the brownstone. I think the push for war has mellowed, but the U.S has ordered the Russian, Chinese and Spanish fleets out of the Gulf," Darren said.

"The Cubans didn't say they were mourning their own people?" I asked.

"Not a mention," Darren said.

"That may mean they're safe." I turned to Jimmy, "I hope my mom got Shannon's message."

"The Tunisian ambassador probably let the Cuban Consulate know we hadn't made it to Queens," Santana surmised.

We didn't have anywhere to go. But we knew this couldn't last, and we would have to leave before we got caught. Jimmy and Bob promised to monitor the official school computers for any indication that security had caught on. Jimmy was certain he could notify us with enough time to get out if there was a problem. Bob had also arranged for us to have fully stocked access cards for food and supplies for the school store. So, money wasn't an issue.

I figured that, when we were safe, maybe we could reimburse the university. I started attending classes. I actually found some of the classes interesting. I was learning both digital and analogue photography. I also attended astronomy and literature classes.

Emily was having fun in her dance and music classes. Abigail was very outspoken in her sociology classes. We all made lots of friends.

In addition to the friends who had helped us, we were making new friends, too. A girl named Serena and her friend Lucille asked me to join their astronomy study group. After the group meetings, Santana would join me looking at the stars.

I tried to stay as close to campus as possible. Santana and I were jointly taking political science from a Professor Brand who came across as anti-establishment. But then, so had Obama until he became Establishment and the Wall Street President.

"When all this is through, maybe we can go here for real," Santana suggested.

"Maybe. It's kind of nice here. Though I'm not looking forward to the winter weather. I suppose we'll be out of here long before that."

"Berkeley has good weather most of the year. It's a little cold in the winter but not like New York."

"I love that you didn't mention Stanford."

"My dad went there. Stanford is a legacy school. My oldest brother is there. My middle brother Angelo could go there if he chooses to." Santana smiled as he mentioned Angelo. "Columbia and Berkeley actually pick students who earn their spots."

"Like us?" I laughed.

"We've certainly earned something, with all we've been through."

"Angelo was your favorite."

"He sometimes tried to defend me to my dad. My dad wouldn't stand for anyone protecting me and Angelo took a lot of heat. He graduated this year. I wonder which college he decided on."

"When this is over, we'll need to go see Angelo so you can catch up on all you missed."

"Maybe we can invite him to join us in Cuba."

"That would be nice." A pang of conscience hit me over planning our future while others might not have that chance. "What about those who were injured?"

"I don't know if anyone was injured. They were closing down the highways pretty fast, and we know there were drills and crisis actors. We haven't heard of any brownstone casualties, other than us. I guess we'll never know the full details of what happened."

"You notice that, like Paddock, we are supposedly dead and can tell no tales. It's a really bizarre world we live in."

"That's for sure." He looked at my finger. "I wish you hadn't taken off your wedding ring."

"I still have it. I can put it back on when we are married for real. Abigail took off hers too, and so did Bruce."

"When people have asked me about mine, I say it's a commitment ring to the girl I love."

"I love you, too. I didn't take it off to hurt you. I took it off to blend in. Besides, I don't need a ring to be committed to you. In all that has happened, the one constant has been you."

"Forever?"

"Forever."

"Then, my ring will count for both of us."

He leaned back on the grass, and I lay with my head on his shoulder.

"I've noticed that Emily is spending a lot of time with Joey," he noted.

"She's making a lot of friends, but she misses Alejandro."

"Alejandro is really taken with her. They are both young."

"They are not that much younger than us."

"I am still concerned that Joey doesn't understand the importance of the age difference."

"Feeling like a protective brother?" I asked.

"Actually, yes."

"I think they'll be okay."

"I'm still going to keep my eye on them."

As we went back to my door, there was a flyer reminding students to get vaccinated for the Engañar flu.

"What's wrong?" I asked, seeing a surprised look on Santana's face.

"Engañar means to deceive in Spanish. Is there really such a thing as an Engañar Flu?"

"I don't know."

Santana knocked on Joey's door. The lights went on. Emily was there. "Emily, what are you doing with—" Santana started to ask but was interrupted.

"We're looking at one of Joey's inventions," Bruce, who was also there, said. "It's a set of glasses that allows us to do more than see in the dark. It zooms in on anything that moves, even insects and magnifies them. Gases other than the norm appear blue. Viruses are too small to see but should create an orangish tint if present in a significant amount."

"Oh," Santana said. "We wanted to talk to you about something."

"Anything new get blamed on us?" Bruce asked.

"Not that I know of. No. It's the Engañar Flu. Have you guys gotten a shot for it?"

"I don't get shots," Joey replied. "I was able to fake my entire vaccination record. My parents didn't want me shot up with aluminum, antifreeze and aborted fetal tissue."

I smiled. I had heard about the controversy. I knew my mom didn't like vaccines. As far as I knew, I'd never been vaccinated—in spite of school mandates, which were often overlooked for well-to-do kids. Years ago, my dad threw a fit when I didn't get the sex vaccine. He tried to force me to get it, saying we needed to promote vaccines for the good of his career. So, I lied to him and said I had been vaxxed. After that, I made a point of avoiding or lying about all other shots.

"Engañar means to trick or deceive. It's just an odd name," Santana said.

"What is that?" Darren, asked coming up behind him.

"The Engañar flu shot. Is there such a thing as an Engañar flu?"

"They claim it's killed six people so far," Darren said. "But I'm Black and vaccines have been found to cause autism at a higher rate with Blacks. I'll take my chances with the flu. I think Bob and Jimmy were going to get their shots tomorrow."

"I'll tell them to hold off. If herd immunity really works, they don't need their shots if so many others are getting them," Santana pointed out.

"I'll mention it to Abigail and Emily," I said "But I think they are avoiding nurses and what not, anyway. The last thing they want is a medical record that could lead to information about them."

"Shannon?"

"I'll talk to her tonight," I said.

"One more thing. Tomorrow is the day of our funerals," Bruce informed us.

"What?" I asked.

"Seriously. It is going to be televised. Your father is flying to New York, along with the rest of our parents."

CHAPTER 10

"This is crazy?" Santana said the next morning. "I can't believe we are going to our own funerals. That's one way they could catch us." We and our group of friends, minus Joey, were in Bob's room, discussing plans.

"We're dead," Abigail said. "We'll be going there as part of a student delegation. They will barely notice us."

"If they know we aren't dead, they'll be on the lookout for something crazy like this from us," Bruce warned.

"Or, if they believe we're alive, they'll think we would use the declaration of our deaths to run from New York and have police stationed at all routes leaving the city," I speculated. "I'm with Abigail. This may be the only time I'll get to attend my funeral, and they better do it right."

Joey came into the room. "This will help." He handed us some gas masks. "The surgical masks half of New York is wearing for the Engañar Flu will only make them sick for no reason."

"I understand most of the deaths during the Spanish Flu were from bacterial pneumonia, caused by masks," Santana noted. "You know a lot of the masks you can buy in the stores come from China and contain multiple viruses."

"Not these," Joey said. "I made them, myself and they have one-way venting pockets so we don't asphyxiate from carbon monoxide poisoning. They have air purifiers to allow us to breathe clean air and protect us from tear gas or mustard gas if they discover us."

"An improvement over the surgical masks, but won't we look out of place?" Bruce asked.

"We're arranging for the others in the Columbia delegation who will be joining us to wear them and so we will look normal. Besides, Professor Brand will be coming with us, and he was impressed when I showed him these masks. He wouldn't wear a medical face mask under any circumstances. So that's a compliment."

"I can't believe you thought Jimmy and I were serious about getting the vaccines," Bob said to Joey. "I've never been vaccinated for anything."

"And my parents knew better, too," Jimmy said. "Turns out, they were right."

We went with Columbia students and Professor Brand by bus to the Saint James Episcopalian Church of New York. There were about forty of us from our political science class, including my friends and several other students. We arrived early.

There were protestors outside, protesting the execution of the Wilderness Five. Professor Brand suggested we go into the balcony to avoid disturbing the families. Most in the crowd were wearing some kind of mask and so we didn't look out of place.

Santana whispered, "You know those masks everyone else is wearing couldn't possibly stop or slow down a virus any more than a chain-link fence could stop an ant."

Security checked our bags and ran us through metal detectors. I was a little nervous, but nobody questioned our identities. Professor Brand explained that we were all Columbia students. Security asked about the masks. Though he wasn't wearing one, Professor Brand said that some of us were concerned about the Engañar Flu and others were wearing masks in support of those with low immune systems. I wondered if he knew that was nonsense. With so many others in the crowd masking, they didn't question the reasoning.

Joey and Bruce were wearing Joey's wacky glasses that looked surprisingly normal for what they could do and see. Inside, before going up to the balcony, I saw Alonzo. Professor Brand went up to him. I kept my head down, though I longed to let him know we were okay.

Alonzo came over to our group to speak more with Professor Brand. The professor turned to our group. "They are refusing to allow Mr. Martina to speak, though he was very close to the teens."

"That's an outrage," a student named Eric said. "We should protest."

"Then you would have to join the protestors outside," Professor Brand cautioned. "This whole mockery of justice is an outrage and a disgrace."

As Brand spoke to our group, Alonzo's eyes caught mine, then his eyes caught Santana's. He looked away, but I sensed a recognition. He nodded.

"I'd be happy to join you and the students in the balcony," he said. "I went to Columbia for a semester in my youth."

"That's where we met," Professor Brand informed the group.

There were murmurs of approval rumbling through the group of students.

A girl, dressed in black, walked towards the front, crying. I noticed she and most of those in black were not wearing masks. I figured they knew the whole flu thing was a hoax and didn't want to mess up their makeup.

"Who is that?" I asked, looking at the girl. My friends from the camp shook their heads.

Shannon whispered to me, "Should I go down there and speak to make this more real?"

"It's better to let it go and watch the show," I suggested.

She nodded.

We all moved up to the balcony. Below, my father came in accompanied by my brother and the woman who had pretended to be my mom in the news reports of the crash or fake crash that supposedly occurred when we were escaping to Cuba. They were followed by Congressman Barillo with his other two sons and a woman I had seen in the news. Santana sneered at his dad. Senator Lindsay Gramcracker walked in, removing his mask as he entered.

"Wasn't he one of those calling for our execution?" I whispered to Santana.

"Guess he came here to gloat," he said.

I recognized Abigail's parents. Also, Emily's parents, whom I recognized from the news reports of the crash, arrived. There were a lot of other young people dressed in black that I didn't recognize, many sniffling. The sad, whoever they were, young black-appareled mourners sat in the reserved rows behind the families and dignitaries. I noticed that rather than having a private family section to the side, the families all chose to be up front, showing off their probably feigned sadness.

Ambassador Sanchez was also up front. I guessed they couldn't stop an Ambassador from expressing his concerns.

I whispered to Santana and my fellow campers, "Do you know any of those other individuals in black behind in the reserved section?"

They all shook their heads. "Never saw them before," Santana replied.

I whispered to Jimmy, who was standing behind Shannon. "Where did they get these people?"

"Rent a Mourner?" Jimmy suggested.

"Isn't it great. They throw you a funeral, and everyone you've never met in your life shows up," Santana joked.

Then someone I recognized showed up and sat beside my dad. It was Matt. His father sat on the other side of Matt.

"Are any of us Episcopalian?" I asked.

"I'm Catholic," Santana said.

Abigail, Emily and Bruce shook their heads. Abigail moved closer to me. "A lot of major funerals take place here. It's not related to religion."

"Oh," I said.

We took our seats. Bruce and Jimmy sat behind Shannon and Abigail, who were to the left of Santana and me. On my other side were Emily and Joey. To Shannon's left were Bob, Darren, Professor Brand and Alonzo. The remainder of the students filled up the four rows behind us in the balcony.

The funeral started with an invocation from an Episcopal priest. Then, the Vice President spoke about how American kids have gone astray because of a lack of morality. He expounded on the supposed sins of youth that had gotten out of hand and had turned all young people into likely terrorists or otherwise depraved individuals. I looked behind me. The students in the balcony were mostly rolling their eyes, motioning with their hands to imply the Vice President was looney, and otherwise whispering insults at him.

Next, Abigail's father spoke about what a beautiful baby she was and how sad it was that she had turned into a terrorist. He warned the crowd this could happen to any child. I noticed Abigail making a throat-slicing motion.

This was followed by a guy who spoke about how he had been dating Abigail until she had fallen for a Muslim, who had indoctrinated her in the ways of ISIL. I whispered to Abigail. "Ever seen that guy before?"

"He looks like one of my dad's interns."

Santana's father spoke of how Santana had gone awry, hanging out with street gangs and some of the more radical people protesting police violence. That got snickers from the students, particularly the African American students, one of whom held up a fist.

Santana's oldest brother Enrique said, "Santana became interested in Cuba and started hanging out with a pro-Cuban crowd. That was when he really went jihadist. After the way Castro treated my grandfather, he should have known better."

I leaned towards Santana.

"My grandfather was one of the mobsters Castro eventually threw out, along with my dad," he whispered. "But I don't know anything about a pro-Cuban crowd. There were a lot of Mexican-Americans in our neighborhood."

My dad took to the podium with a sad expression I'd seen him practice over the years. "Summer was a good kid for a long time. She had a good boyfriend. Then she started hanging out with the wrong crowd. I wish I had sent her to camp earlier. They might have been able to correct her tendencies if only I hadn't waited so long to have her fixed."

"I'm with Abigail. Menendezing him would be too good," I murmured to Santana.

The woman on the other side of my brother, my fake mother, was crying.

Next, my brother got up. "What happened to her was horrible. However, I'm certain that, if the Summer I grew up with had seen what she would later become, she would have asked them to put her out of her misery."

The students with me started booing. Security came over and hushed the crowd.

After Pandar finished, Matt got up. "I loved Summer. However, there was a Russian boy at the school who convinced her that the Russian way was better than the American way. He took her to meetings, Russian communist meetings."

"Russia's no longer communist," I whispered to Santana.

"She started trying to push me into supporting free education, government-funded health care, free speech and ending the necessary wars."

"I thought those were Democratic ideals?" I commented to Santana. "I never went to any Russian meetings."

"Was that what you dated?"

"That was what my dad forced me to date."

"Finally, it got to be too much. I told her she would have to go back to being Summer or we couldn't be together."

Shannon threw an orange that was in her purse down at the podium, landing it perfectly on Matt's nose. Security started looking around the balcony. She sat there innocently. Security questioned some of the students as to who threw the orange.

The students responded with, "What orange?" and "I don't know." Several students shushed security, and the guards finally gave up.

"I can't wait to see what they claim about Bruce and Emily. Maybe the North Koreans or Iranians recruited them," I whispered.

Down the row, I could see Alonzo shaking his head and mouthing "lies."

Bruce's father spoke about how Bruce had taken up experiments with explosives, even blew up his high school chemistry lab. He was certain his son was behind the bridge and tunnel disasters and felt such pain over the losses suffered by so many.

Emily's father talked about how she had been troubled but nowhere near as bad as she became after she met me and Santana and ran away with us. "If she had been able to stay at camp, she would be enjoying herself and looking forward to her future right now," her dad said. He was still the head of the Counsel on Foreign Relations and like Abigail's father, a very strong warmonger. "Getting in with those kids and with the Cuban Government, they learned terrorism. We must not let down our defenses against Cuba. They must pay for what they have done."

The unknown crying girl in black got up to speak. "Summer was my best friend. I tried to warn her about the Russians she got involved with, but she would not listen to me."

"Nice, coming from someone I've never met," I whispered to Santana.

Finally, Ambassador Sanchez spoke. They couldn't deny an official dignitary. As he took to the podium, there were boos from the well-dressed elite crowd of strangers on the floor below.

"The teens who were killed were good kids. None of them were into terrorism. However, they were victims of terrorism perpetrated on them by your government." More boos from the crowd below but cheers from the Columbia crowd in the balcony.

I was glad that Ricardo Sanchez's English was as good as it was.

"They were innocent but murdered by a killer robot without a trial. This was a violation of *The Constitution* your country claims to hold so dear." The Columbia students stood cheering as the crowd below was drowned out by the cheers. We joined them in standing and cheering so as to not look out of place while hoping not to be recognized.

Darren yelled, "Tell them, brother."

I noticed someone from security escorting the Ambassador away.

The crowd behind me chanted, "Let him speak, let him speak."

Following him, Mickey Comet got up to speak. The Columbia students started grumbling insults at her and then sat down as security looked as if they were about to remove us.

"What do you expect from the country that trained them in terrorism?" With that, she got boos from the students and applause from the fake mourners below.

"Something is coming in through the vents below," Joey warned us.

CHAPTER 11

Bob passed gas masks to Dr. Brand and told him to give one to Alonzo. "No questions. Joey sees some kind of gas seeping in. Better to be safe than sorry," he whispered.

Bruce leaned forward and confirmed he had seen it as well.

The rest of us, after whispering repeats of Joey's and Bruce's observations to other students who passed it on, made sure our gas masks were tightly pressed against our faces and that our noses and mouths were covered. Bob signaled for everyone in the balcony to get up and leave. We started for the stairs. Security watched but was probably glad we were leaving. A minute later, we heard screams. I looked back. Mickey had fallen and others were starting to gag. Security looked at us all suspiciously. We moved quickly down into the entry area. "That service was such bunk," Bob said, his voice muffled somewhat by his mask.

People were starting to rush out. Police were trying to hold everyone back.

"Nobody leave," an officer instructed. A line of blue was at the front. We headed for a side exit. Two officers approached our group.

One of the officers ordered, "Remove your masks. We are quarantining this building and we want to see all faces." Before he said another word, he collapsed. Another officer pulled out his gun and collapsed as well.

"Let's go before they bring out the robot bombers," Joey said, putting his little box back in his pocket.

Our group rushed for the door and down the street. From behind, a police car started to approach us, but there was a dense crowd on the sidewalks, spilling into the street.

We pulled off our gas masks and blended in as we and the street crowd, mostly protesters and homeless people, moved away from the officers. Some of the Columbia students grabbed signs and the rest of the group mostly scattered.

Santana, Abigail, Bruce, Emily, Shannon, Jimmy and I held hands to avoid losing each other. "Maybe we should scatter, too," I suggested. "We're more recognizable together."

Before anyone could answer me, a long limo stopped. We couldn't tell who was in it, but someone with a foreign accent called us inside.

"Foreigners," Santana mouthed with a slight smile.

Santana, Abigail, Bruce, Shannon, Jimmy and I got in along with Darren, Bob and Joey. A woman in the front called to Alonzo and the Professor, who had been loosely following us, "How about a ride?" They joined us in the passenger section, where there were two long seats, stretched from the doors to the back.

Behind the driver and facing the back was a computer screen that was silently showing a rerun of the service with Cyrillic subtitles. A radio speaker next to it was broadcasting information in a foreign language. On the sides of the computer and speaker were back-facing seats, one with a man with a bulge in his coat and the other with the woman who had spoken to us. There was also someone up front in addition to the driver but I couldn't see his face.

As I looked away from the front, towards the rear of the car, I saw the Russian Ambassador. He spoke in very broken English, but appeared to say, "I'm so glad reports of your deaths have—"

We all laughed.

My campmates and I sat on the side where we had entered while the Columbia crowd, Alonzo and the professor sat across from us next to the Ambassador.

Bruce said, "Sir. It would probably be best if reports of our deaths stayed as they are."

Professor Brand didn't look surprised by what should have been revelations. "I thought it was you," he said.

"We were framed," I responded, quickly.

"I know. Only a fool would have bought the official story. False flags have been taking place since this country was founded."

The woman informed us, "A number of people have fallen, and they are quarantining the building. They are claiming it was the Engañar Flu."

Joey pulled off his glasses. "These are an invention of mine. It was definitely some kind of gas coming through the vents. If it was a virus, the tint through these would have been different and it wasn't."

"They are quarantining the building, demanding that the survivors get Engañar flu shots," the woman said. "Oh, my name is Ivanova Kornishnikov. I'm an attaché to the Consulate."

"What's in those shots?" I queried.

"Remember when they drugged us at the camp," Santana recollected. "They said that was part of an experiment. Maybe it has something to do with the shots."

The Professor pulled out his cell phone. "I'm calling the department secretary." Apparently, she picked up. "Hello, please send out an email to all my students telling them to see me before getting any shots. It's a long story. Wait to get one yourself as well… Janet, I think there may be a problem with the shots, and they could be more dangerous than the Engañar flu. I want to talk with the students and let them decide for themselves… What?" He looked taken aback. "Send out the email anyway, and pretend I didn't get the Dean's memo. Thank you."

He turned to us. "The Dean has sent out a memo. All students are required to get the shots in order to continue attending classes. No exceptions, not medical, religious or other exemptions."

"The word 'Engañar' means 'to deceive.' It's a trick flu," Alonzo advised him. "Ricardo Sanchez was in there. I hope he is safe."

"It looked to me as if he were escorted to the back after he spoke.

Someone from the NYPD was trying to speak to him. Anyone see where he was when Mickey Idiot was speaking?" Darren asked.

I hadn't seen. We all lightly shook our heads.

"Sir," Bob said to Dr. Brand. "If the shots really are dangerous, we could give water shots to students and pretend they are the real thing."

"That would be completely unethical, particularly if this flu is real. We'll have to discuss it."

"Notice, we are healthy. We left right after the gas started coming through the vents. The people who stayed are the ones who had the problems," Joey said. "That tells me it was the gas, not this faux flu."

"It probably hadn't reached the balcony by the time we left, and the masks may have helped with what reached the areas we walked through. A virus would have stayed on our clothes, our bodies. The fact that it was instantaneously effective below means it spread quickly and harmfully. Still, if we aren't sick, that should have some meaning," Bruce expounded.

"Not only are you brave, you are very intelligent," the Russian Ambassador said.

"We were going to come to your consulate our first night, but it was surrounded by the police," I informed him.

"There was a big scare going on in New York. Terrorists," he laughed. "The robo-bombing put law enforcement and the National Guard at ease."

"Did anyone die in that?"

"I don't know," the ambassador replied.

"It was a set-up," Alonzo related. "A nurse helped move some bodies from a hospital morgue and we called in the alert that you were in the building."

I moved across to where Alonzo was sitting and gave him a hug. "That was brilliant! Thank you. I've been feeling so guilty."

"What about victims in the bridge and tunnel collapses?" Santana asked as I returned to my seat.

"We can't be sure about all of them, but we have word that the majority of them were crisis actors paid to be part of a drill," the ambassador informed us.

Joey gave us a thumbs up, as we already knew about the drills, having seen them online.

"The bulk of the people don't ever question the false flags, and they always put down those who do as conspiracy theorists," Abigail said.

"You particularly pose a serious threat, given who your parents are. Your situation calls into question the Administration, the Congress, some of the technologies your government is using and its war agenda. With your seeming demise, you are significantly safer," he pointed out.

"I just want to go home to Rosa," Emily lamented.

"But we love you here," Joey told her.

"Thank you," she replied solemnly.

"Cheer up, Emily. We'll find a way to get you home," I assured her.

"Rosa terribly misses you, Emily. She's very angry with me for not bringing her to New York with the delegation," Alonzo said.

"I'm glad she's not here," Emily replied. "She'd be hunted, too."

"Today, they were blaming Russian, ISIL and Cuban influences for our supposed conversion to terrorism," Bruce chuckled and then looked more serious. "I'm worried that they will start another war."

"Only on defenseless countries," the Ambassador said. "Anything with regards to us generally is rhetoric or involves proxy wars. In your country, wars are about resource theft, politics and money scams."

"What about Cuba?" Santana asked.

"We have a united front around Cuba. The Chinese and Spanish have joined us. We have agreed to remove our ships from the Gulf only if they leave Cuba alone."

"They are threatening over supposedly being threatened," Joey pointed out the irony.

"Rhetoric, I believe. I'll tell you a secret. We are better prepared for World War III. We don't want it, but we're better prepared and they know it."

Ivanova, who had been half listening to the Russian language radio, turned towards the back. "Mickey Comet is dead," she related. "They are claiming this flu kills instantly."

"But it wasn't the flu. They gassed them," Emily declared.

"We can't prove it, and they'll pay experts to lie," Joey said. "If only I had put a camera in these glasses."

"And the government will see to it there's no autopsy," Santana predicted.

"Our parents were there. Do you think any of them are sick?" I asked.

"Our parents probably were behind it. They probably had fake noses," Abigail responded.

"I like this girl," the Ambassador said. "I hope you eventually get your father's position."

"What? Warmonger?"

"I don't think you would be a warmonger. You might be able to help us bring about world peace."

"Abigail, your mother has been taken to the isolation ward in the hospital. It looks like it's the Henry Kissinger Specialty Hospital," Ivanova said. "She is in critical condition."

"And my father?" Abigail asked.

"I don't know."

"He's the one who deserves to die," she said. She tried to look stern, but I could see some tears forming along the edges of her contacts. She tried to dab her eye area.

"Is there a way we can get to the hospital?" I asked.

"Even if we were to go there, it's unlikely Abigail could get to her mother without disclosing who she is. And that would put you all in danger," the Ambassador warned.

"My mother didn't love me, anyway," she lamented. She couldn't stop the tear that rolled down her cheek.

"Maybe we could dress her up as a nurse and send her in as part of the nursing staff," I suggested.

"She could say she was sent in because of her expertise with contagious diseases," Bruce reasoned.

The limo had very dark glass, but we couldn't be certain outside facial scanners or other devices wouldn't expose who we were.

"I'll have a couple members of my country's security team meet me close to the hospital with your nurse's outfit. They'll escort you in and keep you safe until you are out," the Ambassador offered.

I was almost overcome by the concern of a Russian diplomat for an American teen. The rhetoric between Russia and the USA was so over the top. If our leaders would just shut up with the Russia-hate, our countries might be good friends.

"That's not far from Columbia," Bob said.

The Ambassador dropped most of us off at Columbia and continued to the meeting place with Abigail and Bruce, who was going to assist her. Given his scientific background, we figured he could cover for any slip-ups if they occurred. Alonzo promised to make sure my mom knew we were safe.

We went back to the dorm and waited.

About midnight, Bruce and Abigail returned.

"Is your mom—" I started to ask.

Abigail shook her head.

"I'm so sorry. I know you had your differences, but—"

"She's not the only one."

CHAPTER 12

Abigail took my hands. "Your father didn't make it either."

I hadn't even realized he was in the hospital. All the hatred I had for him seemed to vanish. He was gone. I didn't forgive what he had done to me and my mother, but I felt stunned and saddened that a life had been extinguished.

A memory flashed through my mind. It was of my parents during one of my dad's more peaceful moments. My dad brought my mother a rose and pinned it to her outfit. Then he picked me up and said, "You two are as beautiful as roses." *What had happened to him? Was that all a lie?*

After I saw my mom again, she told me that my dad had once acted like he was devoted to her, as if he had worshiped the ground she walked on. Was what happened to him what happens to men in general? Would Santana someday become like my dad? How could I trust anyone if men who claimed to be in love turned into what my dad had become? Or was my dad that way all along and faking being a good person?

Santana put his arms around me and held me for a minute. Then he turned to Abigail. "I'm sorry about your mom."

"She only cared about her position. She didn't love me. She didn't stop him from sending me to the camp. Emily's parents are gone too."

"Both of them?" I asked.

She nodded.

"I'm sure she'll wake up when we go to your room," I said. I went there with Abigail, and we sat next to Emily on the bed. She opened her eyes and looked at us.

"I had a dream that my mother came here and apologized. She said she loved me and was so sorry for all she hadn't done to protect me."

"I think stuff like that is real," Abigail said. "I'm sure deep down inside, she loved you."

Emily looked at us, without saying anything for several seconds. "She's gone, isn't she?" It was a statement, not a question.

I nodded. "We love you, Emily."

"My father's gone, too?" she asked.

Again, I nodded. "You're in our family now."

"I was never lucky enough to have a sister until the two of you."

"And Alonzo said Rosa misses you terribly."

She was visibly tearing, and then she broke out in a sob. "I kept hoping that they would tell me it was a mistake, their sending me to camp, but I saw them today. They were okay with that robo-thing killing me. They never loved me."

"That image you had of your mother coming to you. Hold onto that. Sometimes people get messed up. Believe that image was your real mother."

She nodded. Abigail and I lay down beside her and held each other until we fell asleep.

Early in the morning, before sunrise, Jimmy knocked on the door.

"What is it?" I asked opening the door.

"Santana. The news just said his brother died."

"Where is he?" I asked.

"Outside in the Southwest field," Jimmy said. "Darren is with him."

I went out there. Darren hugged me and went back to the dorm as I sat down with Santana. We didn't say anything. We just sat there. "Enrique, my oldest brother, was always my father's favorite," he said. "He was one of those kids who was perfect. And he always knew it. Enrique always judged me as being unacceptable. But Angelo, my middle brother, he tried to be good but always had time for me. He didn't hold my craziness against me. While Enrique lied up there, Angelo held back. They couldn't get him to lie. And now he's dead. If I had ever gone back, it would have been to see Angelo."

"I know there's nothing I can say that can make it better. I wish I could take it all away."

"You are my everything. It hurt losing Angelo but nothing like it would hurt losing you. Promise you'll never die, that you'll never leave me."

I knew that not dying wasn't a promise I could make. "Not by my choice," I said. "If I have any say, I'll be here with you forever."

As the sun came up, we held each other. Feelings of loss just wouldn't come where my father was concerned. But if anything ever happened to Santana, that would be my world. He would never be like my father. He didn't have it in him.

"When I was a kid, I had a dog named Fluffy," I said. "He was a Pomeranian. I really loved him. With my mom gone and my first dog, Cynthia, dead, I found Fluffy. He was lonely like me and all I had. He was so sweet, and I really loved him."

Santana watched me as my eyes started to form tears.

"One day, he chewed on my dad's shoes. Dad got so angry. He had to go out and said he would deal with Fluffy later. I was so worried that I hid him in my room that night and made sure he didn't bark. But the following day, I had to go to school. When I came home, Fluffy wasn't there. I asked my brother. He said Fluffy had fallen. But I knew that wasn't true. He looked beaten. He was lying in the backyard barely breathing. I lifted him very careful using a piece of plywood to keep him still as he wasn't moving at all. I had heard you could kill a human by moving them wrong after they had fallen. I walked him over to a vet in my neighborhood and begged him to save Fluffy. He said there was nothing he could do. Fluffy's neck and most of the bones in his body were broken and he suspected internal damage to the organs based on his tests. I stayed there with Fluffy, praying that a miracle would happen. It didn't. I know they say dogs can't smile, but it was as if he smiled as he managed to wag his tail at me, one last time, just before he died." I was sobbing. "I think my dad murdered Fluffy. I kept hoping it wasn't true. But I saw what he said about me yesterday. I think he was okay with me being dead, and I think he murdered Fluffy."

Santana was holding me. He was crying too. "I'm sorry. I wish I had known you before the camp."

"I'm sad that someone I knew died, but I'm not sad that I lost my father. He was a monster." All the anger and hate had returned. "I'm glad that he's no longer in my life. Does that make me terrible?"

"It makes you human. He *was* a monster. My father was a monster, too. I wish he had died instead of Angelo."

"Will we ever become like them? My mom said my dad used to be nice. I don't want to wake up some morning and find that you've turned into someone else."

"If you want, I'll write a pre-nup allowing you to have me executed if I do."

I laughed.

Bob came out into the field. "I have vaccination cards for both of you. It shows you've had the Engañar vaccine. I also have cards for Joey and Darren and all your friends. Oh, and for Professor Brand: I dropped his card anonymously in his mailbox this morning. Joey and I will be volunteering with the shots for the school and we're going to create a distraction and then change out as many of the vaccines to water as we can."

"How did Joey get his device by the metal detectors?" I asked.

"It's not metal, Santana explained. "I know it looks it, but the box and tube are a high grade of plastic. The wire insulation is water. He showed me the schematics after you left with Abigail last night."

"Genevieve was working on some kind of mind-control technology with Bruce's dad. I wonder if she has some thoughts on this."

"Genevieve?" Bob inquired.

"A homeless lady who used to work for Beklet. We met her in the park. She's a genius. But I don't know how to find her," Santana responded.

"Do you think her daughter's painting is still on exhibit at the Met?" I asked Santana.

"Maybe."

"Joey and I can check it out this evening with you," Bob offered.

"Some little girl recognized us the last time we were in there. They might be on the lookout for us," Santana warned.

"We'll bring Darren and maybe Professor Brand. You and your friends can wait outside to verify it's her."

"I like that plan," Santana responded.

Throughout the day, students lined up for shots. The bulk of the undergrad shots were being given out in quick order at the Low Memorial Library. Apparently, they didn't want to bog down Columbia's Medical Center. But there were other locations where the shots were being given too. Our friends were working with the students lining up at Low, but we didn't know to what extent they were able to change out the vaccines. We were pretty sure they hadn't been able to do so at the other locations.

Professor Brand called me, Santana and Abigail into his office. "I wanted to tell you how sorry I was to hear about your families. They've stopped releasing information about the casualties—except that there are now reportedly five-hundred unidentified people in critical condition. I don't know if that's real or fake."

"It should have been my father," Abigail angrily stated. "My mother was cold and uncaring, but not half as bad as him."

"Does that hard exterior fool a lot of people?" Brand asked.

Abigail took a while to respond to the question. "When you are raised by people who care more about what they are having for dinner than about you, you learn to stop showing any concern."

"I'm sorry. I'd be proud to have a daughter like you."

"Thank you."

He looked at me and Santana.

"My father may have loved me once, but not in a long time. I want to feel bad. I should feel bad, but I don't. Not for him, personally. I mostly feel sad that any human being died."

"I saw what your father said. That must have been terrible for you."

"The last day I was with him, he hit me because Matt broke up with me. Apparently, I wasn't the perfect girlfriend. I never hung out with any Russians, and I didn't even like Matt very much, but I was dating him because that's what my father wanted."

"And then he sent you off to be fixed so you would stop thinking and just do what you were told. He must have been an awful human being. I'm not sorry a man like that is gone, but I'm sorry for your loss." Professor Brand placed his hand on my shoulder and I could see the sympathy in his eyes. Then, he looked at Santana.

"The brother who died was the nice one, the one who chose not to lie about me at the funeral. I don't understand why the good brother had to be the one to die."

"I don't have any answers to that. Jacqueline Kennedy was probably wondering why her husband and not some jerk out there who was pushing wars and attacks on minorities, was killed. Sometimes the best die first."

"We didn't blow up any bridges or tunnels," I reiterated.

"I know. I never doubted you. It's a tough thing when the politicians and the media prejudge individuals without evidence. Once the damage is done, it's hard to undo. If there is anything I can do for you, let me know."

"Actually—" I said.

Santana picked up my thought. "We were hoping that you might be free this evening. There is this homeless woman named Genevieve who used to work with Bruce's dad. We thought she might have information on saving people."

"Do you know where she might be?"

"We met her in Central Park, but her daughter has a painting at the Met," Santana replied.

"Bob is planning to have Joey and Darren go there tonight in the hopes of finding her, and we were hoping you could go too," I said.

"I'll arrange to be available. Do you have my cell number?"

"No. Actually, we don't have cell phones, but I think our friends do," I responded.

"I'll give you my number. Have them call me and we'll arrange a time."

"Thank you," I said, as Santana nodded.

Brand wrote his cell number on three cards and handed them to us. Then he looked at Abigail. "Anytime you want a friend or a shoulder to cry on, feel free to give me a visit. I have large shoulders." His shoulders weren't that large, but we got the point of the offer. He wanted her to know she wasn't alone. "Same applies to the two of you," he told me and Santana.

"Thank you," both Santana and I replied. Abigail echoed our "Thank you."

***

That evening, we went to the Met. It was closed. Concerns about the Engañar Flu were causing much of New York to close down.

Across from the Met, people were lined up to get the Engañar shot. It reminded me of the movie, *The Invasion,* with Nicole Kidman. In that movie they were using vaccinations to infect people with some kind of alien consciousness that took over their minds.

I thought back to the way those drugged with the soup had responded to the soundwaves at camp. They reminded me of the people in *The Invasion,* soulless and empty, willing to harm others when told to do so. My friends and I hadn't drunk the soup, and we had had earplugs, or we might have been subject to the same thing.

"Earplugs," I said.

"What?" Professor Brand asked.

"In the camp, they drugged everyone and then they used sound waves. We didn't drink the soup and we had earplugs. But we played along and acted like zombies. They made people in the camp hurt others, some with knives and guns. Everyone did what they were told. We did our best to fake it."

"If you had the earplugs in, how did you hear the commands?"

"We could hear some stuff, but the plugs cut out the bulk of the radio wave technology."

"Let's go get some sound suppressors or earplugs," Joey suggested. We stopped into a Duane Reade store and picked up earplugs for each of us.

"Genevieve was talking about electro-magnetic wave frequencies. Will these screen those out?" I asked.

"There is only so much we can do about that. We can try to build Faraday cages in our rooms though," Bob related.

"Look at that line," I said. Across the street from the Duane Reade was a table where nurses were giving out the vaccines to a line of people that stretched around a block. We watched for a while.

"Look," Santana pointed. In the line, we saw Genevieve.

CHAPTER 13

Before anyone else could say anything, Santana and I bolted across the street, followed by Bruce, Abigail and Emily.

"Oh, my friends," Genevieve said when we reached her. "Toby, Charlene, James, Elissa and Jackie."

I smiled. "You need to come with us."

"But I'll lose my place. This is the line for the free shots."

"We know a shorter line," I said, trying not to cause a stir.

"Where?" The woman behind her said.

"They only have one more vaccine and I told them I'd look for Genevieve," I lied.

"For me?"

"Yes."

"But we've been waiting just as long as she has," the other woman snapped.

"This line will move fast enough," I replied.

Genevieve came across the street where we introduced her to Professor Brand, Joey, Darren and Bob.

"It was so nice of Charlene and Toby to get me," she said.

"Who?" Bob asked and then Darren kicked him.

"Let's go to the North Woods where we can talk," Joey recommended.

"What about the shots?"

"That's why we're going to the North Woods," Joey replied.

"An odd place to get a shot."

"We'll explain everything there." I didn't want to explain or cause a scene with people around and that seemed a good place for a little privacy.

On the way over, Joey showed her his device and explained how it worked.

"You, Columbia students, are so clever."

"Let me show you another of my devices." He put a pair of his glasses on her. "See if you can observe any insects moving on the ground. Minute particles are also magnified. Gases show up in color."

"I can see microscopic insects. What a wonderful invention," she said, taking off the glasses. "But there are no shots out here."

"The shots are a fake. It's not about protecting people," I informed her.

"It wasn't the Engañar Flu that killed those people. It was gas," Abigail explained.

"Gas, but—"

"We saw it with these glasses. It came out of the vents," Joey said.

"I don't understand. You were in the church? James what is this?" she asked, looking at Bruce.

"Let me introduce myself. My name is Bruce Jenkens. You worked with my father at Darkwave."

"But you're—"

"Alive, and I didn't blow any bridges or tunnels."

"We were framed," I said.

She looked at Emily, who nodded.

"Miss. I didn't catch your last name," Professor Brand said to Genevieve.

"Saint Ellis," she replied.

"Miss Saint Ellis. You seem like a very intelligent woman. We could probably use someone with your knowledge on our staff at Columbia. But I need to tell you that these kids know what they are talking about. I was there too. It was not a flu attack that killed those people."

"I don't understand."

"You worked with my dad on some kind of wave technology for mind control. We saw that at the camp. First, they drugged the campers. Then, they used sound waves to get them to do all kinds of things they never would have done in their proper state of mind."

"You are saying they are doing that with the shots?"

"We don't know for sure. But there is something odd about this whole Engañar outbreak."

"Just to humor us, wait a day or two to get your shot. If the herd theory works, you don't need the shot. The vaccine the others get will protect you," I advised.

"True but—"

"And here are some earplugs. They may help." Joey handed her a pair.

"Miss Saint Ellis, do you have a place to stay for the night?" I asked.

"I generally stay somewhere in the park."

"How about I get you a room at the Morningside Inn? Do you have luggage?" Professor Brand asked.

"It's in the same locker we put it in the night I met you kids."

"I'll go with Darren to get it," Santana said. "The rest of you accompany Genevieve to the Morningside. Where is the Morningside?"

"107th between Amsterdam and Broadway," the professor replied.

"Good. Within walking distance of our dorm," Bruce noted.

Santana and Darren got the storage key from Genevieve and rushed off. Genevieve still seemed overwhelmed, trying to take everything in. I was hoping the overwhelm didn't push her into reporting us, but Professor Brand seemed to be charming her. Emily walked next to her and Genevieve held Emily's hand. Good sign.

About the time Professor Brand got her checked in, Darren and Santana showed up with her cart of belongings. "Family," Genevieve told the clerk. "They want to make sure I settle in and am tucked in sweetly."

The clerk went about his business, as if bored by the whole thing.

In her room, Bob pulled out a small laptop from his backpack and set it up. "Wow!" he explained. "I'm now looking at the hospital where the people were taken. I think you should see this."

"Holy," Bruce started to say when he went over to the computer.

"Santana, tell me I'm not seeing things," Bruce said.

Santana looked at the computer. "I wonder if they lied about anyone else?"

"What?" I said, going over to look. "Abigail, you were at the hospital. Did you actually see the other people who died?"

"I didn't even see my mother. I wasn't allowed in the room. There was a special crew already in there."

"Then, you heard about everyone second hand."

"There was some kind of government spokesperson saying who had died."

"I saw them pushing a table down the corridor. The tag on the arm read your father's name." Bruce told me. "The spokesperson told us about the others."

Bruce's observations meant my father probably was dead. And still, I didn't feel anything personal regarding my father. *Is something wrong with me?* But the others were based on an official report.

"Emily. Look at this picture," Bruce called her over. It was a press conference from the night before in front of the hospital. My focus was on someone in the background.

"Oh, my God!" Emily exclaimed. "That's my father, leaving the hospital, alive. What, he faked his death?"

CHAPTER 14

"The spokesperson inside the hospital listed him among the dead when we were there," Abigail said.

"His death wasn't announced in the official press conference," Joey recalled. "The announcements included that Mickey Idiot, Santana's brother, Abigail's mother, Summer's father and others, but not your father."

"Genevieve, you worked with the government on something related to mass mind control. The media is part of it. They are programming people," Santana said.

"Everyone wants to fit in. They don't want to be awake. Genevieve, you were awake, and you saw what happened to you. Being awake is scary," I added.

"Ever since I was thrown out, I have wanted to fit in."

"The fact that you are aware of the process puts you lightyears ahead of those who so want to fit in that they are willing to go along with the lies." I was trying to give her the courage to remember who she once was. If the need to fit in, to think like others, was controlling her, we could all be in trouble.

"I do remember. I tried to tell others what I had discovered and why I thought I was fired. Nobody wanted to believe it. It didn't fit their version of the world," Genevieve related. I relaxed a little.

Emily gave her a hug. "I knew we could trust you."

"The drugs. They aren't the mind control. They make people more susceptible to mind control. I used to avoid vaccines because of the aluminum, formaldehyde and mercury. Those dramatically dull the mind." It was as if a lightbulb had gone off in her head as she spoke.

"My parents didn't get me vaccinated," Bruce said. "They were scientists, and they weighed the risks. But they don't have to vaccinate to simply kill off the population. Look at the contamination that goes into water. The water in thousands of cities across America is more toxic than Flint, and the government isn't cleaning any of it up."

"They tried to drug us with soup," I reiterated.

"We would like you to go over what you witnessed with Joey and Bruce. If we know exactly what they are doing, maybe we can figure out how to counter it," Professor Brand encouraged her.

I looked at her. She looked drained. "Perhaps we should let Genevieve get a good night's sleep and then get started in the morning," I suggested.

Professor Brand looked at her. "I think that is best."

As we walked back to Columbia, Professor Brand said, "What you said about the soup. Be careful of anything you eat or drink. Sealed bottles and personally-made food."

We walked past one of the vaccination lines. A woman was standing there with her child.

"Maybe you should wait to get your child vaccinated," I said.

Santana was trying to guide me away.

"Are you an anti-vaxxer?"

"I just don't know about this vaccine," I said, trying to act nonchalant. "It hasn't had time to be properly tested."

"I trust the government."

"Sometimes the government isn't always right."

"Are you a conspiracy theorist?" The woman was practically shouting at me.

At that point, Santana pulled me away. "Like you said, some people just want to fit in. Some are so eager to join the mass consciousness that they sacrifice their children."

"Like our parents?"

"Not so much. They were among those who should have known. The manipulators."

I nodded.

We went back to John Jay. Shannon and Jimmy were waiting outside Joey's room. "Where did you guys go?"

"We were rounding up a scientist," I said. "Joey and Bruce are going to work with her, starting tomorrow, to undo whatever they are doing."

"I'm in," Jimmy said.

Shannon and I walked up to our room.

"Maybe tomorrow we can go out on the town and take pictures after our classes. I'm supposedly a photography major. We're not really students. We could spend some time enjoying New York," I suggested.

"My parents have heard of the Engañar Flu and they are demanding I come back," Shannon informed me.

"Are you going to? You might be safer there?"

"I'm not sure I trust planes after what happened to yours. They could target me because I'm your friend."

"Right."

"I was looking stuff up online," she said. "On *Truthstream*, they were interviewing a doctor who was working with mind control victims. They were using frequencies to plant words in their head, mostly destructive words."

"Interesting."

"They were trying to make these people appear crazy. They would stalk them and leave obvious clues in their homes to show the people they had been there, but the people couldn't do anything about it or even talk about it or they would be seen as crazy. The victims were mostly women who were alone, who didn't have anyone to help them prove what was happening."

"If we were to go public with what we suspect about this latest vaccine, they'd call us wackos or anti-vax. Even those who have had most of their vaccines and only oppose this one are anti-vax."

"Did you know there's a secret vaccine court through which the government has paid out millions of dollars in damages over vaccines that have injured or killed kids?" she asked.

"I think because there is so much profit in vaccines, they are skipping a lot of safety standards that one would expect them to be using," I said. "I know Robert Kennedy, Jr., has spoken a lot about it."

"If you can't question anything, you can't improve it."

"Right. Even Kennedy has been attacked, even though his kids have gotten all their childhood vaccines."

Shannon looked thoughtful. "Have you thought about going to the hospital to see Pandar, assuming he's there?"

"No. It would be bad if he died, but he isn't a real brother. He let Dad beat Mom and later me. He is so Stockholmed that he can't even see that anything Dad did was wrong. And he'd turn me in if he knew I were alive."

"Now that your dad's dead, maybe he will come around."

"I won't believe it if he does. I'm sure he'll inherit a fortune from Dad, and he'll use it to oppress others. I feel sorry for whomever he marries."

"Do you think your dad left anything to you?"

"Are you kidding?"

"Anything we need to do—besides not take the vaccine?"

"Don't drink from any water fountains or open bottles of water. Only eat food you know is safe. And wear earplugs," I said. I pulled some out of my pocket. "I'm sure Santana or one of the others is giving a set to Jimmy."

"I'll text him to make sure. But will I be able to hear with them in?"

"They cut down certain frequencies and lower volume. They don't cut out all sound. In the camp, without the plugs, there were perimeter barriers that set off major head pain. Without the soup and earplugs, we could hear murmurings through the air but they didn't work until the drugs came."

"Like those people who are hearing voices?"

"Yes, but on a more massive scale. They were probably the test samples, as were we."

"Remember how they tapped Trump's phones before he became President in 2017."

"Yeah. I remember."

"What if they are doing that to the phones at the U.N.? What if something has been said on their phones that has alerted them to the fact that you are alive?"

The thought made me flinch a little. "We can't worry about everything. They already did a second funeral for us. Remember, we supposedly officially died in the Ohio plane crash, originally. It will make them look pretty incompetent if they announce we're alive."

"But they might come after you."

"They might—if they know we are here. Have you heard of any more deaths?"

"They are keeping a lot of the specifics locked down. I'm just hearing numbers. Supposedly four hundred are in critical condition and one-fifty are dead."

"And of course, we're fine."

"They undoubtedly noticed that some students in the balcony escaped. But they also know we won't go public out of fear."

"Those mourners at the funeral were mostly fake. I'm wondering if they are part of a fake death count."

Shannon looked deep in thought.

"Emily's father is alive. We saw a video where he was in the background leaving the hospital."

"We couldn't be so lucky as to lose the head of the CFR." She was being sarcastic, of course.

"For Emily's sake, I'm glad he's alive—no matter how many wars he is likely to start."

"He'll have Abigail's father to help him, unless he's among the one-fifty," Shannon noted.

"What's interesting is that Emily's mother didn't speak and she's supposedly dead. Santana's brother Angelo wasn't going to lie about him and he's supposedly dead. Abigail's mother didn't say a word, and she's supposedly dead. Maybe it wasn't even the gas that did it."

"You thinking they objected and were killed?"

"But my father is supposedly dead, and that doesn't fit."

We decided to sleep on it. That night, I heard some kind of murmuring sound that woke me up. I realized I had forgotten to put back in my earplugs after my shower. I put them in, and the sound went mostly away. This was very much like in the camp. I thought about the extremes they were going to in order to control society. They didn't need to. Most people just watched the MSM and believed. This was for the outliers, the ones who went to the independent media for their news, the thinkers.

The next morning, there was something weird about the atmosphere around the campus. It was sort of a feeling one got from a zombie movie. The excitement and outrage levels were down. It was as if some of the students had gone from activists to mellow overnight. That wasn't the case with all of them. In class, there were very few questions. Most of the students just sat there and took notes. There was a rally in the South Field East. It was much smaller than the previous ones. Most of the students passing by just looked and moved on.

One of the main speakers at the rally was a guy named Everett. "We cannot go along with political assassinations and fear. They want us afraid of the Cubans, of the Russians, of some new version of the flu that is supposedly out to kill us all. We need to look at the agenda. They are invading our privacy, going through our personnel and medical files, looking for anything that makes us a real person as opposed to one of the zombies that simply believes what it is told."

Zombies, the term flowed through my ears. I was thinking something similar myself. On campus, there was less playfulness, lower energy, much lower. But still there were students like Everett. I wondered how many had gotten the shots and how many had gotten the water.

I went to the hotel to see Genevieve. She seemed more lively, sharper, like she had a new lease on life. She, Bruce, Joey and Jimmy were talking about sending out a counter-signal to undo anything that was being broadcast. If nothing else, it would create confusion. "How are you going to get this out?" I asked.

"We were thinking of sending it over the university's emergency notification system."

"Is that operational at night? I think they are doing this when everyone is tired, kind of out of it."

"Good point. We need to have it broadcasting through the dorms at night," Joey noted. "I'll have to make sure it's operational during those times."

"This will only work to counter some of the programming, not the effects of the vaccines," I said.

"Better than nothing," Joey pointed out.

I went back to campus, picked up my camera, found Shannon and we went around town. I photographed the vaccine lines that were still going on. They were shorter today. Maybe, most of the town had already been vaccinated. We walked through the park. I heard some screaming and stopped. A child, maybe six years old, was lying on the ground, blubbering with her eyes rolled upward, foaming at the mouth.

CHAPTER 15

"I don't know what happened," a woman said, trying to calm down and pick up the child. "She was fine, and then suddenly, she started having fits."

"Did she have the vaccine?"

"This morning. Do you think the vaccine had anything to do with it?"

"I don't know," I said. "You should probably get her to a hospital. It might be some kind of allergic reaction that can be fixed."

We wandered towards the Russian Consulate. I noticed a number of traffic cameras in the area and figured it was best not to try to approach the building.

As I was standing at the edge of the park, police in riot gear dragged two guys who could have been college students out of the park.

"We didn't do anything wrong! I was just saying that something isn't right! I wasn't disturbing anyone!" one yelled as a baton struck his back.

"This is police abuse!" the second guy yelled at the officers. He received a baton to the neck.

I started to say something and Shannon yanked my arm and

covered my mouth. I shook her hand off my mouth but realized she was right.

I took a picture discreetly and we walked over closer but behind some of the trees in the park. I wanted to run out there and stop what was happening and hated myself for not doing so, already.

As if knowing what I was feeling, Shannon whispered, "Don't."

The apprehendees were shoved roughly into the police car.

"They are picking up dissenters," I concluded.

"Maybe they had the vaccine and it didn't work on them. Remember, in *The Invasion*, they were picking up and killing anyone who was immune to whatever it was they were putting in people. Maybe it's like that."

"Maybe. There was a rally on campus today. But it was smaller. Joey and Bob estimated that they were only able to replace less than five hundred of the vaccines. That means that the majority of Columbia students were probably injected. They didn't have a choice or they would have been sequestered from attending classes," I noted.

"While some small fraction are hurt by vaccines, the majority are okay. Maybe, if there is something bad in those shots, the same ratios will apply and a large segment of subjects will be immune," she responded optimistically.

"Let's hope so. It would be tragic if New York turned into Stepford."

We walked over to Harlem, a part of the town that was usually a bit livelier. It was unusually calm.

"This doesn't look anything like the Harlem, I've heard about," Shannon said.

"With so many police on the street, maybe everyone is just a little subdued," I noted.

"Wait. Between Jimmy, Genevieve, Bruce, and Bob, maybe we can come up with an antidote. Darren, as a pre-med student, should be able to get samples of the vaccine to test."

A dog on a leash barked and whined at the guy on the other end, who seemed to be totally ignoring the dog, going about his business as if nothing was happening right next to him.

"Bob has a zoology class. Maybe he can do some unauthorized experiments," I theorized.

"Isn't that animal abuse? PETA would throw a fit."

"PETA is the number one dog killer in America. Bob would be trying to save lives. Besides, if the vaccine works on us, don't you think the government will start using it to control all the animals? Now that's real animal abuse."

We walked over to the hotel to talk to Genevieve about this. Professor Brand, Darren and Santana were there. "No need to do it in the zoology lab," Genevieve said. "There are enough vermin in the park. They probably have more personality than the animals in a lab."

"I'll have some equipment brought over here," Professor Brand said. "If they don't know what we are doing, they won't pay attention. Most people are minding their own business."

Santana and Darren agreed to go out to collect some rats, mice and squirrels. "Of course, they would leave this to the pre-med student," Darren griped, going out the door.

"If we get attacked, I expect you to treat my injuries," Santana told him. With that, their conversation disappeared down the hall.

Shannon and I walked back towards campus. As we walked along the street, we saw more individuals being taken by police. "I wonder what they will do to them."

As we got back, Everett was still ranting. Rant may not have been a good word for it as I agreed with what he was saying. The campus police were taking notice, but none of them were acting.

In the dorm, even security seemed more subdued than normal. Shannon started to ask the security guard questions. "How do you like sitting here all day?"

"I get breaks," he said, blandly.

"But aren't there things you'd rather be doing?" she inquired.

"No," he said. "I'm happy." He should have told his face and his voice because he looked anything but.

"Do you read books when nothing is happening?" Shannon asked.

"I used to. It doesn't make sense, anymore. I've got a job to do. Why are you standing around and not going to your room?"

I pulled Shannon away. "We're going now," I said.

"I'm thinking that whatever they injected into them has a strong tranquilizing effect," Shannon guessed. "Maybe it's pure OxyContin."

"We have that in the Los Angeles water supply, and it hasn't stopped the violence," I pointed out.

"Maybe the cops don't drink the water," Shannon said with a lilt in her tone. "After all, most of the violence is coming from them."

"Number one in the country for shooting people," I agreed.

"They have to justify all their military equipment. Now, they have drones."

"And it will only get worse with all these false flags," I remarked. "I bet the police are vaccinating all their officers. But those cops today were anything but mellow. Maybe, they received different instructions."

Shannon suggested she rent a couple of city bikes, using her credit card.

"Have you been using that this whole time?" I asked.

"Nah. Mostly, Jimmy has been treating me to stuff at the campus."

"It's just that, when they see the charge, they'll know we're friends. If they have any suspicion I'm alive, they might be looking for you."

She put her credit card away. "I used it when I first got to New York, but not since, except at a couple of corner drug stores."

"We brought cash. You can have some of mine."

"You don't have to do that."

"When I was on the run, you gave me nine thousand from your college fund."

"But you returned that."

"You've been an amazing friend. Cash is the best way to go, and sometime you can pay me back."

"I have some cash, but I will only take up your offer if you let me return you the favor again if you need it."

"Deal."

We walked along Martin Luther King Jr. Blvd. "I wonder if every large town has one of these?" Shannon asked.

"I'm sure a lot do," I said.

Ahead, some African Americans were protesting the vaccines. "With this latest one, I wish there were more refusing to get vaccinated. It's for a non-existent disease."

"I got vaccines long ago, but I don't ever get the flu vaccine. My mom said she stopped getting the flu when she stopped getting the flu vaccine," Shannon recalled.

I laughed. "Yeah. A lot of others have said that, too."

As we passed one of the protestors, she handed me a piece of literature. I thanked the protester and stuffed it into my backpack. Shannon started reading the one she was handed.

"It's pointing out that Engañar only appeared in the last week, and there has not been enough time for a clinical trial on any vaccine. It questions whether the disease even exists. It also asks for proof of the deaths," she summarized.

I turned to give them a thumbs up. As I did, I saw a team of officers with clubs beating and then tasing the protestors.

CHAPTER 16

The police banged a couple of heads against a wall. I started to rush forward, but Shannon held me back, again. "You don't want a police encounter," she whispered. "You're dead, remember."

I took a discreet picture, hoping they didn't notice. But I felt like a monster for not doing something more. Shannon was right. If we interfered, they would just add ours to the numbers arrested and in the end all our friends would be outed and possibly executed.

There were more than a dozen officers continuing to club the protesters. Next, they dragged the group into squad cars and not very carefully.

"What I don't see are people out in the street with cell phones recording what is going on," I noted.

"There's one," Shannon said. She pointed to a doorway across the street where a guy perhaps a few years older than us was recording the arrests.

After they left, I went over to the doorway where the guy had been standing and knocked. At first there was no answer. I was persistent. He opened it up. He was a very nice-looking African American male of perhaps twenty or so.

"Yeah?" He came across as guarded.

"I saw you recording," Shannon related.

"So. You with the bacon?"

"Just the opposite. I got a picture myself," I said.

Shannon looked a little nervous.

"It's okay," I assured her. "He seems cool."

She looked like she was evaluating him.

"What you want?"

"Just to talk about what is happening in New York."

"What is hap'ning? You blind?" He seemed irritated with us.

"We saw, and we're trying to figure out what's going on. Maybe you could help us," I replied.

"Sure, I've got five minutes." He moved back from the door as he appeared to be sizing us up.

"I'm Sally and this is Shannon," I said.

"Yo," he replied.

"Did you see why they arrested the protestors?" Shannon asked.

"Do cops need an excuse to arrest anyone?"

"We have the same problem with the police where we come from," I acknowledged.

"What's your point?"

"You were watching. Were they arrested because the cops were racist or because they were protesting the vaccine?" I asked.

"Hmm. Could be both."

"Have you seen any other arrests in the last day? "

"Come to think of it, I saw a brother lecturing people in line about the vaccine be'en dragged off, too."

"Have you had the vaccine?"

"F-No. I'm not crazy. Tuskegee. Remember? My great-grandfather was one of the airmen."

"Okay. Well, you seem normal. Have you noticed a difference among anyone you know who has had the vaccine?"

"Difference, like how?"

"Less vocal. Losing their edge? Anything odd?"

"Among my friends?"

"Yeah."

"My friends aren't putting up with that vax shit," he declared. "No wait. My cousin Jacob got it, and he's been acting really mellow."

"Maybe you can keep an eye out. We're watching, too."

"Where do I get in touch with you?"

"We're at Columbia, but we're kind of playing it low until we figure things out. We'll be back."

"You not getting jabbed?"

"Not us. We think the Engañar Flu is a fake. We think they are drugging people."

"I can see that."

"Since, you know we aren't bad guys, I hope, what's your name?"

"Clarence."

"Clarence, it was nice talking to you," I said.

"You chicks are cool." We shook hands with him and said our goodbyes.

As we got back, Everett was still at it, loud and energetic. Students were still crowded around him. I was actually relieved to see that not everyone had lost their spirit.

That evening, Shannon and I went to the football game. Wien Stadium had been designated an emergency treatment center for the "epidemic" and the game was being played in the South Field West. Columbia wasn't the best when it came to football, but I had always liked hanging out in energetic crowds.

The team was doing surprisingly well. It was actually winning. Each time it got a touchdown, the crowd clapped at a slow pace. There were no ruckus cheers.

Professor Brand came up to us. "Have you seen a college crowd react this way at a football game before?"

"I haven't," Shannon replied.

"I'm going to check on the research," he said, taking off.

We continued watching. The other team was Yale, from New Haven, Connecticut. They were cheering and yelling epithets and reacting to everything that happened. Our side lightly cheered and barely reacted to what was going on.

"I wonder how the other team got to Manhattan?" I queried.

"Probably helicoptered in or went the long way around. I'm surprised they didn't blow up the helicopters or bus and blame it on you or Cuba."

At halftime, the band played a variety of patriotic songs. It had been a while since I had been to a football game but the variety of songs at Heritage High halftimes had seemed more modern and less patriotic. The students sang along with the patriotic tunes. Nobody was kneeling to protest the Stars Spangled Banner.

"I think I'm going to throw up," I told Shannon.

"I'm looking for a vomit spot, too," she agreed.

Hands grabbed me from behind. I turned into Santana's arms and almost instantly felt his lips as he came in for a not-so-quick kiss. When we separated, I noticed that Jimmy and Shannon were also making out next to me.

"Genevieve and Darren are analyzing the chemical compounds in the shot," He informed me. "It doesn't contain anything that one would expect a vaccine to contain. It includes something similar to OxyContin but much stronger and with more powerful sedating properties."

"It's amazing people are still able to sit upright and stand," I remarked, looking at the laid-back crowd.

"That's probably because it also contains an offshoot of Luvox, an antidepressant that can cause mania and violence. Among the other ingredients are a heavy dose of something similar to fluoride, graphene oxide and particles that react to electrical impulses."

A flutist screeched his flute. He froze. Everyone around him acted as if nothing odd was going on.

Next, the flutist pulled out something that looked a little like a tuning fork and stabbed himself.

CHAPTER 17

Members of the band and the cheerleading squad walked over him, many stepping on him, as if he wasn't there. Jimmy and Santana were on the field in a flash trying to drag the flutist off without getting trampled themselves.

I pulled out the burner phone I had picked up earlier in the day and dialed nine-one-one as Shannon dialed it on her smart phone. It rang and rang. Nobody picked up my call.

Shannon must have gotten somebody. I could hear her saying, "This is an emergency. A musician has been injured at the Columbia halftime. Please send an ambulance... I am not getting excited... We need an ambulance... Please send one... No, I am staying calm... It's not alright. A person has been injured. Whatever. Just please send an ambulance here fast." She turned to me. "This is insane."

Santana and Jimmy had succeeded in bringing the flutist off the field. Blood was spurting out of the base of his neck. Santana was trying to use his shirt to wrap around the wound and stop the bleeding. "Oxycontin has a suicidal effect," Jimmy remarked.

"This is more like the movie, *The Happening*," I said.

The whole thing was freaky. We waited for an ambulance. Nothing seemed to come. Jimmy suggested getting an Uber or taxi to take the musician to the hospital. We couldn't get anything up on our phone apps.

Outside, we saw a taxi. We asked the driver to take us to the hospital. It was the slowest, most law-abiding taxi ride I had ever had. When we got to the hospital, Jimmy and Shannon suggested we wait while they went in. Jimmy whispered "cameras," to us.

We started to get worried when twenty minutes rolled by and they hadn't returned. When they finally came back out to the taxi, Jimmy said, "It's insane in there. Patients lying all over the floor. We walked through the door to the back room and put him on a cot."

"Most of the doctors seemed to be moving in almost slow motion, as if all the injuries were normal," Shannon said. "But they weren't. One doctor was out of control, knocking patients off gurneys and hitting them with monitors. We locked him in a closet."

Jimmy continued, "We located some supplies and super-glued the flutist's wound as best we could. The doctors never would have gotten to it. There may be internal damage and undoubtedly, loss of blood."

"Let's hope he survives," I worried.

As the taxi took us back towards Columbia, something thumped on the top of the cab, just before we were stopped at a light. The cabbie was about to take off, ignoring the whole thing.

We yelled in unison, "Stop!" We got out. There was a woman's body, lying on the roof of the cab. We looked up and back along the road. We were next to some tall buildings. She could have fallen from an upper floor or a roof. Jimmy checked the woman's pulse and shook his head. Shannon and I were frozen with fear. Jimmy and Santana picked up the body and lay it on a bench. We hoped a relative or friend would find and recognize her.

We had the cab let us out near the game. It was still going on. Nobody asked us for tickets or checked our hands for stamps.

The head cheerleader landed wrong from a handspring. She walked over to her bag, closer to the bleachers, picked up a pair of scissors out of the bag and plunged them into her chest. My group rushed to where she was lying in front of the audience.

The crowd continued watching the game. Nobody seemed to notice us or the cheerleader. The other cheerleaders continued doing their routine as if she was still with them.

Jimmy took off his jacket to try to stop the bleeding from the hole in her chest.

"She's dead," Santana advised, shaking his head as he checked her neck for a pulse. Her eyes were open and motionless.

Shannon backed up, seemingly in shock, then warned, "We've got to get out of here." She ran towards the exit and we quickly followed her. When we got out of the area, Jimmy took her in his arms. Shannon was white, almost like a ghost.

"Is this going to happen to everyone?" she asked.

"She needs to rest. I'm going to take her to the dorm," Jimmy said.

"I—" Shannon started to say.

"Go," I quickly responded. "There's not much we can do here."

"You need some R and R, too," Santana softly murmured into my ear.

"Let's go over to Genevieve's. Maybe, they've found an antidote." I was too shocked to cry. It was all so surreal, like a horror movie. How could this be reality?

"We'll go with you," Shannon said.

When we got to Genevieve's, the whole group was there. "People are killing themselves," I related.

"That happens all too often with psychotropic drugs and these vaccines are loaded with them," Darren said.

Emily, who was sitting in a chair, put her head in her hands.

I put my hand on her shoulder. "We'll fix this."

"But not for those who've died."

She was right, and I had no answer for that.

"This has been going on to a lesser extent for years. Big pharma pays big bucks to Congress and the state legislatures to get away with public experimentation without permission," Sanatana pointed out. "CPS uses them on children and babies. A child is ten times more likely to die under the watch of CPS than with the worst parent."

"I was reading about medical kidnapping," Shannon told us. "Tiffany got me started looking that up when she was telling me about the family law system. In a lot of places, they take children away from their parents so they can try out new drugs on them, all too often killing the kids. Arizona is one of the worst states for that."

"It looks like Big Pharma is doing mass experimentation here," Joey acknowledged.

"And I bet our tax dollars pay for it," Santana remarked. "I've been to Democratic conventions where Big Pharma has shown up with prime rib, Alaskan king crab and Champagne. They own the DNC."

"They own the RNC, too," Dr. Brand asserted.

"So, we are dealing with evil and more evil. No wonder, people are fed up with figuring out which evil is lesser," Shannon added.

"I wonder how much of the missing Pentagon funds went into this city-wide experiment," Jimmy queried.

"Probably billions," Genevieve said. "When I was working at Beklet and Darkwave, the funding coming in was unlimited. Our expense accounts were through the roof."

I noticed that she was starting to sound like a totally different person, more like a professional and less like a homeless urchin. Having a purpose had certainly made a difference.

"How about we take vials of the vaccines to DC and give Daddy and the other scoundrels pushing this a taste of their own medicine? Let them find an antidote."

"They'd hide the antidote from the public like the cures to cancer and heart disease," Santana responded to Abigail.

"Professor Brand," I inquired. "When this is over, do you think you could find a position for Genevieve at Columbia?"

"The University would be lucky to have her. In working with her today, I've been extremely impressed at how knowledgeable and skilled she is. It's a tragedy that her genius has gone to waste for so many years."

"You are too flattering," Genevieve responded. "I think I may be able to come up with an antidote. But here's the problem. First, we have to figure out how to get it to the public in regulated amounts and second, if they don't know a cure has been given to the public, they'll claim the side effects from their own drugs were outweighed by the advantage."

"*Catch 22*," Professor Brand articulated. "She's right. If we tell them we're giving people the antidote, they may try to stop us. But if we don't, they'll say what they did simply cured the fake flu. Still, we need to undo the damage."

"We might possibly be able to put it into the water supply in low doses. But some people will be drinking more water than others," Jimmy considered.

"What if we could put enough in, such that a heavy water drinker would be cured and a lesser water drinker would at least have a little of the antidote?" I asked.

"The results wouldn't be as uniform as I'd like," Genevieve responded.

"How long will it take the drug to wear off?" Bob asked her.

"Probably a week if they don't have any additional doses. We can't rule out that the government won't also put the substance into the water supply, like they did fluoride."

"Is it just a temporary experiment or is this about permanent control?" Darren questioned.

"Good point. What if they are giving long-term suggestions, with the people being made more susceptible by short-term drugging, with the government's possible addition of the vaccine to the water?" I asked.

"That's my suspicion of what's happening. The Darkwave work I was doing wasn't as promising as they would have liked. Unless they found a way to perfect it, they needed some type of catalyst to get past the natural defenses that people have against suggestion. It's the reason subliminal programming only works on a small portion of the population. I am also concerned about long-term health impacts and the possibility that the particles in the drugs, if not deactivated, might make the recipients susceptible to side effects of current and future technology."

"I'm going to set up some kind of multi-wave recording tonight to see if I can pick up on what is being programmed," Joey said. "What wave frequencies were you working on?"

"I'll show you," she said. She pulled up a chart on the computer and pointed to the section of harmonics that she had been working on at Darkwave. "But there is no guarantee that they are still using these."

Bruce and Bob decided to stay with Genevieve and try working as much as possible on finding a solution. Abigail wanted to stay but didn't want to leave Emily alone in her room for the night.

Professor Brand escorted the rest of us back to the dorm. "They always say it's darkest—"

"Just before it goes pitch black," Abigail finished.

"We are coming up with solutions." As he said that, we looked at the sidewalk in front of us. Another body was lying there. I hoped it was a homeless person, simply sleeping. But it wasn't. We continued on.

We expected to see the South Field empty. But Everett and others were there holding a rally.

"I counted eighty injured by the end of the football game. Any other counts?" he asked.

"One hundred and one," someone said.

It must have gotten a lot worse after we left the second time.

"I went to the physics lab. There were at least five bodies there," another person said.

I whispered to Brand. "The two I witnessed reacted to mistakes they had made. I wonder if there is a perfectionist aspect to the process. It would explain the physics building."

"Students' lives matter!" Everett shouted. "First, it was Black lives matter because they were the oppressed. Now, they are killing students."

"These seem to be suicides," someone pointed out.

"Do you think students are killing themselves for no reason at all?" Everett retorted.

I whispered to the prof, "I'm thinking that it is a side effect of some of the words they are using in the programming. Maybe telling people that they need to do things right to be worthy of living or something like that."

"I'm sure those responsible have noticed the deaths," Professor Brand surmised. "If that's the cause, they may try to correct it tonight.

Or it could be a reaction to the specific drugs. I can't believe their goal is to create a suicidal society."

"There is something they want. It's probably more than just the pharmaceutical funding, though that's big. Think of how powerful certain people would be with a society of sheep," Santana hypothesized.

"Think of how easy it would be to invade a country and take its oil if everyone is subservient, and those who get out of line simply off themselves," Darren noted.

"He could be right. Maybe this experiment is turning out exactly the way that they want it to," I said.

"What if we tell students the vaccine isn't even a vaccine," Darren suggested.

"They'll still call us anti-vax," Abigail said. "People are stupid."

"*Men in Black*," Darren recalled. "'A person is smart. People are stupid.'"

"Recently, I've been seeing a lot of collective stupid persons whom I don't think would be any smarter on their own," Abigail said.

"I'm going to need access to the sound lab tonight. Any chance you could help with the keys, Professor Brand? Yours opens more doors than mine. I mean, I could get around the locks. But as long as you are here—" Joey implored.

"I'll go with you. I'd like to see what you come up with."

As they left, I turned to Santana. "Do you think Everett is simply strong enough to overcome the vaccine and programming or do you think he's one of those who got the water?"

"Don't know. But I like him. I hope they don't kill him."

I knew Santana was joking, but there was an element of reality in it.

"What if we counter suggest 'Don't follow suggestions?'" I asked.

"I heard Bruce and Genevieve talking about that. They are also concerned the Deep State actors could have subtly programmed in a passcode that we'll have to break to get the counter to work."

"The longer we wait, the more solidified the suggestions will be."

"It would help to know what suggestions they are using. If people are already programmed, we need to know with what. But I do agree with you about an alternate set of suggestions. The confusion, alone, might cause them to hesitate before following the first command. And if there is a codeword, maybe our friends can pick up on it."

"At least, it's good to have geniuses in our midst," I noted.

"And those geniuses include us," Emily, who had been quiet, acknowledged.

Santana kissed me and went with Darren to their room. Abigail seemed deep in thought as she, Emily, and I went to their room. Jimmy took Shannon to our room. I knew they needed some alone time and Jimmy would be best able to calm Shannon down.

"You worried about Bruce?" I asked Abigail.

"Yeah. I hope he and Genevieve are safe. We don't know to what extent any of us are being watched."

"Bruce is pretty smart. I'm sure he'll keep a lookout," I said, sounding more optimistic than I felt.

"What we were discussing before about how not all the dead are dead. I believed them about my mother. But look at who died. Emily's mom, who didn't lie at the funeral, Angelo, who didn't lie at the funeral and my mom, who didn't lie at the funeral. Your dad was an exception. Do you think my dad let my mom be killed? Or do you think she might still be alive?" Abigail asked.

"I don't know. Shannon and I noticed that too. There are so many questions," I acknowledged. "Let's hope she is alive. Did you know that Barbara Olson was spotted, supposedly arrested, alive in Europe after the crash of Flight 11?"

"That was a hoax anyway. Anyone who believes the official account of nine-eleven is a complete moron." I noticed that Emily was getting bolder in her remarks.

Emily's parents were from the party that was in power at the time of nine-eleven and her father could have been a player at the time. Yet even she didn't believe the official account. Of course, many people from both parties doubted the official stories, especially architects, engineers, firefighters and airline pilots. However, any call for an investigation into the official story was deemed a tin foil hat thing, and requests for investigation of the current events would likely be no different.

Bob knocked on Abigail's door. "I am on my way to help Joey and the Professor, but I was wondering. We saw all those fake mourners at your funerals. What if Joey and I sign up to be crisis actors at the next event in this area; meet the people who are putting the events together?"

"Usually, the trainings are hosted by FEMA. If they find out you're not on their side, they could use the false flag to kill you guys." Abigail advised him.

"We will have to be careful."

"Do you know where to sign up?" Emily asked.

"There's a site. It doesn't tell what's coming up next though."

"Tell us and the Professor before you participate in anything," I advised him.

"I will. And I'll make sure Joey does if he joins me."

I said my goodnights and made my way to Shannon's room.

Jimmy was there. "I'm going to go hang around with Darren. I've suggested that everyone have a buddy with them and that we know where everyone in our group is at all times."

"Good idea. Abigail and Emily are in their room. Bob, Joey and the Prof are in audio/visual, Santana's with Darren and you are joining them. Let's have a minimum of two or three together at all times."

I looked through the window at the field. Everett was still speaking to the crowd that had only dwindled a little.

It took a while for me to fall asleep but I did. A short time later, I found myself awakened in a sweat, an inexplicable fear pulsing through my veins. I ran to Darren's room and knocked. Nobody answered. I went down the hall to Joey's room. Nobody.

I turned and bumped into somebody. Shannon. "What's going on?" she asked.

"I don't know. I just got a weird feeling and ran to check on the boys. They aren't here. Jimmy made this big deal about wanting us to know where everyone was. They wouldn't have just taken off."

Shannon started pounding. Nothing. We went to Abigail's and Emily's room. "It's probably nothing. We just don't know where

Jimmy, Santana and Darren are," I told them when they opened the door.

We looked out the window. Everett was still in the South Field East. But as we opened the window, we could smell smoke. "What do you think's on fire?" Abigail asked.

"Shannon, could you stay with Emily? Abigail and I will go check." I didn't know why I picked Abigail to go with me instead of Shannon. I just had a feeling she needed to be with me.

We went outside. We could see a blaze from a nearby building. We couldn't see where, but I had a bizarre feeling. So did Abigail.

We started running. Soon we were on Amsterdam, running as fast as our legs would take us towards 107th. A blaze was coming out of the fifth floor of the hotel, Genevieve's floor. Her room was on the side where the flames were coming out.

Most of the hotel looked intact. It must have had good construction and a good sprinkler system, I figured. The firemen were forcing everyone out of the lobby. We pushed through and evaded them as they yelled at us and tried to grab us. We made for the stairs and didn't stop until we were at the fifth floor. The stairwell door was open, probably to let out the people leaving the floor and to let the firefighters in. We moved towards Genevieve's room where the firefighters were working.

"What are you doing up here? You have to leave," one of the firefighters said.

"Was anyone hurt?"

"Two people."

"Where are they?"

"They just carried them down the staircase."

"We just came up it. We didn't see anyone."

"The other staircase." We continued down the hall to another staircase and raced down.

Over the edges of the rails, we could see firefighters carrying two stretchers. There were sheets completely covering up the people on the stretchers.

"Oh no!" Abigail cried.

CHAPTER 18

"I've got to look," I said, starting to pull her with me.

She was almost frozen. I let go and ran to catch up with the fire-fighters and caught them on the lowest floor.

"Miss, you can't be—"

I pulled the sheets off the burned bodies. It was impossible to make anything out. The bodies were in pieces and broken apart. I couldn't tell size, race, eye color or anything.

Abigail came down behind me. "No! No! No!"

I had to get her out of there. It was too much. News crews were at the front door. I had seen them as we entered. They might have even gotten a glimpse of our backs when we came in. Hopefully not a telling glimpse. But I knew we couldn't go out that way.

We headed for a back exit. Abigail was sobbing like I had never seen her sob before. "I love him," she kept whimpering through her tears.

The Ascencion School building was right behind Morningside. I pulled Abigail through an open door. Inside, we could see that was where the hotel residents had been evacuated. We put our hands over our faces as if we were concerned about the smoke. A news crew entered the area and we turned to leave before they could set up their cameras.

Abigail's cries caught the reporters' attention. They turned towards us, and I pushed her out the door. This once bold girl was crumbling.

We turned down 108th towards Amsterdam, and then I escorted her along Amsterdam towards John Jay Hall. I knew there was nothing I could say. So, I didn't try.

When we got to Abigail's room, the door opened and Bruce pulled her in.

"Oh my God!" she sobbed. "I thought you were dead."

I followed them inside, relieved that my friend was alive and even further relieved when I saw that Genevieve was inside as well, along with Shannon and Emily.

"I had to distract the guard, downstairs, telling him I thought there was another fire outside and then snuck our little hero in," Bruce explained.

"We saw bodies," I said.

"Those were probably the guys who broke into Genevieve's hotel room. We knocked them over the head and took off with our equipment. Then we heard an explosion. They had something with them, maybe a bomb ready to explode."

Abigail was still crying. She started punching Bruce. "Don't ever scare me like that again."

"I'm sorry. You didn't have a cell phone." He turned to me. "Your new burner is off." I looked at it. The battery was empty.

"Do you know where Santana, Darrel and Jimmy are?" I asked.

Nobody seemed to know. Shannon looked worried. There was a pounding at the door. I opened it and threw myself into Santana's arms.

"You had us scared. We were leaving the hotel, checking the fire, and saw you and Abigail entering. You didn't come out."

"We went through the school."

"Genevieve!" Santana exclaimed, but not too loudly. "Good. Everyone's okay."

"I hope so," I said, and then saw Darren and Jimmy behind him in the hall. Shannon was already throwing her arms around Jimmy.

"Hey, don't I get some?" Darren asked. Shannon and I gave him a group hug. Abigail was still recovering. Bruce sat her down on the bed.

"The good news," Bruce said, "Is that Genevieve is a hero."

"They are using a new psychotropic compound for the primary catalyst. I've pretty much isolated all the chemicals and particles and have found an antidote that I think will work," she announced.

"That's great," I said.

Abigail was now lying on the bed looking up, not speaking. She had thrown her wig down on a chair. Bruce was sitting beside her smoothing her short green hair with his hand.

"So, what is it?" I asked.

"You'll never guess," Shannon replied.

I waited. Genevieve looked at Emily.

"Lemonade," Emily practically sang out.

"You're kidding."

"The citric acid in the lemons and the sugar in the lemonade will counter the effects of the drugs and break down the nanoparticles. But the antidote won't necessarily counter the programming that has already been done," Genevieve explained.

"I'll feel better when more people are sounding like Everett," I said.

"Summer, did you see Everett when you came back to campus?" Santana asked.

"I didn't look." Come to think of it, it was quieter outside.

I went to the window. The southeast field was clear.

"Where do you think he went?" I asked.

"I don't know. One minute he was there. Then Bruce and Genevieve showed up and I was so excited. I haven't looked out since until now," Shannon related.

"There was a crowd down there. They are all gone now," I said.

"Bruce, did you see what happened to Everett and the others?" Santana asked.

Bruce looked out. "When we got back, they were still there."

Darren went and got his computer. "We can't count on the news for anything."

"I can get into the dark web," Jimmy said. "Maybe, there is some information there if nobody else has it."

Darren opened up several pages and frowned.

"What is it?" I asked.

Jimmy leaned in to look. "Holy Yale."

"The game didn't even count. It was just a prep game," Darren said.

"What?" Shannon asked, going over to join them. I was still watching Abigail. "Oh my!" Shannon exclaimed.

Santana and I went over to the computer. She was looking at all the top postings on Fakebook related to the Yale Football team, the one that had lost tonight to Columbia. After the game, five of the players had been killed. Three were shot, one was pushed off a building and one was run over by a car.

From the postings I learned that the events happened late night after they left a not-so-victorious victory party. "Is this even possible?"

"With what we saw at the game, does anyone here believe this is not related to the programming?" Santana asked.

We were all speechless.

"This can't be real," I finally said. But I knew it was. "Darren, can you text Joey at the lab and find out what they've learned about the programming?"

"I just did," Darren said.

A minute later, Darren's phone rang and he put it on speaker. It was Joey. "We're in trouble. If anything happens to us, think of the worst President."

"What?" The line went dead.

Encouraging Shannon, Jimmy, Emily and Genevieve to remain behind—in case the others managed to return, the rest of us left to head en masse over towards Lerner Hall, which was relatively close to John Jay, with just a building in between.

Darren continued trying to reach Joey, Bob and the Prof by phone. There was no answer. As we got outside and started towards Lerner, we saw a team of officers outside and men in suits.

"Those guys look like feds. Look at the bulges under their coats," I said as we ducked back into John Jay.

"Did you forget something?" the security guard asked.

"We were just thinking that you must be hungry with the hours you are putting in here. We were wondering if you wanted us to bring you back some food, bro," Santana offered.

"It's approaching two in the morning. My shift is almost over."

"I'm doing a sociology paper on what it's like to work on campus," Abigail said. "Perhaps you wouldn't mind if I asked you some questions."

The guard shrugged. Darren cut in, "He's probably too busy for this. I noticed there were some demonstrations outside before. Did you do the work of clearing out the protestors?"

"Oh, no. The police and some opposition students came in and the officers cracked some heads."

"Were there injuries?"

"Probably. They were taken away pretty quickly in white vans."

"White vans as in DHS?"

"I don't know. White vans."

"Has anyone been taken away since the protests?"

"You ask a lot of questions."

"Yeah," I said to Darren. "This man is busy. We shouldn't bother him with questions."

"I don't mind the girls asking some."

"Were this building and the South Field East the busiest after the game? I mean you have a radio. Did you hear anything from any of the other nearby buildings or did you have the bulk of the busy work?" I asked.

"Something happened in Lerner Hall a few minutes ago. They said it was under control. Something about a lab break-in and some dangerous individuals."

"Did they catch them?"

"Probably. They just issued an all clear." He pointed to his radio.

"Then, they caught the guys?"

"They didn't say."

"Thank you for your time," Abigail said, trying to sound girlish. "It was so kind of you to answer our questions."

We went for the door. The police and feds appeared to be gone. "I wonder if they got anyone," Abigail worried.

"They would have had some explaining to do if they arrested the professor," Darren said. "And Bob and Joey have student IDs."

As we rounded the front of the building, I saw several officers, accompanied by two men in suits, pulling three guys into a white van. We moved closer. It was hard to tell what the detainees looked like under all the blood that was covering them. An arm hung down from one. It had several tattoos on it. Our guys didn't have any.

"The tan pants were wrong," Darren said. "Bob and the prof were wearing dark pants and Joey was wearing blue this evening. The two with the covered arms had tan slacks."

"They could already have been taken out," I said. "We've got to follow."

Darren put a card into a meter to rent some bikes and we were off following. The streetlights made it easier to tail the van. I hoped the van didn't turn onto the FDR—if it was back up. There was no way we'd keep up on that.

We did our best to follow. The guys were very fast, especially Santana. I wondered if he had done track in school. Abigail and I were bringing up the rear.

We lost them on Wall Street. The vans and our guys made some kind of turn and Abigail and I were too far back to see. We were continuing down Wall Street, looking for the turn when Darren came back and said, "They went into Brexel Pharmaceuticals. Santana followed them in."

"What? How?"

"Cleaning crew. They had a van out back, and as they were carrying equipment in, he stole some stuff and one of their hats and went through the front door."

"They might recognize him," I said. "That's really dangerous."

"I'll see if I can get in there." The voice behind me came from Joey, pulling alongside me on his bike.

"We thought they got you guys."

"We managed to hide out until they left."

"Santana could be in danger," I said.

"Did you get the flash drive from the bushes?"

"That's what you were talking about?"

As we continued towards the building, Joey picked up his cell and dialed Bob. "Get the drive. I'll explain later… Good… Thank you."

"Do you think they were after you?" I asked Joey.

"Probably, but we snagged their instructions."

"Instructions?"

"They were telling listeners to weed out imperfection and extinguish it."

"Like nail anyone who wasn't acting weird."

"Basically."

"Someone attacked the Yale team, the team that lost to Columbia. Three were shot, one was pushed off a building and one was run over."

"Wow. There will be parents investigating."

"And your flash drive is evidence."

"Bob should be able to find it," he said.

We went into the alley behind the Brexel building.

A member of the cleaning crew was looking for something in his van.

"Hello," I said.

He turned towards me and Abigail. "Did you kids steal the vacuum cleaner? I knew I didn't leave it at the warehouse."

"We just arrived. Do we look like we are carrying a vacuum cleaner?" Abigail asked indignantly.

He didn't have time to answer before he collapsed, thanks, I figured, to Joey's device.

We lifted him into the van and Joey took his outfit. "You girls wait, here, for me," he said.

"Santana's in there. I'm going in," I said.

"Green and I will be the lookouts," Darren offered.

Joey took the Brexel access card from a loop on the janitor's belt. "I bet they have retinal scans for the back entrance." Darren held the janitor's eyes open while Joey took a photograph of each.

At the entrance, Joey held the right eye picture against the scanner as he used the card. Nothing. Then he held the image of the left eye against the scanner on his next attempt. It opened. So far, so good.

We each carried in cleaning items we had found in the truck. Inside, closer to the front, an office with a window had a guard, who took a nap at his desk, thanks to Joey's invention.

Joey used the card and the scan to take the service elevator up floor by floor. Most floors were vacant. On the floor below the top, we heard voices. We moved slowly. Footsteps were audible. We went into an office off the hallway. The lights were off and it seemed safer that way.

As we closed the door, a hand reached out from behind and landed on my shoulder. We had been caught. I started to speak, but another hand covered my mouth.

"Shhh." I recognized Santana's voice.

"How did you get up here?"

"The guard down below was a sub. I told him I was, too. I said I had forgotten my ID and needed his help to avoid getting fired."

"He could get in real trouble," I whispered.

"Only if they find out he let me in. It's up to him to cover for himself."

"It's working," I heard a voice say. There was something familiar about the voice and I was furiously trying to recall where I had heard it. "But the reactions are not controlled enough."

"Still, the crowd-size results are excellent," a second voice stated.

"The President is starting to ask questions."

"And you are telling him?"

"That this is a defense project. He still believes those kids blew up the bridges."

It grated on me that I recognized the first voice but couldn't quite put a name on it. The walls may have muffled it a bit, but I wasn't going to excuse my lack of remembrance on walls.

"We need to refine the commands," the first voice continued. "They are having unexpected results. How are those latest kids you picked up?"

"They said they got the vaccine, but clearly the group was unaffected by it. They're in the basement. The lab is preparing an extra dose of the vaccine for them. I'm on my way there, now."

"Will they remember being here?"

"They think they are at police headquarters on a disturbing the peace. Sir, if the new batch doesn't work on them?"

"The exceptions will have to be terminated." That's when I recognized the voice.

"That seems a little strong."

"Are you going to be trouble?"

"No, sir."

The voices dwindled off.

"We have to rescue everyone in the basement," I whispered.

"That was Abigail's father," Santana pointed out.

"I recognized his voice, too."

We looked into the hall. Nobody was out there as far as I could tell. We slipped out the door.

I heard another door open and pivoted to look. "Well, well, well, you two certainly are resilient." It was the Secretary of Defense with a gun aimed at us.

CHAPTER 19

Santana turned to me as we moved in front of Joey. "I told you we shouldn't have come in here," he griped.

"You?" I reacted. "I just wanted to go home to L.A.. It was your idea to stay in New York."

"My bad. After this, we're returning to L.A., immediately."

"Is the show done?" Kreskin asked. "Or do I have to bring in an applause track?"

We turned back towards him. "Look, you don't really want to harm us. Our dads are with the government. They're on your side. What if we just say maya culpa and go along with your plans like good kids?" Santana asked. I admired his lengthy speech.

"Sorry. You can't be—" Before Kreskin could finish, he collapsed, courtesy of Joey's device, fired from around us.

"We're no longer covert," Santana pointed out.

"Let's get to the basement," I said, as we moved towards the elevator.

"You read my mind. That's part of the reason I love you."

"Hey, lovers, we need to get downstairs," Joey said, as the elevator arrived at his call.

Joey used the scan and card to get to the basement. "We have access. This area must be on the cleaning list for when they aren't drugging and torturing kids:"

"Maybe they don't want to leave blood on the floor," I muttered.

As we got off the elevator, we saw a guard by a door, but before he could turn towards us, he was on the floor. We ran to the door, using the scan and the card to open it.

Inside someone in a suit with a big nasty-looking gun asked, "What are you doing here?"

Covering Joey behind us, Santana said, "We're the cleaning crew. We were told—"

"Not tonight. Get out."

"Certainly, sorry for the—" Santana apologized as Joey fired from between us. "Disturbance." Santana looked at me and smiled.

"Let's go," Joey said to the students in the room. Many of them were bloody and injured. "Carry the injured. If you don't want them to kill you."

The reaction was fast. Everett, though covered in blood, picked up the guy next to him. Several other students picked up other injured students and they made their way towards the door. We got to the elevator and could see it coming down from an upper floor.

"The stairs," Joey suggested. We all ran for the stairwell. Santana and I led the way. Joey was behind in case he had to zap someone. We made it to the door of the main floor. As we made our way past the guard, I noticed he was still peacefully sleeping at his desk.

"Bad first day," Santana mused.

As we returned to our friends, the janitor was just coming to but dozed off again. We moved the students into the van, filling it like those old Volkswagen experiments as to how many could fit. We'd done this before but not with so many. There were students holding up students towards the ceiling, all packed tightly. Santana and Joey quickly strapped the bikes up on top. We wanted to drop the bikes off elsewhere to avoid connecting the university to our actions.

Santana took the wheel. He raced for the Holland Tunnel.

"Guys, these people collapse tunnels. Is this one even still intact?" I asked.

Santana who was driving made a quick U-Turn. We headed

towards NYU, where we dropped off the bikes. We took a back-alley tour of New York, dropping off the van behind some buildings in the vicinity of Greenwich Village.

We headed towards the Basilica of St. Patrick's Old Cathedral.

"The door was open perhaps preparing for a morning service. "Padre," Santana, said to the priest inside. "Neciesitamos tu ayuda."

"English," the priest requested.

"We want to start a late-night worship session and were wondering if you have a private room where we could discuss our faith."

The priest seemed perplexed as he looked over the group. "Some of you are injured. What happened?"

Joey stepped forward. "These individuals were protesting the wars, and some officers came and started clubbing them. We need to get them help, but we don't want them beaten again. You're a priest, you have to know what happens to protestors in this city."

"Come with me." He guided us down to the basement. "I'm not going to endanger the church by aiding and abetting some kind of lawlessness up top. And your injuries need addressing."

"Thank you, father," Santana said as we went into the basement.

"Now, tell me, son. Are you and your friends wanted by the police?"

Everett who was bleeding from the head but able to walk and seemingly alert, stated, "My friends and I were speaking against the forced vaccines and the insanity that has gripped this city. We were beaten and pushed into vans and taken to a basement where we were held prisoners."

"It was the basement of a drug company," Abigail interjected.

"You must admit that there have been some odd things happening in this town," Bruce advised the priest. "Have you been vaccinated?"

"No. Some of the vaccines contain aborted fetal tissue. I do not have any vaccines without looking at the ingredients."

"Have you found any oddities with the reaction to the vaccines among people in your congregation?"

"Yes, I have. Is this what this is all about? You are refusing the vaccine and someone did this to you?"

"Yes," I said. I thought about filling him in on more information but decided to quit while we were ahead.

"Look at all the injuries. Someone has an agenda," Everett pointed out. "We'd be dead if our friends hadn't rescued us from that basement."

"Sir, you're a priest. Therefore, you keep confidences. Please keep our existence confidential for now. We really don't know who to trust," Bruce implored.

"We don't even know if it's safe to go back to school," Abigail added.

"We've got to find out what the next round of programming is," I whispered to Santana.

"They will probably wait until tomorrow night. It would be best if we were out of the city by then," Santana replied. He pulled me and Abigail aside. "Your father recognized us."

"My father?" she asked.

"He is involved in this. But he's lying to the President, keeping him in the dark about the real purpose," I related.

"And what's that? Agenda twenty-one or 2030 or 2050 or whatever they are calling it these days?"

"I don't know. But it's something the President wouldn't approve of," I told her.

The priest stepped up behind us, hearing the last couple of words. "The President," he repeated my last words. He looked at Abigail. "I recognize you. You're Secretary Kreskin's daughter. And you're alive." I looked around, concerned others may have overheard. He had spoken lightly. Those who had been abducted were about ten feet away and not focused on us.

"Look, we're the good guys. You must believe us," Santana said, quietly. "Someone with a lot of power is behind everything that is happening. We're just trying to figure things out."

"I was at the United Nations that day. I believe you," the priest reassured us in a lowered voice. "Father Thomas Durham."

"Thank you, Father. These people are trying to kill us." I hugged him.

"Earlier tonight they tried to kill me and a scientist I was working with to find an antidote for the vaccine," Bruce informed the priest.

"Before we rescued these students, we heard them say they were going to drug them and, if that didn't work, they were going to kill them," I added. He already knew a lot. A little more wouldn't hurt, I didn't think.

"In other words, these are Columbia students and you are afraid that, if they go back to Columbia, they will be killed?"

"Something like that," Bruce acknowledged.

"I am not going to go up against the authorities. But you are not formally charged with any crimes. Is that correct?"

"Yes."

"Then, you can stay here for a while, perhaps just a day."

"And you won't tell anyone we're here?"

"If there are parishioners in the basement, it is nobody's business but the church's."

Joey's phone rang. "Bob," he responded. "What? But we threw it there. It's got to be there. I was sure they didn't see us. Look again."

Darren looked at him. "We can't be that unlucky."

"The flash drive is gone," Joey informed us.

"The evidence," I murmured.

"We'll get more," Santana said.

Father Durham directed our whole group towards a smaller room adjacent to the larger basement room. In it were blankets and pillows and some fold-up cots. "I'm going to go upstairs for some first aid supplies, but some of these injuries look worse than anything I can treat with what we have here."

"Everyone is afraid, and we don't even know who the enemy is," I said.

"I know who the enemy is. It's Daddy Dearest. I bet he killed my mother. There was no virus."

"Father, you said you look at the ingredient list for vaccines. Did anyone have an ingredient list for this?" Bruce asked.

"No. Even my doctor said there was no accompanying ingredient list."

"Because this scientist I know did a breakdown and it contains some heavy psychotropic drugs, along with fluoride, magnetic parti-cles, and other nasty stuff."

"This may sound like science fiction," I said. "But they are also broadcasting EMF's and radio wave suggestions. Joey and a professor broke down the code that they were broadcasting."

"Joey told me they found instructions for everyone to eliminate imperfections last night," Abigail reported.

"And then there were attacks on the Yale Football team, which lost to the Lions," I noted.

"I don't know about the broadcasting, but there was a lot of violence and—" Father Durham started.

"Suicides last evening," Bruce added.

"The flutist and the cheerleader both made mistakes before they attacked themselves," I said.

"In my years, I have learned that sometimes information is danger-ous," Father Durham reported. "I suspect that the information you presented at the United Nations had to be discredited."

He believed in our innocence. Relief rushed over me like a warm blanket.

"There is something else odd," Father Durham went on. "I have a large congregation, and I would have expected some of them to be in the areas affected by this new flu. Not one member of my congregation even has a relative or a friend who was injured by it. Isn't that strange?"

We treated the wounds as much as possible under the circum-stances. Darren was in pre-med and reset some of the broken limbs. He probably knew he could be sued but was more concerned with helping than possible later litigation.

A couple of the students, including Everett, looked like they had concussions. We worked to make sure they stayed awake. After Everett's head injury was cleaned up and a bandage was wrapped around his head, he looked like he might actually survive. I had been surprised that he had had so much energy and determination given his headwound. Father Durham got ice to reduce the swelling.

Father Durham pulled our group of rescuers aside.

"Did you park near here?" the priest asked.

"No, but there are cameras everywhere. We did our best to avoid them. There were some sheets and bags in the van and we put them above several of our heads as we walked," Joey said.

"Abigail's father saw us during the rescue. He knows we're alive," Santana related. "They are going to be gunning for us."

"Maybe not," I said. "He is trying to look like an in-charge guy. Our being alive is an embarrassment to him."

Abigail looked down. The tears in her eyes were an indication of the knives stabbing at the heart of my brave friend.

"Any good father would love and protect you, Abigail," I said.

"You don't have to soften it. I know my dad wants me dead or worse. And my mother. He killed my mother."

"My child," the priest said. "There is a Father above who loves you very much."

"Where was he when my father sent me to be tortured or when the dogs tried to make lunch out of me?"

"You're here. Sometimes, he acts in mysterious ways."

I didn't know what I believed. But I was glad the priest was saying these words to Abigail. She needed something positive, some light in her life. Her real-life parents had been so awful. Real or not, believing in a higher power that loved her might help keep the depression away.

She sank down. "I want my housekeeper, my nanny, the one my dad got rid of."

"When this is over, we'll find her," I assured her.

We went back to the injured. Everett was holding an ice pack against his head to reduce the swelling. "I saw you at school. You never participated in the rallies."

"Low profile. We needed enough privacy to try to remedy the situation," Darren explained.

"There is something in those vaccines," Everett told Darren.

"We know."

"What if we put the lemonade in the public drinking water system?" I asked.

"Lemonade?" Joey asked.

"You weren't there. Genevieve figured out that lemonade was the cure."

"It's that simple?"

"Yes. Not the Monsanto/Bayer variety, but the organic stuff. And you can't overdose on lemonade," I said.

"I'm ready for a glass already." Santana faked drinking up a tall one.

"But what we don't know is if the programming will hold if they get the lemonade after the programming has been done."

"Programming?" Everett asked.

"Did you see the game tonight? And the attacks after the game?"

"I saw you carrying that guy off the field and massive injuries on and off the field in the second half. I heard about the attacks on the Yale team and in the physics lab."

"That didn't seem natural, did it?" Santana asked.

"That's what I've been saying. Nothing is looking natural."

"Genevieve found the antidote, but did the other side even look to see if there was one?" Santana asked. "They might try to create a lemon shortage if they discover it."

"Good point. We just make sure everyone on campus is drinking lemonade, come up with a catchy phrase to make it look unrelated," Joey said.

Abigail and Bruce joined our conversation. "So how are we going to give out the antidote?" Bruce asked.

"We're going to set up lemonade stands and get everyone drinking lemonade," Santana suggested.

"So how do we get back to campus?" Everett asked. "Look, I may be injured, but I'm not stupid. I've a pretty good idea who you are. If you're willing to go back, so are we."

"There is some safety in numbers. But let's all keep a low profile. You guys were out in the South Field a lot. Have your rallies indoors for the time being. Avoid being seen. Was anyone taken from the dorms?" Bruce inquired.

"I don't think so," Everett replied.

"I guess they aren't randomly chasing down students. They just knew that you were vocal." Bruce turned to me. "And they don't yet know we are Columbia students."

"Do you think they'll start a facial recognition search?" I asked.

"That depends on Abigail's father and what he tells them."

"He won't take care of us, himself. He'll have others do his killing, as always," she advised.

"When we get back, let's do as before. Everyone hangs out in twosomes or threesomes."

"I like that idea," Everett said.

"In the morning, we have our friends bring free lemonade to the libraries and dorms for everyone going in and out. The Prof should be able to help with that," Santana said.

"I wonder if we could get the church to create a quickie fundraiser with lemonade on campus," I recommended.

"Good suggestion," Father Durham said. "I'll see if we can arrange that. Charity work."

"Then, tonight, we'll have to check out the broadcast, maybe do a counter-broadcast," Joey proposed.

"And everyone, here, keep low and out of sight in case they are looking for us. If any of the dorms get raided, we work together to protect each other," Santana advised loud enough for everyone to hear.

It was already early morning. Joey called the Prof who was just settling down to rest. He was going to make some calls and have kegs of lemonade delivered to campus.

"There are going to be parties tonight," Joey said. "We show up with the kegs of lemonade. Will it hurt if they mix it with vodka in their glasses?"

"You'll have to ask Genevieve," Bruce suggested. "But from what I could see, I think the point is the acid and the sugar. I don't think the alcohol would affect it. But these students are already pretty drugged. If they drink the alcohol, it might mix with the psychotropic drugs."

"They are going to drink, anyway," Joey advised. "We may as well give them the antidote while they are possibly killing themselves."

He had a point. If we told anyone who hadn't seen what the bad guys were doing about the vaccine ingredients, we'd just be called Flat Earthers, tin hat wearers, and conspiracy theorists.

Father Durham stretched the rules to allow some of us to borrow priest and nun clothing to get back onto campus unnoticed in a church van. Once there, we changed and handed back the clothes. They made a few trips until we were all back.

In the late morning, Father Durham and a group of nuns took some church vans to Columbia and offered lemonade to the students while asking for a donation for their charity work. The lemonade was a hit, more so than we expected.

"Why didn't you ask me?" Jimmy chastised Joey, giving him the flash drive. "I figured it out from what Bob said on the phone. I've copied it onto my computer."

"That's cool, man," Joey thanked him. "Bob's down in the Field, handing out lemonade. When he finishes, I'll let him know."

"The question is not so much what they have programmed previously, but what messages they will be sending next," Jimmy pointed out.

"We're going to keep monitoring and we're also going to be subliminally countering the messages on the university stations and some other stations and networks, we'll be hacking into. But of course, I wouldn't hack." He chuckled.

That afternoon, Abigail and I decided to check out the condition of the homeless population in Central Park. We changed into burqas, to try to disguise our identities. With her father aware we were alive, we had to be extra covert.

As we walked through the park, we found ourselves surrounded by officers. "Well, well, foreign terrorists."

"We were born in New York," Abigail lied.

"Su-ure you were. We're going to have to search you," an officer with a captain's nametag, stated.

"This is religious discrimination, a violation of the First Amendment," Abigail declared.

"Strip-search her," the captain instructed two of the other officers.

Abigail started backing up. "Don't you dare."

It occurred to me that their programming had added to their violent tendencies and most brainwashed New Yorkers would sit by and let them do it.

Two officers started to pull on the bottom of Abigail's outfit as she kicked at one of them. They out-maneuvered her.

"Kicking. We'll have to teach you a lesson," the kickee threatened, pulling out his taser.

Two other officers were at my side and I knew they'd react if I tried to interfere. I didn't care. I kicked the taser out of the threatening officer's hand. The two closest jumped on me, pulled my arms behind my back, forced me to the ground, and pushed down on my neck and back. I found I was having trouble breathing and what air was entering was full of dirt. We might die here.

CHAPTER 20

Another officer was removing my headpiece.

As I prepared for exposure, he fell back. I worked to catch my breath and then looked around as I got up. Abigail was standing, assisted by one of several Blacks who were holding branches. The officers were on the ground, looking unconscious.

"Thank you," I choked out a sigh of relief. My lungs and throat were burning from inhaling dirt.

"It's not safe to wear those outfits in New York. The NYPD doesn't like Muslims," one of our rescuers said.

"Charles?" Abigail asked as we started to remove our burqas. "You're right. Good to see you, again."

"Man, if you didn't want to call attention to yourselves, you're going about it the wrong way." He turned to his friends. "It's okay." He looked at our burqas. "I'd get rid of those. They hate Muslims more than they hate Blacks."

"My bad," I said. "I'm good at making mistakes."

We finished pulling off the burqas and handed them to one of our rescuers. We were wearing hooded sweatshirts underneath.

"You?"

I turned to the side seeing a recording had just stopped. "Clarence?"

"Shh. You girls are crazy."

"Thank you for the save. It's good you're saving Muslims—even if we're faking it."

"We're Muslims, too," Clarence related.

"Oh. Good." I realized I had put my foot in my mouth.

"And we haven't been vaxxed. All normal."

"Double good," I corrected, myself. "Except, I thought the Qur'an opposed violence."

"We're allowed to defend ourselves and others, but we are not allowed to retaliate. Where's Shannon?"

"Back at the University. Carlie and I were coming to see you," I told Clarence.

"Thanks for the save." Abigail high-fived Charles.

"Yeah, thanks," I said.

Charles looked from us to his friends. "I told you about that weird rescue."

"Not you?" Clarence asked.

"It was our friends who really rescued him," I related.

"You almost got wrecked, today," Charles reprimanded.

"We got a chance to make new friends," Abigail pointed out the bright side.

The officers started stirring.

"We need to split," Clearance advised.

Several of his friends reached down and pulled off the body cameras from the groggy officers.

Back at Clarence's place, Abigail and I relaxed. Our rescuers had taken off to some kind of meeting.

"Lemonade?" Clarence asked, shocked. "Are you guys shitting me?"

"Seriously," I confirmed. "We have a scientist working on it. We don't know if the people giving the vaccine know there's an antidote."

"That's cool. I think we've got some in the house. I'll make sure my cousin drinks it. But I don't think those cops who are beating people up are going to drink it."

"What have you observed since yesterday—besides us getting attacked?"

"Violence, craziness. Some couple driving down the street today started yelling at each other about who was messing up. The next thing, they were outside their car beating on each other. The guy pushed the woman in front of a moving car. The driver braked and tried to stop but couldn't stop in time. Next thing I knew, the driver threw himself through his windshield, and he wasn't the only one. All kinds of craziness like that going on."

"Did you hear about the Yale football game?" I asked.

"Yeah. Several Lions got picked up this morning for taking out some Bulldogs. Looks like Harvard will be moving up in the ranks. Are you sure Harvard isn't behind this?"

I started to smile at that and then realized this was real life, not just some insane movie you could laugh at.

I handed him fifty dollars.

"Hey, I don't need your money."

"It's for lemonade for your friends and anyone else you think may need it. It may not reverse the programming, but then again it may help."

"Programming."

"Like MK Ultra brainwashing programming."

"I figured. The government's always pulling nasty shit. They're behind this?"

"We think some of them are."

"You chicks, stay tight."

"Stay safe and take care of yourself," I said. "Oh, if you can video anything safely, do, but they may come after anyone they see recording."

"I've got lots of video, and they aren't getting it. I know how to keep out of sight."

"Good."

We said our goodbyes and then headed back to the dorm.

The students at Columbia were starting to look more normal, less zombielike. They were having discussions, no longer in a monotone, and were questioning things. There were still a lot of zombie-looking types, though. I hoped tonight's keggers would take care of that.

When we went into John Jay, I noticed that the lemonade on the security counter was out. I was about to go looking for Jimmy when he arrived with another five-gallon container.

We got together in the lounge down the hall from Jimmy's room. This time, the prof, Everett and a couple of guys from last night, named Nick and Justin, joined us. Darren, Santana and I were going to two back-to-back parties and Justin and Nick were going together to two other ones. The goal there was to make sure that as many students as possible had lemonade with whatever they were drinking and to insert flash drives that would fit with the various styles of music and would also, of course, contain subliminal suggestions. Supposedly subliminals weren't effective on a normal basis, but for those drugged, they might have a greater impact.

Jimmy and Bob were going to try to block and decode incoming frequencies or radio waves to the University while Joey and the professor were going to try to create a counter signal for the entire campus. We were thinking a good message would be, "Calm down and be nice to everyone."

Bruce was going to make sure Genevieve, Abigail, Shannon and Emily stayed safe. He was joking about how we gave him the tough job.

As we walked to the first party, I asked Santana, "Will those who haven't had the antidote even show up to a party or will they be back in their dorms perfecting their next papers and suicide plans?"

"We may not be able to get everyone. But at least we'll get enough, between this and the lemonade in all the dorms," he optimistically replied.

"The Professor dropped off two fifty-gallon containers at each of the campus libraries," Darren said.

First, we went to a party in the Brownstones for Sigma Alpha Epsilon. It was relatively mellow. Half the students were drinking lemonade straight from some of the ten five-gallon containers that had been sent by the prof. Everyone was looking uptight but not programmed. "Perfectionism may mean staying sober," I remarked.

The boring music flash drive fit with the selections they were already listening to. "We've got to get to the next party." Santana grimaced. "If I have to listen to one more minute of elevator music, I'm going to die."

The second party we went to was in the FLS Brownstones. It was the Sigma Alpha Phi party, that was well attended and a bit on the wild side. In fact, it was a little reminiscent of the fun parties in *Animal House*. A fifty-gallon kegger of lemonade had already been delivered and it had already been mixed with grenadine and one-fifty-one.

Everyone seemed to be having a ruckus time. The music was loud and awesome. Joey had put together a dynamic combination of punk rock and new rock on a music track with low-level subliminals. "Abigail would love this party," I said.

After we switched the music, the party got even wilder. Several students started chanting, "Fight the Establishment." Others joined in. Next, a group of students called for removing the security guards from the campus, pointing out that their existence was a concession to the New World Order.

"What did Joey put on that flash drive?" I asked. "It certainly doesn't sound like peace, love and goodwill."

"Whatever it is," Darren said. "I support it." He looked at me. "Lighten up. They are ready to take on the very guys who are trying to kill you."

"And they could get killed helping us," I warned.

"If the numbers are massive enough, maybe not," Santana tried to reassure me.

"I hope this is different than the message that is being broadcast in Harlem," I said. "Black activists are already under attack and all

Blacks, Muslims and Latinos in New York have a target on their back. I wish we could do something about that while we are here."

Someone turned on a TV screen. It was a video of students being beaten up in the east field and dragged away in the white vans. "I downloaded this from Instagram," one student said.

"It was up on Fakebook for about two minutes before the censors got it," another recalled.

"Yeah. The Fakebook AI censors, created by that foreign genocidal government, figure that anyone who posts pictures of violence is suicidal. Our government tries to locate the posters so it can silence or kill them, itself," another contended.

"Maybe they can make a difference as long as they don't get killed," I conceded.

Before leaving, we suggested a march on City Hall on Monday. I thought that might quale any dangerous actions on their part. We pointed out that the Establishment is in their private resorts on weekends.

"Yeah. They've stolen all the money that should go to free college and are vacationing on it. City Hall, Monday!" a student, who seemed to be prominent, announced.

"City Hall, Monday!" echoed throughout the room.

That might have redirected or delayed any reactions. But the energy was still a little concerning.

"Maybe, we ought to see what effect the subliminals have had on the conservative partiers," Santana suggested.

As we went back towards the more conservative party, we saw streetlights going out, being hit with stones. A guy on the roof was cutting some kind of electrical or cable wires. I recognized him as one of the guys at the boring party. A nearby cell signal tower collapsed as students started cutting into it with drills and smashing parts of it with golf clubs.

"This could get interesting," Santana said.

"As long as New York doesn't go down overnight."

"I could go for that," Darren crowed.

"The establishment blew up bridges, tunnels and part of the FDR.

Do you really think these students could do worse? At most, these are prank attacks," Santana pointed out.

"The others were talking about actually standing up and protesting," I noted.

"Notice that the leftist students are planning a more honest protest than the uptight sneaky middle of the roaders," Santana observed.

"Yes, but the leftists, the good guys, could get killed at City Hall."

"If they do what we discussed, nothing will happen before Monday." I wasn't even sure Santana believed his last remark.

Darren, who had gone up to get a closer look, came back. "You see, when tight-ass whiteys create trouble, they're sneaky and dishonest. They are hoping someone else gets the blame for what they did because they want to pretend to be so law-abiding when they are the worst criminals of all."

"I know," I said. "More whites are arrested for drugs, but more blacks are incarcerated. Whites usually get acquitted or manslaughter if they are prosecuted at all for killing people. Blacks usually get the death penalty."

"Capital punishment takes too long to please the swine. In this century, the police just shoot Blacks and other minorities, while claiming to support equal rights, and that's the end of it. No expensive trial, no rights, no attorney, just a bullet in the back," Darren contended.

"Our society is really messed up," I agreed.

When we got back to John Jay, there was a party in the third-floor lounge. People were drinking lemonade and some of the hard alcohol they had smuggled into the dorm. Most of the students were mixing the two. Everett was there, speaking to the students. "We must take back, not just our university, but our city, our country from the tyrants who have stolen our democracy. Does anyone really believe there are free elections in the U.S?"

The crowd yelled, "No!"

"Exactly. We may have to take up pitchforks. All our leaders know they were appointed by the global elites, not elected. And when someone does surpass the rigging and win, the global elite yells, 'Russia, Russia, Russia—' even though Russia has nothing to do with our elections."

"We know that," a student named Carl said. I recognized him from last night's detained group. "I backed Bernie Sanders but was too young to vote. The DNC had my brother's name removed from the voters rolls here in New York and then finally it was admitted that they had deliberately done that. The elites only lose the general elections when they don't rig them enough. When the left stays down, the Democrats have to super-rig or lose."

"It's all the same," Everett said. "We are just replacing one master from the global elite with another. Even Bernie Sanders gave up the ghost and didn't call them on their crimes. They are all in it together."

"This is a real discussion," I whispered to Santana. "I wish that the middle-aged generation saw what was going on."

"They've been programmed, not necessarily by drugs and EMFs but by the media, by Raquel Madcow and others. Anyone who tells the truth loses their job in the MSM. A lot of the honest journalists have gone to RT or do pirate videos," he pointed out.

"Or to Bitchute, like Debbie Lusignan, the Sane Progressive did. But it is interesting that our generation, when not brainwashed by educational institutions, are willing to look at what everyone else is sweeping under the rug," I said.

Hearing our discussion, Darren interjected, "We may have been really young at the time, but we all learned from Hillary's theft of 2016 from Bernie Sanders. In past years, Americans have found honest spokespersons such as Chris Hedges, David Swanson, Glenn Greenwald, Cindy Sheehan, Debbie Lusignan, Dennis Kucinich and Cynthia McKinney. Instead of the MSM, our generation is listening to Jimmy Dore, Jason Bermas and Ryan Cristian. We know the MSM lies for the corporate elite, brainwashing the public with their fake news."

"I've noticed that we also get support from the much older generations, like Genevieve's," I pointed out.

"The seniors and our generation are pretty much in tune. It's the generations in the middle who don't want to disrupt their pretty lives with facts that contradict their right to be ignorant," Santana contended.

"Do you ever wish you were asleep?" I asked Santana.

"Maybe. But I don't want to be like Arial." Arial was a girl at camp who had ratted me and Santana out to camp counselor Marco, who tied us to a tree and later almost killed us, but was eaten by his own attack dogs.

"I wonder what ever happened to her."

"She's well programmed. She'll fit right in in Washington."

"With my brother. Together, they'll have fun taking money to promote the wars and killing in the Middle East."

"My oldest brother is just like them. I miss Angelo."

"It's terrible that the good ones were supposedly killed. Abigail's mother wasn't evil like her dad. Of course, my dad was at the kids' camp. He was definitely not one of the good guys. I wonder why they killed him."

"Abigail said it was a tag under a cover. We don't know if they faked his death or if it was real."

We went back to Abigail's and Emily's room.

"How did it go? Are they ready to kick some butt?" Abigail asked.

"More so than I expected. I think Joey changed the message," I told her.

"That was probably my doing. I told him flower people can't stand up to the New World Order," Abigail confessed.

"The students I just saw are anything but flower people. They're ready to launch a war on the Establishment."

"Good. That's an improvement," Abigail said.

"This waiting for another disaster to drop: do you feel it too? Like a lull in a storm?" I asked.

"The other side is probably taking the time to regroup and plot," Santana speculated.

"I want us to go home to Rosa," Emily lamented.

"If I could, I'd put you on the first plane," I said.

"I won't leave without the rest of you," Emily replied, firmly.

"We'll find a way to make that happen," I consoled her. "Where's Bruce?"

"He and the professor are in Jimmy's room cooking up a plan for getting into the water supply," Abigail informed us.

"That may be what it will take," I said.

"The prof has a friend he's going to talk into giving us a tour of the Hillview Reservoir, but he's off work until Monday night," Bruce said, returning.

"So, until Monday night, we may have to live with the city's programming."

"By the end of tonight, much of Columbia and Harlem will have the antidote," Bruce said.

Genevieve, who was sleeping on the bed, woke up and smiled at our group. "I really appreciate the energy of your generation. My generation has really let you down."

"Not as much as the generations in between," I said. "The generations that are now in their 30s, 40s and 50s are much more willing to go along with the status quo."

"A lot of them have well-paying positions and don't want to rock the boat. It won't be long until they are on the outside, just like us," Bruce said.

"Where is Joey?" I asked. "I want to have a discussion with him about his message."

"Don't get strung out about it," Abigail said. "Anything they do, the Establishment has coming."

"I'm not worried for the Establishment," I clarified.

Santana sat down in a chair and pulled me onto his lap.

"Think of it this way," Jimmy said, entering the door with Shannon and the prof. "We may get to survive the night. If they kill us, they'll have to fight Columbia."

Shannon slapped his sleeve.

"You guys take care of my girl while the prof and I try to save the world," Jimmy instructed us.

"Upward and Onward, James Bond," Darren joked.

With that the prof and Jimmy were gone. Shannon sank onto the bed beside Genevieve. Emily curled onto a mattress on the floor next to the bed.

"Why don't you guys get some sleep?" Santana said. "Tomorrow could be a long day."

"Santana, if they were drinking the lemonade, why were they so open to the suggestions on the disk?" I asked.

"Your question contains the answer," Genevieve said. "When the underlying drugs are out of their system, the suggestions will talk to the parts of a person who agrees with them."

"That's why the more refined students are doing dirty underhanded stuff because that's who they are and the more rebellious students are talking revolution because that's who they are?"

"Exactly. If they have had the antidote, they won't do anything they don't have a natural inclination to do—unless it relates back to the programming while they were under the influence of the drugs," Genevieve responded.

"Then, the programming the bad guys did." I rolled my eyes, realizing that the speaker defines who is bad or good. "That programming could override the counter-programming we do."

"With them no longer under the influence, it will likely still be there in the background, but may have lost its power. I guess we'll see," Bruce said.

"There is also the programming from the media," Abigail reminded us. "People have been programmed from birth to believe what the media tells them. Our generation has broken away for the most part, but most people haven't. We may also have been brainwashed by what the media said. Did we actually look at the damage that happened our first day in New York? Maybe there is something we missed. Some evidence of how the tunnels and bridges and that section of the FDR blew."

"You're right. We need to do that," I agreed.

"If they did it with one of the sonic weapons I was working on, there won't be a lot of evidence, but there will be a lack of evidence of explosive devices," Genevieve said.

We all put in our earplugs, and Shannon and I went to our room. "Shannon, we've been best friends for a long time, but everything you've done for me is above the call of a friend."

"We're sisters. We always have been."

"I feel the same."

That night, I dreamed about the beatings my mom had received, Dad's threats to kill me and my mom, the deaths of my dogs, being pulled away from my mom in the motel room, my dad hitting me over the break-up with Matt and being tased and kidnapped by the bounty hunter to the Gulag camp. My dream flashed to a night when my mom rushed me out of the house with her following.

Dad managed to grab Mom's hair and pulled it hard. She slipped and fell. She cried out, "Run, run."

I hesitated, worried about my mom.

"Please run."

I obeyed. I knew that it would be worse for her if I stayed. But if I had been stronger, I'd have found a way to stop him from beating her and removing her from my life.

As I ran out the door, I could hear Pandar ask Dad, "Do you want me to catch her?"

Just before the door closed, Dad responded, "Make her pay."

I hid in the bushes near the house. I was shaking with fear I'd be caught. But I felt guilty, too, as I also heard him yelling at my mom, beating her.

I wanted to go back to rescue her. I could see Pandar looking for me. He was about to find me. A squirrel climbed into the yard, distracting him. He took a stone and killed it. He had learned well from Dad.

I continued hiding, praying that my mother would be alright. Pandar went through the gate, apparently thinking I had run out through it as I cowered for hours.

Finally, I worked my way towards the door. Mom was in the kitchen. Her forehead was bleeding. Bruises were forming. She saw me and motioned me back out. I closed the door, mostly, but I could hear Dad coming into the kitchen to speak to her, more politely and in a calm voice. "You know I'm trying to do my best for you and the kids."

"Summer's a good girl. She tries so hard. Even harder than Pandar tries. Please, treat her better."

"I'm trying," he responded. The rage was gone.

I went back in. My mother flinched a little.

"My little girl. It's your bedtime," my father said.

"Right, Daddy," I said to appease him. "Can Mommy tuck me in?"

"Go," he said to my mom. She went up with me. She was shaking. When we got to my room, she held me.

I sobbed, angry at myself for not being stronger, for not finding a way to stop him from hurting her.

"It will be alright, honey. I'll keep you safe."

But she couldn't. Not after my dad had her forcibly removed from my life with the support of the police and family court system after she had almost died from one of his later beatings. That was the same dad who beat me in her place after she was forced out of my life, the same dad who pushed me into dating Matt and sent me to the Gulag camp after Matt and I broke up. All the time in camp, I so wished I could see my mom again.

My dream switched to my rushing into Mom's arms as she got out of Shonnon's car the night she and Shannon rescued me and my friends after we fled the camp.

That was the happiest moment of my life.

I woke up and looked around. It was morning. Despite the memory of my dad and brother that I'd suppressed, it was the best night's sleep I had had since coming to New York.

Emily was in my room. "Santana brought me here and asked that I bring you to the third-floor lounge after you woke up and got ready."

"What's up?"

"I don't know, but it sounds serious."

I got up, took a quick shower, dressed and went with Shannon and Emily to the lounge. Our basic group of twelve (including me and the prof) were now present. "How bad?" I asked, looking at their faces.

"We blocked their signal coming to the campus while they were sending out their message. Also, in Harlem and at NYU, we managed to do some blocking and re-messaging, too," Bob stated.

"Don't forget all the lemonade. The church made sure that it got to residents on the other end of Manhattan. They made special care to get it to the NYU students and staff," Jimmy reminded us.

"I also sent numerous keggers over there," the prof related.

"And what I'm not yet being told is—"

"Their message," Bob replied. "You guys may want to sit down. We countered it, but not until it was broadcast across the island with the exceptions I mentioned."

"I'll take it standing," I said. Santana stood right beside me.

"It was about you. They told people to eliminate the Wilderness Five terrorists who blew up the bridges."

CHAPTER 21

"Were they broadcasting images?" I asked.

"The technology did include pictured images," Genevieve said. "I've been looking over the data this morning. They are images of you as you looked speaking at the United Nations."

"Did they have our location?"

"It told them to look for you in Manhattan," Bob informed us. "Abigail's father must have talked. The programming didn't get to Columbia. It was blocked here. This is probably the safest place in the city for you to be."

"Don't the guards go home at night?"

"We've been delivering a lot of lemonade to them, and we've got counter programming playing in the lobbies and over the sound system. The subliminals are quiet enough that they will likely give them headaches."

"What's the counter programming?" I asked.

"The Wilderness Five are national heroes. We owe them our lives." Jimmy said. "Our new message. No images, of course."

"And the counter-message you released publicly last night?"

"It was the same one played at the parties, encouraging everyone to stand up to the Establishment," Bob responded.

"I recommended against that too, Summer," the prof said.

"However, it might come in handy now," Bob pointed out.

"Any results?"

"In certain parts of Manhattan, particularly Wall Street, violence is way up," the prof related.

"Wall Street?"

"Investors have been attacking stockbrokers over the weekend while the Market is closed," Jimmy explained.

"I don't know that that's a bad result," Santana remarked. We all looked at him. "Just injecting a little humor. All right, it's not funny."

The prof provided the good news. "But around Columbia, NYU, Greenwich, and Harlem, violence is way down."

"So, our counter-programming was a success among us peons," Joey surmised.

"The lemonade, too." Shannon smiled.

"Doesn't anyone feel like we're being out of integrity using the very kind of programming we are upset that they are using?" I asked.

"Ordinarily, I am opposed to that kind of programming," the prof agreed. "Right now, we are doing our best to save lives and mitigate a terrible situation. We are countering something that is turning students into killers. Remember those Yale players. If we are saving lives and not hurting people, I'm in. But no more suggestions with a potential side effect of violence. I would suggest you five stick close to the University. We don't know what will happen on the outside."

"What about the facial recognition programs?" Santana asked.

"We are continuing to counter-program everyone on campus and the risk is more limited here, but you might be at risk anywhere else from that," Bob advised.

"If you leave, do so under cover. When you go to classes, maybe you could wear glasses in addition to caps," Joey suggested.

"What about the water supply?" I asked.

"The trouble will be getting all the necessary organic lemonade?"

"Raid a pharmacy for ascorbic acid pills and a grocery store for cane sugar," Shannon suggested. "Cane sugar can't be genetically modified."

"But getting all that into Hillview might be difficult," the Prof worried. "It's in Yonkers, about twenty-two miles northeast from Columbia, but the tunnels and bridges off the island that are still up are being monitored and all cars are being stopped."

"Maybe, they're protecting them against real terrorists. Aren't they more of a threat than a group of teens?" Shannon asked.

We looked at her. I could see it in her eyes as it suddenly hit her that almost nothing was protected from real terrorists. Even the TSA procedures were designed to harass the public and had never stopped a real terrorist attack.

"What if we take over an MSM station and encourage everyone to drink lemonade and to send flowers to the Wilderness Five?" Bob suggested.

"The media is a real problem. They have their own form of programming. They have been constantly telling the public about the importance of sending kids to places, like those camps in time to stop them from turning into terrorists like you," Joey explained. "We've tried hacking into them, but the anchors are strongly pre-programmed with Benjamins."

"So, no matter what we do, the media will continue to program the public that we are terrorists and to get them to send their own kids into torture," I said.

"On campus, most of us know better than to trust the media," Bob reassured us.

"We also have the problem of the camps. They are torturing teens in those camps, every day," I lamented. "We came here to save kids from those camps and now many more may die in them."

"Fastest growth industry in America. But I don't think that's all it is," Bruce said.

"Abigail's father was talking about a plan that was behind the President's back. It didn't sound like it was tied to any of the wars in the Middle East. We need to figure out what their endgame is," Santana advised.

"Clinton, Bush and Obama lied about a lot of stuff to set the stage for mass surveillance and more and more wars to follow them. Maybe we could bug my dad's office and expose what is really going on," Abigail suggested.

"That would entail going to D.C.," Bruce said. "Not safe."

"We fight them on their home territory," Abigail clarified.

"They are programming New York. Maybe you guys would be safer in D.C.," Darren pointed out.

"If you are to get out, we will need a diversion," the prof said. "And if you think facial recognition is bad in New York, imagine how much worse it will be in D.C."

"They still don't have Seth Rich's killers," Darren pointed out. "We don't even know who killed JFK or his brother or son."

"We do know who killed Seth Rich," Santana and I both said at the same time.

"I guess you do," the prof said.

Sunday went relatively smoothly. Father Durham visited the campus after his service. He met me and my friends in the second-floor lounge at John Jay.

"Thank you for your help," I said.

"No. Thank you for yours," he told us. "There was a wave of extreme violence Friday night that ended last night. Everything around the Basilica has calmed down since we started handing out the lemonade. And this morning, the sun was out, and the people all seemed relaxed, happier."

"It's calmer here, too," I said.

"Wall Street and Park Avenue could use some lemonade. My congregation plans to bring it over there later today and tomorrow during business hours."

"How about to the United Nations? We don't know how many of those got the vaccines," I noted.

"Your Ambassador Sanchez came by the church, today."

"He's out of the hospital?" I asked.

"Apparently, he never went in it. He exited through a side door after they escorted him from the stage."

I breathed a sigh of relief. "They were securing the doors when we got out. We almost didn't escape. I'm glad he left before they gassed the place."

"He hinted that you were there, though he didn't mention your names."

"Joey invented glasses that allowed us to see the gas entering the hall. We got out quickly. We thought it might be aimed at us." I felt reassured that Ambassador Sanchez got out. "So did he say anything?"

"Just that he was worried about five special teens who had the courage to tell the truth. He said that, if I saw you, he wanted me to help you in whatever way I could. He did mention, as you indicated, that they tried to secure the side door to the chapel. He was already out when he saw you leaving."

"Did he have some lemonade?"

"Lots. And he was taking back several pitchers to the United Nations to share with his colleagues."

I smiled and Santana high-fived me.

"On Tuesday, I've been asked to visit a parish in Pennsylvania. I was thinking of stopping the van by here to get a quick look at my favorite campus."

"Is that a kind of invitation?" I asked.

"If someone gets into my van while I'm not looking, well—that will be a surprise to me."

Emily hugged him, followed by me and then Abigail. Shannon and Bruce shook his hand and Santana high-fived the priest.

***

The next morning, I went to my photography class and then to St John's Chapel. Because of the help the church was giving us, I was feeling more religious than normal. Thanks to Father Durham, we were also receiving help from St. Paul's, which was also distributing lemonade.

As I was returning to John Jay across the college walk, I saw Emily. She was coming out of the Miller Theater, next to Broadway. Across the street was Columbia's Bernard College. Most of those hanging out on that section of Broadway were students. Campus security was also there. Suddenly, she caught someone's attention.

Three people jumped out of their cars and charged security. Security tried to hold them back as Emily moved towards me and I moved towards Emily and took her hand, turning back towards the center of the campus, but more and more people stopped their cars, got out and joined in running after us.

CHAPTER 22

In a flash, groups of Columbia Students jumped in front of those rushing after us. A fight ensued. The people from the cars were especially violent.

I briefly looked on, wondering if I should join the fray, but I had to think about Emily's safety.

We ran towards the Low Library as several people chasing us were closing in. We were about to be captured. I thought about blocking our hunters while Emily escaped. As I turned, dozens of students from Columbia grabbed our pursuers and more that followed and threw them to the ground.

In Low, we went down into the basement. There was a tunnel beneath the building connecting Low to the Butler Library. Another tunnel connected Butler to John Jay. But the door below Butler and the other tunnel doors were supposed to be secured, and I knew we might be trapped.

As we got to the door, Bob opened it and we rushed through it to Butler and then to John Jay and up to Emily's room to alert Abigail. Bob was on the phone to Darren, Joey and the prof.

From the window in the room, we all watched a fight ensue on the campus. More and more people seeking to apprehend us started ignoring threats from campus security and rushing onto the campus. In response, more and more students came out to confront and block them.

Then, from the street, nearby residents from Harlem started running onto campus to assist the college students. New York's finest, dressed in riot gear, started pushing their way onto the campus and Columbia's security pushed back. Students didn't budge.

The police pointed their guns into the crowd, but before they could fire, Columbia students from all sides trampled them. Police guns fired into the air. I prayed that none of the bullets would hit any of the students.

"Santana and Bruce are safe," Bob said. "They're with the prof. He's getting them over to the athletic center. We are going to all meet at Mudd, away from the fighting."

"Shannon and Jimmy?"

"They're on their way back over here."

As we watched, the Columbia students were holding their own. Security had rushed out from all the buildings in force to remove the uninvited from the campus, but by now there were hundreds invading the campus, including a great many police officers.

The Columbia students and Harlem residents moved out forming a wall pushing the intruders onto Broadway. Other pursuers were coming from Amsterdam and another wall was pushing them back. Columbia students blocked all access points from West 114th as well. It was as if we were protected in a human-walled palace.

Darren brought up some Football Jerseys that had been donated and we put them over our clothes.

"Thank you, Father," I heard Bob say over the phone.

"What?"

"Your ride will pick you up at Mudd. He's bringing clothing from his church. You're getting across the field in Football Jerseys and can change later."

I kissed Genevieve, goodbye. "I hope we get to see you again soon," I said.

"I love you," Emily told her.

"Thanks for being like a second mother for a little while," Abigail said.

We made our way across to the Hamilton Building and then crossed into the steam tunnels, where Jimmy and Shannon met us. Through a series of interconnected moves, we managed to make our way to the Dodge Fitness Center, where we met up with Bruce, Santana and Professor Brand. We continued on to Mudd Engineering.

We were guided into a classroom, where we changed into nun and priest garbs. I hugged Shannon and Jimmy.

"It's not goodbye. We're coming with you," Shannon informed us. She and Jimmy, reached for two extra outfits and put them on. She turned to the prof. "See that Jimmy is excused from classes until he's back."

"Sure thing."

As we exited, we saw Father Durham in a church van. Father Jimmy sat in the front. Shannon sat behind the driver so she could smile at the police monitoring the Washington bridge and whoever was taking the money to cross it.

In a short time, we were in Fort Lee, New Jersey. We continued on to Philly.

Father Durham drove to a Cathedral close to downtown. "I need to stop here for a meeting tomorrow evening. They have accommodations for us."

"They knew you were bringing guests?" Jimmy asked.

"I told them, yesterday. Today, I explained that I would be coming a day early."

"I don't know how we can thank you," I said.

"By surviving and saving those other teens being sent to the camps."

"You said you were at the United Nations," I recalled.

"My nephew was in one of those camps. My sister had been hesitant to send him there, but the school counselor and her husband insisted it would help him. He came back horizontally. In a body bag."

"I'm sorry." I felt like crying, knowing that we had failed in our mission to close the camps.

"That must have been rough, man," Santana commiserated.

"When they saw his body, it was hard to recognize it. He had been beaten and tortured. My sister couldn't handle what she'd done and took an overdose of sleeping pills, by accident. Now, she's with my nephew. You save the rest of the teens if you can."

"We're trying. It seems the establishment is pulling out all stops to prolong the torture and killing," Bruce related.

"A new bill to close them was sponsored, but it's not going to make it," Jimmy advised us.

"What?"

"It's a show. I saw online that the vast majority of Congressional donations come from weapons manufacturers. They're not going to regulate camps that brainwash kids and turn them into zombies, ready for the next war or false flag attack. Most bills that are introduced are done so for show. The authors never intend for their antiwar bills to be signed into law."

"Is there anyone on our side now? George Miller retired. Kucinich and McKinney are no longer in Congress," I pointed out.

"We need to replace all of Congress and get Kucinich and McKinney back in there," Jimmy said.

"I couldn't agree more," Santana declared.

"Can you imagine our parents having this discussion?" Bruce asked us. "My parents couldn't care less about the plight of American teens."

"Mine are cool with killing teens, including their own daughter. At least, my dad is. My mom was a go-along," Abigail said.

"My parents thought kids were stupid and needed specialized training to be acceptable," Emily said. "If my dad is alive, maybe my mom is too."

"Everybody in Philly is going to assume that you are new priests and nuns in training. Make sure they don't overhear these discussions. The less said, the better. Look serious and relatively quiet while we are there." Father Durham cautioned.

"Amen," Santana said. "They spoke Latin in my church. I speak Spanish. I used to just sit there and hope to assimilate whatever it was the priest was saying."

"I gather your father didn't send you to a Catholic School."

"He wanted to show he was a regular guy whose sons were enrolled in regular schools."

"I wish they had given him a course in how to be a father," the Father criticized.

"The trouble with our fathers," Santana said; "Was that they know what kind of fathers the public wants them to be, but inside they were nothing like that."

"I can't imagine how horrible it must have been growing up as you did."

"At least we have you, Father." I smiled.

"Amen," Shannon said. "Jimmy and I were lucky to have our parents, but I saw what Summer went through. Her father was a psychopathic abuser."

"In my experience, those are the ones who get custody. That's why I'm opposed to the current divorce system. The church also has reasons, but I am opposed because I've seen violent abusers getting full custody and good parents being completely pushed out of the picture. That is no way for children to be raised."

As Father Durham spoke, it hit me that, with all the scandals about priests, there still were some good ones, just as in any profession.

That evening, after dinner, Jimmy said he wanted to go to the library to do some research on some matters pertinent to the church in Manhattan. Santana, Shannon and I agreed to accompany him.

"So dedicated," Father Durham said, in response to our decision to do work during the evening.

The news on the radio had made no mention of the situation at Columbia and we were worried for the Columbia students.

At the library, we went to the computers to sites and channels not even close to what the government called mainstream to get some real facts. Santana had lifted a card from someone leaving the library. I was kind of surprised that, in addition to hot-wiring cars, he was also good at lifting wallets. He only took the card and then told the gentleman he had dropped the wallet.

We watched live videos in a private room. Students were winning the standoff with the local authorities. In response, the military had been brought in.

I froze as we watched armed soldiers aim their guns at students. I looked for our friends. I hoped they weren't on the dangerous side of those guns.

A shot was fired. A student screamed as blood squirted out of her shoulder. As students came to her rescue, the soldiers were confronted by catapults flinging horse manure from the rooftops of the various buildings.

Helicopters swooped in as students launched homemade rockets into their gears to bring them down.

Then the tanks arrived. "This is because of us!" I freaked. "We're not even there, and they could all die for us."

The tanks were greeted with hoses spraying grease, mud and glue, covering the scopes, blocking any way for the occupants to see out. With the tank visuals blocked, students jumped up on the tanks and threw lit cherry bombs into the scopes, the exterior weapons and anything that had an opening for the fireworks.

Loud cheers across campus followed student victory after student victory. The military was losing the war.

The military brought in armed drones flying above campus, possibly looking for us. Some students knocked down some of the military drones with slingshots. One uploaded video of a downed drone showed it had X-ray technology. The government was definitely looking for us.

Another drone started to tear-gas the students. The staff brought out gas masks from the science labs. Most student warriors quickly covered their faces and continued the resistance.

The Air Force tried doing fly-overs with planes that were met by massive fogs created by newly created high-power fog machines aimed up to where the planes were attempting to fly. As the planes came lower towards campus, student-made water cannons took them down.

As far as I could tell, nobody had been hurt. Some servicemen or women had to parachute out and were captured by students who showered them with mace. The prisoners of war were cable-tied and taken into a university basement. As one live feed went down, another one would go up to allow us to keep watching.

Students were following government recommendations on masking and so the identities of the student militia were unknown. The videos were put up under names like Blue Lion and Golden Victor. I had a strong feeling that Darren, Bob, Joey, Genevieve and our favorite prof helped mastermind the victories. I just hoped they weren't injured, fighting for us.

Apparently, thousands of students managed to call home and their parents started calling their elected officials. There were reports from members of Congress asking parents to stop calling their phones and faxing their offices. They said they couldn't conduct business with all the lines being tied up.

Raquel Madcow ranted:

The parents calling the Congressmen and Senators are terrorists who must be apprehended and locked away under the NDAA.

Madcow played recordings of angry calls demanding that members of Congress stand with Columbian students or resign. There were threats of recall and of creating a blacklist of leaders needing to be removed in the next election.

"Clearly, Russia has invaded the minds of Columbia parents. A well-placed nuke on the Kremlin may be required to restore sanity and protect our leaders."

Finally, amidst the loss of the war and the escalating anger from the parents, who were still being called terrorists by the news media, the President stepped in and called off the invasion of Columbia.

No excuses were made for the invasion. Though government subliminals had called for taking us out, the government, still, had not publicly stated we were alive.

It wasn't long before all the uploaded videos of the victory were off the Internet.

The regular news stations spoke of an uprising of terrorists on campus that had been quelled, but there was no coverage of the war on the actual channels.

"Score one hundred for Columbia. Score zero for the New World

Order," Jimmy cheered. "But if the government cuts Columbia's funding in response to its loss, the university will need extra donations to replace those funds."

"It's a good thing we left when we did," Santana smiled. "And a priest helped us escape. Maybe miracles are on our side."

I shook my head.

"If we had been found there, they might have blown up the campus," I said. "You saw what they did to the prison where we were held in Cuba."

On the way back to the Cathedral, we walked by Independence Hall and stopped.

"Can you imagine how our forefathers would react if they were here now?" Jimmy asked.

"Earlier this week, I spoke with a student from Africa, who said our forefathers never leave us," Santana replied.

"In that case, maybe our ancestors will help us stop what is happening to the other teens," Shannon hoped.

"I try to be optimistic, Shannon, but sometimes I just wonder if Deep State is so powerful that nothing can defeat it," I confessed.

"We won at Columbia. Or rather the students won. Even if the news won't cover it, they defeated the most powerful government on the planet. The pictures showed armed tanks and fighter planes, and the students stood up to them and won. The bad guys tried to control our minds and failed."

Jimmy's phone rang. He put it on speaker. It was Joey. "Plan lemonade is a total success!" he announced.

"You guys are great. We saw videos," Santana agreed.

"Of course. We did great, and lemonade is now Columbia's official drink—sometimes with a little extra."

"Cool," Jimmy said.

"Also, we think there is something odd about the explosions from the day you spoke at the U.N.. I've been talking to the guys in the geophysical lab. The Earth's vibrations didn't match a series of explosions that would have taken down bridges and tunnels."

Before Jimmy had a chance to respond, Joey jumped in again.

"Tomorrow, I'm going to relax and eat an ice cream cone on the way to go brook fishing, maybe I'll even have nine—so I don't get bored."

"Joey," Jimmy tried to clarify.

"Have to run. I'm bored. Bye."

"Joey doesn't eat ice cream," Santana recalled.

"Think about what he said," Jimmy commented. "Cone. Nine."

We smiled. "Coney Island at nine on the Boardwalk. But we're supposed to be here," I said.

"It's only a couple of hours away," Jimmy pointed out. "Maybe, we can borrow the van tomorrow and take 95 to 278, bypassing Manhattan. They may still be looking for us there, and if they think we've gotten out, they won't think we were stupid enough to go to Brooklyn."

Father Durham had no problem with our borrowing the van. He was exceedingly trusting. Shannon, Emily and Jimmy were staying behind. Jimmy would be using the Philly Library to do additional research while the rest of us went to Coney. Somehow Jimmy had managed to get more burner phones so we could safely communicate. Most had been removed from the market. We knew our prior phones could have been compromised by Stingrays or other fake cell towers. Jimmy and Bruce put together a police radar detector that also monitored police radio frequencies.

We had allotted extra travel time and traveled through Stanton Island to Brooklyn. Even with traffic, we were at the Boardwalk at eight-thirty. We brought clothing we had smuggled out to the van in our football bags during our escape. Once we got close to the pier, we changed. We also went into a shop and purchased some souvenir T-shirts and new caps so as to have a somewhat different look than before. We had brought the boxes of contact lenses and switched the eye colors a bit. At nine, we spotted Darren on the Boardwalk. He escorted us to a Funhouse where Bob, Joey and Everett were waiting.

"Okay, we're in Brooklyn," Joey said. "Let's start with the Brooklyn Bridge. It's about thirty-six miles away, but the most famous."

We moved towards the parking lot and got into the van. "Now, speak," Santana said. "How did you handle the water facility?"

Joey smiled. "We managed to get our hands on a truck that looked like a delivery truck. Bob broke into the facility's computer system and put a delivery on the schedule and then crafted some documents that looked legitimate. The prof distracted his friend who was in charge of security there while we unloaded some highly concentrated ascorbic acid and sugar into the water. I think the vaccine dulled the senses and nobody there was on their toes, concerned about the kinds of things you would expect the security to focus on."

"So, they did themselves in," Abigail said. "Poetic justice. You could have been real terrorists and they would never have known."

"If they are watching the Brooklyn Bridge, we probably should not be driving this van right up there," Santana advised. "Let's find an old vehicle, pre-2000 on these streets."

"Easier to hotwire?" Darrel asked.

"That too. Post 2010 vehicles can be hacked. Did you read Vault 7?"

"I memorized it," Bob said.

"Wow," Santana responded. "You must have a photographic memory."

"Something like that," Bob replied.

We drove down several backstreets. On one street, he found a Dodge station wagon from the sixties. Being good at picking locks, Santana was inside in less than half a minute and had the car running in a couple more.

Bruce had taken over driving the van. We parked it close to the Boardwalk parking area. Father Durham had a handicapped placard that we gladly made use of to avoid overtime parking problems and got into the station wagon with Bob driving.

Manhattan was connected to the world through twenty-one bridges and fifteen tunnels. Reportedly, all on the eastside had been blown. Skipping the collapsed Hugh Carey Tunnel and other former bridges and former tunnels along the way, we headed towards the Brooklyn Bridge. We were more visible in the daylight though Santana pointed out that we would be less suspicious than at night.

"There must be millions of homeless people and kids here," I observed.

"And cops will be cops. Look at that one clubbing that homeless kid over there," Darren angrily spouted.

Surprisingly, the officer walked away as Bob stopped. The kid was covered in blood. His mother was next to him, crying and holding his bleeding head.

"We need to get him to a doctor," I said.

"I have no insurance," the woman related. "My husband cut it while I was in the hospital. He told our son he'd kill him if he told the police what he saw my husband do to me."

"What about the family assets?"

"The judge gave them all to my former husband. We've been living on the street."

Santana and I both pulled some money out of our pockets as Abigail got some bandages from a convenience store across the street. Darren started wrapping the kid's head and checking his eyes.

"I'm sorry. I wish I could do more," I said, knowing they'd be in more danger if they stayed with us.

"Thank you. You've done more than anyone else in a long time."

Santana gave her some more money. "Take care of yourself. You deserve so much better."

The woman hugged Santana and then me and Abigail.

"We have to be going," Joey advised.

I knew we had to get out of there before the officer returned.

"You should probably find another place before that jerk comes back. You don't want to be around for act two," Darren warned.

The woman escorted her son away as we got back into the station wagon.

The area surrounding the Brooklyn Bridge was completely blocked off. On both sides of the start of the bridge, there were multiple guards. The road leading to the bridge and the side areas close to the bridge were blocked off. We noticed that the areas close to the Manhattan Bridge were, also, barricaded off. From our observations, the bridges had collapsed over the East River and the parts next to the river had turned to rubble, but the parts of the bridges leading up to the rubble were still intact. Looking at the closed ferry landing, Bruce remarked, "You'd think with the bridges down, they'd keep the ferry open."

Maneuvering through side streets and traveling a little off road, on sidewalks and through a couple of fences, we made it to Front street, parking near the corner of Main, about a block from Brooklyn Bridge-Pebble Beach Park. We walked to a section of the Pebble Beach Park near the closed Carousel. We had a good view of where the Brooklyn Bridge and Manhattan Bridge would have crossed the East River—had they still been there. Some businesses were open but the park and the streets were mostly empty, probably because of the loss of the main tourist attraction and the closed roads. Joey, Bob and Darren all had phones that could do video.

Though there had been more guards on the lower side of the bridge, there was only one visible guard on the outer blockade on the Pebble Beach side. Joey used his device to knock the guard out and then took his uniform.

"Nice," I said. "Handy device, great plan."

We moved through the first blockade. Inside there were more security guards, including three guys in suits, clearly Feds. We tried to stay out of their view.

"I heard on the MSM, they've announced they're planning to rebuild this bridge fast. Do you see any rebuilding equipment?" Bob whispered.

"This is bullshit," Darren said. "Something insane is going on here."

All but one of the guards and the three suits went to look at a vehicle with a driver who was arguing with other guards on the blocked road on the Brooklyn side of the destroyed bridge. Joey used his device on the remaining guard and pulled him out of our way. We went further past the barricades onto what was left of the bridge with our friendly security guard taking the lead.

As we got past one of the final barricades and stepped under what appeared to be some kind of green sheeting, something appeared before our eyes that wasn't there before. "Guys," Bruce said. "Does this look like a fallen bridge to you?"

The Brooklyn Bridge stood before us intact.

CHAPTER 23

The Brooklyn Bridge was shrouded in some kind of dark covering, but it appeared to be standing all the way to Manhattan as always. As we backed up and exited the covering, there was no appearance of the bridge crossing the water and the part just before the water again appeared to be rubble.

"The collapse was an illusion or is this?" Joey asked as he walked forward and touched the intact bridge with us following him.

"No. The illusion is that it's gone," Bruce said. "We're looking at holographic projections, enhanced by a green screen. There are some who believe that the planes that hit the World Trade Center were also projections or holograms. I don't buy that theory, but there are scientific and engineering principles that would have made the official narrative impossible."

"In other words, they are projecting fallen bridges and collapsed tunnels, while the media manipulates the public," Santana summarized. "Look."

Above the bridge was some kind of camouflage covering to disguise it from the sky.

"Let me get this straight," I said. "There were no fallen bridges?"

"At least not this one, and I'm willing to bet the others are also intact. We need to locate the projectors because I have a feeling that all these problems can disappear with them," Bruce advised.

"What if we cut through the covering?" Santana suggested. "It's a screen, isn't it?"

"We don't have the tools. From the air, the covering probably looks like water. From Brooklyn and Manhattan, rubble up to the water is being projected."

"I felt the blasts," I recalled.

"Did you feel it or hear it?" Bruce asked. "I know I heard it and my body reacted. You?"

"I don't know. But what about the smoke and debris in the air?" I asked.

"Easy to create without collapsing a bridge," Bruce noted.

"I got video online of the supposed collapse," Joey told us.

"I did too, and I'm now recording that it didn't collapse at all," Bob said. "My video beats your video."

"But not my new video. It's awesome. I cut you out so you don't look like a clown."

"Where do you think the projection is coming from?" I asked.

As we stepped outside the sheeting, again, everyone looked around. Bob put on his glasses. "That building over there," he said, pointing to a tall building about a half mile away. "And from its position, it can also project onto the Manhattan Bridge and create a holographic illusion for planes flying over both as well."

Bruce spoke up. "There is bound to be a counter projection on the other side of the river, also. Well-placed mirrors and green screens could be enhancing the visibility of the projections."

"What about the FDR?" I asked.

"The vehicles closest to the damaged areas were semis. What if they were driven by stunt drivers who bailed as they overturned, dumping debris?" Bob asked.

"Much of the chaos was caused by the pile-up and crashes of cars approaching the damage," Darren noted.

"And the sound of the explosions?"

"There are government-operated loudspeakers throughout the city," Bob acknowledged.

"And the damage to the road? It wasn't all debris. The buildings swayed," Santana interjected.

"Projections, like this one," Bruce surmised. "But we could be wrong. This could be the only fake."

We moved out of the blockades and waited in the park, acting like tourists, as Bob went over to the building and returned.

"It contains a number of government offices. Security was checking the purpose behind all visits and verifying that individuals had the right to be there. I looked at the list of offices. Guess who is in the Penthouse?

"Darkswamp?" Santana asked.

"Exactly."

"Darn," Darren said.

We moved around to the back side of the office building trying to figure out how to break in and turn off the projection. As we continued watching, Emily's father slipped out the door and into a limo.

"We need more time to plan our entrance," Joey said.

"Let's check out the Queen's Midtown Tunnel," I suggested, finding myself worried about being trapped in a high-security building.

"That would be easier to disguise. They just need to cover and block the entrances. Most planes won't be checking it from the air," Bob pointed out.

"If we are going to drive the station wagon further, we need to do something about the license plate," Santana finished. We moved back to the vehicle and watched as he switched the license plates.

"I'm not giving up on this building. Every security system has a flaw." Joey wasn't a quitter.

"How about the city's power generators?" I suggested. I'd seen that in enough movies.

"They'll have a backup system, I'm willing to bet," Bob said.

"Can we access both?" Santana asked.

"It would help to have the building plans," Bob related. "Let's check out the Queens Midtown Tunnel, first."

We drove past the Williamsburg bridge, also seemingly fallen, into Queens and this time switched into a Lincoln Town Car, 1972.

We stopped at a consumer warehouse and picked up a drone. Joey attached a remote-control camera and applied some silver mirroring to it so it would reflect back at the cameras and create momentary confusion for anyone looking in its direction.

The entrance to the Queens Midtown Tunnel was similarly blockaded. It appeared to be destroyed until the drone got past security and behind the screen. Watching the images the drone sent back, the Midtown Tunnel looked undamaged. But to be sure, we flew the drone in further. Joey looked towards the location of the screening and back towards the best projection point where another tall building was located. Again, Bob checked out the building and found that it had a Darkswamp office.

"We know Darkswamp is heavily involved. We need to monitor their conversations and figure out what they are up to," Joey suggested.

"How are we going to do that?"

"You're dealing with Columbia University. We've got engineering students and high-tech students," Bob pointed out.

"But which ones can you trust?" I asked.

"Probably not the preppy legacy students," Joey surmised.

"The students in Alpha Sigma Phi seemed pretty rad and ready for revolution," Santana recalled.

"I could really dig those guys," Darren said. "They were cool."

"They are. Several are in my classes," Joey agreed.

Bruce had been fairly silent, observing and listening. "I think I could rig up a local power failure, but someone would have to be ready to break into the building and kill any backup generators."

"Father Durham needs the van back by morning," Abigail said.

"I can handle the driving," Santana boasted.

I chuckled, knowing his usual driving speed.

"If we could turn off the projection aimed at the Brooklyn Bridge during the beginning of traffic hour today, a lot of people would see it," Bruce said.

"Of course, they'd cover up the reappearance and get their news media to tell people they were seeing things," Darren commented.

"And people will believe what they are told, not what they see with their own eyes," I said. "Challenging, but we'll figure something out."

"My dad was an electrical worker and used to take me along when he worked on powerlines. I can help," Everett offered.

<hr>

We did a little shopping and got two sets of wire cutters and other tools. We drove back to check out the building we believed was projecting the images of the collapse of the Brooklyn and Manhattan Bridges. Bruce and Everett went to work on the power situation.

Santana pointed out the cameras on the outside of the building. "They have shielding around the outside with only a small opening to hit the cameras." Joey was pulling out a slingshot.

"Nobody could hit it from here with a slingshot," Bob said.

"I was my neighborhood champion."

Bob pulled out the drone. He attached a sharp blade to it for shattering the lens.

"They'll see that coming," Joey said. "Let me slingshot it. They won't know what hit it, maybe a drive-by."

Darren and Abigail started taking bets. Abigail was betting on Joey. Darren was voting against. A couple of minutes later, Abigail was ten dollars richer.

"Want to take a bet on the other cameras?" she asked enthusiastically.

"That's okay," Darren conceded.

"Darn. And I thought I was going to be rich today." She snapped her fingers, as if disappointed.

We tried to stay out of sight as Joey continued to take out cameras towards the back entrance. We could see something behind the building that looked like a small power complex.

A minute later, we got the text from Bruce on his new burner phone. "Done."

We started moving towards the building. The door locks must have been electronic as they were unlocked as we entered through the door we'd seen Emily's father exit earlier.

Abigail stayed lookout, outside, along with Darren. Joey, Bob, Santana and I headed for the staircase. We could hear confusion from the front, where security was located. Low wattage emergency backup lighting was on and some people had flashlights. It seemed as if everyone was rushing past us, looking for the way out.

We waited until the bulk of the occupants had passed before we moved up the stairs, close to the sides, turning our heads towards the wall to avoid recognition. At times, we had to backtrack and hide in doorways and cubicles on the various floors to avoid being noticed.

At one point, the full power went back on and then out. "They've got the back-up generators," Santana surmised.

We got up to the top floor and located the computerized projection units. There were several projectors aimed in different directions. Bob pulled out a permanent marker. "Let me," Joey said. He wrote "False Flag" backwards and upside down over the now unpowered projector bulbs and then covered the lenses. We quickly rushed down the stairs, knowing the ones behind the illusion would have started heading this way the moment the projections went out or the words Joey wrote appeared. Santana and I were ahead with Bob and Joey following.

As we reached the bottom, I felt the barrel of a gun, pushing into my back. "My, my, Ms. Tanner. You keep popping up alive." It was Kreskin's voice.

CHAPTER 24

"Sir!" I was trying to stall for time, but suddenly the gun moved from my back. I turned. Bob had hit Kreskin with a tire iron. Kreskin was unconscious, bleeding from the head.

"I came prepared."

"Let's get out of here," I encouraged. We raced out of the building, joining our friends outside, and rushed towards where we had parked the Lincoln. Once in it, we barreled around the area to try to lose any strays and then started heading back towards Pebble Beach. We could see the traffic on streets not far from the Brooklyn Bridge going gaga over the sudden reappearance of the enormous, undamaged structure that the power failure had caused—though it was still covered in some kind of cloth.

People in Queens rushed past security, climbed up the arches and ripped the shroud off the bridge. It looks as if hundreds had joined in. Across the river, we could see a crowd storming a building on the Manhattan side as well.

"Look, they've figured it out," I said.

"How are they going to get out of that one?" Bob asked. "Tell the public not to believe what they see with their own eyes and feel with their own hands?"

"I'm sure the media will come up with something," I responded.

"And they'll believe it," Santana said from the driver's seat.

"Time to hit the media stations," Everett suggested.

"We're already outlaws. I'm still hoping to survive this one," Bruce said.

"Shit," Santana reacted.

"Double shit," Darren said.

Red and blue lights were flashing behind us. "Do you think it was from the break-in?" I asked.

"I'm banking it was the second stolen car," Santana replied. "I should have changed the plates." Santana stepped on the gas. "Hey, this car has power, more than it should. No wonder someone didn't want to lose it."

"Probably freaked when it disappeared," Darren said.

We headed south, then east, then north and west. We did several more turns and picked up more police tails. As we rounded one corner, we spotted a dumpster and threw most of the rest of our stuff into it before rushing past and before our followers saw what we were doing.

A police helicopter overhead ordered us to stop. We headed for Brooklyn Bridge Park and Pier One. "Everyone, roll down your windows," Santana instructed, "and brace yourself. Everyone in front, cover up to prepare for shattered glass."

"I saw this in *Ruthless People*," Darren said, rolling down the window beside him.

Somehow bracing ourselves didn't relieve the impact with the railing and the fall into the water. "Don't get out until it submerges," Santana told us.

"Good thinking on the windows. Alleviates the pressure, even if the car does fill up faster," Bruce said.

"The faster the better, given they undoubtedly already have people preparing to dive into the water," Bob warned. "Anyone here that can't swim underwater?"

A couple of minutes later, we were submerged. The car must have had some openings through the floor as it filled up from underneath at a relatively fast rate. I wasn't expecting that.

As we swam from the car towards the shore, some good Samaritans were swimming towards us from different directions. I shook them off one who tried to help me and pointed to the car as if someone was inside and I was part of the rescue. Bruce followed my lead and the others did likewise. The swimmers dove towards the car, trying to figure out whether someone was stuck inside.

With the distraction, we managed to swim away to the shore. Our guys pulled off their shirts and Abigail and I stripped down to our undies, treating them like bathing suits. On shore, we tried to look like regular high school students out for a swim in the East River.

We had left most of our belongings in the church van.

Joey looked at his device that had also taken a swim. "When it dries out, it should work. Or else, I'll make a better one."

"How did you hang onto that?" I asked.

"I tucked it into my shorts as I was swimming. We lost a lot of tools though. We can replace them."

We went to the dumpster and pulled out our backpacks, that our Columbia friends had filled with the remainder of our things from Columbia, as well as their own backpacks. "Extra sets of earplugs are in there," Bob boasted.

"Good idea in NYC," I remarked, putting mine in.

Santana spotted an older VW Wagon. "Looks about the right age to be easy," he noted.

There was no driving towards the crowd on the bridge. It had filled the streets—in spite of Feds and guards trying to clear the area. We parked on the other side and walked towards Pebble Beach, again. Darren pulled out some binoculars and passed them around.

As I looked through them, I said, "They are almost rioting at that building on the Manhattan side."

Joey looked through the binoculars. "You're right. They have figured it out. That's got to be where the Manhattan projector is. And they're forcing their way in. Score one hundred for the people."

We stood and watched for a while. "They broke a window at the top and threw something out," Darren observed through the binoculars. "That couldn't have been easy with that thick glass. I bet it's the holographic projector from the Manhattan side."

"Go for it!" Abigail cheered at people rushing towards the Manhattan Bridge.

"Now we have the other bridges and tunnels to handle," Santana said.

"They look ready to take on the system. We may not need to," Bruce observed.

Suddenly, pain exploded in my head. I noticed my friends holding their heads too as were others around us.

CHAPTER 25

"Your earplugs." Santana felt my head. Mine were in, but that didn't stop the pain.

"You have them in?" Bruce asked Santana.

"Always, around here," Santana replied through clenched teeth.

"They're not helping," Abigail groaned.

Around us, people had fallen to the ground, but we were still standing.

"They're helping, but not enough," Joey said.

We went into a sports store. Everyone inside was unconscious on the floor. My head felt like something was hammering at it, but I could still stand. We went for the gun section and the guys grabbed full sound suppressors and handed them to us. The pain subsided as I put mine on. I felt a rush of relief throughout my body.

"Cameras," Bob mouthed. He tapped Joey and waved at the rest of us to go towards the front.

Out front, troops were marching in the streets. We hid behind window displays and watched.

As the troops finished passing, Joey and Bob joined us with some hats and we moved out. "The recordings went bye-bye," Bob informed us.

People were lying unconscious on the bridge and floating in the water. Troopers were picking up fallen people on and about the bridge, including those hanging from the bridge and putting them into white vans.

"DHS," Darren mouthed.

"What was that?" I asked the group.

"Soundwave directed energy," Bruce surmised. "Notice the military didn't move in until everyone was affected. Maybe it's off now." He took off his suppressors.

"Don't!" Abigail exclaimed.

"I'm fine. It's safe, now."

"You could have been back in pain with just the plugs, again," I noted.

"They aren't going to want to deactivate the troops."

"Where do you think they're taking them?" I asked.

"I don't know," Darren replied. "I suspect someplace large, like a stadium."

"Rescue!" Everett wanted to charge. "We rescue them like you did us."

"Suicide," Bruce advised.

"We'd need an army," Santana pointed out.

"Glad we had the plugs," Everett said.

"Really. Or we'd be just like them." I pointed to the bodies being loaded into the vans.

"The bridge is still standing," Bruce said. "They might have stopped the people who rushed onto it, but we took down the projections and the bridge is fully visible. The illusion is gone."

"But at what cost?" I asked. "I'm so tired of people getting hurt because of what I do."

"It's them," Santana declared. "You're still taking everything on yourself? Please stop."

"They got the Manhattan Bridge while we were in the shop." Everett pointed to the other visible bridge, now empty of people.

"If we hadn't exposed this, they could have faked the destruction more often, elsewhere. Now, they have to readjust their plans," Bob purported. "We may have saved lives."

"There are a few people in the water. I need to rescue them," I said. I worried that we had hesitated to long. I hadn't been alert enough to notice if they were in the water when we went into the store. A person could pass very quickly from drowning.

"*We* need to rescue them," Santana corrected me. The East River was definitely not clean, but we jumped in, again. The troops were focused on people on the Brooklyn Bridge, not those in the water.

We tried to stay out of view of the troops who were doing body-removal on the bridge. For once, my swim team skills came in handy. I wondered if the troops were in some kind of trance themselves as they didn't even look our way.

Together, we pulled out half a dozen people. Bruce shook his head when it came to several. We worked to try to push the water from the lungs of those we got to the shore and also did some CPR. By the time we were done, all but one were breathing and we could feel their pulses.

Darren shook his head, looking at one man we couldn't help. His skin had turned blue and he was very stiff.

"He may have been dead and floating before the sound attack. This is New York. Not a lot of compassion here," Darren said.

Most of the river people were coming to, but they were still rather out of it. We put the people from the river into the VW wagon and drove them to a hospital in Connecticut. We walked into Emergency as if we owned the place. Santana led me into a storage closet where we grabbed some medical coats. We took some gurneys out to the van and started loading them up.

"Hopefully someone will treat them in the ER?" Bruce said. "Hospitals are not what they used to be."

Santana drove back to the church van, where we said goodbye to our Columbia friends before heading back to Pennsylvania at top speed. I was a little worried about being caught but the radar and police radio monitor and radar detector Bruce and Jimmy had put together helped us avoid obstacles and tickets.

The Columbia students planned to dump the stolen van on a back street on their way back to Columbia where they would be working on a strategy to make all the bridges and tunnels visible and try to rescue the prisoners. Darren and Bruce had both gotten video of the people being picked up and hauled away. We planned to see if the church could help with demanding the release of the detainees. Our hope was they were just knocked out but still alive.

Additionally, we were all going to try to find out what the plan was that Kreskin didn't want the President to know about.

On the way back to Philly, I asked, "If the debilitating frequency was similar to what they used at camp, why didn't our earplugs work like they did in camp?"

"They probably used more amplification than at camp, which covered a smaller area. And these are different plugs than we had there. They did help. We were the only ones who didn't lose consciousness in the area," Bruce speculated.

"They only picked up the people at the bridges. How are they going to explain the collapse of the people who weren't right at the bridges?" I asked.

"They'll say they should stop doing drugs," Abigail surmised.

"And indoors, such as the store. Why didn't the walls provide protection?"

"Maybe the radio or source playing the canned music, inside, directed the same soundwaves to those inside—or maybe they were powerful enough to penetrate the walls," Santana responded to me.

I looked at the car radio. "Do we dare?"

Abigail turned it on, as she pointed to one of her earplugs. We all still had them in. The media was talking about how exciting the reconstruction of the Brooklyn Bridge was.

"Exciting. It wasn't there this morning and suddenly the bridge is intact? This is bullshit," Abigail said. "Darren's right. Let's go punch out Raquel Madcow."

Bruce smiled and gave her a kiss on the cheek. "The media brainwashing starts, again."

"And even if all the bridges and tunnels are exposed, they'll just keep lying," I presumed.

"The problem isn't just the officials doing the bad Deep State stuff. It's also the media that couldn't tell the truth if it landed in their studios," Santana said.

Santana's burner phone rang. "Nice try, guys." It was Jimmy. "Why couldn't Engañar have taken out Raquel Madcow?"

"I guess we can't expect a lot from a non-existent flu," I said.

"When I get out of this, I'm going to get my own TV station and go all Debbie Lusignan," Abigail said.

"The military carried off hundreds, maybe thousands, of people somewhere. We need to locate them," Santana advised him.

"Joey called and told me. We're all working on it. Word is they're at Citi Field where the Mets play. There is more but I'll tell you when you get back. Drive carefully," Jimmy said.

We were already in our Holy clothing as we parked near the Cathedral and walked over to Independence Hall, where we met up with Jimmy, Shannon and Emily, who were also dressed in similar clothing.

"So, the truth starts to come out and the news media covers," Bruce critiqued.

"If Kreskin fired a machine gun at a group of pregnant women in the middle of Times Square, they'd talk about what a public service he was doing in assisting with population control," Jimmy remarked.

"It's not as hopeless as it seems," Shannon said.

"After the guys got back to Columbia, Joey made a contact within the Defense Department who is ready to blow the whistle on Kreskin," Jimmy related.

"How do you know he's not a fake?" Bruce asked.

"He thinks Joey is Gucifer Seven. He is going by the name Green Dragon but wouldn't tell Joey his real identity. So, I did some checking on his IP. He's Hans Larken."

"He was the chief assistant in the Department when Daddy first came there. Then Mario Johnson impressed Daddy and got promoted past Larken," Abigail informed us.

"Even if it's revenge against Kreskin, we could use the help," Bruce said.

"According to Green Dragon, Larken, Kreskin's flying back to D.C. tomorrow, and then he's having a big meeting with Emily's dad. He was going to fly back tonight but something came up, and he decided to delay his return."

"The Brooklyn Bridge or getting hit in the head?" Santana asked.

"Hit in the head?"

"He was holding a gun to Summer's back. If I had the tire iron instead of Bob, he wouldn't be returning to D.C. at all." Santana was visibly upset.

I put my arms around him and gave him a quick kiss. "You are awesome. We all did our part."

"Emily, your dad was there too," I said. "We saw him coming out of the building in Brooklyn where they were projecting the fake image of the fallen Brooklyn Bridge."

"He was healthy?"

"Looked that way."

"Any sign of my mom?"

"Didn't see her. But she might not be involved in faking false flags."

"I hope she's alive, but—" She started to cry.

"I hope so, too." I put my arms around her.

"Emily, she went along with sending you to the camp. Don't forgive her. She deserves to rot in hell," Abigail told her.

"I don't believe in hell."

"Too bad. It would be nice if there were some eternal torment for all our parents." Abigail turned to me. "Except your mom."

I thought about how I missed my mom. At least, she was alive, even if she wasn't here. I was glad she was in Cuba and was hoping she stayed there.

I broke out laughing and then felt guilty about laughing. "That poor guy who spent all that time souping up his car. If we get out of this alive, we'll have to reimburse him."

"Car?" Shannon asked.

"We deep-sixed it. Literally," I said. "I hope he has insurance."

We went back to the van and got our stuff. As we walked on the sidewalk towards the Cathedral, we saw a black car with darkened windows. We moved into a doorway as it passed. The windows were heavily shaded. Men with bulges in their suit coats got out and went into the church.

"I didn't think we slipped up with the van," Santana lamented.

"We had on our priest and nun clothes when we were traveling in it," Bruce pointed out. "And we had different license plates in New York."

"We're worried about us? Maybe, they know Father Durham helped us," I fretted. "We have to protect him after he risked so much to help us."

"You don't think they would go after a priest, do you?" Bruce asked.

"Our government routinely blows up churches, hospitals, schools and wedding parties. Do you really think it's beneath them to harm or even kill a priest?" Abiail responded.

Our group moved closer to the church and saw other priests protesting as Father Durham was roughly escorted out.

CHAPTER 26

"I don't know anything," Father Durham insisted as he was being dragged away.

"You're coming with us," one of the men demanded, as he shoved Father Durham into the black car.

"I wonder if they thought the white vans were too noticeable and switched to black cars," I queried.

"We have to do something," Shannon declared.

"Where's Santana?" I asked, as the car took off.

In the bushes, near where the car had been stopped, I saw movement. Somebody in his underwear was slowly getting off the ground. A priest, or rather Jimmy, smashed the guy from behind with a lid from a trashcan that was beside the street ready for pick-up, probably the next day.

"Now, I'm going to kill him." I knew what Santana was up to and was very worried.

Jimmy came up to us as his phone rang. He answered. It was Santana's burner phone. The voices I heard were not Santana. "Everyone quiet," Jimmy urged, though I suspected our end was muted.

"Turn right at the Avenue of the Arts. We're going to the Ritz-Carl-ton," a voice instructed.

Shannon looked up the location on her map. It wasn't more than a mile. We started running in that direction as we continued listening. "If you so much as make an expression of discomfort or utter a word, I'll pull the trigger."

It sounded like the car stopped. I didn't hear much else except "2905."

We continued running. We passed a depot with lockers. Quickly, we stuffed our things into several lockers and kept running. We were debating about whether we were better off dressed like priests and nuns or students. We decided to wear the habits in and pull them off later.

The 29th floor required a key card. A guest got in our elevator and used his keycard to go up to the tenth floor.

Our five-finger guy was missing. "Do you have the time?" Bruce asked the man. As the guy looked at his watch, Emily reached into his pocket and took his key card. But it wouldn't take us above the tenth floor.

We took the elevator down into the basement to look for the service area.

We searched for a closet, where uniforms, anything that might help, was stored. A waiter came out of the room service kitchen. "Sister," he said to me. "I think you have the wrong floor."

"Our guide pushed the button to take us up to the 29th floor to join another father from our congregation," Jimmy lied. "But we didn't get out in time and we wound up down here."

"We let our Father down." Shannon started to burst into tears.

"No problem. I'm going up to the 30th floor and will drop you off on the 29th on my way."

"Thank you," I sighed.

As we got off on the 29th floor and the elevator continued up, I saw Santana in the corridor, waiting outside the room. I punched him. "You jerk. I was so worried about you."

"That means you care, bonita madonna. You do know I love you and would never leave this world before you finally marry me."

"Oh, you know how to butter me up. Growl. I love you too, jerk."

"Is that a 'yes' to my proposal?"

"Um, I think we're trying to save Father Durham." Butterflies were jumping in my stomach in spite of the precarious situation. Santana always knew how to get to me.

"If romance is handled for the moment," Jimmy interrupted, "Let's figure out how to save Father Durham. You're the driver?"

"And a low-level agent, which is why I'm waiting out here."

"They didn't notice their man had changed?"

"He was also a Latino, though nowhere near as handsome. Racist white officers think we all look alike. Handy, right?"

"We need them out of the room," Emily demanded. Abigail was clearly rubbing off on her. My little adopted sister was becoming more assertive.

"Yes," Santana agreed.

"Do what you do in school when you want everyone to go to the beach," Jimmy suggested.

"Brilliant," Santana said. "Where is the fire alarm?"

"There are sensors in the ceiling," Bruce observed. "We just need a fire."

"Anyone have anything they want to burn?" I asked. I looked around and saw trays of empty plates with covers. I didn't know if the napkins had flame retardant on them.

Bruce pulled out a Coney Island Map he had picked up in a souvenir shop. "Anyone have a match?"

"I have a lighter," Jimmy said.

"You don't smoke," I reminded him.

"Lucky for you, I go to concerts."

Bruce had a little rubber cup with the bottom missing that he held between the door and his ear. We took turns, listening.

"What about cameras?" I asked.

"I suspect this is one of those floors where they want privacy," Bruce guessed.

With my ear to the cup, I could hear, "You gave sanctuary to a group of thirty kids Saturday morning. We have the videos."

I guessed we weren't as clandestine as we had thought.

"My church doors are open to all. If some kids came in there, they would have been welcome. But I don't recall whether any kids came in."

"We have the satellite images."

"There may have been kids in the Basilica. But what does that have to do with me? "

"You have given aid and support to enemies of the state."

"If you are concerned about enemies of the state, then why have you brought me to a hotel and not to a government building?"

Before they could answer, the fire alarm and sprinklers went off from the flaming map Jimmy was holding up high.

The rest of us backed against the wall on both sides of the door as two men came out with guns in their hands and looked at Jimmy as the door closed behind them. A second later Bruce and Santana had them on the ground, knocked out with food trays that were waiting in the hall to be picked up.

Well, not quite out. Santana grabbed the gun from the one who was starting to snap out of it and knocked him over the head with it while Bruce used the cover to hit the other guy again and then requisitioned his gun.

We stayed off to the side of the door. A moment later, a third guy came out and was knocked to the floor. We waited. No more noise came from the room.

"May I go now?" we heard Father Durham ask. Nobody answered. A second later, we were through the door, untying him. He had bruises on his face, a black eye and a split lip. Sprinklers were flooding the hall as we rushed out the door, down the fire escape and past incoming firemen.

As we left the building, Jimmy got a call from Darren. "The Mets were playing tonight and there was a mix-up with tickets. The audience was already full when the paid ticketholders arrived."

"Duh," Abigail reacted.

"They gave the paid ticket holders a raincheck for tomorrow morning for a special practice game."

"What about the detainees?" I asked.

"Columbia students brought them lemonade and spoke to them.

Those people really believed they went to the stadium to see the game —well, all but a few, who insisted that they woke up there."

"So, more mind control?"

"They probably injected them with something to make them forget what they had seen?"

"And the bridges?"

"All back up. Fast construction. Tunnels operational as well. Too many people, not in the stadium, witnessed the transformation."

Santana drove us back to the Cathedral, collecting our backpacks from the locker on the way. He parked on a nearby side street.

The other fathers were very happy to see Father Durham return.

"The guys who collected him are rogue federal agents. They took him to a hotel and worked him over. He needs a safe place to recover," Bruce related.

One of the Fathers offered a solution. "My sister has a cabin not far from here. She only uses it in the early summer. It's empty the rest of the year. She sometimes lets me borrow it. You can follow me there."

"Father Browning, isn't it?" Santana asked.

"Yes, it is."

"Gracias."

"Thank you," the rest of us said in unison.

"May God be with all of us," I added, trying to sound more nun-like, though I'd never been in a Catholic church before late Friday night or early Saturday morning.

Before taking off, we asked that word be sent to the congregations in Queens to distribute lemonade. Father Browning made some calls and promised that this would be done.

After Bruce got a key to the cabin from Father Browning, we followed the father at a bit of a distance as he drove through trees and hills. I was hopeful that we weren't going by any of Pennsylvania's numerous nuclear power plants. I didn't see any along the way. Limerick, one of the leaky ones, wasn't on our route.

Finally, Father Browning honked as he passed a driveway and

continued on. We continued on too. This was preplanned in case of satellite footage.

"This van may have tracking," Bruce noted.

"Then we need to find a place to dump it and then make our way back here." Santana pulled to the side of the road and Abigail, Bruce, Shannon, Jimmy, and Emily helped Father Durham towards the driveway to the cabin. Santana looked at me. "You're not going?"

"I'm with you. Remember our discussion in the hotel hallway?"

"I was concerned I was pressuring you too much."

"I'm not ready to get married or engaged. But you know how I feel about you."

He nodded and continued on. We circled back closer to Philly, found a shop and bought a moped. Our money might run out sometime, but we had each brought enough from Cuba that we still had a comfortable margin.

I continued driving the car for a while as Santana followed in the moped. I pulled off the road and joined him. We kept under the cover of the trees and continued on. The moped was slower than a motorcycle. We stopped at a fast-food restaurant that was hidden from the sky to recharge it. Then we were off again. When we reached the cabin, Father Durhan was resting on the couch and our friends were helping to apply ice to his bruises.

"The refrig is fully stocked with all kinds of good stuff," Emily enthusiastically announced.

"That makes things easier," I said, remembering the traps that were being used for food at the camp, food I had refused to eat.

"We aren't far from Bryn Mawr, but at least we didn't go by Limerick," Jimmy related.

"Limerick is that plant that leaks so much it needs to be shut down, right?" I queried.

"It's really bad. But we got SONGS, Diablo and Indian Point shut down," Jimmy recalled.

"That was fun," Shannon jumped in. "I remember riding with my parents to SONGS for the protests when I was a kid. Some speaker, possibly the mayor from some town like Solana Beach in San Diego County talked about how he had given his kids organic milk, thinking it was safe. When he tested it, it was off the charts, radioactive because of Fukushima fallout."

"My parents were also cool." Jimmy smiled. "Because I wanted to be a surfer, they were active in trying to close down SONGS."

"The milk isn't necessarily safe from radiation—even now," Santana pointed out. "You were right to skip it at camp. Right after Fukushima hit the U.S., Lisa Jackson, the EPA Acting Director, closed down our country's radiation monitors, and nobody but the universities and independents were doing any monitoring. Berkeley's results showed Californians should stay away from leafy vegetables and milk. The organic milk is at highest risk because the cows are eating the possibly radioactive grass growing outdoors."

"I saw on the Environmental Reporter's site, you know Michael Collins, that the rain was really bad as late as January 2015," Shannon recalled. "I do worry about the radiation in the ocean."

"We surfers may have a shorter life span but a more fun one," Jimmy noted.

Emily changed the subject. "We got help from the Columbia students. What about the college students here?"

"Not all Millennials are necessarily on our side," Santana replied.

"Bryn Mawr is now taking guys," Shannon announced. "I've been thinking of going there after high school. They are number one in the country for getting girls into grad school, and science is really big there."

"Isn't that in an elite area?" Bruce asked.

"They heavily recruit foreign students, who may be more supportive of us."

"I'm making a tomato basil and mushroom soup," I said. "Any other preferences?"

"I think I saw some frozen apple pie," Santana replied.

"Apple pie, tomato basil mushroom soup, anything else?"

"I saw some Cherry Kijafa in the cupboard," Jimmy noted.

"We'll have to leave some money for Father Browning's sister to replace what we take," I said.

Father Durham tried to sit up, but we encouraged him to stay down. "Tomato basil mushroom soup and apple pie?" I asked him.

"That would be wonderful. I haven't properly thanked you for rescuing me from those federal hoodlums."

"Dealing with federal hoodlums seems to be a daily event for us," I replied.

"Maybe next time, we'll just replace the government," Santana teased.

"You're making light of it, but you kids put yourselves in danger to save me. 'Thank you' doesn't express the extent of my appreciation, but thank you, anyway. If you hadn't rescued me, I wasn't going to talk, and I am certain they would have killed me. I know you are being watched." He pointed up. "And you will be blessed for your courage and good deeds."

"You saved us before we saved you," Bruce reminded him.

"Pay it forward," Emily said.

Santana started a fire in the fireplace, after we had a vote, while hoping that it wouldn't call attention to the cabin. Jimmy had checked and found that somehow the cabin had escaped having a smart meter, which would have told the government and hackers how many lights we had on and where we were using the electricity. Emily helped me with the dinner and everyone said it tasted good. All of us but Father Durham sat in front of the fire and relaxed, talking about possible plans for the future.

Drinking wasn't my thing, but the Kijafa tasted like cherry juice, and I felt like I deserved a drink after all I had been through. The buzz it gave me made it a little difficult to deal with Santana so close. He had his arm around me whenever he wasn't eating.

I worried that Emily might feel like the odd one out with Alejandro still being in Cuba. "I'm sure that Alejandro is thinking of you. Perhaps you can send him a card in a sealed envelope to let him know you are okay."

"I sent him a couple from Columbia. I didn't put my name on them, but I signed 'Love,' followed by a comma and a blank line. I couldn't tell him where I was. Do you think he'll wait for me?"

"I think he adores you. He'll wait as long as it takes. I'm sure of it."

She smiled and leaned back, looking dreamy-eyed, probably thinking about Alejandro.

"I'm serious about wanting to marry you. I was ready before we came back to the States. And I'll be ready whenever you say the word," Santana said.

"I'd like to wait until I'm at least eighteen—unless we have to do the emancipation thing. Also, college is supposed to be tougher for married couples."

"We could arrange to go to the same university, maybe Berkeley, and get an apartment. We won't have the usual economic issues. I have a trust fund from my late grandfather."

"So do I, but I am not sure about Berkeley. It's a great school, but—"

"I've been trying to talk her into Bryn Mawr because she'll get a good pre-veterinarian education. Did you know that President Woodrow Wilson taught there?" Shannon joined in.

"You mean the white supremacist who showed *Birth of the Nation* in the White House before winning a Nobel Peace Prize?" Santana asked.

"The Prize was for helping create the League of Nations. Besides, Barack Obama who bombed more civilians than any other President before him also got a Nobel Peace prize," Shannon replied.

"True. We could do with a peace President for a change. They all seem to be for war," he agreed.

"Except Carter. Also, Kennedy was going to pull us out of the Vietnam war, and his death was the reason it continued and expanded," I reminded them.

"I am amazed at how much you kids know," Father Durham said. "I think your generation is the smartest one yet."

"Thank you," we said in unison. Emily went over and gave him a hug. He tried not to grimace from being touched, but I could tell he was in a lot of pain.

***

We girls got the larger bedroom, though it only had one queen sized bed and there were four of us. The guys and Father Durham were to take the smaller one, but it had two twin beds. Father Durham elected to stay on the couch. We gave him some extra blankets and a pillow. We offered to pull the couch out into a bed, but he declined the offer, clearly in too much pain to want to move.

"You were only in danger and hurt because you helped us, Padre," Santana said.

In our room, I looked at Emily. She was holding up well. It must have been tough on her maybe losing her mother but not knowing for sure. Abigail had it equally tough. The only parent who came close to loving her was reportedly gone.

"Have you thought any more about looking up you're former housekeeper, Philomena?" I asked Abigail.

"Only about a million times," she said. "I'm going to have to find her."

"When we are out of this, maybe we can all help locate her."

"When I was younger, she was more of a parent to me than either of my parents. I just hope my daddy didn't harm her."

That had occurred to me as well, given how cruel he seemed. I didn't know for sure that my father was gone, but I still couldn't work up any feelings of personal loss. I still felt guilty about not feeling guilty or sad over his reported death.

"I saw Spotlight," Emily said. "Father Durham and Father Browning are nice. They aren't at all like those priests in the movie."

"I am sure the majority of priests and ministers are really good people. It's the exceptions you hear about."

"Our parents are the exceptions to human beings. Cold and evil," Abigail said. I realized a part of her wanted her mom to be in the same category as her father so she wouldn't hurt as much about her mother's supposed death.

I wished I could help Santana. It almost broke my heart to think of what he must be going through. Of all those from our families who reportedly died, Angelo was the best. Santana believed Angelo would have stopped what was happening if he had known in advance where their father had sent Santana. Santana didn't even get to speak with his brother after we escaped the camp. He planned to, but Angelo's cell had been disconnected, and Santana couldn't call him through the house phone while evading their dad.

I hadn't yet sent any mail to my mother. She knew I was alive. I resolved that tomorrow I would send her a note, anonymously, of course, that she would know was from me. As crazy as things were, we were still blessed to have people, good people, in our lives who cared about us. The five of us had survived the worst kinds of torture and attempts on our lives and we cared about each other as if we were brothers and sisters, though I wasn't about to think of Santana as a brother.

I had my mother back and Shannon and Jimmy. Tiffany was out there, still caring about me. Emily had Rosa and Alejandro. We all had Alonzo, who had gotten close to my mom. I expected that one day, he just might become my new dad. We also had the Columbia students, particularly Joey, Darren and Bob. There were others there, like Everett and Professor Brand, who had been kind to us and there was Clarence from Harlem, and of course, Genevieve.

Adding to all those, we had Father Durham and Father Browning and our friends in the Tunisian and Russian delegations. Maybe there was a God up there somewhere. It seemed sad that people had to wait until they died to find out if God was real, especially when there was a possibility this was all there was. But if there was nothing else, at least I had my mom, Santana and lots of friends who loved me and whom I loved.

The next morning, Santana, Jimmy and Bruce awakened us with breakfast in bed. "You girls cooked last night and we decided we owed you one," Santana said.

They had prepared us potatoes, stuff with mixed vegetables and glasses of orange juice. "I know you don't eat eggs, Summer. Is this alright?"

I was almost crying. "It's beautiful," I said. I looked at Abigail. She was crying. Shannon looked like this was nothing new to her. Emily was munching hers right up and a minute later, asked for more. We laughed and Santana went back to get her additional food.

Shannon and Jimmy were smiling and joking around, almost like an old married couple. Compared to us, they had been together a long time.

"I heard from Professor Brand. He's got a friend, a lady friend, who teaches social justice at Bryn Mawr. I gather he had a coded discussion with her. She's willing to help," Bruce informed us.

"Did you get her name?" I asked.

"Jacqueline LaMont."

"More good news. There is wired internet here. I set up a VPN and did some digging. Found some really interesting stuff," Jimmy said.

"So, the profs got a girlfriend," Santana commented.

"She is one of the most respected professors at Bryn Mawr. She has encouraged a great deal of civil rights legislation in Pennsylvania. Apparently, she did a lot of work with State Senator Leach," Bruce informed us.

"I remember him. He was big on youth rights and on crediting teens for social justice work," I recalled.

"The prof mentioned that."

"I was kind of hoping that he and Genevieve would hit it off," Emily said. "Genevieve shouldn't have to be alone."

"Matchmaker," Santana joshed. "I'm sure when this is over, Genevieve'll find someone special of her own."

"We can take credit for one match," Bruce said.

We looked at him.

"While Everett and I were cutting the powerlines, Everett mentioned that he and Bob had really hit it off."

"I didn't realize Bob was gay," I said. "That's cool. Their personalities are so different that they complement each other."

"They're above eighteen. So, their fathers can't send them to Camp to get fixed."

I thought about Jamie. "I wish we could have saved Jamie."

"They broke him. If we could have found a way to get out of there earlier, maybe he would have survived. He lost his will to live. Otherwise, he would have fought when they put the noose around his neck," Santana contended.

"Jimmy, what did you find on the Internet?"

"Oh, I've been waiting for someone to ask."

"Sorry," I said.

"Yeah, romance takes precedence over saving the world," Santana joked.

"On the Dark Web, I picked up a brief thread through a backdoor to some kind of official discussion about an upcoming change in Administration. The channel disappeared almost as soon as I saw it."

"As in impeachment?" I asked.

"I don't know if impeachment was involved. I suspected it was more of a coup from reading it. Abigail's father was mentioned as a successor. He is in the line of succession."

"My dad is planning to take out the President and everyone in between in the line of succession?"

CHAPTER 27

"I didn't get clarity on the how or the what of the planned coup," Jimmy stated.

"What does it matter? The President is just a figurehead anyway," Santana pointed out.

"The current one is a loose cannon. He only does what they want nine-nine percent of the time. That one percent is critical to those who oppose him. They want someone who will answer one hundred percent to the real powers," Jimmy contended.

"Who was part of this thread?" Shannon asked him.

"It was one of the people in the CFR, calling himself Rhino."

"My dad's the head of that," Emily reminded us.

"I know. The CFR was actually easier to tap into on the Dark Web than some of the other players in whatever is going on. They use the Dark Web to throw its users off base."

"What more did they say?" I asked.

"The thread disappeared really fast, faster than an InstaChat item."

"We need to look for someone working with Emily's dad called Rhino," Shannon guessed.

"That was an online alias, not a real name. There's more. There was something about how New York had worked and D.C. was next."

"The brainwashing or the false flags or both?" Bruce asked.

"Not clear."

"So, we were the excuse, but the fake pandemic, the mind-control vaccines and false flags were an experiment for a larger operation?" I asked. "Is it time to contact Dennis Kucinich and Cynthia McKinney?"

"I want them to stay alive. These people are playing for keeps," Santana replied.

"The defense industry has a history of Wellstoning anyone opposing them," Shannon pointed out. "My parents said they were planning to vote for Paul Wellstone and then they killed him, his wife and daughter, the pilot, co-pilot and his staffers after he voted against the war on Iraq. That was a threat to anyone in Congress who planned to oppose the military industrial complex."

"Edward Kennedy and Robert Byrd were supposed to be aboard his plane. Of course, they're now dead, despite having missed the plane," Santana said.

"Mark and David Wellstone got the proof that their father's plane was blown out of the sky, but even the DNC wouldn't touch the truth," I expounded on Shannon's information.

"Of course not. The DNC is bought off by the defense industry," Santana reminded us.

This was a discussion I had had many times with Shannon and was part of the reason I was so disillusioned with my father's party. I planned to register as NPP, or no party preference, when I got to be old enough to vote.

"Any more from Green Dragon, the whistleblower?"

"Not yet."

***

Santana and I rode the moped down the hill and picked up a car, which of course, we planned to return later and went back to the cabin.

Father Durham still needed recovery time. Emily offered to nurse him. Jimmy and Bruce decided to stay behind to cover the Net. Santana, Abigail, Shannon and I took off towards Bryn Mawr.

Bruce was correct. Bryn Mawr was in an elite area of multi-million-dollar mansions set in the hills about ten miles from Philadelphia. The school mostly consisted of castles, some with a history of ghost stories.

Although we touted ourselves on not being superstitious, Shannon and I avoided the Senior Steps entrance to Taylor Tower, just in case, since we were considering later becoming students at Bryn Mawr. The legend of the Senior Steps stemmed from threats made by former President Woodrow Wilson, who had an office right by that entrance. He got tired of hearing students trampling up and down the stairs. So he issued a statement that anyone but a senior who used those stairs would not graduate. That turned into a superstition.

We looked for and found Professor LaMont's office. The school staff was very courteous. I made up a phony name for myself and told them I planned to apply later this year.

Professor LaMont was expecting us. Apparently, Professor Brand had communicated a relatively clear picture of what was going on to her.

"You kids are in quite a pickle," she remarked. "You're innocent, and yet, the media and government have already proclaimed you guilty of numerous crimes."

"They also have reported us officially dead though they know we're alive," I pointed out. "They subliminally told New Yorkers to finish us off."

"We die a lot," Abigail noted.

"That spells danger as they could kill you off and claim you were dead all along."

"We think they might be planning a coup against the President."

"Stopping a coup is a little difficult. They know who you are. That makes infiltration out of the question. It would help to have someone currently on the inside, like Smedley Butler, who exposed the planned coup against FDR."

"Any suggestions?" Santana asked.

"Professor Brand indicated there has been a full media blackout, but the Columbia Students are aware of the situation."

"This may sound crazy," I stated. "And if someone told me this, I'd think they were crazy. But along with everything else, we've discovered that what happened to the bridges and tunnels was just an illusion."

"An illusion?"

"We went with other students yesterday and found out that the Queens Midtown Tunnel and Brooklyn and Manhattan Bridges never collapsed but were covered with screen cloth, and a projected hologram was used. Very scientific, but who would believe it," I expounded.

"Professor Brand would. He told me that they used some high-tech to falsely frame you. That must be what he was speaking about. It also explains why they were able to rebuild the Brooklyn Bridge in minutes. I have a nephew in Brooklyn who forwarded me a video that appeared on InstaChat."

"So, Joey's video got out?" I asked.

"Yes, it did. You will find you have a lot of underground supporters. Half the students at Bryn Mawr are asking questions. The Espionage Act threat garnered the attention of young people all across the country. If telling the truth could do that to you, it could do it to anyone."

"As in 'First they came for Assange. And then they came for –'" Santana started a variation of the poem.

"That's precisely what the talk around campus is. We have a large social justice network here."

"Have any suggestions?"

"Rally the students."

"What?"

"I hear you have the students at Columbia behind you. It's important to rally the students on a national level. Get as many as you can to speak out and demand answers."

"Santana and I have a legalistic problem. They're gunning for us," I pointed out.

"But Shannon and your Columbia friends don't have that problem. Is that correct?"

"They're in the clear so far. But yesterday, the feds beat up a priest who helped us, and they likely would have killed him if we hadn't rescued him."

Several others who came to the office with her were certain their parents would join in as well.

Professor LaMont drove us back to the cabin after we dropped off the borrowed car and joined her in hers, being careful to avoid being seen under the cover of the trees.

LaMont spent some time talking to Father Durham. Jimmy called Professor Brand and put him on speaker.

"The Columbia students are not taking this sitting down. More are doing research. The FDR was not damaged. A cloud of debris was released. There were closures but no damage."

"What about the injured?" Santana asked.

"Nobody knows anyone who was actually injured. It calls into question whether all the deaths from the gas in the church were faked or whether everyone was a crisis actor."

"As go-along as my mom was, I wouldn't believe she would have agreed to faking dying. She liked being the wife, the living wife, of the Secretary of Defense." Abigail shook her head.

"I want to think my mom faked it, but I don't feel it. The dream was so real of her coming to me after death," Emily lamented. "If you find out I'm wrong, I'll be happy."

"I don't think Angelo would have faked his death. My other brother might have but not Angelo."

"So that leaves the possibility that they were killed or were forced to play dead," Brand surmised.

"My father might have faked his. He was that cold of a human being. We know Emily's faked his," I responded.

"There is another option. There could have been a coup within the coup," Jimmy suggested. "Some of the greedy people could have been eliminated by greedier individuals. I'm not saying that happened to your father, Summer. But he was on the other side of the political Spectrum from Abigail's father."

"I'm just glad my mother is safe," I said. "Do you think you could track down Abigail's former housekeeper and nanny, Philomena Rodriguez?"

"I'll try locating her on the Internet." Jimmy looked at Abigail with a reassuring nod.

I could see a glint of joy mixed with fear in Abigail's eyes.

"You can wait to make actual contact until after it is safe," I told her.

I looked at Emily. She closed her eyes. "Rosa loves me. She is my mother, now." There was a waiver in her voice as if it was a sadness that the mother who had raised her could have saved her but didn't.

"And we're your sisters and we love you, too," I said, touching her shoulder and then giving her a hug.

"The Columbia students are reaching out to students at colleges throughout the country. They are sending videos and discussing the mistreatment of the Wilderness Five," Professor Brand informed us.

"A number of Bryn Mawr students have already contacted other universities. UC Berkeley, UC Santa Cruz, Nevada State, Arizona State, NYU, USD, and Georgetown students are particularly interested in your plight," Professor LaMont laid out.

"Georgetown? I would have expected that to be more establishment," I said.

"They couldn't keep the progressives out," Jimmy gloated.

"There is the six-degree issue," Professor LaMont noted.

"Six degrees?" Emily asked.

"Everyone is six degrees from everyone else in the world. Basically, your friends and their friends and so on to six degrees includes everyone on the planet," Professor LaMont explained.

"I've met the President," Abigail said.

"That means I'm two degrees from the President and three degrees from everyone he knows," Professor LaMont commented.

"When we figure out what is going on, we do need to get all the students we can to Washington," Santana said.

"And the students will have to wake up those parents who care," Shannon interjected.

"That was the plan students at Bryn Mawr were suggesting," I said.

"I'm willing to bet most parents will care," Jimmy contended. "CPS wants the world to believe all parents are bad so they can steal and traffic the children for all that HHS money."

"Which is why good parents don't have a chance in court," Santana noted.

"My parents have a policy. If CPS comes to the door, don't answer." Jimmy held up two thumbs.

"Your parents have always been great," Shannon told him.

"And yours." I had always been envious of the relationship between Shannon and her parents.

She put an arm around me. "They love you, too."

"I'd feel better if I picked you up, tomorrow, than you taking someone else's car there." Professor LaMont had undoubtedly guessed that today's borrowing was unauthorized. I wondered if she knew of Santana's history of similarly borrowing his dad's cars.

Later that evening, I told the others, "I like Professor LaMont. She encourages free thinking. She doesn't tell her students the answers. She lets them discover their own answers."

"That's the best way to teach and get the message across," Bruce noted. "If you tell someone something, they'll treat it as opinion. But if you assist them in coming to their own conclusion, they will make it their own. I understand that Berkeley has switched from teaching thinkers to training followers."

"Let's hope the students there aren't so far gone that they believe the government's lies about us," I responded.

"They're trying to brainwash students at all the universities," Father Durham related. "Whether the students can see through the brainwashing is a sign of the strength of their characters."

We made salads and three veggie pizzas and ate them quickly. We had picked up some corn syrup-free drinks for the cabin. We knew most corn in the USA contained dangerous defoliants and caused cancer.

After dinner, we gathered and discussed the findings among ourselves.

Jimmy's phone rang. He put Joey on speaker. "Until they cut us, Columbia was broadcasting and exposing the truth. Some students are planning to march on and take over three New York news stations."

"Good luck with that. If they get arrested, the government can do anything to them."

"They figure if they can just take them over for a minute tomorrow, it will have an impact others won't forget."

"And they could wind up in prison, brainwashed and powerless," Jimmy warned.

"The people need some wake-up juice. They wake up for a little bit and go back to sleep. Sleep is easy. Being awake is hard for the masses. They need to wake up in a way that they can't forget," Abigail asserted.

"The fact that anyone bought the official story of the bridges shows how far gone society is. We even believed it without questioning until we found out otherwise," I added.

The next day, Santana, Jimmy, Shannon, Emily and I dressed like Bryn Mawr students, complete with college sweatshirts and caps. Bruce and Abigail stayed behind to watch developments remotely and for Bruce to work on the computer. I suspected they also wanted some alone time. Father Durham, who seemed to be doing better, planned to get more rest and to study his Bible.

As Professor LaMont drove us to Bryn Mawr, she decided to swing by Independence Hall, which was a bit out of the way, but we were glad she did.

A demonstration of thousands of students had been planned. Penn State had gotten into the loop and their students were cutting class to protest our treatment and demand closure of the Gulag camps and schools.

"I'm not going to stop," the Prof said. "There is a risk they will use facial recognition to check out people in the crowd. I just wanted to get a glimpse. One of my students will stream the speeches live when they start."

"Students protested other wars by the millions, and yet it had no impact," Jimmy reminded us.

"While the state has been trying hard to break family bonds in the U.S., overall parents dote on their children even more than they did in the 60's or even at the turn of the Millennium. And the seniors who have protested before have joined them," Professor LaMont reflected.

"With legislation attacking boycotts and protests, won't some be scared?" Shannon asked.

"There is courage in numbers. And Americans are fed up with the tyranny of the few," Professor LaMont replied.

"I hope you get to be my Prof if I go to Bryn Mawr," Emily said.

"Bryn Mawr is the most underrated university in America. I was offered a fellowship at Harvard and turned it down to teach here. Professors are more free to teach the truth at Bryn Mawr."

"I've heard about the pressure, elsewhere. Professors are being fired or retired for telling the truth about nine-eleven or about the Israeli-Palestinian situation."

"In America, there are serious complications for telling the truth about Palestine. Look what the Democratic Party did to Cynthia McKinney and she was a six-term congresswoman."

"She's my hero," I said. "She is still running around the world saving lives."

"And the mainstream media never covers her," Santana pointed out.

"Were you old enough to remember how the U.S. Government didn't care or help out in any way when the Israeli Military held the six-term Democratic Congresswoman hostage for eight days as it tried to extract a false confession from her?" LaMont asked me.

"I know about it. It was before I was born, but I researched it because, as I said, she is my hero. The Israeli government imprisoned McKinney because she was bringing medical aid to the children of Palestine on a boat. The Israelis had fired on and rammed her prior boat. She and Galloway later brought aid by foot, but the Israelis refused to let them bring more than the supplies they could carry."

"And when her father was dying, she skipped the next boat to take care of him. That time, the Israeli Government killed a number of those trying to bring medical supplies. They thought she was on board and were aiming for her," Shannon said. "She is my hero, too."

"Bryn Mawr is definitely the place for you. Half of the country doesn't even know who McKinney is."

"You can't be a true liberal and not be a fan of Cynthia's," I declared. "She and Kucinich tried to stop the attack on Libya that killed so many people and turned the country from an equal protection, free society into a slave state." I turned to Santana, "When I tried to discuss McKinney with my dad, he told me to shut up."

"Guess he's not a liberal. I don't think I ever heard my father talk about her. I know he's not a liberal," Santana said.

"I had thought liberal was a term that has gone into disrepute with much of your generation, thanks to the media," Professor LaMont commented.

"That's because of the 'Neoliberals,' who are the same as the 'Neocons.' There's essentially no difference between Democratic and Republican Senators in terms of their political philosophy."

"In Congress, Adam Schifty makes the neocon philosophy sound comparatively leftist," Santana remarked, sarcastically. We all laughed in agreement.

"Santana and Summer, I am curious how the children of Marcus Tanner and Congressman Barillo wound up so—" She paused. "Knowledgeable and cynical regarding the Democratic Party."

"That's why they sent us to the camp," I replied. "Notice they didn't send our siblings." I may have come off too strong on that, as I thought about Santana's brother. Santana had to be hurting, knowing his better brother Angelo was dead. I could only hope that his death had been faked like Emily's father's. I didn't want to share my hope with Santana as it might turn out to be false.

"Two of our siblings spoke at our fake funerals. They lied," Santana said.

"That had to have been horrific," Professor LaMont sympathized.

Santana and I nodded. "I knew what kind of person Pandar was before. He watched as my mother and I were beaten and he didn't care. I feel sorry for anyone he winds up marrying."

"He'll probably marry someone who hates other women until she winds up the brunt of his beatings," Santana remarked.

"Seriously," Jimmy said. "The person he chooses will probably be someone who even hates her own mother."

As we approached Independence Hall, our path was blocked by National Guard Troops.

"We need to protect the students," I said.

"They'd bomb the place if they knew we were here," Santana advised.

From where traffic was blocked, we could see the troops firing rubber bullets into the crowd, along with tear gas.

CHAPTER 28

A heavy spray of water hit the troops. Apparently, the students had accessed the water system.

"I'm not wanted," Jimmy said, jumping out of the car.

"I'm going with him," Shannon announced, leaping out to join him.

Seconds later Shannon called me on her cell and I put it on speaker. The water spray was continuing and apparently, the students had a heavy power source as active electrical wires were being thrust onto the ground where the troops were marching. I worried about all the criminal charges that could be leveled against the students—even though it was self-defense. Even just resisting arrest could land them in jail.

I could hear screams from the troops as they backed up. The students put up barricades as they moved away from the street.

From Shannon's phone, I could see that many of the students were prepared with gas masks, safety glasses and protective coverings.

"I hope they don't bring in war planes," I worried.

"I don't think they'd dare," Santana reacted as hordes of people from the immediate area started rushing the troops in defense of the students. Storekeepers, sight-seers, customers, mothers and fathers, homeless residents of Philly, and businessmen and businesswomen were hitting troops with briefcases, purses, backpacks and other items being carried.

We watched as the troops retreated. "This is a public relations nightmare. Someone must have called them off," LaMont speculated.

"We're on our way back," Shannon informed us. "Meet you at Race and Sixth."

Continuing on to the college, the professor informed us, "Today, at Bryn Mawr, the students are meeting in McPherson Hall's Goodhart Auditorium to discuss the camps and what they consider an attack on America's youth. They don't see you as terrorists but as heroes, falsely accused. Still, make sure you avoid being recognized for your sake and the college's."

"Wow. That's awesome," I enthused. "Thank you."

"It wasn't me. They were talking this way before yesterday's political science class. A secret that the college isn't telling is that the College Board sneaks us AP results before they are released to the public, which is a complete violation of the rules. We start checking out the top scorers and send them encouraging letters years before they have to apply. I looked and found we sent a letter to you, Summer."

"I didn't get it. I only have a GED. I flunked my pre-calc final right before I was sent to the camp, but the professor changed the result to reflect my prior quizzes."

"We send the letters based on the AP scores, not on what some high school prof does. You got fives on your AP exams, including calculus, U.S. and European history, psychology and government and politics exams. Those are especially important. You're an AP Scholar—even though you didn't finish high school."

"I didn't get the letter."

"Did your dad want you to go to Bryn Mawr?"

"No. He wanted me to go to Harvard with Matt, the worst boyfriend of my life."

"Who also spoke lies at the funeral," Shannon pointed out. "You are so lucky you aren't with that creep, anymore. I never liked him."

"I'm the lucky one," Santana told her.

In Goodhart Auditorium, we watched from the back. Nobody seemed to recognize me under my Bryn Mawr cap, or if they thought I looked familiar, they instantly dismissed it. Santana was also unrecognized, though I noticed a couple of girls did a double-take.

Though Bryn Mawr had gone co-ed, there weren't many guys. In my opinion, even with half his looks hidden under the cap, Santana was still the hottest guy I'd ever seen.

The primary speaker and moderator was Sloan Sharmin, who was apparently very popular, given the applause she received. We started by viewing live footage of demonstrations at Columbia, Cornel, Brown and Harvard.

At Harvard, one of the last vestiges of the elite of the elite, students were protesting our treatment and the treatment of America's youth in general. A warm sensation went through me—until officers began pounding students with mace and billy clubs. The elites were actually attacking their own. The video switched to the Indy Hall demo, held by students from various Pennsylvania universities. Penn State was especially well-represented.

At the Independence Hall Rally, an African American girl, who appeared to be in her late teens, was boldly speaking as she moved back and forth across the stage. "Are we going to let out-of-date warmongering elitist rulers from our parents' generation demonize and torture our generation and our younger siblings while we do nothing to help save American teens and youth?"

The event was clearly taking on the middle generation. In a way, the generational attack was unfair. There were a lot of educated indi-viduals in our parents' generation. It was really about us versus the elites and the truth versus the media lies.

The second speaker, a guy with a Penn State sweater, focused on the media. "How many of you used to think Raquel Madcow was something other than a corporate whore? She is the highest paid news liar, and she earns her money by lying about virtually everything."

In my view, this was a much more properly placed criticism.

He spoke about how a former news commentator named Keith Overlord had once been more honest but had since become a corporate war-hog, pushing lies to distract people from real issues. The speaker continued with a call to watch only the independent media and for students to think for themselves. "We've got to demand our parents turn off the MSM. Tell them if they don't, you won't come home for Christmas." That was greeted with cheers.

The speaker continued, "We've seen the evidence of the lies about the bridges. Today the President, himself, idiot though he is, has demanded an investigation into the false flags and has declared the attack on Manhattan 'a false flag event.'"

"What?" I asked, turning to Santana. "This means we could be off the hook for terrorism?" I whispered.

Shannon and Jimmy looked our way in surprise as well.

"There's still the Espionage Act," Santana whispered back. "I don't think he has the brains or power to stand up to those in his own Administration calling us terrorists."

"We could take to him what we have and ask for a pardon—in case they keep coming after us," I responded.

"With the support of all these college students, that's a possibility."

Despite the crowd, I gave Santana a sitting hug. A couple of girls seemed to glare enviously, but it didn't look like they recognized us.

The next speaker from Penn State, Sheila Merreck, addressed the issue of the camps. "Long ago in 2007, George Miller had hearings about the body bags and torture coming out of the Gulag Camps and Schools. The House passed legislation to regulate them, but it never passed the U.S. Senate. You know why? It was because leaders from both sides of the aisle are taking contributions from the owners of the camps, large contributions. The Gulag industry is the fastest-growing industry in the nation. We've had Presidential candidates and Presidents who have received money from the Gulag industry and some have been part owners of these programs. What is the purpose of torturing, raping and even killing kids in schools that have no books? We have evidence of a strong connection between the Gulag industry and the defense industry. Are these schools preparing future mindless puppets to work in private and government forces to be sent into foreign lands for an agenda to kill innocent children, or to even kill our own citizens here in the USA? Remember, the Contras were formed, not to take over Nicaragua, but to kill the innocent and blame the killings on the Sandinistas. George H.W. Bush, the guy who didn't know where he was when JFK was shot, was involved in the U.S. Government deals that set up the Contras."

I put my lips to Santana's ear. "She just gave the answer. The money is why the defense industry is fighting so hard to keep the truth about the camps quiet."

"And why they are going so far to blackmail our leaders into supporting them," Santana whispered back and then kissed my ear.

A shiver went from my ear down through my spine. "I love you," I murmured.

"Ah, you're just excited about others seeing past the smoke and mirrors. Now, me, I really, really love you," he countered.

I lightly punched him in the arm.

Shannon, who was on my other side, mumbled. "You two stop carrying on, or you're going to call attention to yourselves."

Jimmy whispered past her, "Get a room."

I made a face at him.

The broadcast speeches went into government greed and how the youth had had their future stolen from them due to the high price of colleges, the health care crises, the exportation of jobs, the destruction of the environment and so on. Several students at the Indy Hall rally called for war on the ruling class—though I was sure they meant their declarations in a non-violence sense.

The final speaker, Natasha Bramwell, declared, "The reason Occupy Wall Street was such a failure was that the adults running it were weak. They didn't like the tear gas and the threats on their freedom. We're fighting for our lives, which will be worthless if this continues. The elites have declared war on our generation and now it's time for us to rise to the challenge or die in the ashes they've cast us into."

"I always blamed Obama for the fall of Occupy Wall Street. He and the bankers told the mayors to close it down as it was making him look bad," I whispered to Shannon.

"But the Occupiers didn't have to give up," Jimmy replied.

"We are the awake generation," Natasha continued. "We are the best educated generation in history. Long before entering high school, most of us had more knowledge than most of the middle-agers, watching Raquel Madcow, will learn in their lifetimes." That got a standing ovation from all the viewers in the auditorium.

I hoped this would not become an agist movement. We needed all ages to oppose the torture programs.

After the video of speeches at Indy Hall ended and attention turned to the university event, Sloan went to the microphone, again, and spoke to the crowd. "Now what are we going to do?"

There were standing microphones in two aisles and lines of speakers at each ready to speak.

"My name is Clara Nardin. I say we march on Washington. It's less than two hours away. We fill the trains and rally on the way."

That was met with an audience-wide applause that turned into a standing ovation.

The next speaker, Naleen Johnson, suggested we co-organize with other northeastern universities to have the schools in Maine start the train journey from the northeast with others joining as the train got to their cities or connecting cities. She noted that we might fill up several trains. "While on the trains, we can start the momentum going and by the time we get to Washington, they'll know we are coming."

The speaker that followed her called for student convoys from the West Coast and other areas. It was noted that it would take a couple extra days for the West Coast activists to a arrive.

Some students possessed copies of Paul's videos that Diego had broadcast from Cuba of the torture and sexual abuse at our camps and the little kids camp. It was suggested copies be distributed to all colleges and universities.

Sloan pointed out that we all must watch for provocateurs during the event. She reminded the students of how following the 2017 Inauguration, reporters were arrested with charges that could have netted them sixty-six years in prison and their only real crime was reporting on the Inauguration.

Jordon Nash told the crowd, "The provocateurs will try to make a peaceful demonstration violent, and we'll get the blame. We must make sure that does not happen. We must be vigilant and protect each other. We students are all brothers in the matter."

By the time the rally was finished, the students had a plan. The coordination was the only question. It was decided that the following week on Tuesday, when the Senators would be in their offices, would be the best time for the event. It was suggested that students should demand school credit for attendance.

Afterwards, Professor LaMont led us back to her office. "You may not have planned it this way, but you are changing the world for the better."

"That's because we're really cool wonderful individuals," Jimmy joked.

"You may be wonderful, but Professor Brand has sent some homework assignments for you, Jimmy," Dr. LaMont informed him.

"No rest for the world-savers," Jimmy responded. "I brought a few of my books but left others back at Columbia."

"We have a bookstore here. Let me know what you need, and I'll pick it up. Now, Summer, what would you have been studying if you were in school?"

"Biology, zoology, holistic approaches to medicine and some other assorted subjects. I got my GED. I need whatever basic courses will assist me in getting into veterinary school."

"And I want lists from you, Santana, Shannon and Emily," she said handing them some sheets of paper. Santana rolled his eyes.

"Darn," Emily said.

"You're fourteen. If you keep up your studying, you'll fit right in here at Bryn Mawr."

That visibly cheered Emily up.

The rest of the day, we observed some of the classes and also sat in Dr. LaMont's office and watched videos from rallies taking place at Midwestern and West Coast universities. She brought us some "healthy food," as in organic. There was enough left over that we snacked on it the rest of the afternoon. The rally at Berkeley was very encouraging. The students marched from Sproul Plaza to People's Park, reminiscent of what took place during the sixties. Santana's name came up prominently in the speeches.

After school, Dr. LaMont drove us back to the cabin. Bruce and Abigail had also been watching the speeches. Bruce had managed to tap into HAARP, his daddy's project. "I think HAARP is planning a real-time disaster in D.C. on Friday of next week," he said.

"They're probably expecting us to show up there and take the blame," Santana surmised.

"You kids might want to stay back on this one," Father Durham encouraged.

"Or maybe, we can get to the President beforehand."

"The President?" the priest asked.

"Abigail's father said that there was something they were doing that the President didn't know about," I reminded him.

We were startled by a knock at the door. I worried it could be the feds. Emily, Bruce and Abigail took Father Durham into the boys' bedroom. Jimmy and Shannon hid in the girls' bedroom.

I stood next to the door and listened for sounds. Santana grabbed me and dragged me behind the couch. It was too late to turn out the lights. Everybody was hidden, but if it was the feds, they'd do a search.

CHAPTER 29

Professor LaMont got up the courage to find out who it was. She went to the door. "Who is it?" There was no answer, just another knock. She pulled the chain across and opened the door a little. "Who are you?" The response was quiet enough that I couldn't make out the words.

Professor LaMont closed the door, removed the chain and opened the door. "Are you sure you weren't followed?" I heard her ask.

"Father Browning dropped me off three miles back." I recognized the voice and jumped up from behind the couch.

"How the heck did you get here from Cuba?"

"Boat, car and lots of hitch-hiking?" Alejandro said.

A fraction of a second later, the bedroom door sprang open and a blur of a fourteen-year-old girl rushed past Santana and me and was twirled around in Alejandro's arms.

"She didn't miss you at all," Abigail teased.

"Does your mother know you're here?" Professor LaMont asked.

"I called Alonzo when I got to Trenton, and he was ready to kill me, but he told me about Father Durham being taken from the Philadelphia Cathedral and beaten. I figured he was leaving out details about you. So, I went there, spoke to Father Browning, and here I am."

"I get the feeling I'm going to have to share my twin bed," Santana said.

"How's my mom?" I asked.

"Scared. She wanted to come, but everyone told her she'd be putting you at greater risk if she showed up. They'd definitely follow her to you."

"The students here are planning a march on Washington," Santana advised him.

"I'm in."

"You're not even here legally."

"True, but at least I'm not wanted by the feds, yet?" he pointed out.

"I'm making vegan lasagna and salads. Anyone want to help me in the kitchen?" I asked.

Santana raised his hand. In the kitchen, he noticed that I was a bit nervous. "Don't worry. They'll be fine."

"Alejandro is younger than either of us and Emily is almost a year younger than him."

"I know. They are young but very mature for their age."

"Emily had to grow up overnight in the camp. She needs to just be a kid, again."

"Both are very grounded."

"I know. I just wish I could protect her."

"She's like a kid sister to you," he said.

"Exactly," I responded.

Professor LaMont came into the kitchen. "I hope you kids will be safe here."

"So far, so good. But you never know. That could have been the feds. Our lives are that crazy."

"You know how to get in touch with me if something comes up."

"Yes. And we really appreciate all you are doing."

"I've got to get back to read the papers my students turned in today."

"You aren't staying for dinner?"

"Another time, but thank you for inviting me."

"I was thinking that tomorrow, we could use the audio-video lab to make videos that could be aired during the march on Washington," Bruce suggested, as we escorted her to the front door.

"But they might trace those to Professor LaMont," I cautioned.

"We can have them uploaded elsewhere," Santana suggested.

"But the digital footprint."

"If they trace it, how are we supposed to know whom all the students are lending our equipment to?" she pointed out.

I was optimistic but a part of me was sad. I was so blessed to have friends, but I still missed my mother and my dog. I kept telling myself that somehow, we'd make it safely back to our new home in Cuba.

The next day, we crowded into Dr. LaMont's car. She showed us to the audio/video lab. Bruce and Jimmy figured out how to work the university's equipment. The five of us who had been through the camps made speeches regarding what we had experienced since our U.N. presentations. Naturally we left out any information regarding anyone who had helped us and the locations where we had stayed.

Jimmy, Shannon and Alejandro interacted with the other students, getting a feel for the situation. However, after a short time, Alejandro rejoined us in the computer lab. Alejandro's skills with the dark web exceeded those of Jimmy and Bruce. He had learned to get around the more extensive obstacles thrown up by the Cuban government on their web. Interestingly, the private carriers in the U.S. were going the way of Cuban Internet because of the loss of Net neutrality in the States.

Alejandro worked on locating a back door to the CFR and in particular looking for any emails and information from Emily's father. Emily worked with him on information leading to passwords for her dad. Alejandro focused on a particularly troubling email between Emily's dad and mine from a couple of weeks back.

*"From: **Tanner** <Tanner@CA.gov>*
To me: Chair@CFR.Gov

I want guaranteed reinstatement and more control or I'll go to the President."

---

*"From: **Victor Hattan** <Chair@CFR.gov>*
*To: **Tanner** <Tanner@CA.gov>*
*You are playing a dangerous game. We will all profit and gain power, but do
not cross us or there will be consequences.*

There were a number of other emails. There were references to
"Operation Overhaul." Abigail helped Alejandro figure out her dad's
password. A couple of emails between Abigail's father and Emily's
dad read as follows:

*From: **Victor Hattan** <Chair@CFR.gov>*
To: **Secretary** <Kreskin@defense.gov>, me
Is everything in place for next Friday?"

---

*From: **Secretary** <Kreskin@defense.gov>*
To: ***Victor Hattan*** <Chair@CFR.gov>
*New York experiment, a success, except temporary. It stops working after a
few days. That will be long enough. Looking for exterminatables who have
slipped through our hands. Formula was effective in shortcutting mind
control operations. Will be dropping nanoparticles via air filter day before
D.C. event."*

Bruce explained to us that from that and other emails, it appeared
that the mind control formula would be transmitted by nanoparticles
dropped from the sky or through the vents in D.C. on Thursday. *But
where specifically in D.C.?*

CHAPTER 30

"Jimmy picked up some possible references to a coup, yesterday. Could Operation Overhaul be about the overhaul of the U.S. Government?" I asked.

"Maybe they are planning to put those nanoparticles in the air vents of the government buildings and take control of everything," Bruce suggested.

"From the comments about the effects wearing off, they probably think that was natural and don't know about the effects of the lemonade and counter-programming," I said.

"So do we set up a lemonade stand outside Daddy Dearest's office?" Abigail asked.

"If the President isn't involved, we notify him," I proposed.

"Excuse me. He's a whacko," Santana countered.

"Wacko or not, he might be the only one who can help us. He called off the war against Columbia," I reminded them.

"It looks like my dad really is in charge, doesn't it?" Emily asked.

"Sorry," I said. "It does. Clearly my own father is involved, too."

"Unless he's dead. I did see the name tag on a stretcher," Abigail recalled.

"But they said Emily's father was dead, too, and he's alive."

Of course, from the emails, it sounded as if my dad had gotten greedy. They might have followed through with the threat. It was impossible to know for sure.

"The United States, the nation where the dead keep coming back to life," Alejandro quipped.

I laughed. "How many times have we died, so far?"

"At least four, but who's counting?" Santana commented.

"I'm going to dance lab," Emily said. An escape from the discussion about her father was probably for the best.

"If you want to continue this—" Alejandro looked at Bruce. "I'll watch my girlfriend."

Bruce took over at the computer. He looked through more of Emily's dad's emails. "Apparently, Emily's dad is heavily invested in Darkswamp. It's looking like he's running the company behind the scenes. There are some emails documenting his investment return. As we suspected, Darkswamp is profiting heavily from the Gulag camps and schools and not just because of what they used the camps for. They are making billions from convincing parents to send their kids to the various programs."

"Is that any surprise, given the fees they charge for sending kids there?" I asked.

"According to this figure, my parents paid seven-hundred thousand dollars to send me off, and there was an agreement for cooperation that looks like it involved research. My dad is currently a top engineer for HAARP. I have some strong suspicions about what kind of research he is helping them with."

"You think Darkswamp has its own HAARP facility?"

"HAARP has a great many locations, other than the primary one in Alaska. It looks like Darkswamp has full access to HAARP and has been developing its own weapons based on HAARP's. Here's another email from Abigail's father to Emily's father."

"*From:* **Secretary** <Kreskin@defense.gov>
To: *Victor Hattan* <Chair@CFR.gov>
Three T coming your way. Reported missing.

"T for trillion?" Abigail asked.

"That explains the missing money from the Pentagon budget. There was also missing money before nine-eleven," I noted. "Cynthia McKinney exposed that."

"Wait, there is an email to a General Richards from Kreskin," Bruce observed.

"You're in Kreskin's email?" I asked.

"Yep. It talks about him and another lower-level general becoming the chairman and vice chairman of the Joint Chiefs of Staff after the demise of the current Joint Chiefs."

"They are planning to take out the Joint Chiefs? Maybe creating a military coup, as well?" I responded. I didn't think anything else could surprise me. "But Kreskin is the head of the Defense Department and the Joint Chiefs are under Defense."

"Kreskin doesn't make the appointments of the senior military leaders, though they are under his Department," Bruce explained.

"What if they are planning to make the Pres, the VP, the Speaker of the House, the President Pro Tem of the Senate, the Sec of State, and the Sec of the Treas all look crazy from whatever the nanoparticles do?" Santana suggested. "With the chemical compound they used in Manhattan, they could do that—or they could outright kill them."

"But how would Kreskin get rid of the heads of the Joint Chiefs and those between them and the generals plotting the coup?" I asked.

"Another false flag. The President convenes Congress for a War session and brings part of the Cabinet and the Joint Chiefs with him," Santana replied.

"Even with a VPN, we couldn't warn the President by email as someone is bound to read and probably intercept his emails," Bruce pointed out.

"Doesn't he Twittle in the middle of the night?" Santana asked

"You suggesting we reply to one of his posts?" I responded.

"It's a possibility," Bruce suggested.

"They'll work fast to break through the VPN," Santana warned.

"We could send something like 'Kreskin planning an FF & to take Pres via succession,'" I suggested. "And then get off, right away."

At the end of the day, we shared our discussion with Professor LaMont and our friends.

"Hold off. Let me check the student enrollment to see if there is anyone related to the President whom he would listen to," she suggested.

"Here's the other problem," Jimmy noted. "If we share our concerns, they'll hold off and make him look paranoid for thinking this is going to happen—if he believes us. They are good at that."

"And hacking those emails could have serious legal consequences for you," Professor LaMont pointed out. "If you go public, they'll use this to make you look worse."

"We can't sit on this. We saw what my dad did to me. Imagine what he'll do to the country if he becomes President," Abigail warned.

"Actually, we think it's Emily's father who is in charge," Santana contended. "Emily, how does it feel to be the daughter of the behind-the-scenes ruler of the not-so-free world?"

"She should ask for an increase in her allowance?" Jimmy joked. Even Emily laughed.

"You think you might have someone who knows him among the student body?" I asked Professor LaMont for verification of her earlier suggestion.

"If not, maybe Columbia does. But the student records are confidential. Giving anyone else access to the records could get me terminated for cause. The same for Dr. Brand. Even going into the records, ourselves, is risky."

"How long will it take you?" Jimmy pushed.

"At least through the weekend."

Back at the Cabin, we were surprised by another knock at the door. It was Father Browning.

"I got a visit from someone, named Napoli, who claims to be

connected to the Secret Service. He heard about the incident with Father Durham and wants to speak with you."

"I bet he does," Abigail said. "Probably collect us for more of what Father Durham went through."

"The Secret Service is an agency that protects federal officials," I pointed out.

"My dad is a federal official. One of his Secret Service thugs turned me over to the guy who kidnapped me to the camp," Abigail stated.

"The fact that they are contacting Father Browning could mean that they are closing in on us," Bruce warned.

"How much did he know?" Santana inquired.

"Just that Father Durham had been tortured and he wondered if Tom had given us a clue as to your whereabouts."

"What did you tell him?" Santana asked.

"That we were surprised that he had been tortured, and that he left right after Tuesday night and hasn't contacted anyone at the Cathedral since."

"In other words, you lied," Santana said. "Can you do that?"

"I phrased it in a way that could be viewed as true. He did leave Tuesday night and he hasn't called the Cathedral since."

We nodded.

"Then, you think it's a trap?" he asked.

"Most definitely," Abigail warned. "Who knew about the torture besides the torturers and those for whom they were working?"

"Any chance he followed you here?" Santana inquired.

"I don't think so. I didn't even bring my own car. I borrowed a vehicle from one of the parishioners I've known for years and left my car at his place."

"Just so long as your parishioner doesn't get tortured," Jimmy cautioned.

"He's a former wrestler."

"Speaking of former wrestlers, anyone think of contacting Jesse Ventura?" I asked.

"Very high profile and outspoken. Odds are he's being watched," Bruce replied.

"He's a former governor, Navy Seal and he hosted the show *Conspiracy Theory*," Santana recalled. "He investigated a lot of stuff."

"Their investigations were pretty credible, too. Ventura investigated one of my dad's operations," Abigail noted.

"What about *TLAV*?" Emily asked. "We've sent them information before, and it went viral."

"The footage Bob and Joey got of the bridges would be great if Ryan Cristian showed it," I said.

Jimmy was on the phone in a minute to Joey. We listened to their conversation over the speaker. "Someone claiming to be Secret Service approached one of the fathers. We think it's a trap."

"He's not the only one showing interest. A guy, known as Piro, Twittled to have the students at Columbia asking around for information about you. Claims to be a 'good guy' friend of yours."

"I don't trust anyone who identifies themselves as a 'good guy,'" Jimmy said.

"I formed a Twittle account, supposedly at Oxford, under a VPN. Sent Piro a private message saying I might know someone who knows something, but for all I knew he is an assassin," Joey related.

"We're also looking for someone close to the President who can interface with the President. We have reason to believe they are going to pull off a coup next Friday, earlier if they know we know. They are talking of putting nanoparticles with the drug into air vents on Thursday. There is also a talk of putting lower generals in charge of the Chiefs of Staff while Kreskin becomes President," Bruce expounded.

"Do you know how long the line of succession is to the Secretary of Defense? He'd have to get rid of quite a number of people."

"We know," Jimmy replied. "Let me know what you find out."

"Sure thing. Same to you."

After they hung up, Bruce commented, "You do know the government has vans and equipment that could listen through walls and burner phones. If they are outside, they know what we are discussing."

"We've got to hope they didn't follow Father Browning," Santana responded.

"I'm going to get my parishioner's car back before anyone drops by his place," Father Browning said.

We said our goodbyes to Father Browning. We stayed up late, talking about what to do. What if they were watching us, listening to us? That would put them steps ahead of us. The march on D.C. was scheduled for Tuesday.

Emily suggested we make s'mores in the fireplace. Father Browning's sister had marshmallows, chocolate bars and graham crackers in the cupboard. Alejandro had his first one and seemed to be enjoying a bit of American culture.

———

We were just turning in for the night when Father Browning knocked on the door, again. When we opened it, he seemed in severe distress.

"I parked down the hill and actually borrowed a bicycle to come up here. Haven't been on a bicycle in years."

"Your car?"

"No. The Jonesmores's, my parishioners."

"I don't understand."

"They're dead, I think. He and his wife."

"What?"

"I went back and saw a blaze. I parked down the street and walked towards the house. Bodies were being taken into an ambulance. They were covered with sheets. Dead. The ambulance took off without a siren. I went back to the car and drove away as fast as possible. A boy down the hill lent me his bike and promised not to say anything if I got it back by morning."

"Don't go back to the Cathedral," Santana advised. "Go anywhere else. Santana gave the Father a thousand dollars for expenses. "And get rid of the car."

Father Browning looked at the money. "I can't take this."

"Don't use cards. Use cash only. If you have any left over, consider it a donation to your church."

After Father Browning left, Santana advised, "We need to get out of here. It's only a matter of time before they make our location."

I turned to Father Durham.

"I'm strong enough to travel."

"But where?" I asked.

"I know a place," Father Durham said.

In addition to our belongings, we took the laptop belonging to Father Browning's sister that Bruce and Jimmy had been working on. We figured we could return it to her later. It had some of our data on it and we didn't want to leave anything behind that might implicate Browning and his sister.

As we made it a few feet from the cabin, an eerie feeling struck me. I looked back and Santana did the same.

As we did so, the cabin burst into flames.

CHAPTER 31

While the cabin, along with its bricks, stucco and metal turned to ash with amazing speed, I noticed that none of the foliage nor trees around the cabin caught fire. Plastic trash bins, just outside the back door, weren't in the least bit melted.

"The smart meter," Bruce said. "This happens a lot."

"I heard about that. They've observed the same phenomenon in Northern California," I recalled.

Bruce grabbed a fallen branch that was thick with leaves and swept the ground behind us, erasing our footprints. "Some people think the smart meter explosions were an accident. They were designed that way. They intentionally didn't put any surge projectors on the smart meters and they turn all the wiring so hot the houses turn into furnaces," Bruce expounded as we moved away from the cabin. "I've seen the paperwork. They are also controlled remotely."

"I checked. This house did not have a smart meter," Jimmy countered. "They would have known right away the cabin was occupied and which rooms we were using if it had had one. Directed energy or HAARP?"

"This was not an accidental fire?" Alejandro asked. We looked at him. "Got it. We better move fast."

"They'll be sending a clean-up crew," Santana warned. "As in any survivors are the clean-up."

"Right," I agreed.

In the background, we heard sounds, like cars. We kept going through the trees.

"They will still be able to pick up our tracks. We need to find a way to lose them," Santana pointed out.

We saw a stream, small and shallow. We stepped into it walking downstream a ways. My feet were soaked and getting very cold but, like the others, I continued on. Father Durham was moving well. I knew he must still be hurting, but he was making every effort not to show it.

"One day, we are going to find time to relax," Santana reassured us.

Emily looked like she was going to cry.

"Emily, I will do whatever it takes to keep you safe," Alejandro assured my friend.

"We've made it this far," I told her. "There must be a purpose behind it."

The silence was broken by angry barks.

"Not the dogs, again." Abigail let out a sob and then silenced herself.

"It would be nice if Hope were here," Santana said.

"No. I wouldn't want Hope to fight off another pack of dogs," I countered.

Where the stream dwindled to nothing, there was a park with a bonfire that was surrounded by teenagers.

"Let me try this," Santana suggested. He approached the group. "Hi. My friend, here." Santana pointed at Emily. "Found out her mother is in the hospital in Philly and our car broke down. If anyone could give us a ride, we'd appreciate it and make it worth your while."

"Why are you carrying so much stuff?" one boy asked.

"We don't know when we'll get back to fix the car."

"I'll give you a ride," a second boy said, glancing at Emily. He looked Santana's age, maybe a little older.

"Yeah, you would offer to help the pretty girl," the first boy complained. "You're my ride."

"Charlotte can give you a ride, won't you, Charlotte?" the second boy asked a girl who was with them.

A girl in the group replied, "Sure."

"All right with me," the first boy responded as he let out a smile.

"There are nine of you. I hope you don't mind being squished or having half of you sit on the other half's laps?"

"No problem," Bruce replied.

Once in the car, the driver introduced himself, "I'm Roger and you are the Wilderness Five plus a priest? Are you a real priest?"

"Yes, I am," Father Durham answered him.

I was a little concerned about our identities being blown. I looked at Santana. He looked uncomfortable, too.

"Don't worry," Roger said. "I recognized you from your U.N. photos. Good job. You guys are my heroes. My high school class is planning to go to Washington on Tuesday."

I felt relief.

"Now, do you really want to go to a hospital?"

"There is a place we could go to, but it's a longer drive from here," Father Durham replied.

"We need to warn him about what the bad guys are doing," I said.

"Warn?" Roger asked.

"They beat up Father Durham to try to find us. And they just burned down a cabin belonging to the sister of another father. You might just want to drop us off in Philly at a hospital and pretend you didn't know who we are," I advised him.

"Hey, I'm not a gutless wonder. My dad's a cop, and if they attack me, they'll have him to deal with."

His words made me more than a little nervous. *Could they use his father to get to him or could his father make him talk?*

"Don't worry," Roger said, looking in the mirror at me as if reading my mind. "My dad's one of the cool ones. He turned in some of his fellow officers for attacking a Black teenager last week. He says he'd rather lose his retirement than be involved in thug activities."

"Your father sounds courageous."

"He also doesn't believe the official story about you guys. He said he's seen things while on the force in Philly that would shock anyone. He claims nobody would believe a lot of what he's seen."

"He might be a good guy to have on our side," Father Durham said.

"The more people we involve, the more people we put in danger," I warned.

"We've learned some shit, I mean stuff," Santana said, looking at me, "That nobody would believe unless they had seen some of the crazy stuff we've seen. Even your father might doubt it."

"Try me," Roger said.

I looked at my friends. Did we dare trust this guy?

Emily was the one who spoke, apparently deciding she could trust him. "We think they are planning a coup against the President. We don't like the President, but someone more evil is planning to take over."

"Who?"

"My father," Abigail responded.

"That's right. Your father is the Secretary of Defense."

"And my father," Emily said. "He's the head of the Council on Foreign Relations."

"Weren't the Obamas on that Council?"

"Obama took us from two wars into seven," Santana pointed out. "My father's a congressman, and he went along with that sh—stuff."

"How do they plan to do this?"

"We don't have the whole plan, but it involves lower generals pushing out the Joint Chiefs and eliminating everyone in the line of succession down to Abigail's father," Jimmy expounded.

"How are they going to do that?"

"Did you hear about all the craziness in Manhattan last weekend?" I asked.

"Yeah. That stumped the whole country. Several members of the Columbia Football team are in jail."

"It wasn't their fault," I contended. "They drugged everyone and then gave them suggestions via radio wave technology."

"Wow. I've seen some ScrewTube videos on that kind of stuff," Roger said.

"They are planning to use nanoparticles in the air vents some-where, maybe in the Capitol, to drug some people. We don't know exactly who or where. Next Friday was mentioned for the coup and Thursday was mentioned for the nanoparticles in some private emails we weren't supposed to read," Jimmy continued, apparently trusting that Roger wouldn't turn us in for hacking crimes in addition to all our other attributed crimes.

"But if they find out we know, they may alter their plans and then, nobody will see it coming," Emily warned.

"*Catch 22*," Santana commented.

"Okay, so we have to save the free world by keeping that crazy guy who is President in power and stopping people who are even worse, and we have less than a week to do it," Roger verified.

"Right," I said. "But they wouldn't hesitate to kill anyone helping us. At least, if something happens, someone else knows." It was a hint for Roger to take action if we were caught.

"No. I need to make sure you guys stay safe. My dad taught me that, if you help someone, you take responsibility for keeping them safe."

"I like that," Santana said.

"You could already be in danger," I advised. "Even by now, the bad guys could have spoken to your friends and have a lock on your car."

"My friends are rebels. If someone in authority starts asking ques-tions, they'll claim they didn't see anything. I'd do the same if I were the one still at the sleepover."

"Plausibility. Even if you help us, it's best if you can't lead them to us," Jimmy said.

"Do you have one of those smart meters at your home?" Alejandro asked.

"No. My dad wouldn't allow it."

"Smart man," Jimmy said. "No pun intended."

"At first, I thought that was how they burned down the cabin we were staying at—like happened in those bizarre California fires," Bruce noted.

"Wow. I've heard of stuff like that. But to actually see it. Wow."

"It had to be something else, though," Bruce corrected his earlier supposition. "Jimmy noticed the cabin didn't have a smart meter."

Father Durham joined in the discussion. "These kids are correct in telling you that you are in great danger. Another priest assisted us. It was his sister who owned the cabin we were in. He borrowed a car from a parishioner to come see us. When he got back to the parishioner's place, the parishioner's house had burned down. He returned to the cabin to warn us. Shortly after that, his sister's cabin was burnt to the ground."

"You're a priest, and I know you have some kind of vow of truth. I mean, I believed the others, but it's good that you have the facts, too."

"Watch out for someone claiming to be from the Secret Service," Bruce warned. "A Secret Service agent named Napoli visited the other father and asked questions right before the fire incidents happened."

"My evil daddy has Secret Service protection," Abigail said. "It was probably one of his Secret Service puppets."

Roger dropped us off in northern Philly and gave Jimmy his cell number, email address and home address. "If you need anything, man, let me know."

"Thank you for helping us," Emily said. The rest of us gave him our thanks as well.

"Anytime. Just call."

We walked several blocks before Father Durham took us off to the right a few more blocks, then another right and then six blocks later to a street on the left that opened into an industrial park. We went up to a warehouse and he knocked. I looked around. I didn't see any cameras in that area. Someone looked out through a viewer in the door and then opened it. A middle-aged man with a similar appearance to a muscular version of Gregory Peck's in *To Kill A Mockingbird* stood before us.

"Tom, what are you doing here?"

"We need a place to hang out for a couple of days, very private. Thought you might be able to help."

"Of course."

He let us in. He reached out and shook our hands, one at a time.

"I'm Shane. I owe Father Durham my life. Anything I can do for you, I will."

He led us through several doors interconnecting the warehouses. "It's by luck that you caught me here on a Friday night. I've been spending most of my evenings and weekends in Chester. I was just finishing up the inventory."

"Shane owns all these warehouses here. He's a very hard worker," Father Durham explained.

"And I owe it all to you. Did Father tell you about me?"

"He didn't, but I'm sure it's an interesting story," Shannon said.

"When I was getting my MBA, the school was so tough, I developed a really bad coke habit. I couldn't get off of it. I broke into an office to support my habit and was running from the police. Father Durham took me in, helped me break my habit. When I was clean, he found an attorney to supervise my turning myself in. I got a bargain: informal probation for six months. Then Tom, Father Durham, helped me turn my life completely around, introduced me to someone in the warehouse business, who apprenticed me. Pretty soon, I had my own set of warehouses. I sell stock, legitimate stock, out of a couple of them and rent out the rest to other businessmen."

"All the warehouses in this area belong to Shane," Father Durham advised us.

"They keep telling me I should get more security, but people I deal with are pretty honest. After my past confrontations with the police, I don't like cameras around my business locations. Some of my tenants have their own cameras monitoring inside their warehouses."

"That's a great story," I said. "It shows that anyone can turn his life around and become a real success."

"I'm very proud of Shane." Father Durham patted him on the shoulder.

"Your example is the kind that could give hope to anyone who knows about it," Shannon commended him.

"Helping the Heavenly Father help others is why I became a priest. I have had some concerns about the scandals in the Church. I do read the papers. The scandals relate to only a small fraction of the priests out there but reflect badly on all of us. Most of us use our positions to help people in need. Watching someone like Shane turn his life around makes it all worthwhile."

"I'm Catholic," Santana said. "But if I became a priest, I couldn't marry Summer."

Father Durham laughed. I was sure I was blushing. The others laughed, too.

"That is a downside to being a priest."

"There is an upside, too," Shane joked. "The more men that become priests, the more girls for the rest of us."

"But then the girls become nuns and it evens out," Father Durham teased back. "Shane, we need to be invisible for now."

"No problem."

We followed Shane to a delivery truck and got inside the back.

"There might be satellite tracking of all the vehicles leaving this part of Philly," Bruce said. "It would be best if we didn't go directly to wherever."

"Satellites? This sounds serious," Shane said.

"Let's say the forces of ultimate evil are after us. That's close enough to the truth," Father Durham said.

"This is a delivery truck. I can make some stops by some stores on the way home. Let's stop by a few truck stops and restaurants. I'll carry an empty box in and come back with food and supplies for the weekend."

At the first stop, Shane came back with a variety of sandwiches, both meat and veggies and some soft drinks and bottles of water. We had had dinner at the cabin, but I was still hungry, maybe from all the nervousness. We chowed down. Naturally, being a vegan, I had one of the veggies.

I looked at Emily. Alejandro was doing his best to keep her calm and relaxed, but she had a look of a deer caught in the headlights.

"We've had more help on this trip than most people have in a lifetime," Santana told her. "I think someone above *is* on our side."

"I know someone up there is on our side," Father Durham said.

"You are all good kids, and you will see that God's hand is guiding us, even when it doesn't look like it."

Though I wasn't Catholic and I doubted any of my friends in the truck outside of Santana, Shane and Father Durham were, Father Durham's words provided me with a sense of peace. His words could have been said by anyone in any religion, but it was great to have him reassuring us. Also giving me a sense of peace was Santana's arm around my back. Whenever I was with him, butterflies would chase each other around in my chest and stomach.

"We'll make it through this," Santana declared. "Summer and I have a date at some time in the future that I'm not going to miss." Now, I was blushing, again.

Shane definitely took the long way to wherever we were going. For music, he even turned on some old anti-war songs that were fed to the back where we were. Finally, he took us to a very large garage that contained a collection of vintage cars. The inner door to the garage connected to his house.

"You've done very well for yourself, son," Father Durham told Shane as he guided us into the house.

I noticed Shane had a smart TV in the living room. We stayed out of view of it while Bruce whispered, "Please unplug that TV for your own safety."

Shane complied.

"I have a non-smart TV in the dining room," he said. He turned that one on.

A news story caught our attention.

"Detective Redland of the Philadelphia Police Department is demanding answers." The camera flashed to Detective Redland.

"Cars do not just explode for no reason. The witnesses said there was nothing wrong with Roger's car before it mysteriously vaporized. I am demanding answers, and I am demanding them from Washington."

CHAPTER 32

We stood there in shock. "Oh my God. He was nice enough to help us, and this is what they did to him." I was visibly shaking.

Santana put his arm around me and guided me to a couch. Emily looked close to fainting herself. Alejandro put his arms around her and they both dropped onto a loveseat. Emily was sobbing and Alejandro, with tears in his eyes, kept his arms around her as he tried to comfort her.

"HAARP?" Abigail asked Bruce. "Or the car thing from Vault 7?"

"It looks more like the new laser technology. Victims don't see it coming. The defense industry is really proud of it. Lasers are invisible and soundless. They can blow up airplanes, vehicles and even houses. Then, there is the Hutchenson wave technology, developed by Dr. Hutchenson and based on the Higgs field theory, also suspected in those California fires," he reported.

"It's a scary world," Father Durham comforted. "If not for God, I'd be terrified. Roger was a very good soul. I'm sure he will be looked after."

"Even with God, I'm terrified," Santana said.

Jimmy was on his phone. "Thank goodness, you answered," he said. He nodded at us and paused. "Snake Plissken, I heard you were dead," he joked. "Clearly, car thieves serve a good purpose." That all sounded reassuring. He started to laugh and then caught himself. "I'm sure he does. They are after you now. Make sure you stay out of sight and safe. They don't give up easily." He paused again. "Smart idea… Right… Sure thing. See you Tuesday or maybe before."

"He's alive," I breathed, hoping my relief was valid.

"The car was stolen. He went into the underground parking at a Target and someone took off in his car. Didn't make it far."

"These guys are playing for keeps," Bruce said. He looked at Shane. "Are you sure you want to risk helping us?"

"This makes me want to help you more," Shane replied.

"I told you he was a good man," Father Durham said.

"Did they do that to your face?" Shane asked Father Durham, looking at the bruises.

"They would have killed me if these kids hadn't saved my life," he responded.

"What you do for Tom, you do for me."

"He's saved our lives more than once," I related.

My friends nodded.

"Tell me what you need. Computers? Internet?"

"We need a way to the President," Abigail remarked.

Shane seemed taken aback.

"We think there is going to be an attempted coup," Santana explained.

"I don't particularly like this President," Shane responded.

"If you think he's bad, you should see what my father will do if he becomes President."

"Your father?" Shane asked. "Wait, you're the Wilderness Five!"

We slowly nodded.

"But you're alive."

"And the bridges didn't fall. It was an illusion, like our deaths," I explained.

Shane looked at Father Durham, who nodded, and then sat down, trying to grasp what was going on. "If what they did to that car was any example of their ability, they could have downed the bridges."

"We've been to the Brooklyn and Manhattan Bridges. They never collapsed. It was all projection, mats and media lies. The Columbia students have footage," I continued.

"I heard something about a standoff at Columbia and then nothing."

"That's because the media doesn't want you to know," Santana said. "They kidnapped quite a number of Columbia students and Father Durham helped us save their lives."

"And not a word about it on the news."

"There is never any real information on the news," Santana pointed out.

"This presents a whole change in my view of the world." He looked down, thinking. "Make yourselves at home. You've seen the kitchen. The bedrooms are upstairs on the second floor. The one furthest from the staircase is mine, but you are welcome to the rest of them. In the hall just off the living room, there is a room with a desktop, two laptops, printers, sound synthesizers and camera equipment. If you go back towards the kitchen, you'll find a door that opens onto stairs to the basement. There is also a back staircase from the bedrooms and upper floor that goes down to the basement."

We got up and he gave us a personal tour of the place.

As we checked it out, Santana continued, "Tuesday, students from all over are planning to travel to D.C. Any chance we could borrow a truck or van to get there?"

"If you'd like, I'll personally drive you," he said.

"Kids, it's getting pretty late, and you haven't slept since early in the morning. How about you get some rest and we continue on with this tomorrow," Father Durham advised.

The next morning, I walked into the computer room as Jimmy was speaking on the phone with Joey, I assumed, about Roger's car. "Is there any way to defeat these laser weapons?" Jimmy grimaced. "But by then it's too late, isn't it?... When will that be ready?... In other words, in the meantime, they can take out any car, any building, any person and all we can do is watch. I can hardly wait until they put the technology on police drones." He shook his head and held up his free palm in seeming exasperation. "Great. That's all we need...He was alive, last night. Don't know about this morning...Thanks...You too."

As he hung up, I noticed a mug filled with something dark. I sniffed and detected a chocolate odor.

"It's hot chocolate with almond milk," Jimmy said.

"Where are the others?"

"Bruce is working in his room on a laptop and Abigail's with him. Santana and Shane are making breakfast. Shannon, Emily and Alejandro are in the living room."

The sound of a piano floated through the air. I recognized Chopin's "Minute Waltz." I followed the music. Emily was sitting at the piano with Alejandro beside her looking more than pleased at his talented girlfriend.

After she finished, she got up, and Alejandro started playing old Elvis Presley songs. I guessed that those were still popular in some Cuban circles.

Shannon and Emily started dancing. They looked happy as if everything was normal and the world wasn't going crazy. I wished I could somehow stop time and make their joy and lightness last forever.

Hands went over my eyes as the smell of food wafted into the room. When Santana's hands were removed, Shane held a plate with what looked like an omelet and fresh cinnamon rolls and another plate of pancakes, smothered in steaming maple syrup.

"No glyphosate and the omelet is vegan," Shane said. "The pancake mix came from Europe. Also, vegan."

"Oh!" I responded, grabbing the plates. Emily and Shannon turned and looked.

"When you finish, there's lots of food in the dining room," Shane said. I followed with Santana as Shane led the way. A few minutes later, Shannon, Jimmy, Emily and Alejandro joined us. Shane and Santana took some plates up to Bruce and Abigail and to Father Durham, who was still resting, and then came back to join us.

And to drink, there was lots of lemonade. "We thought that it would be good to keep a minimal level of the antidote in our system," Santana explained.

I kissed Santana on the cheek.

"Joey has glasses that can see the lasers, but he doesn't yet have an invention that will tell us when a laser is about to be fired from a distance," Jimmy announced.

"Can't they also fire them from satellites?" I asked.

"Probably. Defense contractors have done promotionals for the DOD, showing successful laser technology fired invisibly, silently from planes. Of course, the contractors and government are always ahead of what we're informed about," Jimmy said.

"So, if they see us, they can just fire an invisible laser and vaporize us?" I asked.

"Basically," Jimmy said. "One more bit of good news. The Columbia and NYU students have convinced the Port Authority to come clean about the bridges. Well, not quite clean. The Port Authority had to have known all along they hadn't fallen. But they are finally admitting they were never blown while pretending to be surprised."

"Then, they are only after us for the Espionage Act, again?" I asked.

"Which carries the death penalty." Emily looked fallen.

"Em, it's a step in the right direction. They can try to nail us with the Espionage Act, but without the fake deaths and injuries on the fake bridge and tunnel collapses, much of the world will still be with us, right?" I said, trying to reassure her.

Santana smiled. "I wish I could say the problem was over. We both know our government blackmails and controls the world or rather Deep State does. As far as Deep State is concerned, we are the country's number one enemies. And the news media is still not broadcasting the latest Port Authority report about New York."

"What should we do?" I asked.

"The only solution is a revolution," Abigail said, coming into the room. "Seconds?" she asked. Shane got her two more plates of food, which she gobbled up as if she hadn't eaten in a week. "What? Being terrorized makes me hungry."

"The President could pardon you," Shannon noted.

"If he's still the President when this is all over and if Deep State doesn't order him not to, like it did with Snowden and Assange," I reminded her.

"I could still Menendez my dad, and then they'd have to get another figurehead."

Father Durham laughed. "The bit about honor thy father means honor the person your father would be if he isn't violating every other Commandment. I still don't condone parent-killing, though."

"I don't even know whether my dad's alive or just faking his death," I said.

"The emails we saw give them a reason to off your father, Summer. I'm not saying that's what happened," Bruce stated, entering the room. "I haven't seen any indication he's alive. He doesn't seem to be prominent right now, but he could be operating behind the scenes." He looked for a reaction from me, maybe to make sure I wasn't even more upset by his remarks.

I felt numb where my dad was concerned. He was okay with my torture and death.

Bruce continued. "I don't mean to be impertinent or to hurt anyone. All but one of those connected to us who are supposedly dead either didn't speak at the funeral or had a beef with others running the show. What if they decided to use the flu of ridiculousness as an excuse to off anyone who wouldn't cooperate with Deep State?"

"By Deep State, you mean my father, right?" Emily asked.

"He's clearly a major player. He may or may not be in charge," Jimmy said.

"What about Father Browning? Is there any way to know if he's safe?" Father Durham asked.

"If he's safe, he's out of touch. I guess that as long as we don't hear of his demise or his fake demise, he's probably fine," Santana said.

Shane turned the conversation from the issue of death. "I spoke to one of my food distributors this morning. He distributes organic lemonade with cane sugar. I told him I had heard that the students going to the Capitol next week were pushing natural drinks, such as lemonade over hard drinks and that he could create a lot of good will by distributing free lemonade at the Capitol and White House."

"How about the Pentagon and the FBI?" Santana asked.

"I'll suggest those to him. So far, he seems interested."

"Anything new on the Net?" I inquired.

"There is stuff about a backup plan involving laser technology," Bruce informed us.

"Like what they did to Roger's car?"

"That was the impression I got. Another defense contractor has plunged ahead with the research and testing of new tech. If the nano plan doesn't work, they'll simply create a false flag and blame it on Cuba and Russia."

"Cuba and Russia?" Alejandro asked, furling his eyebrows.

"That's what they said."

I looked at Alejandro. Along with his family, my mom was also in Cuba. We had to stop that plan.

"We already know my dad's a major part of the plan. Couldn't we expose him in advance? Without him, it would fail," Abigail proposed.

"I've leaked the emails to several reputable online sources, such as *TLAV*, *The Grayzone*, and Jason Bermas," Bruce said. "But I don't know as they'll even receive them or publish them without verification if they do get them. Several of the independent online news outlets are airing the footage Joey and Bob took of the Brooklyn and Manhattan Bridges."

"How about the footage of the battle for New York?" I asked.

"They've aired that as well."

"Since the worst of those emails comes from mine and Abigail's fathers, couldn't that be considered a leak, even if it was a hack, making it okay to publish?" Emily asked.

"Maybe. Everything Wikileaks published were leaks from verified sources and not hacks. That didn't help Julian," I pointed out.

"In the midst of saving the world, how about you guys relax some?" Shane suggested. "There's a pool and a steam room downstairs in the basement."

"The basement?" I asked.

"This is Pennsylvania. We get snow here. There's an outdoor pool and an indoor pool."

There was a part of me that felt guilty about the idea. There was another part of me that just wanted to refresh myself, stop worrying for a little while and relax. We had a lot of help trying to save the world. Even James Bond needed a break.

So, wrong as I felt it was, we took Saturday off. In the pool downstairs, we played Marco Polo and had water fights. For a little while we were just teenagers, regular teenagers, without a care in the world.

Santana pulled me into the steam room. Our relationship was steamy enough, but the added steam and sweat seemed to build up the passion. Santana's lips found mine and I never wanted to let him go. I laid back on the bench. He pulled himself over me. As his lips and mine were intertwined, I felt so warm and safe inside, that all our troubles melted away.

His hands rubbed my shoulders and I knew that both of us wanted so much more than just to kiss. I had to fight my urge to let the relationship go further. I knew that once I let it go too far, there would be no pulling back. But I didn't want to pull back, to stop. Our lips separated and his moved across my face, kissing my cheeks, my nose, my neck, my shoulders, my arms, my stomach, my thighs.

He started to play with the strap on my top. I knew he wanted me like I wanted him. He kissed my shoulder again, and all I knew that he was the only love I would ever want. Being here with him was so right. I was kissing his neck and chest as well, not holding back when the sound of the door opening disrupted the mood.

"Sorry," Bruce said. Abigail giggled as he closed the door.

I sat up, feeling the need to recover my resolve to wait. "Hey Santana, you play eight-ball?"

"Me? I could lie." He looked a little frazzled by the interruption.

"Good, I'm challenging you. There's a table in the rec room on the third floor."

We went upstairs. Apparently, Jimmy and Shannon had the same idea. Fortunately, there were two tables. Shannon suggested taking bets. She was betting on me to defeat Jimmy. Jimmy wasn't ready to take her up on that one.

"Ouch," Santana said. "You must be good."

"It was my one vice," I admitted.

Santana and I played and found we were evenly matched. We finished with me ahead by one game.

After lunch, we went into a mini-theater that was on the third floor. "The ceiling can be pulled back. There's a glass covering," Shane informed us. "However, I know you are concerned about satellites. So, we'll keep it covered." The movie we chose was *V for Vendetta.*

"This is what we need. A full national movement," Jimmy said.

"I think that's what we are hoping for," I pointed out.

As I watched the movie, I could see the similarities to the current society were very strong. We had the false flags, the lack of freedom, near total surveillance, a corrupt media and a corrupt government. In the end, it was the detective, who had tried to stop V, who eventually pushed the button to destroy Parliament. He had gone from a state of being asleep to being fully awake. The people who filled the street took back their government and that's what made the difference.

We were watching the credits when Jimmy's phone rang. "You may have to get a new burner phone," Bruce told him.

Jimmy put it on speaker mode. It was Roger. "My dad wants to help. He is hoping to meet you and locate a solution."

"Is anyone monitoring your calls?"

"No. Even my dad thinks I'm contacting you by email, and he's letting me play dead."

"Wise move," Santana approved.

"We have to be very careful with respect to any meeting," Jimmy said. "You saw what they did to your car."

"Right. I was thinking we could meet in a very public place, where you would have an escape route if someone else shows up."

"That would be good."

"How about outside Sweet Greens at the Suburban Square Shopping Mall off Thirty," Roger suggested.

"When?"

"One hour."

I encouraged Shannon, Abigail and Emily to wait behind with Father Durham. Alejandro, who would be monitoring the Internet, also agreed to stay behind.

"I've been left behind enough times. I'm going," Emily stated.

I pointed out to Shannon and Abigail that we might need someone available to rescue us later if something unexpected happened.

"You better keep my girlfriend safe," Alejandro ordered.

"Then, we better," Santana replied.

To make things safer, Shane and Jimmy, whom the feds were not officially searching for, were to wait outside Sweet Greens. Shane gave Emily his phone so the rest of us could listen as we watched the meeting from nearby.

As Roger approached Jimmy, he turned back and looking away from Jimmy towards some other guy, yelled, "It's a trap."

CHAPTER 33

The guy Roger was looking at appeared confused as he pointed to himself. Jimmy and Shane moved away through the shops as two men grabbed the recipient of Roger's warning and slammed him to the ground.

From our vantage point, we knew it would only be a moment before we were found. We moved into the Banana Democracy Shop and picked up some clothes to theoretically try on in the dressing rooms, disappearing from view.

The phone fell as Emily went into the dressing room and the connection ended. As pre-designated, we proceeded towards the meetup site, a couple of blocks from where the car was parked.

Jimmy and Shane weren't alone. A tall man accompanied them as they walked towards the meeting location. Jimmy didn't appear to be in any distress.

Emily's phone rang. "It's okay," Jimmy said. Santana and I moved out towards them, leaving our other friends behind around a corner.

"This is Roger's dad," Jimmy explained.

"Sorry for the situation, but they tapped Roger's line. I'd get rid of your phone. Roger is working to distract them right now."

"Are you sure he's safe. They blew up his car," I said. "And they attacked that poor man he pointed at."

"I have a friend backing up Roger in case they pull anything. Let's go somewhere to talk." I turned in the direction of the others and nodded. They joined us, and we walked down the street into a Starbucks and sat down.

"My name is Duane Redland," the tall man said. "I've been doing some research. What I've turned up is interesting. A private corporation is trying to commandeer the assistance of the various police departments. You and your friends are still officially dead, but clearly they know you're not and are looking for you. The situation with the bridges and tunnels should have raised some red flags, but it's as if the department isn't listening to anyone but the guys from Darkswamp."

"Do you drink lemonade?"

"Lemonade?'

"It's the antidote to a mind control drug they are using. We have a scientist who used to work at Darkswamp that analyzed the contents and came up with citric acid and sugar as the antidote," Bruce explained.

"I take those in my iced tea."

"That's how the Columbia students were able to stop acting crazy," I said.

"Roger says Darkswamp is planning a coup?"

"My psycho dad is planning to become President," Abigail stated.

"You are Abigail Kreskin, correct?"

"Yes."

"Do you know the plan?"

"You saw what they did to your son's car. Stuff like that could be in the plan. We also believe they plan to use nanoparticles of the mind-altering drug in the vents in D.C. They may be planning an attack on the Joint Chiefs as well as the Presidential line of succession down to Kreskin," Santana expounded.

"Your father's a Congressman?" Duane inquired of Santana.

"Yes."

"If any other kids told me this, I'd think they had a vivid imagination, but when you add together kids of top U.S. officials disappearing and being declared dead with reappearing bridges, it bears more weight. Some of what I've seen at the department already had me convinced that something is very off. Your explanation isn't any stranger than everything else going on."

"We've learned to be cautious, but a lot of good people have believed and helped us," Santana told him.

"My son is one of them. I also have a fellow officer, a Lieutenant on my force who is ready to believe. His name is Kevin Warren."

"The odds are not great at stopping the bad guys."

"Your odds just got better. You're Shane Dresden, aren't you?" he asked our escort.

"Yes, sir."

"Shane is a good businessman and has a good reputation in the community," he said, looking at us. "He's always come across as pragmatic and rock solid."

"I had my wilder days," Shane admitted.

"I'm sure we all did," Duane replied. "I understand the students are going to D.C. Tuesday morning. I suggest we already be there."

"That's what we were thinking," Santana said.

"I would get rid of the burner phone as quickly as possible. They were monitoring Roger's call, but I don't think they were able to track your location."

Jimmy pulled the battery, dropped his phone on the ground and smashed it. Then he picked up the pieces in a paper napkin, undoubtedly for throwing away later.

"Here is a number you can reach me at. They won't have this. Text me first. My old handle years ago in the CB era was Wild Dog."

"I'll be Snagglepuss," Santana said. We looked at him. "Hey, when I was bored, I sometimes watched old cartoons."

"You need to be very careful. The men who were watching my son a minute ago are some pretty nasty dudes. Warren is making sure he stays safe. I suggest you slip out the back door in case they catch me coming out the front."

We nodded, shook his hand and thanked him.

When we got back to Shane's, Shannon threw her arms around me and told me not to leave her behind again. I felt worn out.

"It's good you weren't there. We were almost caught in a trap, but Roger and his dad were prepared."

I wished I could keep all my friends safe so I didn't lose anyone else. Though I missed my mom and my dog, I had it much better than Emily and Abigail who might never see their mothers again or Santana who might never see his brother Angelo again. I had been doing my best to stay positive and I had found myself being more negative than I liked.

I left the others discussing the events in town and to make whatever decisions they wanted while I took a long, hot shower and then went to bed.

Right after I turned out the light, I heard a knock on the door.

"May I come in?" Santana asked.

"My bouncer took off and so I have no resistance," I joked.

He opened the door and sat on the bed. "I don't know how you do it," he said.

"What?"

"Staying strong. You are there for everyone and you're a real leader."

"Leader? Me?"

"Haven't you noticed? Everyone is looking to you for leadership."

"I would have said they are looking to you."

"We make a good team."

"How are you holding up? You've been through even more than I have, and you haven't let on how much it must be hurting you," I said, leaning against him.

"Keeping busy helps."

"It's helped me too. I just got worn out tonight."

"Same. The others will fill us in in the morning. Are you sleepy?"

"Exhausted but still awake."

"Mind if I keep you company? You are my lighthouse, my anchor. I probably don't tell you enough, but you have become the center of my world."

"You are always saying the right things. Well—now you are. When I first met you, I thought you were a jerk. Then I realized you were faking being a jerk and were really nice. Then I realized I was crazy about you. Then I realized I love you. My biggest fear is losing you in this insanity."

"Then you have nothing to fear." The reassuring look in his eyes almost made me believe all was well.

"Unless you take too many risks."

"My priority is to keep you safe."

"And I'll be doing whatever it takes to keep you safe," I echoed back.

He leaned in and started kissing the side of my head down to my neck and my collarbone as he continued talking between kisses. "Then, we're at cross purposes. I'm putting your safety first and you're putting mine first. What should we do about it?" he murmured.

I could barely breathe with him kissing me like that. It was as if the world had stopped. I managed to stumble through some words. "I guess we'll have to both keep safe." I had never been the forward type when it came to romance, but it was all I could do not to pull him in and rip off his shirt. "You know I'm trying my best to stay a virgin." I couldn't believe I said it like that.

"I respect that," he responded, continuing to kiss me, continuing to drive me crazy.

"Yeah," I scoffed.

"Seriously. I can wait. But I would like to be able to touch you and kiss you, properly, of course. It will make the waiting—"

"Harder. You're driving me crazy." I finally said what I was feeling.

"Remember *Twilight*?"

"So, now you're a vampire?"

"No. But Edward was willing to give up what he wanted most to keep the woman he loved safe."

"And that's what you are doing?"

"I want you. I mean I really want you. But I will wait for that until you are ready, whether it's a month or a year or ten years."

"It won't be ten years. I'll be eighteen in two."

"Right now, that seems like a lifetime, but I can handle the wait."

"I do love you. I just want it to happen when we aren't running from stuff or trying to figure out where we want our lives to take us."

"I don't care where it takes us, as long as we are together."

His lips were now on my neck. I pulled back, then turned my lips towards his and pulled him closer. When our lips separated, I said, "I've dated before."

He pulled back and looked into my eyes. "I know."

"But I was never attracted in this way to anyone I ever dated. This is new territory for me," I continued.

"I never dated seriously. There was never anyone, not like you. It's not just that you are beautiful, which you are, or smart, which you are, or sexy, which you are. I used to laugh when I heard that line about two halves of a whole. It's more than that. It's like you are my whole, like I'm empty when you aren't with me. I never thought I'd need anything, but I need you, Summer."

"I need you too. I never thought I would need anyone, either, but I do you."

He kissed me again and then studied my face with his eyes as his forefinger traced my jaw. There was so much warmth in his eyes they could have started a fire.

"However, if you ever want your freedom, that's one good reason to wait," I added.

"That's not going to happen."

"I'm glad you came to my room." I meant it. I didn't want to let him go.

"I hope that's not a dismissal," he said, kissing me again.

"Actually," I hesitated. This sense that it could all end at any moment invaded my thoughts and I tried to brush it away. "Would you misunderstand if I asked you to stay here tonight—not so much tempting each other—but just hanging out?"

He took off his shoes and kissed me. "I get it. Even if it's just platonic, I always want to be with you. Tonight, tomorrow night, as long as we can, on whatever terms I can be with you."

"When I was a little girl I used to believe in those fairy tales about happily ever after. Then, my mom left and and my dad forced me to date Matt. I wanted to please my dad, but I thought I was going to have to settle for what I didn't want."

"No wonder he went wacko. He probably wanted you but knew deep down inside that he could never have you."

"Thank goodness, I didn't wind up with him. I'd go through it all again, the camp, the running, the Cuban prison and all to wind up with you, no matter what happens in the next few days."

"Thief. You stole those words out of my mouth. You'll have to give them back." With that, he kissed me, like there was no tomorrow.

Every time we embraced was like the first time. No better. I felt like I was falling off a cliff, safe in his arms. The butterflies were doing somersaults and handsprings and jumping for joy inside of me. I don't know how long the kiss lasted, but when it was over, he kissed me again. Eventually, I laid my head on his shoulder and fell asleep, this time dreaming of him and me.

In my dream, it was our wedding day. Shannon, Emily, Abigail and Tiffany were my bridesmaids. All our friends, from my school, from Cuba, from Columbia and the others I had met since leaving the camps were there. Father Durham was presiding, but it was a civil ceremony. Alonzo was walking me down the aisle as my mother watched.

We got to the front and then suddenly, the scenery changed from light and flower pedals to the Capitol with Marco, the camp torturer, dragging Santana away and my father locking me in a room with my kidnapper, the guy who had tased me, cable-tied me and taken me to camp in the trunk of his car. Then Matt appeared in a groom's suit.

"No, I don't want you, Matt! I want Santana!" I yelled at him.

"Wake up, Summer." I felt myself being shaken. The image was still there. "Wake up. It's a dream." I felt lips on mine, lips I loved. They soothed me, reassured me that everything would be okay. Somehow, it would be fine.

Sunday, the net carried the story about the disappearance of a priest,

Father Browning. Had they killed him or had he gotten away? We had told him to disappear.

I thought of how they had blown up Roger's car. We learned from Duane, that he had found four more officers willing to help. He was to act as go-between. The others had no information about who we were with or our new burner phone numbers. We still had the one Jimmy had given us to take to Brooklyn. It was not the one we had spoken to Roger on. We were avoiding compromising that phone as we hoped to hear from Father Browning on it, but no such luck.

Bruce was working on the Twittle issue. As usual, he was using a VPN and remote servers to make it look like we were in Australia or another distant land—not Russia, as Russia was being targeted by the continuing new Red Scare, used by Democrats to explain their losses.

Jimmy contacted Duane on one of his spare burners. We found that most good people were willing to help in spite of the government looking for us. Duane's position and his life could be in real jeopardy if his department discovered he was helping an enemy of the state.

There really were a lot of good police officers, I thought. The police had the highest rate of domestic abuse of any profession and there were always officers targeting Blacks, Latinos and Persians, but Duane was one of the whistleblowers trying to clean up the Philadelphia police. Undoubtedly, because of his efforts, he was likely already a target of hate-mongers in the department. He wasn't part of any of the oppressed groups, but he had a conscience.

I thought back to the men who took my mom away that last night before she was absent from my life for all those years. One of them was a police officer. The LAPD officers who always supported my dad were in sharp contrast to the type of officer Duane appeared to be. I thought about the word "appeared." So often, what appeared to be true was just a diversion, sometimes the misdirection was good as when we were locked up in Cuba and the government pretended we were dead to protect us. Sometimes, it was bad, like the Secret Service agent who had pretended to be on our side when speaking to Father Browning.

I thought about Joey's insider contact, Green Dragon. It sounded Chinese. Maybe it was someone born in the year of the dragon. I wondered whether Joey had made any headway. Bruce placed a call to Joey and put the phone on speaker so we could both talk.

"Anything new from Green Dragon?" Jimmy inquired.

"Got another email from him. He wants to know what we know so he can come up with a plan to take to the President."

"We've had people pretend to be our friends and turn out to be really bad guys," I said.

"I'm exercising caution."

"We may have six of Philly's finest on our side. I can never be sure though," Jimmy told him.

"What happened to the other phone?"

"We got set up yesterday, but our contact found a way around it."

"What have you heard from Father Browning?" I asked.

"Nothing. The prof got a message from LaMont, saying Sparrow is okay."

"Sparrow as in brown?" Jimmy questioned.

"That's my hope. She didn't clarify."

"Everything set for the march on Washington on Tuesday?"

"Yep. Our favorite profs are going to be there, too."

"Watch for anyone trying to sabotage the trains."

"How will we stay in touch? Will you have Net while there?"

"Got a laptop with a portable wifi connection," Jimmy informed him. "Not using it now, but in Washington we can communicate via InstaChat. Everything disappears quickly—though not necessarily. And they could black out the Internet."

"Download all videos before they disappear, then."

"Joey, can you look up whistleblowers on the Philly PD and give us a sense of who can and cannot be trusted. Look up anything you can on—" I started to ask.

"We need to be careful. They may have receivers on towers outside Columbia. They've watched us in the past. No names."

"Sorry."

"More trouble. Had a flash drive full of info. It's disappeared."

"You think someone took it?" Jimmy asked.

"Maybe someone is double-dealing. We were careful when we went to the Basilica. How did they find out we had been helped?"

"Interesting. What was on the flash drive?"

"Copies, not the doctor's work, but copies of some of the footage we got in Queens and elsewhere and some of the information we've gotten online. None of our plans."

"In other words, trust nobody we can't be sure of," I said.

"Exactly."

"If they know students are coming by train, they may plan a counter. Be very careful. And have an alternative travel plan," Jimmy advised.

"Plan to. We'll definitely keep an eye out."

I went to find Shane. "Do you have access to some satellite computer equipment so we can be connected in D.C?"

"There's a ton of it in one of my warehouses. Just tell me what you'll need."

Jimmy had gotten a message. Everything seemed all set for Tuesday's train trip. However, Joey still needed to ferret out whether he had a mole. For all we knew, we might have one, too.

Jimmy contacted Duane, again. We would be meeting Duane later that day. Shannon insisted on going along this time. We decided to leave Shane behind in case not all Duane's friends were trustworthy. Shane was planning to have a cryptic email exchange with Joey to make arrangements to pick up the students from the train station. He had VPNs on his computers and said he knew how to be surreptitious in his messaging.

Alejandro talked Emily into hanging out with him on one of the last days before we would either succeed or possibly die trying. I tried to talk Abigail and Bruce into staying behind, but Bruce insisted that he wanted to be there for any technical discussions. Father Durham was studying his Bible and was planning to do some religious stuff. Since I wasn't Catholic and had no intention of becoming Catholic, I didn't inquire.

Shane loaned us a BMW sports utility vehicle. Jimmy drove while the rest of us huddled down under tarps. We decided to meet at Bryn Mawr in the gymnasium.

Professor LaMont, who joined the meeting, had received a message she believed was from Father Browning. He believed he was in danger and was safely staying away from his normal hangouts.

"Good that he is safe. Father Durham will be very relieved," I said.

"I'm sure you are, too," she agreed.

"Enough people have gotten hurt over helping us," I said. "I don't want that ever to happen again."

Duane introduced us to David Sands, John Turloch, Norman Cummings and Mack Highland, four of his fellow officers. "Roger will be taking the train Tuesday as will Mack's son and David's daughter. We want to make sure those students are safe."

"We have a problem," Bruce said. "There is a possible mole. Someone stole a drive from one of our friends at Columbia. It wasn't critical, except now it is possible, if there is a mole, the bad guys may suspect some of our plans."

"Did it mention the train ride?"

"It didn't mention our plans. But, if there is a mole, he would likely know about the travel arrangements by now."

Together we worked out a plan to try to protect the students taking the train. Shane would be picking them up when they arrived for the event. Next, we worked on the plan for D.C.

"They will probably be looking for you, maybe even checking vans and cars. You may be dead in the eyes of the public, but not in the eyes of the men who threatened my son and me."

"I think we should go there Monday, saying we were checking into a police convention. We'll take two cars for future police cadets," John said.

"The hotels have video and are highly watched," Santana pointed out.

"It's the most monitored city in the country," Bruce remarked.

"You can't go in as yourselves," Duane pointed out.

"What if we disguise ourselves approaching the Capitol and drop the coverings right before we speak on the steps?" I suggested.

"There's the laser weapons, that could take out a person without any notice," Bruce reminded us.

"We'll have to keep an eye out for any planes in the area," Duane advised.

"Also, lasers are line of sight. They can go through metal but mirrors could be used to defeat or confuse them," Bruce noted.

"We also have to watch for provocateurs," Santana pointed out.

"My dad has command of lots of those," Abigail noted.

"You mean people who try to make your group look bad," Duane interpreted.

"We need to make sure nobody goes inside the Capitol or has any weapons," Santana advised.

"I can have a line of students from Bryn Mawr blocking all entrances from anyone promoting violence," Professor LaMont offered.

"We could probably get the Columbia Football team to help out with security as well," Jimmy suggested.

"I know where we can get detectors to scan incomers for weapons. We'll tell everyone that we're afraid of FBI insurgents and they'll understand," John said.

"And how about a check-in tent for equipment or supplies that students and people don't want to carry?" Duane recommended.

"It will have to be watched to make sure that nothing is planted," David advised.

After discussing the best approach, we decided to take off Monday for Georgetown University. Dr. LaMont had enlisted the assistance of one of the profs there. Duane and John would give us escort, while David and Mack would work on other aspects of the operation. Genevieve and Professor Brand would be accompanying the Columbia students.

Professor Brand and Joey had located a Columbia student whose mother worked in the White House. The goal was for the student's mother to get Abigail in to speak with the President. The girl had told Professor Brand her mother could arrange for student passes. We guessed that the feds might already be suspecting Duane after they blew up his son's car. Instead, John Turloch would be accompanying the students to the White House, saying he was protecting their security.

Bruce didn't like the idea of Abigial going to the White House without more backup, such as himself. Duane felt that Bruce's presence could call attention to her identity. Bruce disagreed, pointing out that he could disguise himself.

"I can do this," Abigail told him. "Trust me. I need to do this. Duane and John are right. It puts me in more danger if you come."

John assured Bruce that he would do whatever it took to protect Abigail. Bruce was still uncomfortable with the idea.

We already had fake IDs from Columbia. Jimmy managed to create fake identification cards from Bryn Mawr for us all as backups while we were there. The prof was theoretically inattentive to what Jimmy was doing with the cards. Duane said he normally would have to stand against such activity but, to prevent a coup, he considered himself and his group to be acting undercover.

Jimmy and Shannon would be talking on the radio from Georgetown. Santana and I would be leading the rally and hoping not to get arrested.

The students from Columbia would include a great niece of the U.S. President. She would be leading a contingency group at the Capitol.

Emily would be standing by to help us pilot a plane to get out of the area if there were a problem. Emily's amateur flying abilities had saved our lives when we were on the run in Mexico. Our police helpers were going to come up with a plan to make sure there wasn't a coup at the Pentagon and hopefully arrest Abigail's and Emily's fathers.

The plan seemed plausible. But I knew very well, plans could change. We started back to Shane's,"I am still worried about the flash drive. They likely know we know they are planning a coup d'état," Jimmy worried.

"It would be better if they didn't know, but they have no way of knowing how much help we are getting. Remember the 2016 election? Clinton had the cheating in place, but didn't count on the Bernie Sanders supporters staying home and so many others voting for what they thought was change," Santana reminded me.

"What they thought was change but didn't get," Jimmy pointed out.

"I wish we knew for sure Father Browning was doing okay," I said.

"Professor LaMont seemed pretty sure," Jimmy tried to reassure me.

"Is this car registered to Shane?" Bruce asked Jimmy.

"No. This is a model that was on loan to him," Jimmy responded.

"Good. See that drone up above following us?" Bruce pointed out the back window.

CHAPTER 34

High in the sky, a drone was tailing us.

"How did it make us?" Santana asked.

"Some kind of imaging. It could have been at the gas station. They have video cameras. Or they could have been doing a search via satellite?"

"Think it has a laser?" I asked.

"We need to get out of here ASAP," Bruce warned. We were driving through an area with trees. "Let's try the mirror effect. Pull over under those trees."

Jimmy complied. Bruce pulled a large mirrored car cover out that unfolded several times, covering the SUV.

The covering was larger than the vehicle. We moved under the trees towards a clearing. "Everyone out in case it doesn't work," Jimmy instructed. He put the car into neutral and we all shoved it into the clearing. A second later the drone was visible through the trees right before it blew up.

"You were prepared." I breathed a sigh of relief.

"Have to be with what they keep throwing at us," Bruce replied.

The drone and laser had been silent. There had been no notice of when the weapon would be fired, but it was deflected.

"Won't they be sending another one to replace that one?" Santana asked.

"That's why we're taking a side trip through the woods," Jimmy said. "Santana, you want to drive?"

We laughed. Jimmy was a pretty wild driver, but Santana was the one with the reputation. Santana jumped behind the wheel, and off through the forest we went, staying under cover as long as possible, moving only onto highways when trees were covering them.

"It probably won't be safe to drive this back to Shane's," Bruce said. "But we'll have cover for driving until pretty close. When you are close, park it off the road out of site. Shane can pick it up later in a truck."

There was enough cover for us to walk back, without being observed from above, but not without some fear.

When we got back, Santana said, "We've got one night of freedom. What would you like to do?"

"Party and dance," Emily suggested enthusiastically.

"I'll second that," Alejandro said.

Shane had some balloons in the basement. We filled them with helium. Then, Santana put the end of one into his mouth and sucked in the helium. A second later, he was sounding like Mickey Mouse.

We pulled out New Year's poppers, horns and hats, even though it wasn't New Years. Though we didn't speak of it, we all knew this could be the last party of our lives.

Shane had a confetti machine that dropped confetti all over us as a lighted disco ball turned, making the recreation room look like something out of a fantasy movie.

Jimmy found some of his favorite old Green Day songs on Shane's vinyls and we sang and danced to "American Idiot" and "On Holiday."

Even Father Durham seemed to be enjoying himself, watching as we goofed off. We were laughing and celebrating so hard that we thought someone in our group had turned out the lights when the power went out.

"Who did that?" Shane asked.

Nobody copped to it.

"Come on," Santana advised and then whispered. "Shhh." Power-out light detectors were on.

As I tried to size up the situation, nearby footsteps could be heard inside the house.

CHAPTER 35

We were on the third floor. Shane quietly led us down the back steps, to the basement into a room with couches and pictures on the walls.

"They have bunker buster bombs. I don't know if they'll use them. At the least, they'll raid the place," Bruce warned.

Shane removed a picture from one of the walls and pressed a button that had been behind it. What had looked like a solid wall opened. We moved into a what I believed was a safe room as he put back the picture. He pulled a lever inside the safe room. The wall closed, and we could feel the room going down. It opened onto a larger safe room. The power down there was on.

"This part of the house has an independent backup system and the house, itself, also has a backup system, which is not on yet. We're connected to a tunnel that leads into the woods. There is an exit to the outside if needed." He pushed a button on the wall. "The basement side is now locked. If they look behind the picture, it won't do them any good."

"I thought you were legit?" Santana asked.

Father Durham shook his head. "Whatever you are into isn't any worse than what the government is doing."

"Some of my cargo is no questions asked," Shane explained. "Priest-penitent privilege?"

Father Durham covered his eyes. "I don't see anyone here to negate it."

I looked around and saw video monitors portraying images of events in the house. Shane explained that he had cameras that worked automatically when the power went out and were based on an infrared viewing system. Troopers moved up the front stairs, armed with guns, big guns. There were a lot of men, perhaps a whole Green Barret or Seal team. They clearly meant business. At least, we were all together.

"I wonder how they found us?" I pondered.

"Duane?" Jimmy questioned. "I thought I could trust him, but he was the only one who knew about Shane."

"Except the phone call to Roger was made from here. Maybe they figured it out. Or maybe the mole from Columbia," Santana suggested. "Of course, it could have been Duane."

"The car?" I asked.

"No. Jake reported it stolen earlier today, and it isn't tied to me."

"Also, we parked about five miles away in the woods and there were other homes closer to the car than this one, if they uncovered the branches we put over it."

"It was me," Father Durham said. "I'm so sorry."

We looked at him.

"I found one of those voice changers among your stuff, and I called the Cathedral to ask about Father Browning. They must have traced the call."

"It's alright, Father," Shane warmly told him.

"We were worried about him, too. Dr. LaMont has assured us he's okay. But if they find our stuff—" I started.

"I moved it down into the safe room earlier today. Also, two laptops in addition to the one you brought," Shane told us. "Just had a weird feeling. It's in the closet over there," He pointed to one of several closets. "I was going to tell you when you returned, but you rushed up right away to the rec room, instead of going to your rooms when you got back. So, I forgot."

"What phone did you use?" Jimmy asked.

Father Durham handed him a phone. Jimmy took it and smashed it.

The intruders were going through the basement.

Shane turned on the speaker. "Whoever called from the phone is gone. There's no trace of the kids."

Another trooper said, "Get some swabs and check the DNA. We should have the results by Friday. I suggest we station one of our cars down the road to watch the driveway in case they return. It looks like someone was throwing a party upstairs."

"Maybe the group is hiding out by breaking into vacant houses," a third trooper speculated.

As the troopers left, the power inside the house came back on. An outside camera showed someone positioned by the side of the house.

"What's that?" Jimmy asked as Shane looked at an outline of the house with a picture of a person.

"It's a heat detector. They left someone inside."

"I don't get it," Santana said. "You have no cameras outside your warehouses, and yet you have the ultimate security here at your home."

"Outside my warehouses, it's public. I don't like to be observed wandering downtown. The city already has too many cameras invading privacy. The house is private property, and the only one who would be watching the videos is me. It doesn't have Ring cameras. Those are monitored by the police. However, I didn't actually create the security here. I purchased if from a gentleman who moved to California. He was former CIA and very paranoid, always afraid of being attacked. The city doesn't even have the real specs for this place."

"Good precautions," Santana said. "My dad voted for the NDAA in spite of the fact that eighty percent of his constituents said they opposed it."

"That's the one that allows them to grab any American citizen for indefinite detention for life without any rights or trial, isn't it?" Shane asked.

"Yep. Let it never be said that my dad puts his constituents first."

"The power that's on is the back-up power, which automatically goes on twenty minutes after a failure unless it's turned on quicker. The city power is still off."

"Can they tell if we turn on the computers?"

"Not in this room. And their man in the house can't hear us."

"Unless he has that equipment that can hear through walls," Bruce noted.

"There is extra shielding here."

"I thought it was over-cautious or paranoid that you moved our stuff down to the basement earlier," Alejandro said. "You really are intuitive."

"That and cautious. After what happened to Father Browning and your friend Roger, it seemed like a good idea while most of you were out."

"Can you tell anything about the man they left behind?"

Shane hit a switch and turned on a video. "The camera doesn't show a red light and he probably doesn't know we're filming him."

"I recognize him," Santana said. "He's one of the thugs that was beating up Father Durham in Philly."

"You're right," I said, taking another look.

"I'll never forget that face," Father Durham said, touching part of his own face that was still recovering from the bruising. "That doesn't mean I do not forgive," he added, apparently realizing that he was sounding a little unpriestly.

"Now, they came here looking for us," I noted. "But they don't know for sure whether we were invading this place or here with permission."

"I'm sorry I caused you so much trouble," Father Durham told Shane.

"No," Shane said. "You're no trouble. We're safe. This safe room has cots in the closet, running water and a refrigerator with food. It was meant to withstand most fires."

"The fires they were having in California burnt the steel and porcelain to ash but not the trees," I told him.

"You do get that those weren't normal fires, don't you?" Bruce said.

"There is also filtered air here in case of a radioactive disaster, like Limerick going TMI."

"Good to know," Santana responded.

"Of course, it's soundproof."

"That's good," Jimmy said as his phone beeped. "Apparently the signal isn't blocked." He looked at the phone. "What is this? Does anyone know what this message means? *'The Mother of all Winters is coming to D.C.?'*"

"She can't!" I freaked.

"It's a code," Abigail told him coming over to me and giving me a hug. "Don't worry."

"Code for—" Jimmy started to ask.

"My mother!" I exclaimed.

CHAPTER 36

"Mom had Alonzo use the codeword 'Winter' when we were in the Cuban prison and Alejandro's family was keeping mom, Emily and my dog Hope safe."

Jimmy continued to speak more quietly with Joey while I continued to panic.

"That means Alonzo will be there protecting her," Alejandro assured me. "She'll be fine."

"It's one more person to worry about." The assurances weren't working. I was terrified. "She'd probably risk her own life to help me, and having to make sure she stays safe will make it a lot harder."

Santana put his arms around me. "It will be alright."

"I lost her for most of her life. I just found her again. I can't lose her." I was practically sobbing.

Jimmy put away his phone. "We have five police officers, eleven of the smartest teens anyone has ever seen, a priest, a top entrepreneur, two professors, a scientist and thousands of students. Your mom will be fine," Jimmy said, but not convincingly.

"Thousands?" I asked.

"Actually, I think tens of thousands are planning to come," Jimmy said.

"Tens of thousands?"

"That may be an underestimate."

"All for us?" Emily asked.

"For themselves, actually. By protecting you, they are actually protecting themselves from your fate."

"And the kids still in the camps. They are doing it for them, too," I said.

"I'm doing it for you," Alejandro told Emily.

We decided to rest as we would be taking off in the morning. I woke up to Jimmy's voice.

"I've been monitoring the Net. Look." Jimmy turned to InstaChat. Posters were putting up pictures of themselves with signs, saying, "I'm with Summer" or "I'm with the Wilderness Five." He turned to a page someone had put up with a petition with more than seven million signatures demanding the United States drop any prosecution of us. The petition called us heroes who deserved to be honored.

"Wow!" I reacted.

"The parents who are having their children kidnapped to the programs are being called child abusers, and there are calls for removal of kids from any parent who has sent any of their children to the wilderness camps, schools or other behavior modification programs," he continued.

"In other words, no matter what, we've already made a difference," I summarized.

"Remember, there was a bill introduced to close down the programs after your U.N. speeches. Already fifty members of the House, including some of the most pro-war congressmen, have signed on and a companion bill is being sponsored in the U.S. Senate."

"I thought that legislation was dead," I said.

"Friday hasn't happened yet. If they institute some kind of blackmail or mind control, that will be the end of the legislation," Abigail advised.

"She's right and the leaders who had sex at the little kids' camp will definitely do whatever they are told to do to avoid exposure," I suspected.

"Those slobs," Shane said. "Any man who would have sex with children deserves to go down. Even at the worst of my drug problem, I would have found that appalling."

"Pedophilia is rampant in Congress," Santana said. "It's especially bad in the California legislature. You should have seen some of those pictures."

"Emily's, Abigail's and my dads were on the videos of the kids' camp," I told him.

"Terrible," said Father Durham. "In the church, I spoke in favor of terminating the status of the pedophiles after the *Boston Globe* broke its story. Individuals who do engage in that behavior need psychiatric treatment, not to remain a status symbol to parishioners."

"Sodom and Gomorrah," Jimmy remarked.

"I agree. We cannot teach the word of God if we don't obey it."

"A very enlightened priest," Bruce approved.

"I never had much respect for priests because of all the ridiculous hellfire stuff, but you aren't so bad," Abigail said.

I smiled. I had never believed in the hellfire talk, either, and I likely never would. This world had enough hell. God's plan, if there was one, had to be much better and not about hanging out on clouds playing harps.

Jimmy flashed on the latest *Ron Paul Liberty Report* video, talking about the biggest tax increase in American history. It was bipartisan legislation that gave all the millionaires in Congress, the Executive branch and the Supreme Court multi-million-dollar tax credits, paid for by increased taxes on the middle class.

"Are you sure we want to stop the coup?" Santana asked. "Maybe, we should cheer it on."

"You think this is bad? You should see what will happen if my father takes over."

"What we need is a real coup. Throw everyone out," Jimmy remarked.

"In states like Georgia and Florida, they are arresting priests for feeding the homeless," Father Durham said.

"That's nothing. Reporters are being arrested regularly for simply reporting the news, not committing crimes, just telling the truth," Jimmy pointed out. "And some countries, backed by the USA, are executing reporters by the truckload."

"Isn't that why we're being nailed with the Espionage Act? For telling the truth?" Abigail asked.

"What is interesting is that you kids are from opposite sides of the aisle, but you basically agree on the issues," Shane observed.

"It's not about partisanship. It's about truth. What is bad are the people who don't want to talk about what it going on because they claim reality is party-based," Abigail explained.

"If Dennis Kucinich and Ron Paul ran on a joint ticket, they'd win," Santana noted.

"Would it matter to you which was at the top of the ticket?" Father Durham asked.

"I'd prefer Kucinich at the top, but I'd vote for a Paul/Kucinich ticket, if I live that long," Santana responded.

"Agreed," I seconded. The others nodded, too.

"If Dennis's wife were a natural-born citizen, I'd vote for her for President," Shane said.

"How about Jesse Ventura for vice president?" Abigail asked. "Imagine Ventura running with Kucinich?"

We looked at her. "Just because my parents are right-wing Republicans doesn't mean I don't think Dennis is cute, and he's shorter than me."

"'If there's any hope, it's in the Proles,'" Santana quoted.

"*1984*," Father Durham said. "Eric Blair wasn't just a writer. He was part of high-level discussions about the direction America, Europe and the power elite were planning on taking Western Society. It was a warning of what he had learned about the plans our leaders had for us. While *Animal Farm* was about Russia, *1984* was about us."

"This is weird. Most of Pennsylvania is blacked out," Jimmy said, looking at the Internet. "Is there a purpose or is it a test of some plan for later this week? We may have one of the last standing computer lines."

"It works off receptors from satellite feeds twenty miles away and doesn't depend on the local services. It must be in one of the sections that's still up," Shane told us.

"Usually, they don't do something for no reason. Who or what is in Pennsylvania?" Santana asked. "Is there a VIP or something important going on in Pennsylvania?"

Jimmy used Duckduckgo to search 'visiting Pennsylvania.'"

"Five Star General Brad Nester is staying at a hotel near Independence Hall, the same one where they tortured Father Durham."

"They'll recognize us, sneaking in to find out what's going on. And it could be a trap," Shannon warned.

"Duane," I said. "Let's call Duane and see if he can get some of his fellow officers to protect the General. Forward Duane the emails about the planned takeover of the Joint Chiefs to show Nester. He and whoever goes with him can say they got them anonymously."

"I'm already calling him," Jimmy said. After the call and the forwarding of the emails, there was little for us to do but sit and wait.

"Anyone have some cards?" Santana asked.

"Poker or fish?" Emily debated.

"Poker. We'll play for crackers," Abigail suggested.

"Good. I don't like crackers. I won't mind losing," I said.

Surprisingly, the father joined us. And even more surprisingly, he won.

"You've played this before?" Bruce asked.

"I've been around quite a bit. Before I became a priest, I did a fair amount of card-playing. It's not like we are gambling for real."

"True," I said. "You can have what's left of my crackers."

"Anyone for Fish?" Emily asked. This time she was the big winner. This gave her a smile, something that warmed my heart, given how frightened I was inside.

Finally, Jimmy's phone rang. He put it on speaker.

"Good call," Duaine said. "We got there just as some thugs were trying to break into the general's room under cover of authority."

"What did you do with them?" Jimmy asked.

"Not much. We held them until some people the General trusted got there and locked them up."

"Do you think the lower generals will be warned by virtue of the arrests?"

"That's the interesting part. General Nester said that this is one advantage of the NDAA. The thugs are being held in Virginia without notice to any attorneys or any of their partners in coup-making. They've been stripped of their wires and telephones."

"Excellent." I felt weird saying that as I totally opposed the NDAA and indefinite detention.

"It's better," Duane continued. "We let slip the emails about the planned coup to the General and he'll be watching. It was clear the men were coming to assassinate him as they had their guns aimed at him when we barged in. He's, now, on alert. Lower-level generals, now unlikely to advance, have been quietly placed under observation."

"Double excellent," Jimmy said. "See you tomorrow, if we can get out of here."

"That thug still there?" I asked.

"Yep," Shane said, looking at the monitor. "Also, they are stationing people down the street."

"We'll work on a plan," Duane said.

I thanked Duane. "You've renewed my faith that there are some good officers out there."

"There are a lot of us. You just don't hear about us in the news."

"Say 'hi' to Roger for us," Emily requested.

"And keep him safe. He's already on their hit list," I reminded him.

"Will do. See you tomorrow."

"Tomorrow," Jimmy confirmed.

The next morning, the man inside the house and the one outside were gone when I woke up.

"They left the house an hour ago," Shane said. "Something funny is happening with the electricity upstairs. I don't have a smart meter, but it's looking as if something is affecting the wiring."

"The fires. They couldn't use the smart meter and so they might be trying some kind of wave technology or a directed energy weapon," Bruce guessed.

"Fire. Not something I like happening to my place," Shane said.

"I'm sorry we brought you so much trouble," I apologized.

"It's fine. This place is over-insured and they haven't yet canceled my fire insurance. If they pull something, I'll be able to rebuild. The under-basement is protected from most of whatever sci-fi technology they decide to throw at us." He flipped another switch. We could see on the monitor a section of the garage lowering and sealing itself. "There are a few vehicles I'd like to preserve."

"How far underground are we?" Santana asked.

"Probably not far enough to survive a direct nuclear hit. Those underground cities won't provide as much protection as your government thinks if their locations are known and targeted."

"I hope they are," Abigail said. "In fact, I'd be willing to publicize their locations. The pigs should have to suffer the consequences along with the masses."

"Part of why I love you." Bruce kissed her cheek. This was the first time I had actually heard him say he loved Abigail, but it had been obvious since right after we escaped the camp that he was smitten with her.

"I noticed your place has battery-powered sprinklers, but water won't hinder the kind of fires I've seen on the news," Jimmy informed us.

"You are aware. A lot of people in your age group are asleep," Shane proclaimed.

"More of us are awake than you'd think," Jimmy answered.

"I avoid arguments with the sleepers. If the average person saw what was going on, they'd feel some responsibility for doing something and they'd feel guilty for doing nothing and choose to go back to sleep. I'm not doing much of anything but I'm fine with that." Shane looked at Father Durham, seemingly to see if there was disapproval.

"You do enough, son. You didn't have to take us in."

"I'm about to do more, aren't I? You are going to need my vans to get into D.C. with the police escort. I have a couple with false floors." He looked at Father Durham. "Not for anything illegal but just to protect certain cargo. Since they're looking for you, you'd be best out of sight when we enter the city."

"Your vans are at your warehouse?"

"I have multiple warehouses, now, and I actually have a fleet of trucks and some very loyal and 'awake' truck drivers. Useful, huh?"

"Shades of *Smokey and the Bandit*," I joked.

"Hadn't thought of that one. But yeah."

He pressed another button that I guessed was an emergency alert. "Premature, but if they are going to start a fire, we might as well get the authorities here as quickly as possible. We should take off during the diversion."

"We've got Her Majesty's Secret Service Agent Double O Ten," Santana joked.

I smiled. Clearly, we watched a lot of the same movies.

"Not so fast. Usually, the other double 0s die and Bond has to save the day," Shannon pointed out.

"In that case, you're the new Double O Seven. Moore passed away, and the current one doesn't make it."

"Your mother would be proud, James," I teased.

"I thought I was James," Jimmy said. "It's okay. I'll be Luke Skywalker."

"Captain Kirk, here," Santana said.

"Hey, I wanted that one," Bruce joked. He didn't joke that often, and I enjoyed seeing him lighten up.

"The fire's starting," Jimmy noted.

CHAPTER 37

"Look on the monitor, right in the center of the house," Jimmy pointed out. "The metal on the doorknobs is melting. But the carpets and the furniture are fine so far and the plastic covered camera is still recording."

"Not for long. The whole house is likely to turn to ash," Bruce advised.

"The trees outside will probably be fine, like in other recent fires," Jimmy remarked.

"I'm counting on that," Shane said. "Though in a real fire, the trees burn first."

It wasn't long before a string of fire trucks pulled into the driveway. By then, the fire had spread and the carpets and furniture were also on fire. The metal inside the house was continuing to melt.

"What about keepsakes?"

"I lost my most important keepsakes when I was doing drugs. My remaining important ones are the cross and Bible Father Durham gave me. Those are down here."

Shane opened another door. "Pick up what you want to bring."

We put on our backpacks, complete with laptops. Outside the door was a tunnel, a number of bicycles and an electric surrey with three double seats.

We put our stuff into the back of the surrey. Shane got into the driver's seat with Father Durham beside him. Bruce and Abigail sat in the middle seat and Alejandro and Emily took the back. Santana, Shannon, Jimmy and I rode the bicycles.

Being athletes, Shannon, Jimmy and I easily kept up with the surrey. So did Santana. Santana hadn't talked a lot about his life before the camps, but he always seemed physically fit and he had been faster than me in following the DHS van in Manhattan. The exit from the dirt path at the end of the tunnel to the road was about five miles away. From there, we kept riding under the trees in the direction of Philly.

Finally, we reached a large storage area. Inside was a van, an old firetruck and a much more modern large ambulance. "There is always a need for volunteer firefighters and transport to the hospital." We piled into the back of the ambulance and Shane drove us towards Bryn Mawr, staying on dirt roads under the trees until we were far away from where he lived.

As we arrived at another warehouse, the door flung open. Inside there were several large moving vans in addition to trucks and two of our friends from the Philadelphia Police Department.

Duane spoke to a couple of men. We stayed mostly silent and out of sight. Officer John Turlock and a driver Shane referred to as Reggie got into the front of a "Money Express truck." Shane explained that "Money Express" was one of his businesses. Companies contracted for safe transport for bank deposits and such. Shane and Reggie were bonded. Shane said that Reggie was one of the "awake" people who could be trusted. Clearly, he wouldn't be using the truck for a real money delivery in the next two days.

"They burned down my home," Shane told Duane as the two got into the front of the ambulance.

"I saw it on the police radio. Glad all of you made it out alright."

Inside the ambulance were cots, with sheets and paramedic outfits. Those of us who were recognizable got under the sheets or hid under the cots while Shannon, Jimmy and Alejandro dressed as paramedics.

We went south to Virginia and then up Highway 29 towards

Georgetown. On Highway 29, Shane turned on the siren. I was certain this was illegal but so was everything the goons, who were taking over the country, were doing.

"Georgetown is a Jesuit University," Father Durham informed us.

Crossing the Potomac, a feeling of hanging between success and ultimate disaster enveloped me. This could be where my journey ended or where my future began.

CHAPTER 38

After crossing the Potomac, Shane turned off the siren. "They might have satellite imagery, and so I'm pulling into the MedStar Georgetown University Hospital." He stopped in Emergency and went inside to speak with someone. When he came out, he drove us to the Jesuit Cemetery, where we were carried out under sheets into the chapel.

Inside, Father Browning was waiting. I threw my arms around him. "I was so worried. I know Professor LaMont said you were okay, but I didn't have any details."

"She planned much of this but was worried about leaks," he said. My other friends crowded around him, hugging him.

"I was praying for your protection. He is watching over us," Father Durham said.

"And He brought all of you here safely," Father Browning noted.

We're not out of the States safely yet, I thought.

We dressed in black Jesuit robes and made our way over to Copley Hall where we would be spending the night. One of the priests escorting us gave us a map of tunnels running under the campus. We met up in the back of St. Williams Chapel, on the first floor of Copley Hall.

"The Church is not particularly pleased with your Government, but will not officially oppose it. You are safe here," Father Browning assured us.

"I hope your sister had fire insurance," Jimmy said to Father Browning.

"She did. It was to be canceled as of next week. Good timing on the part of the feds."

"We saved her laptop," Jimmy said.

"She will be grateful for that," Father Browning replied.

"Have you been here most of the time since Friday?" I asked.

"I arrived on Saturday."

"They burned down Shane's home, too."

"I'm sorry. But you have performed a wonderful service," Father Browning told Shane.

"He certainly has," Father Durham agreed.

"In the Bible, those who lost from doing good works were often repaid sevenfold," Father Browning said.

"Right now, we're just hoping to stay alive." But I wasn't so sure of our prospects for longevity.

"Have faith," Father Browning encouraged.

A girl who slightly resembled stock images of Snow White entered the Chapel. "This is Mary Jo. Her mother is a Secretary in the White House," Father Browning told us.

"My mom promised to take me and my roommate Jasmine on a tour of the White House tomorrow morning. We may even get to meet the President." She smiled sheepishly and then handed Abigal a new student ID, a pair of heavy glasses and a red-haired wig to match her picture.

"Green hair, red hair, you are still beautiful," Bruce told Abigail. He put his arm around her. Alejandro did likewise with Emily.

"Did Bob put this together?" I asked her.

"Yes, Bob. He's really nice and his friend Joey's so cute."

I smelled romance in the air. "They're both really nice. So's Darren."

"I know. I introduced him to my real roommate Taylor, and they have been together almost every minute since."

"Does anyone else know your plans?" I inquired further.

"I didn't even tell Taylor."

"Good. The fewer who know of our plans, the less danger," Santana interjected.

"Thank you for your help," I said.

We were allotted fifteen rooms on the fourth floor. Apparently, students who had been on that floor had been moved to the first floor and other dorms under a pretense that rooms were being modernized. I didn't think we had that many people working with us, so far.

Food was brought up and we all sat around having planning sessions in the fourth-floor lounge, drawing diagrams of the security for the Capitol, listing ideas for getting me and Santana on the steps as speakers and making sure that Abigail could be rescued after attempting to speak with the President or in case she was recognized before she had the chance. She would be accompanied by Mary Jo and John.

We discussed getting the help of General Nester. Jimmy had gotten an email from Nester saying he is watching for another assassination attempt. We were hoping the disappearance of the assassination team in Philadelphia wouldn't alert Kreskin and Hattan that their plot had been uncovered. We also hoped that the plotters hadn't cut a deal with Nester. We didn't trust anyone in power not to sell out.

An overwhelming fear suddenly encompassed me, and I felt the need to get outside for some fresh air and alone time. My fears kept creeping up—almost like a premonition.

Shortly before evening, I dressed in a Sari and head covering. The school supported students of all religions. I went to look at the Potomac. I made it out to the Chesapeake and Ohio Canal and sat down beside it. Walking didn't help. The fear was getting stronger. I watched a tourist boat about to cross the Potomac coming towards the Capital Crescent Trail which separated the Chesapeake and Ohio Canal from the Potomac.

Shannon and Jimmy were suddenly by my side. "You didn't think we'd let you go out in public alone." She put her arm around me.

"Would it be awful if I said I was scared?" I asked.

"I'm scared too," Shannon said.

"I'm definitely scared," Jimmy added.

"Summer, you are the bravest person I've ever known," Shannon told me.

"I didn't realize there were scuba divers here," I said, watching a diver with a black box jumping into the river from the trail as the boat took off.

"They're everywhere," Shannon said.

"There is something odd about him and that box he's holding." The diver was swimming towards the boat, slowly, as if to look more casual, but he was close enough to the surface of the water that I could still see him. *It couldn't be some kind of sabotage, could it?*

As if compelled, I quickly lowered myself into the water throwing the Sari back onto the shore. I still had my underwear on. I raced across the Canal and the trail and dove into the Potomac. My swim team skills came in handy again. Was there a VIP on the boat who was now in danger? Was this just my imagination or paranoia?

Suddenly, I realized I wasn't the only one in the water swimming after the man. Shannon and Jimmy were coming up behind me. I was the fastest of us three, though, and soon I caught up to the diver. He was attaching something to the underside of the boat.

I tried to pull it off. He grabbed me around the throat and tried to strangle and drown me at the same time. I fought back, but he pulled out a knife and a second later his hand was pulled back.

My attacker was now fighting with Jimmy. Shannon was on the swimmer's back, helping Jimmy.

I went for the attachment to the boat and managed to pull it off. I moved it away from the boat and its path.

Blood. I saw blood in the water.

Jimmy! The distraction resulted in my losing my grip. The device or whatever it was went down, down, down. I swam back towards the boat and where I had last seen my friends.

I was suddenly yanked hard. It was Jimmy getting me out of the way of the boat's path as it passed. Shannon was beside him.

Jimmy was bleeding, pretty badly from his left shoulder. As the water washed away blood, more appeared on him. It looked like a very bad slash.

A second later, an explosion below rocked the area and the water shot up above me. I could see the boat rolling over as I was submerged in the aftermath.

CHAPTER 39

I regained my strength and resurfaced.

The explosion had knocked the boat onto its side and passengers were in the water. Jimmy, Shannon and I started helping people get to lifesavers and rafts that had been on the boat, had self-inflated and were in the water. It looked as if some of the crew had been injured but were alive and rescuing people as well.

There was one passenger I wasn't taking to a raft. "Take a deep breath and hold it," I instructed.

I held onto her and dove down, down, down, swimming under the surface as far and as fast as I could towards the Capital Crescent trail, ran across it and then swam across the canal.

As I got her ashore, we weren't alone. A couple of troopers threw blankets over us and pulled us into a military jeep.

The jeep stopped at Healey Family Student Center. We were told to stay while our military escorts got out and went into the hall.

Of course, we weren't going to stay put, but it was almost as if they were letting us escape.

Recalling the tunnel system map we'd been given, I grabbed my escortee and we went down via the nearest entrance. We resurfaced in the backstage section of Georgetown's Davis Performing Arts Center.

In a dressing room, we found costumes. We quickly got into them, added wigs and hats, and moved towards Copley Hall to our Fourth Floor Suites.

As we entered, I saw Duane and Shane holding down Santana. They released him, and he ran to me, taking me in his arms. "I was going after you, but these two thugs held me back."

"Thank you," I told Duane and Shane as Santana pulled back, visibly irritated.

"Remember our promises," he complained.

"And they helped me keep mine."

Santana turned to my mother and smiled. "Hello, Mrs. Tanner. It is a pleasure to see you again."

CHAPTER 40

"Your scary life is going to be the death of me," Mom half-scolded.

"I've been hoping it won't be the death of me," I replied.

"Whatever is happening tomorrow, I hope you are going to stay out of sight."

"I'm going to stay out of sight of any airplanes and drones, I think." She folded her arms across her chest.

"Jimmy and Shannon are still at the river," I informed the group.

"No. We're here," Jimmy said entering the room. "You know the tunnels also connect to Copley Hall. You didn't have to get out at the Performing Arts Center."

"I'll remember that next time. Do you know who those military guys were?"

"Nope," Jimmy replied. "But I'd say someone is keeping tabs on us. They let you go."

"You think they were giving us rope to lead us to the rest of you?"

"They took off after you got out. But they may have been watching from before. Hopefully we don't get blamed for that explosion."

"What happened?" Santana asked.

I went over to Jimmy and examined his shoulder which had been bandaged with a shirt pulled tight and tied. It was still bleeding through it. "We need that stitched," I advised.

"At least, Jimmy survived. I don't think that other guy's going to make it," Shannon told us.

I turned to Santana and Duane. "Someone tried to blow up my mom's boat. I detached the bomb, but it blew up on the floor of the river, knocking over the boat."

"Sounds like you were a big hero," Duane said.

"No, Jimmy was. He took on the saboteur and saved us all."

"My heroes," Shannon said.

"You were pretty heroic yourself," I contended as Jimmy was saying something similar.

"Let's hear it for the Heritage High swim team," Shannon beamed. "What were you doing on that boat?"

"Trying to be covert coming here. It was going to the trail and I planned to leave the group to finish getting to Georgetown."

"They were probably following you from the moment you entered the country," Duane surmised.

"Hello, Mrs. Tanner," Bruce said, opening the door. He was accompanied by Abigail, Emily and Alejandro.

"Hi. It's good to see the four of you intact."

"You missed all the fun," Jimmy teased.

"Yeah, you're all wet. Wish I had been at that party," Abigail teased back.

"Be glad you weren't," Shannon advised.

"Emily, you've really grown in the last few weeks. Rosa misses you so much. She's been trying to get permission to travel to the U.S., but it's the Americans who are blocking her."

"Figures," Abigail said.

"Juanita and Alvaro miss you Abigail and Bruce. And of course, you, Alejandro. They said to keep you safe and out of trouble."

"They aren't mad at me for sneaking out of Cuba?" he asked with a smile in his voice.

"Oh, they're definitely not happy about it. But they love you. They are also trying to get visas."

"I had to be here for Em," he asserted.

My mom re-crossed her arms.

"See. She's safe, happy." He pointed to Emily smiling.

"My understanding is that you all have been anything but safe."

"With all due respect," Santana told my mother. "We've all been getting a wonderful college education. We've been at Columbia, Bryn Mawr and now Georgetown. And we've even been getting instructions in morality from two priests. We have the finest law enforcement protecting us. You couldn't ask for a better education for your daughter."

My mother's arms were still crossed and held firmly across her chest with her hands attached to her sides.

"Okay, we could have had a more boring education. But we've learned a lot." Santana flashed a smile at her.

My mom finally let out the laugh she had been holding in. "It's hard to stay upset with you kids. You are all so amazing."

Santana's smile grew into a broad grin. Emily and Alejandro came over and hugged my mom.

"How is Alonzo doing?" Alejandro asked.

"Worried about you. Otherwise, okay. He's at the Cuban Embassy here. And he said for you to behave yourselves, stay out of trouble and stop saving the world."

"After tomorrow," Alejandro replied.

"What is going to happen tomorrow?"

"We're saving the world," Jimmy interjected.

"Abigail is going to meet with the President and we are going to try to expose a coup d'état planned by her father."

"I hope that Summer is nowhere near the action."

"I won't be in the line of fire for the laser action," I said.

"That doesn't sound good."

"Look, we don't want to be on the run or hiding out for the rest of our lives. We aren't just 'saving the world' as you put it but also saving ourselves."

"I understand, but I still worry."

"Mom, except for maybe those military guys and anyone watching satellite footage of the Potomac, they may not know for sure you're at Georgetown. We should probably keep it that way for now."

"Since when did you get to be my mom?" she teased.

"Since you missed most of my childhood," I said. From the look on her face, I instantly knew the hurt she still felt over those lost years, and I wished I could take it back. "I'm sorry. It wasn't your fault. It's the broken system. But it forces us kids to grow up faster."

She reached out, tears in her eyes and hugged me.

———

Since my mom's arrival, we'd adjusted the bedrooms. Shannon, who would have been my roommate, was staying with Mary Jo so that I could have time with my mom.

———

Later, while the others were preparing for the next day, I sat in my room with my mom. It was a nice evening as we looked through the drapes at the stars.

"Do you think they can see in?" she asked, looking out at the sky.

"Maybe. But I'm tired of being afraid. That's why I went to the Potomac—even though I was wearing a disguise until I saw the diver with the bomb."

"It wasn't just my life you saved. You saved everyone on that boat. I may not always show it, but I am so proud of you. And I am very impressed with your friends." She laughed. "Santana looked like he was ready to kill to get free to rescue you."

"He's really wonderful."

"It's more than a crush or first love isn't it? I mean, you really love him."

"Yes. I do. I know I'm young, but I know how I feel."

"Have you?"

"No. We're both waiting. We're only sixteen. We have lots of time, I hope."

"You've got a good head on your shoulders. He's the kind of guy worth hanging onto."

"I know."

"Years ago, before your father, there was a guy I should have hung onto."

"Not Daddy?"

"No. My father chose him."

"Sounds familiar. I almost fell into that trap."

"With the first guy, I was convinced that other things were more important and I let him go. It was a huge mistake. I only realized too late how much I cared. So, when the challenges come up, just go through them together while you wait for the right time, which will hopefully be in ten years."

I laughed. "I think we'd like to find the same college so that we don't wind up getting separated while we are finding ourselves."

"Smart. You really are very mature for your age."

"What about you and Alonzo?"

She smiled. "He makes me happier that I've been since I was a teenager, with the exception of when I was raising you."

"Happier than that other guy you didn't wind up with?"

"Much." She looked thoughtful. "There's one catch. Alonzo's adoption of Santana is about to be finalized. Would that be awkward?"

"Awkward!" I exclaimed. "That would be so cool, Mom. I have you. Emily has Rosa. Abigail, Bruce and Alejandro have Juanita and Alvaro. Santana doesn't have anybody but me. He just lost the only brother who cared about him. I keep telling myself that he's not just interested in me because I'm all he has."

"Oh, honey. If you could see the way he looks at you. It's so much more than that."

She hugged me, and we both found ourselves crying. "I'm so glad I have you back, Mom. You don't know how much I missed you. I know it wasn't your fault, but I used to dream that you would come and take me away."

"I wish I had."

"You were there when I most needed you. We never would have escaped from the camps if not for you."

"I helped, but you were already free."

"And they were hot on our trail. Abigail was near death. You saved us."

There was a knock on my door.

It was Santana. "I hope you don't mind. I just wanted to see how you are doing."

"Great. We've been talking about you."

"I haven't committed any felonies or gotten arrested today," he teased, half-smiling.

My mom shook her head, smiling back. "I'll let you two talk."

After my mom left, Santana sat down next to me by the window.

"I hope your mom doesn't think I'm a bad influence."

"She likes you. And Alonzo likes you too."

"He's more of a real father than my own dad," Santana said.

"She said the adoption is close to finalized."

"Really?" Santana sounded excited. "That's great."

He saw the expression on my face, which should have been more enthusiastic. I wanted to punch myself over my unspoken reservations, knowing he needed this.

"Oh. He and your mom. Is this a problem?"

"No. I think it's great that you'll have Alonzo. It's just that, if they wind up getting married, we'd be like brother and sister."

"Oh. At least you would find out quickly whether it was too much to be living with me."

"I don't think it would be too much. But with my mom supervising me and Alonzo supervising you, it would just be weird."

"Got it. But think of it this way. We'll be in the same country, wherever that is until we go to college. We're still going to apply to the same colleges, aren't we?"

"That's my plan," I said.

"If it bothers you at all, I can still turn down the adoption? I'll do whatever you want."

"No. You need Alonzo and he needs you. I'd never interfere with that. I'm just being silly."

"I just want to be around you."

I smiled. He put his arm around me.

"It will be so nice when we don't need to worry about anything but our parents," I said.

"Just so you know. No matter what our parents do, you will always be a girlfriend and not a sister to me."

"Same here. Or you know what I mean."

"Yeah."

"I'd like more time with you where nobody will walk in before tomorrow." My biggest regret about possibly dying on the steps of the Capitol was all the moments I wouldn't have with Santana.

"Me too. Let's get out of here."

He grabbed a pillow and two blankets and guided me down into the tunnels and we wound up in a room below Healy, I think. But he didn't stop there. He put one blanket over our heads and took me outdoors to a secluded spot under some bleachers. We laid down on one blanket, partially hid under the other, and peaked through the bleachers at the stars. He pointed out his favorite constellations and talked about stories and myths of lovers who had been separated and found each other again.

"Most of the Greek myths ended unhappily for lovers. I don't want to wind up like that."

"Let's create our own myth," he suggested.

"You start."

"I know. Once there was this beautiful princess. She was the most beautiful princess that had ever lived. And there was this prince, who had never met a girl that really excited him. He wasn't interested in guys either."

I laughed.

"Anyway, this prince was sent to a nasty dungeon where there were monsters that sucked the blood out of people. He was afraid he would never find a beautiful princess."

He looked at me.

I continued the story. "A princess was being forced to marry a rich jerk that she didn't love. She felt that if she didn't, her father would hate her. He told her it was her duty. But she didn't marry the rich jerk, and so he sent her to the dungeon, too."

"And then the prince saw her and instantly fell in love."

"But he was really mean to her." I crunched my nose.

"That was because the monsters would only let him be around her if they thought he didn't like her."

"And she hated the way he talked to her, but every time she looked at him, something happened inside of her. And then she realized that he was the one who had risked his life to help her without her knowledge when she was thirsty and hungry."

"And that was because he loved her from the moment he saw her."

"And when she realized he was a really nice guy and was only pretending to be mean, she realized she loved him too."

"But then they had to escape to be together."

"There were others who needed protection. So, they took their friends, who were also prisoners, and escaped from the dungeon. And the handsome prince saved the princess's life over and over again."

"And she saved his."

"But they were not safe. The monsters came after them."

"But the prince and princess and their friends gallantly fought them off."

"Again and again and again."

"And finally, they got to be together."

"Forever and ever and ever," I finished.

"But it's not the end. It will never end. See those stars up there?" He pointed to a number of stars that looked as if, put together by themselves, they would form a heart. "That's our Constellation."

The sensations that went through my body were impossible to fully describe. I was tingling and at the same time had an image of our hearts being connected, turned into one. "I love you," I blurted out.

"I love you more."

"You want to bet?"

"Yeah," he said. "You're my heart, my center, my north, my south, my east, my west, my home, my world."

"And you're mine. Sometimes when I'm with you, I feel like there is only one of us."

"Namaste," he said.

"Yeah. Namaste, but more. I used to hear that true couples

completed each other, that together they were as one person. I get it with you."

"You are the most important part of me, the part without which I couldn't exist."

I laughed. No other guy I had ever met would say the things Santana was saying—even if he felt them. "A shrink would call us pathetic. But it feels good. I want to be with someone I feel this way about."

"If love is insanity, I'll take insanity," he continued. "As long as I'm willing to let you go if that's what you want."

"I don't want. But I also need to be willing to let you go if that's what you want."

"Never. I know that teens our age make all kinds of promises that they later change their minds about. It's not going to happen with me. This is real." The look in his eyes told me he meant it.

"It's probably because all we've been through has taught us what's important."

He leaned over and kissed me and the world stopped. I didn't want it to restart, not ever. I wanted to be like this for always. We didn't speak these words out loud, but we both knew that this might be our last night on Earth.

We lay there in each other's arms for hours, just staring at the stars, holding each other, whispering our love for each other.

I thought about what my life would have been like if I hadn't gone to the camp. It would have been awful. I would have lived a life I had hated, never again seeing my mom, never finding Santana and never helping to rescue my friends. The good that came out of my being kidnapped to Camp Torture was the most unlikely thing in the world and yet it almost made the nightmare worthwhile. If I had to go through it all again just to be with Santana, my mom and my friends, I gladly would have done so. And now, I might be able to save more lives.

Images of the fire and Paul and the blue team burning to death, of Sonya being gang raped and bleeding to death, of Jason being electrocuted, of Jamie dying by hanging and of the bodies of John and Charlie and the little kids' graveyard rushed to my mind. I pushed them away. I wanted only to think of Santana in these last moments.

A noise snapped us out of it. I sat up and looked around. "Sorry," Jimmy said. "Your mother had some fears that something had happened to the two of you. I just meant to check quietly to reassure her."

"What time is it?" I asked.

"It's one in the morning. We're going to be up by eight."

"Promise me that you won't do anything stupid tomorrow," I said to Santana. "I want to be back here or somewhere with you tomorrow night."

"Let's both promise we will do what it takes to be together after tomorrow and forever."

"I promise."

"The only thing that would get in my way of being with you tomorrow is if I have to protect you with my life."

"Don't! Please don't," I implored him. "Stay safe and I'll stay safe."

"Deal." He kissed me and I kissed him back, silently praying that this wouldn't be our last night together. He helped me up and escorted me back with his arm draped around me as mine was around him.

At my room, he kissed me goodnight. As I stepped in, my mom gave me a hug. "I was young once. But I was never in a situation like this, and I never had what you and Santana have. I know it must be hard for you to say goodnight with tomorrow coming up."

"It is. Thank you for understanding, Mom. Would it disappoint you if I said 'I'm scared?'"

"I'd be scared if you weren't scared. I've never been prouder. I keep asking myself what I did to deserve a daughter as incredible as you."

"I love you, Mom."

"I love you, too."

The morning began with Santana knocking on the door. My mom opened it. He brought in a tray of food for me and my mom.

What do you do with a guy who brings you breakfast in bed? I asked myself.

As my mom pulled out the change of clothes Duane had brought her the night before, she said. "Take good care of my daughter today. I'll be at the Capitol, but you two always seem to wind up with extra plans."

"I will protect her with my life," Santana assured her.

"You better not," I reacted. "Remember your promise of forever." I looked at my mom, whom I knew was listening to every word while pretending not to.

"I want you both safe," my mom said, going into the adjoining bathroom to change. Abigail's and Emily's room was connected on the other side. "I'll be with Abigail and Emily."

After she left, Santana sat on the bed and started spoon-feeding me some fruit. This guy was so unbelievable. "Amorcito, Tu Eres mi vida y tu me vuelves loca."

"I think you just told me that I drive you crazy?"

"I also said you are my life. And yes, you do drive me crazy."

"Not as crazy as you drive me. Together, forever."

"Together forever," he repeated.

Santana went to check on Bruce and Alejandro while I got dressed. We all met in the Fourth Floor Lounge. Shane had taken off early, along with Reggie for part B of our plan, picking up the students when they arrived.

Mary Jo was bright and sparkly. As previously decided, John would accompany Mary Jo and Abigail to the White House in one of the police cars Mack and David had driven to D.C.. Bruce again said he wanted to go along to make sure that Abigail was safe, but John and Duane pointed out that, even disguised, two Wilderness Five teens would be more identifiable than one. John assured Bruce he would keep Abigail safe. He reminded Bruce about the facial ID technology that, when at its best, in places like D.C., could generally get around disguises.

We prepared for an impromptu press conference later that day at the Capitol. We planned to dress as priests and nuns, hoping they hadn't caught onto our trick, just to get across town. We planned to get lost among the crowd if anyone was watching.

Another surprise was that Jimmy had paid his friend in the L.A. area big bucks to teach him how to print fake IDs. He printed us all Washington State Drivers' Licenses. The TSA didn't accept them for airlines, thanks to the Real ID Act (or rather no thanks to the Act), but we weren't flying that day. We just needed to get to the Capitol and, if necessary, escape to the Cuban Embassy, hoping it did not bring war upon the friendly country.

All was well until Jimmy's phone rang. He put it on speaker. It was Joey's phone calling, but Darren was the one speaking. "Taylor said she was sure Mary Jo was the one who took the flash drive. And she said she saw Mary Jo sneaking off to see someone who looked sort of like a fed before she left for Washington."

"Mary Jo!" I exclaimed.

"Mary Jo knew most of the plans. But Taylor didn't know about the plans for the White House as we were keeping everyone who didn't have a major role on need-to-know. Taylor thought the reason Mary Jo took off early was to meet the fed. Taylor didn't want Joey to be hurt by learning about the guy. When Mary Jo didn't make it back to catch the train, Taylor felt she needed to tell me so that I could carefully explain to Joey about her not showing. Look we need to run or we're going to miss catching everyone at the depot."

"Right. Keep everything on the need-to-know. See you there," Jimmy replied.

Bruce was beside himself. We tried to call John, but there was no answer on his cell. "We need to get to the White House."

Duane agreed. "If more than a few of you go, you'll be more easily spotted. Santana, Summer, Bruce, I'll escort you and Father Durham to the White House. I could use a legitimate priest. Emily, Shannon, Jimmy, Father Browning and Katherine, can you handle the Capitol?"

We all nodded consent to Duane's plan.

Attired as a nun and priests, Santana, Bruce and I got into the back of a Philadelphia police car, along with Father Durham in the front. David Sands, Norman Cummings and Mack Highland would be staying with the others.

We all knew we could die but, if we didn't get there in time, so could Abigail. Duane had a police radio on, listening to any alerts.

He briefly turned on NPR.

"We have a special report. A train carrying hundreds of students has exploded in Pennsylvania."

I froze.

CHAPTER 41

"¡Mierda y doble mierda!"

"The explosion has left very little behind."

"No!" I thought of the loss of life. *This can't happen.* Had the plan gone awry? Santana held my hand. Mary Jo would have known about the planned train ride. Once again, we hadn't been able to circumvent trouble, and our plans to save lives had done the opposite. We certainly hadn't been able to save the train and whoever was on board.

"The identities of the passengers are not currently available. There were transfers, but it is believed that students from most of the northeastern colleges, Harvard, Yale, Brown, Columbia, NYU, Princeton, Penn State, Bryn Mawr and Havertown were traveling towards Washington D.C. We will bring you more on this later."

I was sobbing as Santana held me.

"They vaporized the train. You think it was something like Athena?" There had been a Lockheed advertisement selling the Athena plane to the U.S. Government. It was silent and the laser was invisible. In the ad, the object below was there one minute and gone the next without a trace of what had disappeared it.

"Lasers are directed light. It could have caused a chain reaction explosion. It seems more likely it was a missile," Bruce, who was usually calm, exclaimed, "Abigail! We have to get to Abigail."

I found myself praying. Even though I wasn't Catholic, I was hoping there was some kind of God up there, somewhere, and that the presence of the priests would help. Santana used an additional burner phone that Duane had picked up. He tried calling Shane, Joey, Professor Brand and Professor LaMont. Their phones went straight to voicemail.

Then he tried calling Jimmy and put it on speaker. "Yeah, we heard. Nobody is picking up. Let's hope no news is good news. You could be heading into a trap."

"We have to save Abigail!" I cried.

"We're not turning back," Bruce declared.

We pulled into the White House gate. "I have three priests and a nun who want to bless the President and join him in praying for those students on the train," Duane told the guard.

"Just a minute," the guard said.

We waited. They weren't waving us through. Some military personnel came out of the White House and got into several jeeps. They drove towards the gate.

I thought back to the planned coup to replace the Chiefs of Staff. Had it already happened?

The driver of the first jeep spoke to the guard and then to Duane. "You're Officer Duane Redland from Philadelphia?"

"Yes, I am."

"We need you and your passengers to follow us. Do not deviate from the route. We have three additional military jeeps that will be beside and behind your vehicle."

I noticed that the passengers in the jeeps were armed with riot or attack gear and were carrying very large guns. I knew Duane wasn't going to do anything funny.

Will we disappear into permanent indefinite detention? We were wanted for violations of the Espionage Act of 1917, a capital offense.

We tried to reach Jimmy, but suddenly we no longer had any signal on either Duane's phone or the burner phone we were using.

Santana held my hand tightly in a seeming attempt to reassure me.

I wondered if Mary Jo had told them about Georgetown and if troops would be pouncing on Copley Hall. Was my mother in danger, along with the rest?

"It will be alright, my children," Father Durham said. "Have faith."

"It's kind of hard to have faith when assault weapons are being waved around," Santana responded.

"Remember Daniel and the lion's den."

"I'd prefer lions to being surrounded by guys with guns," I replied.

"They might try to make you disappear, but there are people on my force who will ask questions if I disappear," Duane said.

"Do you think Roger is okay?" I asked him. Duane hadn't said much since the radio bulletin came on.

"Yeah. I think he's okay. I'd feel it if he weren't. Friday night was the first time his car had ever been stolen. That car thief saved my son's life. Makes me wonder if maybe your group is blessed."

"But the train. If people died because they were trying to stop us," I lamented.

"You aren't responsible for the evil deeds of others," Father Durham said.

"Your father blamed you for a lot of stuff, didn't he?" Duane asked me.

"Oh yes. If everything wasn't perfect, it was my fault."

"I've tried to let my son know that, whatever happens, he is still a good kid, and to do better next time if he fails."

"I really admire Abigail. She rebelled and did a lot of stuff I never had the courage to do."

"You want to dye your hair green?" Santana asked. "I'd still love you, but I prefer your hair's natural color."

"Maybe blue. Until the camp, blue was my favorite color."

"I cringe every time I see a blue shirt," Bruce reacted.

"What you kids must have been through. And you are still out there, trying to save teens currently in the camps. You could have stayed safe in Cuba. I understand other countries have also offered you asylum," Duane said.

I knew much of our discussion was for distraction. Inside the car, we couldn't be sure that any of us or anyone else was safe.

Our vehicle was escorted into a warehouse and the door was shut. "We should have brought Shane with us. Maybe he could talk warehouse to the army," Santana tried to joke.

The man from the lead jeep got out and came back to us. "Would you please follow me." His armed buddies stood by our car as we got out. They all escorted us to a room with chairs and desks.

Inside were Abigail, Mary Jo, John and two other military guys with big guns, who stood up as we entered and saluted our military escort. I ran to Abigail and hugged her. Bruce was right behind me. I moved aside so he could hold her in his arms.

The officer in the lead looked at Duane's holster and said, "I'll need to take your gun."

"I'm a police officer, and I don't give anyone my gun without a name and a reason."

"My name is Captain Carlton. I think I outrank you. We don't want any trouble."

"Detaining us is trouble."

"May we please have your gun, sir?"

Duane seemed to think about it for a second before handing over his gun.

"They got mine too," John informed him.

The military men at the front sat down again.. Captain Carlton and the men following him left.

"What's going on here?" Duane asked John.

"Your guess is as good as mine. They stopped us at the gate and brought us here."

I looked at the men who had been seated at the front of the room when we arrived. They were the men from the jeep who picked up my mother and me. I believed one was a lieutenant and the other was a corporal.

"I saw you two yesterday," I told them.

The corporal nodded, but otherwise they didn't reply.

"They picked my mom and me up at the Potomac and escorted us as far as Healey."

"Thank you guys for giving my friend a good escort. You can drop us off at Healey or some other nice spot if you like," Abigail proposed.

The men didn't show any reaction or emotion.

I looked at Mary Jo. "So how much did you tell them?"

"Nothing. They brought us here."

"I mean before."

"I told my mom I wanted to tour the White House with my roommate and that I'd be coming to town today. Of course, she isn't my real roommate."

"Your real roommate claims you took Joey's flash drive."

"What? Taylor said that?"

"And she said you met with a fed."

Mary Jo's mouth opened wide, giving the appearance of shock.

"The train blew up," I continued.

"No?" she cried. "Joey was—is he alright?"

"I don't know. They say hundreds of students were killed."

"No!" she exclaimed, seemingly in shock. She was very convincing.

"We have to get out of here." She turned to one of the men watching us. "My boyfriend was on that train. I need to know if he is hurt."

Santana watched her, seemingly appraising the situation. "There is a mole somewhere at Columbia."

"You think it's me?" She stood up and slapped him.

He shook it off, came over to me and whispered, "I believe her."

"So do I," I whispered back. "And that means we have no idea who the mole is."

Santana put his arm around me. It probably looked weird, given that he was wearing a priest's robe and I was wearing a nun's habit. Bruce, also dressed as a priest, had his arm around Abigail.

Clearly we were from a provocative sect of Catholicism—or not. It probably didn't matter as I was sure they had already made us. We were told to sit down.

Duane and John had their arms folded and were studying the guards and the room.

Father Durham pulled out his Bible and appeared to be praying.

"What do you think they intend to do with us?" I whispered to Santana.

"At least, this isn't the same crew that was torturing people or trying to drug the kids in the camp," Santana said cheerfully, undoubtedly for my benefit.

"They seem to be waiting for something."

"Maybe the torture crew," he quietly replied. I got the impression he was joking, but it wasn't funny, given the circumstances. "Just so long as they don't separate us."

"So far, they seem to be bringing us together."

I could hear sounds outside the room.

"Why are you bringing me here?" It was my mom's voice. "We have rights."

"Sir, I want an attorney if you are going to detain us." That was Jimmy.

"Ow. Young lady, please do not kick me, again."

"Let us go and you won't get kicked again." That was Emily.

"And if you do anything to Emily, I'll kick you, myself." That was Alejandro.

The door opened and the others were brought into the room. The newcomers were Jimmy, Shannon, Emily, Alejandro, my mom and Father Browning.

One positive thing was that nobody was touching or handcuffing any of us. I had read about interrogations where the key factor was whether the person was free to leave. I was certain we weren't. Though, unlike Chelsea Manning, we hadn't been stripped and forced to stand naked in a cell for hours at a time.

Is this all to create a false sense of security or so that Kreskin can come in, machine guns firing and eliminate us, along with his daughter?

"Darling," my mom uttered.

I got up and went over to hug her. "At least, we're alive so far and we haven't been hurt or injured."

"What is going on?" my mom asked.

"None of us made it inside. We were brought here from the gate. And personally, I believe Mary Jo when she says she isn't the mole."

"Taylor," Mary Jo growled. "She's the one who lied about me. She showed up late for the semester and walked in like she owned the place, putting the moves on Darren."

"Wasn't Taylor with the students who were coming in from Columbia?" Jimmy asked.

"Have you been able to get hold of Joey?" Santana replied with a question.

"Just his voicemail."

"Call him back and leave a message. Something like, 'Don't trust Taylor.' If he's alive and he better be, maybe he'll listen to it," I suggested. "If our phones are working again.".

Why weren't any of our friends from Columbia answering when we were able to make calls? They can't be gone. And here we are captives. We need to be finding them.

But there was no way to do so. Though we weren't cuffed, the guns were enough of a deterrent that we weren't likely to leave.

We sat and waited. My mom tried to make a phone call. At least, whatever had been jamming our cell reception before had ended. The corporal came over and said, "We need to remove your telephones, at least temporarily."

In the camps, we hadn't had access to working phones either. At one point, Marco had handed me my cell phone back with the unremovable battery removed.

"We have a right to an attorney," Santana said. "I have *The Bill of Rights* memorized. 'Congress shall make no law respecting an Establishment of religion or interfering with the free exercise thereof or—'"

"My parents will pursue my disappearance as will Shannon's," Jimmy declared.

"I am familiar with *The Bill of Rights*. For now, just hold on. Someone will be in here to speak with you, shortly," the lieutenant replied.

Half an hour passed, and still nobody was there to explain what was going on or whether this was an indefinite detention.

I thought back to the case of Tammy Rief, which I had checked out more thoroughly over the Net after my escape. She had gone to Hillary Clinton's Secretary of State's office to give them information proving her son had been internationally sex trafficked through the San Diego Superior Court to a ring operating out of Australia. Then she went home to Alabama and to a beauty parlor to have her hair done. At the beauty parlor, an off-duty sheriff who happened to be a Grand Dragon in the KKK, along with someone who had flown in from San Diego, where public officials were believed to have actively participated in the international sex trafficking of Tammy's son, raided the parlor. The Grand Dragon deputy sheriff told the beauty salon owner she and her family would be killed if she told anyone they had grabbed Tammy. Despite the death threats, the beauty salon owner talked, and Tammy's family found out what had happened to her. Tammy was held in solitary indefinite detention for ninety-one days before being illegally taken to San Diego for a longer lock-up, a secret jury selection and other unlawful proceedings, all in violation of the *U.S. Constitution.*

Is this what will happen to us? Are we going to just disappear? There was no beauty salon owner to notify anyone of our disappearance. But there were a lot of us, and we would be missed.

Finally, I asked, "Is this one of those NDAA indefinite detention things?"

We all watched the redundant response. "You'll get answers shortly." After speaking to us, the lieutenant started studying his own phone for text messages.

"So far, they haven't water-boarded us or stripped and tied us to a tree yet. That in itself is good news," I said.

"That's coming," Jimmy joked. Shannon gave him a dirty look.

My mom gave me a hug. "I'm so sorry I didn't save you from camp."

"At least, I made friends and I might be able to save more lives. Or at least, I was hoping to save more lives before we wound up here."

"You will," she tried to reassure me. "Alonzo will be looking for us and Shannon and Jimmy's parents will fight for their kids." She looked at the troopers. "This is bound to become an international incident, too, if you don't let these kids go."

"I want to, again, assert my Constitutional right to an attorney," Jimmy demanded.

"As do I," Santana echoed.

"Didn't your father vote for the NDAA?" Jimmy asked him.

"Sí, mi padre es un cerdo."

"I'll second that sentiment. Nuestros padres son puercos grandes." Abigail glared.

"Let's acknowledge that all our fathers are pigs," I stated.

My mother was trying to look neutral, but I could tell she was holding back a laugh.

"My dad is okay?" Jimmy said. "He and Shannon's and Alejandro's dads are excluded from the pig comment."

"I'll second that," I related. "Your dads are really cool."

Duane and John weren't joining in the conversation.

"And the fathers here are good guys," Santana said.

"But they don't have any real children," Abigail pointed out. "So, they can't be Padres Puercos."

"There might be some who would disagree with you about me," Father Durham told her.

"I can be a real puerco at times, particularly early in the morning." Father Browning commented.

A few minutes later, Captain Carlton came back in the room, closed the door, and said something I couldn't hear to the guy I suspected was the Lieutenant.

The Captain turned towards us. "I understand you provided some emails between some generals, Mr. Hattan and Secretary of Defense Kreskin. We would like to know more about how those emails were acquired."

We didn't say anything. We certainly didn't want anyone to get into trouble for illegal hacking. The government always seemed to care less about truth than about punishing whistleblowers and anyone telling the truth.

"I'd like to speak to my attorney," Jimmy said. "That's not an admission of guilt. Just a Constitutional right."

"Don't worry about that."

"Is that what they told Bradley Manning?"

"We're trying to get at the truth."

"And I'd be happy to talk with you after I see my attorney," Jimmy replied.

"These are kids," my mother said. "They are not criminals. They are on your side."

"Clearly, there is some confusion here."

"Okay. Go," I said. "Unconfuse us."

There was a knock at the door. The lieutenant went to open it. He saluted someone outside the door.

General Nester walked through the door. We all stood. "I hope my men haven't been overzealous," he said.

"Sir, what is going on?" I asked.

"Those emails indicate a matter of treason may be taking place. Now, you are all minors and I'm sure we can forget what method was used to gain access to them if we can verify that they are valid. Tell us what you know."

"It seems that Hattan's password to his email is coup1now. Kreskin's is mklpf10. From there you can see what the generals are saying, if they haven't changed their passwords," Jimmy expounded.

"Our fathers were included in those emails, and so technically it's not hacking," Emily said.

"I'll accept that. But this is a very serious matter. We can't just accuse the Secretary of Defense of planning a coup."

"What about the generals?" Santana asked.

"An hour ago, I put them into a brig after my men observed clear interactions with them and Hattan and a conversation that verified the plans indicated by those emails."

I looked at Emily. It appeared they had evidence on her father.

"We have reason to believe that Darkswamp is involved. The pretend attack on those bridges was orchestrated by Darkswamp," Bruce informed him.

"I saw the footage. Sometimes we wind up in bed with corporations that are not altruistic. There will be a recompense, but not a public one."

"Someone blew up a train," Jimmy interjected.

"We're looking into that and following the trail. We believe we can connect that to contractors who had special arrangements with those generals."

"Our friends were on those trains," Jimmy pointed out.

The Captain looked at his phone and whispered something to the General.

"I believe we have a special guest here."

The door opened and a guy, I had never supported but was glad to see, walked through it. Shannon's mouth opened very wide.

"Mr. President," General Nester said, saluting. "It is thanks to these teens that we have been able to stop a coup."

"But is it stopped?" Bruce asked.

"They were planning to put a mind-altering chemical into some air vents, wipe out certain people in the line of succession and put Kreskin in charge of the country. Do we know that that plan is off?" Jimmy asked.

The President replied, "I'm having the White House ventilation checked and members of Congress have been asked to meet outside the Capitol until the building and ventilation system are secured. I understand you have a demonstration planned."

"Yes, sir," I said. "But we're wanted individuals. Espionage Act, 1917."

"And Darkswamp has a habit of shooting lasers and directed energy weapons," Bruce pointed out.

"The military should be able to do something about that problem, can't it General?"

"We'll do what we can," Nester replied.

"I'd like something more certain," the President responded.

"Yes, sir."

"The Espionage Act," Jimmy reiterated.

"You're pretty smart kids. You've probably heard that I can pardon pretty much anyone I want."

We looked at each other.

"So today, I'm issuing eleven full pardons for everyone in this room."

This time, my mouth fell open.

"Thank you," we all said with Emily going first and the rest of us echoing.

We walked up to him and shook his hand.

"I will also be issuing some medals of honor. You are very brave youngsters. If you are interested, I'm sure there's a place for you in government service."

We nodded. Even if he wasn't the President I would have chosen, it was still an honor to be told that.

"And we do not discriminate against green hair," he chuckled as he looked at Abigail.

"What is going to happen to our fathers?" Emily asked.

"That is another matter. Are you worried about them?"

"They sent us to Gulag camps," Abigail declared. "Throw away the key."

"Some, but not all, of our fathers sent us to Gulag camps," Jimmy interceded.

The President laughed. "They'll have to have a trial first." That wasn't something I'd been expecting him to say. I didn't think he was big on trials.

"I am being helicoptered to the White House. If the Captain could take you to your event at the Capitol, I believe you have some speeches to make."

"We have friends who were taking a train here. We don't know how they are."

"I will have my people check into it."

We all started to walk out a back exit of the warehouse. There was a helicopter behind the building, but I didn't see anyone inside it.

We were accompanied by the officers who had been guarding us, the General and the Captain as we escorted the President to his helicopter. We were walking casually and the military personnel had warmed up to us, though they didn't say much of anything in the presence of the President. Abigail and Bruce were talking to the Captain as we proceeded.

From the side of the warehouse three figures emerged. They were Kreskin and two men in uniforms with guns pointed in our direction.

CHAPTER 42

Kreskin's gun was pointed directly at the President. "I wouldn't draw any weapons or you all lose your President."

"Today is D Day and you lose," Santana responded as he moved in front of me. Alejandro moved in front of Emily and Bruce moved in front of Abigail, who was between me and the Captain. I tried to push Santana out of the way, but he held me behind him.

"Back away from my daughter," Kreskin ordered Bruce. "Get her," he told the men.

Kreskin's escorts, holstering their weapons, shoved Bruce, Santana, and me aside and grabbed Abigail from where she was standing next to Captain Carlton. Bruce got up and fought one of the men and got knocked back by the other with a blow across his face. He fell to the ground. This was followed by a kick to Bruce's head.

Santana jumped on the guy who had pushed me and they struggled as Abigail pulled free, went to Bruce and started to kneel down. But the one who had hit Bruce dragged Abigail away to her father. Santana's attacker knocked him back and pulled out his weapon, aiming it at Santana. So far, no shots had been fired.

It occurred to me that the moment shots were fired, the whole military would hear the shots and come raining down—unless they thought those were in the line of duty.

I said a silent prayer for Santana and Abigail as I tried to conjure up a plan. None came to me—except to rush between Santana and the gun, which I did, as he pulled me down, covering me with his body.

"Don't expect a reprieve, Mr. soon-to-be former President. I have witnesses that these terrorists pulled off the coup and were killed in self-defense. Of course, if it came out I shot you, the opposing party would declare me a hero, but anyone saying I did so would be a conspiracy theorist. And don't expect your Secret Service detail to save you. They're earning bigger bucks on my payroll and are busy being distracted, picking their noses. Now, my daughter. I'll give you an out. Do you have a hug for your old man?"

"Certainly," she said, smiling.

As Kreskin held the gun pointed at the President, his daughter gave him a hug that was interrupted by the sound of a gunshot.

Kreskin stumbled back as Abigail pushed up her father's gun in his weakened hand, causing the shot he then fired to miss. In her other hand was a gun.

Instantly the distraction was enough to give our escorts, minus the Captain time to draw their guns on Kreskin's escorts.

Father Durham checked Kreskin's pulse and shook his head.

I felt for Abigail. I rushed to her and gave her a hug.

"Good work," the President said, looking at the Captain.

The Captain replied. "I seem to be missing my gun. I hope there won't be any repercussions for allowing a minor to relieve me of it."

The President took a breath, looked up and then chuckled a strained laugh. "I think the repercussion is you'll have to join our heroes at the White House for a ceremony to give you all metals."

We smiled, but it was a mixed smile for me. I knew that Abigail must be hurting. No matter how much she hated her father, she also had to feel something for him.

Bruce got up and shakily rushed to Abigail. He pulled the gun out of Abigail's hand and put it on the ground like it was a vial of some disease and then he hugged her. "I love you," he said and then kissed her.

"I could get into this," Santana said, taking me in his arms and kissing me right in front of my mother and the President. We were joined in the event by Emily and Alejandro and Shannon and Jimmy.

"They should make a movie out of this. When I was a kid, all good movies ended with a kiss," the President said.

The General escorted the President to his helicopter and joined him inside. I had a feeling some Secret Service agents were about to get fired. The President again thanked us and waved as he and General Nester took off with the Lieutenant piloting.

We piled into a van outside the warehouse. The corporal returned our phones and gave Duane and John back their weapons and then got into the driver's seat. Captain Carlton got in back with us.

About ten minutes later, we all walked up the Capitol steps. A podium and microphone had been set up. Alonzo was next to the microphone. He gave my mom a hug as we all lined up to speak and support our friends.

Behind us, most of Congress was present, seemingly making a show of cheering us on.

"They got a message that there was a possible problem with the ventilation inside and were asked to stay out here," Alonzo explained.

"I suspect those on the payroll of the Pharmaceutical-Military Industrial Complex are not happy about this," I replied.

Over the speaking area was an awning with a mirror facing away from us. "That just might take care of any laser," Carlton, who had arrived to watch our speeches, informed us. "We also have planes flying up there, ready to shoot down any unauthorized aircraft, particularly aircraft flown by any defense contractors. But if you repeat that, I never said it." He gave me a hug. "Go get them."

There were ropes separating our area from crowds of students and their families. It was manned by the Capitol police. A burst of joy rushed through me as I saw Shane, Joey, Bob, Darren, Professor LaMont, Professor Brand, Genevieve, Clarence, Charles, and Everett pushing to get through. I waved at them to come forward and the Capitol police let them pass.

"Plan B worked," Joey said. "We got everyone already on the train into Shane's fleet of trucks just before Philly and Shane had more trucks waiting for the students arriving from elsewhere in Philly. Frank, Kevin and Clay, three more honest cops in Duane's department, used their positions as officers to assist the transfer. The plotters blew up a mostly empty train."

"I guess my paranoia wasn't really paranoia," Santana related.

"You're not paranoid if they're really out to get you," I said. "But what about the those left on the train."

"The students bought out almost all the seats on the train and most other customers were told to wait for the next train. In spite of our emptying the train, there were casualties, but the number was low," replied Shane.

"Any loss is one too many," I lamented.

The others nodded solemnly.

"Where is Taylor? She lied about Mary Jo," I related.

Darren didn't look happy to hear that.

"She was right here. I'm sure she'll surface, again."

"This is a huge crowd," Santana pointed out.

"When they blew up the train, a lot of parents caught the next flight to D.C.," Joey explained.

"Look my parents are here and so are Jimmy's," Shannon said.

"They didn't have enough time to fly in from the West Coast after the train announcement," Santana noted.

"I guess they were worried about us." Shannon and Jimmy ran past the ropes and hugged their parents. I went with them and got a hug as well.

A hand in the crowd reached out and grabbed my arm. It was Rosa. "Let her in," I told a Capitol Policeman. "In fact, let them all in. They're our friends."

Rosa hugged me and ran to Emily who was rushing down the steps to meet her. Rosa picked her up in her arms. "How's my little girl?"

"Bigger now."

"I can see that."

"I get to come up, too?" Roger, now in front, behind the rope, asked.

"You kidding? Your father is looking for you," I said. "Thank you for everything."

He smiled.

"You haven't forgotten me," came a voice I recognized in the crowd. I strained to look for her as I moved past the rope into the crowd, again. "Here," her voice came. Tiffany was standing with her parents and her little brother. "My parents insisted on coming along. "

"Come join us, all of you," I said to Tiffany and her family.

We walked up to the microphone. "You ready?" Santana asked.

The Capitol police pulled barriers forward to right in front of where the podium was on the steps.

"I'm ready," I said, butterflies bouncing in my stomach, as I prepared to charge through with my speech. With Santana at my side, I felt I could do anything. But before I could say anything more, I saw three of my heroes on the steps above, three former members of Congress were speaking with the other members of Congress. I put my hands to my face, barely able to hold in my excitement.

"How did they get here?" I asked.

"Well, kiddo," Alonzo said. "Since you were risking your lives to speak here we decided to ask the leaders you most admired, Dennis Kucinich, Cynthia McKinney, and Ron Paul, to come and join you. It was your mother's idea."

I waved at them and they waved back.

"And there is another surprise," Santana noted. He pointed to former Congressman George Miller moving through the crowd as students shook his hand. The police let him through, and he climbed up the steps to join the congressmen behind us.

I looked up at the mirrored arch I and the members of Congress stood under. It only provided superficial security. We could be lasered from the front or the side, if security was lax. It wouldn't stop a missile. I told myself we were safe, but I knew we weren't.

As we all stood behind the microphone, a man I recognized as Congressman Barillo walked up to us. "So, this is Summer. I am pleased to meet you."

"Get out of here," Santana practically growled. "You sent me off to be tortured."

"I didn't know what they would do."

"You knew. And I saw your speech at my funeral. Very touching. Is Angelo really dead, or was that a lie too?"

Congressman Barillo bowed his head a little. "We couldn't save him."

"I bet. There was no Engañar virus. You let them murder my brother. I never want to see you, again, as long as I live."

"I'm still your father."

"Not anymore," Alonzo stepped in and said, "The Cuban Government has terminated your rights and granted me full custody."

"This is America."

"And even in America, I'd die before I had anything to do with you again. I bet some of those out there are your constituents. Would you like to see what they think?"

Barillo walked away. As I turned to look behind us again, I saw another uninvited guest. I went over to Captain Carton and pointed out Emily's father. The Captain got on his cell. A minute later two soldiers came up and spoke with Hattan. I put an arm around Emily. "Are you alright?"

Rosa put an arm around Emily too. We stood there as what looked like an argument ensured. Hattan was escorted down the steps. He stopped as he passed where we were standing. "Emily, you are still a minor."

"She is my daughter, and I will not have you speak with her without her permission," Rosa firmly stated.

"She is not your daughter. She is mine, and my government will stand behind me."

"We'll see about that," Alonzo said.

"Mr. Hattan, sir," Alejandro jumped in. "I guess now is an appropriate time to mention that one day I plan to marry the girl who is no longer your daughter." I had to hold back a laugh, and I noticed Santana was trying his best to hold one back as well.

"Over my dead body."

"And you're not invited," Alejandro declared.

"Is my mother dead?" Emily asked.

"Yes." There was no emotion in his voice.

"Did you kill her?"

"How can you—" he started to say and then stopped talking. The soldiers escorted him away from the speaking area.

George Miller came down the upper steps and shook my hand and then the hands of my friends. He had previously met Santana at a Democratic gathering.

George Miller, a twenty-term Congressman, addressed the crowd.

"Years ago, I sponsored bi-partisan legislation to regulate behavior modification programs. These brave youngsters have come here today to tell you about what happens in these programs and why they need to be regulated. Summer Tanner, Santana Barillo, Abigail Kreskin, Bruce Jenkins and Emily Hattan."

The audience cheered. "I give you Summer Tanner."

I stepped up to the podium.

It was very quick. As she stepped from the crowd, I knew something was about to go down, but before I had time to react, Santana was standing between me and Arial. I tried to push him out of the way as multiple shots rang out.

CHAPTER 43

"Santana!" I screamed.

Santana was still standing, but Captain Carlton, who had jumped in front of both of us, fell to the ground. When I was able to look past Santana at where Ariel was standing, she was being held by Darren and Joey. A Capitol policeman had her gun.

An officer cable-tied her hands as several of the Congressmen, including George Miller, who was right by us, were leaning down and trying to assist Captain Carlton.

As the Capitol police pulled Arial away, I said into the microphone that hadn't been turned off. "Wait. They have been using mind control drugs on Ariel for months. She doesn't understand what she is doing."

"I understand it!" she shouted. "You destroyed our camp. They were making us into something, and you wrecked it."

"They were torturing and killing teens. You, yourself, were beaten and dangled off a cliff by a rope tied to your feet. Remember?"

"That was a learning experience," she shouted.

People in the audience uttered sounds of shock at her words. The police continued taking her from the scene. A path was cleared for paramedics to bring a stretcher up for Captain Carlton, who fortunately was conscious. He was having trouble speaking as they carried him away, but I could hear him get out the words, "Go for it, Summer."

"That's what they did to us. They tortured us and expected us to love them when they occasionally showed a minimal amount of mercy. I saw campmates die, brutally. They died by electrocution, hanging, burning to death, being shot by counselors, and bleeding to death after being gang raped. They had forced fights where students were encouraged to do real damage. A great many teens have died in these camps. They hog-tied us, stripped us, put us in boxes, dehydrated us, starved us, and forced teens to choke on our own vomit. A lot of girls are raped, and a great many teens and pre-teens die in these programs. But our camp was not unique. This is happening throughout the whole behavior modification system of camps, schools, treatment centers and other facilities. Every last one needs to be closed down.

"The problem is a basic one in our society. Teens are treated as property, chattels, who must behave in a certain way. It's only an additional step to torture them and tell yourselves you are doing it for their good. Courts regularly give children to violent rapists and abusers. Courts choose not to listen to the kids, not to care what the kids want, because they are kids and have no rights. Why must college students incur a lifetime of debt to take classes and why is there a charge for life-saving health care? Our government goes into other countries and bombs hospitals and schools. The majority of casualties in Afghanistan, Iraq, Libya, Yemen and Palestine have been women and children. It's time we minors have rights, starting with the right to vote and have a say in our government. If we are old enough to be forced into torture, then certainly we are old enough to elect our leaders and to run for office ourselves.

"It was the Columbia students who saved Manhattan a week ago. They stood up to the media's brainwashing and lies and put themselves at risk to take a stand for what was right. I don't know what happens to some people when they leave college. Too many become complacent, don't want to think, but even if you don't want to think for yourselves, don't listen to the corporate media con artists who make money off lying to you. Listen to your sons and daughters who are open-minded and fighting for all our rights. And it's time the USA adopted the United Nations Convention on Human Rights and joined the other member nations of the International Court of Criminal Justice."

The speech was a lot different from what I had intended to say. I suddenly realized that everyone was applauding very loudly. The crowd started chanting my name. Looking out at all the students and the parents, I realized that maybe America could heal the wrongs that had been committed against my generation.

Santana stepped up and got his own applause. "Isn't Summer great?" The crowd applauded. "I just told my father who sent me to the camp to take a hike." More applause from the crowd. "And yet it is complacent partisan voters who are willing to keep electing leaders who don't care about them. My father voted for the NDAA, again and again. He voted to fund genocides and to eliminate habeas corpus. If there is a reason to throw out members of the legislature, it should be their voting records that are diametrically opposed to the needs of the American people.

"We don't just need to regulate behavior modification programs. Summer is right. We need to close them down. We also need to arrest everyone who has been involved in torturing teens at those facilities. And all psychologists and school counselors who recommend sending children to these camps should be fired without tenure and/or have their licenses revoked. And the best way to clean everything up is to once again elect honest leaders who are not on the take, people like George Miller, Dennis Kucinich, Ron Paul and Cynthia McKinney.

"Ask yourself why you would vote for a candidate who has already voted to lock you up without rights or even a trial under the NDAA? Why would you vote for a candidate who does not support your right to health care while he or she is fully covered for life? Why would you vote for a candidate who thinks it's more important to invest in bombs than in you and your families?" Each sentence was met with more applause.

"As for parents, if they are real parents, why do they have to pay someone to kidnap you and take you to a place to be tortured so you will become the kind of child they want? Do people like that deserve any parenting rights? Shouldn't sons and daughters who have been shipped off to be beaten and tortured by others be able to determine who will educate them, who will raise them and what they will be when they grow up?"

The applause was thunderous by now. The crowd started chanting, "Close them down."

Bruce got up. "My parents are scientists, smart enough to know better, but that didn't stop them from sending me off to be tortured. My parents work for a program that is supposedly doing weather modification. But if our government would stop destroying the environment, why would the planet need weather modification? If you look at the patents on their project, it can be used as a deadly weapon. We need a ban on all weather modification devices and weapons that can be used on America and American citizens."

That drew a strong applause.

Abigail went up to the microphone. But right before she spoke, she turned, apparently seeing someone coming up beside her. "Philomena!" she exclaimed leaving the microphone to hug her former housekeeper. They were both crying. Tears were very rare for Abigail. I knew there was a really soft side to her, but as she cried, I got more of a glimpse of the little girl who just wanted someone to love her.

"Speak, carina. I'll stay right here."

"It's hard to speak when I'm crying," she whimpered. Alonzo gave Abigail a handkerchief, and she wiped her tears.

"I wasn't like Summer. I wasn't the perfect child, who got sent off to be tortured anyway. I was wild and rebellious. I didn't approve of what my father was doing. He was blowing up children in other lands. That isn't okay, and I coped by rebelling. So, my father, who was responsible for the deaths of thousands—maybe millions—of children, sent me off to be tortured for my offense of partying and dying my hair. I shouldn't speak ill of him. He's dead. I should feel bad that he's gone. Any death is terrible. But I can't help thinking of all the children who died as a result of what he did and all the dying that would continue at his hands if he were still alive. All young victims deserve to be mourned. I have also been told my mother is dead. She was kinder than my dad, but she didn't raise me. Too often, rich and powerful parents don't even raise their own kids. They are too busy being elitist public figures to know how to be parents. They don't have time to be good examples of human beings at home. So, they send their kids to Gulag camps or schools. Most of the teens at my camp were from rich families. What gives adults the right to send their children off to be starved, dehydrated, stripped, gagged, drugged and raped?

"Ariel, who just shot Captain Carlton, is an example of what these camps produce–if we let them break us. Having been practically eaten alive by guard dogs, I couldn't even walk when I left the camp. Paul Saunders, the son of the camp director, carried me to where my friends could help me escape. Then he died trying to rescue others. There are no doctors at those camps. I was given penicillin to which they knew I was allergic, but they didn't have much else. These camps and all the behavior modification programs are violations of the International Bill of Human Rights and of the Convention on the Rights of the Child. Every one of the Gulag School and Camp administrators should be brought before the Hague for crimes against humanity. Of course, this country needs to sign the ICJ. And Santana and Summer are right. Children should have the right to choose who raises them. My father sent away the one person who loved me, Philomena." She pointed to her former housekeeper. "Today has been insane but in so many ways, it's the happiest day of my life. And it will be even happier if—" She turned to the members of Congress who were standing above her. "If you will do something, today, to stop the torture of American kids and teens in behavior modification programs."

It wasn't just the crowd that was applauding. So were many current and former members of Congress at the top of the stairs.

Emily wrapped things up. She looked over at her father who was standing in handcuffs on the side with his military escorters, watching the event. They had apparently agreed to let him see what his daughter had to say.

"In addition to eliminating these programs, can we also disband the Council on Foreign Relations?" The applause was so thunderous and long that I thought it would never stop. "The CFR is the biggest terrorist organization on the planet." The applause got even louder.

There were shouts of "Right on" and "Speak, sister."

"I was thirteen when I was placed in the camp. I learned quickly to be cooperative. Those that weren't cooperative were subjected to the worst of the torture. Some even died. My friend Sonja was gang-raped under the supervision of the counselors and bled to death. What parent pays twenty thousand to seven hundred thousand dollars to have their child gang-raped? It's impossible to believe the parents don't suspect what is coming. If the camps were good places, we wouldn't have to be kidnapped. We'd go willingly. I'd like to see a memorial, a national monument, erected for all those who have died in these programs. Imagine what they would have become if they hadn't died. I'm going to read a partial compilation of names and the reported causes of death.

"Geoffrey Vorhies, age thirteen, Chris Scheck, age thirteen, Jonathan Avila, age sixteen, Ashley Shaddox, age fourteen, Chad Franza, age sixteen, Dionte Pickens, age fourteen, Ryan Lewis, age fourteen, Victoria Petersilka, age fourteen, Ian Mulhare, age sixteen, Karlyle Newman, age sixteen, an unknown male of sixteen, and an unidentified boy and girl of unidentified ages died by hanging."

Emily continued reading a long list of names, ages and causes of deaths, that included deaths by restraints, hanging, dehydration, electrocution, lack of medical treatment for fatal conditions, suffocation, being shot trying to escape, suicides, fire, downing, heat exposure, freezing, and many other unnatural causes. After reading the list, she concluded. "This was just a partial list of the deaths that have been reported. Each of these lives and others who died in these programs mattered. I ask the members of Congress out there to ensure these young Americans will not have died in vain."

We all surrounded Emily. She looked at me, indicating that she wanted me to say something.

I did. "Let's all have a minute of silence for these and all other victims of these Gulag camps, schools and facilities."

A couple of members of Congress whispered something to George Miller. At the end of the moment of silence, he spoke again. "I have been told that legislation has been introduced in both houses to stop these abuses and that there will be a resolution calling for the erection of the monument Emily has called for." More cheers went up from the crowd. "What has happened to American teens in these programs has cast a dark cloud over America's commitment to human rights. Let's show the world we can do better."

After the event, we went back to Georgetown, along with our Columbia friends, Genevieve, the professors, the priests, officers who assisted us, my high school friends and their families, my mom, Alonzo, Philomena, Rosa, Shane and Roger. The university made accommodations for all of us. As we were celebrating, Ambassador Sanchez showed up with a four-legged friend who jumped into my arms, practically knocking me down.

"We got special permission to bring Hope into the country."

It was like old family week. While I had been glad that Hope was out of danger, I had really missed him. He had saved my life more than once when we were escaping the camp.

As Juanita and Alvaro Martina walked in the door, Alejandro hung his head a little as he walked up to his parents. His dad looked like he was going to lecture Alejandro on taking off to the States, but then gave him a hug, followed by a hug from Alejandro's mother.

Ina, Medhi and the Tunesian Ambassador arrived. "Thank you for saving our lives," I told them.

"We're all part of the same family," Ina said.

We got word that Captain Carlton had made it out of surgery. Emily's father had been denied bail because of the seriousness of his offense. The Democratic leaders were, again, calling on Congressman Barillo to resign from Congress. Word was he had, again, refused. Missing from everything were Santana's mother and Bruce's parents.

Shannon explained. "I looked up Santana's mom. His dad has a stay-away order preventing her from seeing her son, just like happened to your mom."

"Our next step should be to reform the family law system to allow mothers to be mothers."

General Nester dropped by to speak with my mom. It looked serious. They came over to me, and he addressed me. "Good work,

Summer. You are a beautiful young lady. I expect great things from you." He walked off to speak with my fellow escapees.

"Are you going to be in any trouble because of that restraining order?" I asked my mom whose eyes were starting to tear up a little.

"No. But I am going to have to take care of that before we go back to California."

"We're going back to California?"

"If you want. There's no hurry."

"What about Alonzo?"

"I haven't said 'yes,' yet."

"Do you love him?"

She avoided answering. "But there is you and Santana, and I want to do the right thing."

"Santana and I are fine. It's time, you had some happiness, too."

"How would you feel about going to Italy?"

"Italy?"

"Alonzo might get a diplomatic position there. He plans to speak to Santana about it."

"If Santana is going to Italy, I guess I need to learn to speak Italian. But what about my other friends?"

"I'm sure we can figure something out, if we wind up going there."

"What are the universities like in Italy? We all passed our GEDs, and I might be able to get into college there. I am still planning to study veterinary medicine."

"We'll check. I know Cuba has some excellent programs. Lifespans are longer in Italy than the U.S. It probably has good medical and veterinarian schools."

I went over to Darren, who looked a little down. "I'm sorry about Taylor turning out to be a plant," I said.

"That was a shock. But I've got a long way to go to get through medical school. It would have been a bad idea to get serious at this stage."

"Right." I gave him a hug. "And you're a great guy. Any girl would be lucky to have you."

"You think?"

"I think."

"Just not this one," Santana said from behind me.

I laughed and gave Santana a hug. "Have you talked to Alonzo?"

"I told him that I would only go to Italy if you went to Italy. Together, forever."

"Together, forever. Can you teach me Italian? It's not that far from Spanish."

"We can learn it together."

"I like that," I said, as he gave me a kiss, right in front of everyone.

Dr. LaMont and Professor Brand were clearly hitting it off well. She kissed his cheek. At one point, Professor Brand went over to Genevieve. I didn't know what he said to her, but she looked very excited and hugged him.

As I walked over to her, I could see she was wiping away tears from her eyes but had seemed happy at what he had told her. "It looked like you got some good news or did you?"

"The best. I've been offered a fellowship at Columbia. I'll be able to do research and teach physics. I owe it all to you and your friends."

"No, you don't. You got that on your own merit."

"I never would have met Professor Brand and the Columbia staff if not for you putting us together. Thank you. You have given me back my dream and my purpose."

I hugged her. Santana and Emily walked up. "What's up?" Santana asked.

"Tell them."

"I'm going to be teaching at Columbia."

"That's wonderful. Then I'll have a reason to go to Columbia. I passed my GED," Emily told her.

"I think that Rosa would like you to live a little first," I advised her.

"You don't think I've lived a little these past months, what with the camp and being on the run?"

"I think she wants you to enjoy being fourteen for a little while. Columbia will be there when you are ready for it."

"Maybe Rosa can come to New York with me."

"Maybe." I had a feeling Ricardo Sanchez would arrange it, if necessary.

I noticed that Bruce was very attentive to Abigail. He was probably afraid that she would get depressed when confirmation of her mother's death and her shooting of her father sunk in. It would probably be rough at times for her, but she and Bruce had something very real and she had been reunited with Philamena.

Shannon, Jimmy and Tiffany were running around making sure everyone was having fun. Jimmy was handing out food and Shannon and Tiffany were trying to get people to dance. "Thank you," I told them.

"We didn't do anything for you that you wouldn't do for us," Shannon said.

"You saved my life and you brought my mom back to me. Then you saved me again and again. I am so lucky that you are my friend."

"Hey, you were there for me when the other kids ignored me and kind of shunned me at school. You had a big part in helping me become who I am."

"And Jimmy, you're a great guy. But at Columbia, you better be loyal to my best friend or I'm coming after you."

"New York is terrible for surfing. I'm going to be spending all my vacations in California with Shannon. Besides, when have you known me to look at any girl but your best friend?"

"True."

My mom and Alonzo announced their wedding plans, and the event turned into a real celebration. My mom, apparently, had taken my advice.

"You may be my step-brother, but you are not my brother."

"And you're not my sister," Santana agreed, giving me a hug.

At the end of the evening, everyone was happy.

After I said goodnight to Santana, I came back to my room to find my mom was already there, waiting for me.

"Darling. I didn't want to say anything during the celebration, but General Nester did some checking on something for me and I need to tell you."

I sat down. It looked serious and I suspected I knew what it was. "Is it about Daddy?"

"He's gone. I'm sorry."

"Abigail told me about him, but I knew they were faking some deaths. I don't have any feelings about him. I should, but I don't. Every time I think of him, I think of what he did to you and me. Am I an awful person?"

"No. You've been through so much. Once, there was a good side to him. I don't know if it was real or fake but there was some good there."

I nodded. "I'm glad I have you. And Alonzo is wonderful. I am so glad you said 'yes.'"

"Me too."

The next day, we were to go to the White House for a medal ceremony. It wasn't just us five. He was also giving medals to those who had helped us stop the coup. It was to be a large ceremony.

I was getting ready to leave for the event when there was a knock at my door. I wondered if it was Santana or one of the others. Mom opened the door. It was Pandar.

"Hi, Pandar, it's good to see you. I hope you are well," Mom said.

Pandar walked right past her, pretending she wasn't even there. "Hi, sis."

"Hi. You're really going to ignore Mom, like that?"

"It's fine," my mother said. "I need to see Alonzo. You look good, Pandar. Take care of yourself." She went out and gently closed the door, seemingly to give us some privacy.

"They read Dad's will this morning. You didn't come."

"No, I didn't. I don't care about his will."

"That's funny. He left everything to you."

"What? He hated me. You were his favorite."

"He signed it when you were dating Matt. It was part of some kind of deal with Matt's dad. He just never got around to changing it."

I was more than a little stunned.

"If you don't want the money, you can refuse it."

I looked at Pandar, the brother who had let my dad almost kill my mom, who had ignored the beatings I had received, who didn't care that my father had sent me off to be tortured.

"No. I'm going to take the money. It's got to be in the millions. I'm going to give half to eliminating the camps and the other half to the person who really deserves it, who took his beatings and only showed us love, our mother."

"And what about me?"

"You get what you gave. You are so much like our father, it's unbelievable. Do me a favor and close the door on your way out, and don't come back through it."

"But, sis."

"Goodbye, Pandar. And this time, make it a last goodbye. I don't want to see you again."

He started to speak and then turned towards the door. "One day, you'll wish you had a brother."

"I lost my brother, long ago," I said. "But I've gained several real brothers."

As he opened the door, Santana came through. "Want me to throw out the trash?"

"I already did. Bye, Pandar."

"I hope you and your lowlife friends fry. I understand that Mickey Comet announced that you've been charged with the Espionage Act. That includes the death penalty."

"Let me assist you out," Santana said, grabbing Pandar by the collar, pushing him out the door and slamming it behind him. "Guess he didn't hear the announcement that went out earlier today that the President has signed our pardons."

"You would think the son of a former Gubernatorial aid would know that the death penalty is not applicable to minors, anymore. I used to think he was perfect, not real perfect but obnoxious perfect."

"As it turned out, you were the one that was perfect, and you just didn't know it," he said, putting his arms around me. I pulled his face towards mine and kissed him. It was meant to be a quick kiss, but I found that I couldn't stop kissing him. There was something mesmerizing about him that got to me every time.

"I love you," we both said at the same time as the kiss was followed by a hug.

"It's been confirmed that my dad is dead," I informed him.

"Are you alright?"

"Yeah. He was never a real father. And now I've got my mother back, the parent who really loves me."

"And I've got a new father I respect. When we were in that camp, who would have thought it could turn out this way." He stood back. "You're going to be the most beautiful girl in the world when you receive your medal at the White House. I'm going to be the envy of every guy who sees you on TV."

"Like all the girls watching won't be salivating for a shot at you."

"I only have eyes for you."

"We better get going before you distract me so much I'll forget about the ceremony."

There was a knock before my mom opened the door. "You ready to go?"

"As ready as I'm going to be," I said.

At the White House, we were all escorted into the Oval Office for a special ceremony. Hope accompanied us. There were video cameras inside from various news services. The mainstream news media had boycotted our event at the Capitol, but were out in force at the White House. Only a few newsmen were allowed inside due to lack of space. Diego, our favorite reporter from Cuba, was one of them.

Captain Carlton entered in a wheelchair with an IV and some monitors attached. At his side was a physician.

"They released you?"

"No, they just brought me here. I'm not allowed to exert myself. Right after the ceremony, I'm back in the hospital, flat on my back."

At the start of the ceremony, the President again stated, in front of the TV cameras, that we were all pardoned. He announced to the world that Abigail had saved his life, though he was surprisingly tactful enough not to say how. He called her America's greatest heroine.

Mickey Comet was not in the room, though reports of her death had also been overstated or else she was on her second life. She was probably busy hoping everyone would forget her earlier comments.

The President held up the pardon documents for the cameras and gave us copies.

The cameras zeroed in as I and my friends from the camps and those who had assisted us in defeating the coup got our medals. Genevieve was sparkling as she got hers. It was so good to see her finally getting the recognition she deserved.

The President had another announcement. He held up an executive order, closing all teen behavior modification camps, schools and programs for the press to see. "Congress could take years to pass the proper legislation," he informed us.

Before we left the Oval Office, the President asked to speak with Santana, Abigail, Bruce, Emily and me privately.

"You kids are young, but you have proven that you are survivors with high morals and the skills to get good results. Our intelligence agencies could use you. We could even set up a special division for your group. We would protect your safety while allowing you to work on important federal matters."

I didn't know what to say. Santana answered for me. "That's a wonderful offer, sir. May we have time to think about it and discuss it among each other?"

"Take all the time you need. You've been through a major, really major, bigly experience. Get back to me when you've had recovery time."

EPILOGUE

Before we left D.C., I had a visit from the lieutenant who had been guarding us at the warehouse. With him was a black German shepherd. "My name is Lieutenant Tarley. I'm sorry I didn't feel free to speak the other day. I knew my superiors were planning to explain things, and I didn't want to say anything that might contradict them."

"It all turned out well," I replied.

"I'm here for another reason. I understand you are good with dogs."

"Dogs?"

"You adopted a wild dog at the camp, tamed it and gave it the love it needed."

"Hope's a great dog. He adopted me."

"I have a dog that I picked up over in Afghanistan that I can't take back with me on my duty in the upcoming war. I need someone to take care of her. She's very sweet."

"I'm going back to Cuba for at least a while. My mom's getting married in Havana."

"But you are taking your dog. One more wouldn't be too much trouble. When I'm done over there, perhaps, we can meet up or if the two of you have become attached, she can stay with you. I need to be able to trust that Love will have a good home."

"Love?"

"It's not a name I'd normally pick, but she was so loving, it just fit her."

"Love and Hope. It's up to Hope," I said. "Let's go outside. He's getting some exercise with Santana."

Outside, Lieutenant Tarley released Love, who ran over to Hope. Quickly they started playing together.

"I guess Hope's got a friend for the time being."

"Thank you."

"One thing, Lieutenant."

"Yes?"

"Wars are dangerous and innocent civilians too often are shot. Please be careful to survive and also please don't kill any civilians and especially don't kill any kids."

"I'll do my best."

"That's all I can ask."

The flight to Havana was like a party with our close friends and family on board. When we arrived in Cuba, it was time to prepare for the wedding. It was great being able to go back to Cuba without having to look behind our back to see who was chasing us.

We had been on the run for so long that it was unusual not to have someone trying to kill us. A part of me kept wondering if the plane was going to explode. At every jolt, I found myself feeling I was back in the experience of running for my life.

Juanita Martinez knew one of the top dress designers in Cuba. Her name was Lativa Gomez. It only took her two days to alter her most beautiful dress into a wedding gown for my mom.

"I feel like a little girl," my mom said. "I'm so nervous. I hope I'm doing the right thing."

"I like Alonzo, but if he ever starts treating you like Dad, he'll have to deal with me. And Santana will also make sure he stays in line."

My mom laughed. "He's nothing like your dad."

My mom had me give her away. It was cool, a daughter giving away her mom. Emily, Abigail, Shannon and Tiffany were bridesmaids. Santana was Alonzo's best man.

The wedding was outdoors on the lawn of the Presidential Palace in Havana. As she threw the bouquet, I think Mom was hoping I would get it. At sixteen, I knew what I wanted, but I was still a long way from being ready to get married. It was Abigail who caught it. No surprise, it was Bruce who caught the garter.

"I hope that you don't feel bored now that we've survived the camps and everything Deep State threw at us." Santana said.

"I could use a rest. It will be nice to relax before our next adventure."

"Our next adventure? Are you thinking of taking up the President's offer?"

"I doubt it. The country had done a lot of regime changes and thefts of foreign countries. And I don't trust his advisers. We wouldn't want to be working for the kind of bad guys who just finished trying to kill us."

"True."

"I've been thinking about the medical child trafficking they are doing in Arizona and elsewhere, you know, taking kids away from their families to turn over to Big Pharma for experimentation."

He nodded. "That is a serious problem in the U.S. and Big Pharma can be really nasty as we found out in New York. What do you think? We should wait four or five weeks for our next adventure?"

"How about eight? That way we can enjoy the sun and a couple of months of freedom before we wind up running for our lives again. Mom and Alonzo will have a long honeymoon in Vinales and we wouldn't want us to take off before they come back. "

"So, you're game?"

"As long as I get to be with you. Together, forever."

"Together, forever." And with that, he kissed me like it was the first time, but this was the most tender and passionate kiss yet, and I knew that we really would last forever.

Special Bonus: Emily Hattan's Full Speech at the Capitol

"In addition to eliminating these programs, can we also disband the Council on Foreign Relations? The CFR is the biggest terrorist organization on the planet.

"I was thirteen when I was kidnapped in the middle of the night by a bounty hunter and placed in the camp. I learned quickly to be cooperative. Those that weren't cooperative were subjected to the worst of the torture. Some even died. My friend Sonja was gang-raped under the supervision of the counselors and bled to death. What parent pays twenty thousand to seven hundred thousand dollars to have their child gang-raped? It's impossible to believe the parents don't suspect what is coming. If the camps were good places, we wouldn't have to be kidnapped. We'd go willingly. I'd like to see a memorial, a national monument, erected for all those who have died in these programs. Imagine what they would have become if they hadn't died. I'm going to read a partial compilation of names and reported causes of death.

"Geoffrey Vorhies, age thirteen, Chris Scheck, age thirteen, Jonathan Avila, age sixteen, Ashley Shaddox, age fourteen, Chad Franza, age sixteen, Dionte Pickens, age fourteen, Ryan Lewis, age fourteen, Victoria Petersilka, age fourteen, Ian Mulhare, age sixteen, Karlyle Newman, age sixteen, an unknown male of sixteen, and an unidentified boy and girl of unidentified ages died by hanging.

"Brandon Hoffman, age seventeen, Angela Miller, age seventeen, Valerie Heron, age seventeen, Richard DeMaar, age sixteen, Ashlie Bunch, age fifteen, Roger Benson, age fifteen, Benjamin Lolley, age sixteen, Matthew Loebach, age sixteen, an unknown fifteen-year-old girl, an unknown seventeen-year-old teen, and Logan Volpe, age fifteen, died by suicide.

"Philip Williams, Jr., age fifteen, was severely beaten in the *therapeutic* boxing-ring prior to death. Nicholas Grant, age sixteen, was beaten to death. Eric Futelle was murdered by two other teens at his Gulag School. Kiley Jaquays, age seventeen, Jeremy Gualin, age fifteen, Tammy Edmiston and Katherine Lank, age sixteen, fell or were pushed to their deaths. Fatal fight victims included Danny Matthews, age seventeen, Anthony Parker, age sixteen, and Cristian Gonzales, age fifteen."

"Aaron Bacon was beaten, tortured, dehydrated and starved to death at sixteen. Michelle Sutton died from dehydration at fifteen. Gregory Jones, age thirteen, died from a fall after being dehydrated in temperatures exceeding one-hundred degrees for nine and a half hours. Other heat stroke victims included Ian August, age fourteen, and Shanice Nibbs, age seventeen.

"Joy Evans, at seventeen chocked to death. Bryan Jones, age fifteen, died by electrocution. Gina Score, was run to death at the age of fourteen.

"Nicholaus Contreraz, died of cardiac arrest at the age of sixteen after instructors continued to harass him and force him to exercise even though he told them he was sick. He was put into restraints and died.

"Other restraint deaths included Leroy Prinkley, age fourteen, Joshua Ferarini, age thirteen, Wauketta Wallace, age twelve, Roxanna Gray, age seventeen, Diane Harris, age seventeen, Anthony Green, age fifteen, Dawn Perry, age sixteen, Jason Tallman, age twelve, Casey Collier, age seventeen, Thomas Mapes, age seventeen, Jamar Griffiths, age fifteen, Shinaul McGraw, age twelve, Jeffrey Bogrett, age nine, Earl Smith, age nine, Eric Roberts, age sixteen, Bobby Sue Thomas, age seventeen, Rochelle Clayborne, age sixteen, Melissa Neyman, age nineteen, Jimmy Kanda, age sixteen, Chris Campbell, age thirteen, Robert Rollins, age twelve, Sakena Dorsey, age nineteen, Jeffrey Demetrius, age seventeen, Kelly Young, age seventeen, Dustin Phelps, age fourteen, Laura Hanson, age seventeen, Mark Draheim, age fourteen, Andrew McClain, age eleven, Tristan Sovern, age sixteen, Mark Soares, age sixteen, Edith Campos, age fifteen, Kristol Mayon-Ceniceros, age sixteen, Jerry McLaurin, age fourteen, Joshua Sharpe, age seventeen, Michael Ibarra-Wiltsie, age twelve, Sabrina Day, age fifteen, Randy Steele, age nine, Willie Wright, age fourteen, William Lee, age fifteen, Tanner Wilson, age eleven, Stephanie Duffield, age sixteen, Charles Moody, age seventeen, LaTasha Bush, age fifteen, Matthew Goodman, age fourteen, Jamal Odum, age nine, Orlena Parker, age sixteen, Jerry Trivett, age seventeen, Maria Mendoza, age fourteen, Garrett Halsey, age thirteen, Travis Parker, age thirteen, Linda Harris, age fourteen, Shirley Arciskewski, age twelve, Mikie Garcia, age twelve, Martin

Anderson, age fourteen, Joey Alteriz, age sixteen, Angellika Arndt, age seven, Darryl Thompson, age fifteen, Faith Finley, age seventeen, Alexis Richie, age sixteen, Michael Owens, age sixteen, Corey Foster, age sixteen, Joseph Winters, age fourteen, Paige Lunsford, age fourteen, Kenneth Barkley, age fifteen, Shaquan Allen, age sixteen, David Hess, age seventeen, Paul Choy, age fifteen, and Jeremiah Flemming, age fifteen.

"Michael Wiltsie, a sixty-five-pound boy, was suffocated to death at age twelve by a three-hundred-pound "counselor" who sat on him until he stopped breathing. Deaths by medical neglect or malfeasance included those of James Roman, age fourteen, Omar Paisley, age seventeen, Kristen Chase, age sixteen, James White, age seventeen, Roberto Reyes, age fifteen, Candace Newmaker, age ten, Kevin Rider, age fourteen, Katherine Rice, age sixteen, Tony Haynes, age fourteen, Erica Harvey, age fifteen, Autumn Bear, age fifteen, Willie Durden, age seventeen, Dillon Peak, age fourteen, Rocco Magliozzi, age twelve, Alex Cullinane, age thirteen, Caleb Jensen, age fifteen, Brendan Blum, age fourteen, and Dyskeha Streeter, age sixteen.

"Brad Glickman, age fifteen, Connie Munson, age fourteen, Dawn Birnbaum, age seventeen, Lorenzo Johnson, age seventeen, and Astrid Valdivia, age thirteen, died or were murdered (mostly shot) attempting to escape their respective programs.

"Jonathan Lenoff and Peter Cooper, whose ages were not released, died by fire.

"Lyle Foodroy and Robert Erwin, age fifteen, Robert Zimmerman, age seventeen, Charles Lucas, age sixteen, James Lamb, age fourteen, Bernard Reefer, age nineteen, Eric Schibley, age seventeen, Danny Lewis, age sixteen, David Sellers, age fifteen, Shawn Diaz, age fifteen, Ryan McCandless, age thirteen, Joseph Bolt Jr., age seventeen, Carnez Boone, age fourteen, and another unidentified fourteen-year-old girl drowned.

"Deaths by freezing included Joyce Howden and Lorene Larhette, age seventeen, Aaron Grey, age sixteen, and Alex Lansing, age seventeen.

"Dawnne Takeuchi, was killed at eighteen when she was thrown from a semi-truck. Harry Rutledge, age fifteen, Christopher Hill, age seventeen, and Cailin Lee, age fifteen, were run over by trains. Grace James, age seventeen, Daniel Huerta, age seventeen, and Khali Todd, age twelve died in traffic accidents.

"At sixteen, Corey Baines was killed when his head was crushed. Carey Dunn, age fifteen, was killed when building materials fell on her.

"At fifteen, Janaia Barnhart died but the cause could not be determined because of destroyed evidence. Other cases where the causes of death was either covered up or unknown included Mario Cano, age sixteen, Leon Anger, age seventeen, John Garrison, age eighteen, Carlos Ruiz, age thirteen, Matthew Meyers, age unknown, James Shirey, age fourteen. Kasey Warner, age thirteen, Lenny Ortega, age twelve, Elisa Santry, age sixteen, Natalynndria Slim, age seventeen, Sergey Blashchishen, age sixteen, an unidentified fifteen-year-old girl, Levi Snyder, age fifteen, and Del-Quan Seagers, age fifteen.

"This was just a partial list of the deaths that have been reported. Each of these lives and others who died in these programs mattered. I ask the members of Congress to ensure these young Americans will not have died in vain."

ACKNOWLEDGMENTS

This book and the prequel were written in 2017 during the November NaNoWriMo. To my surprise, many of the fictional elements in this book have taken place or become more exposed in more recent years in one form or another, including a flu agenda, vaccine mandates, side effects, assassination attempts on the President, intelligence agencies conducting secret operations without the knowledge of the President, and the attacks by the feds on the free speech of university students.

It was the National Youth Rights Association that brought the deaths, torture and injuries of teens in the behavior modification (Gulag) schools, camps and facilities to my attention. That organization of youth activists has worked for decades to protect and expand the rights of young Americans and to educate the public. Their website can be found at http://www.youthrights.org

There is no place in our society for the torture of children. The fact that elected officials are mostly turning a blind eye to the torture, deaths and abuse in the Gulag programs is indicative of how corrupt and purchased America's elections have become. An exception to elected officials doing nothing to stop the torture was former Congressman George Miller, who held hearings about the programs and got the House of Representatives to pass legislation to regulate them, a bill that died in the U.S. Senate. California and Colorado have attempted to regulate the camps, but such regulation has not stopped the abuses. Teens and pre-teens are regularly sent out of state to these programs, too often never to return.

Young Americans are never given credit for their natural intelligence. A system of dumbing down has overwhelmed the educational systems. John Taylor Gatto, who was formerly New York's Teacher of the Year, warned about the dumbing down process taking place in America's Schools in his books, *The Underground History of American Education* and *Weapons of Mass Instruction*. Instead of creating thinkers, most educational systems are now creating followers and teaching students to stop thinking while the finest professors are being fired for telling forbidden truths. Free speech is now under attack at universities across the country and it's up to all Americans to demand a restoration of integrity and freedom to the system.

Every nine seconds a woman in the USA is assaulted or beaten. Yet, American courts, particularly those in California, routinely give full custody to violent abusers and exclude protective parents from the lives of their children, limiting the protective parents to expensive monitored visits, where any visits are allowed. The absence of the protective parents from the lives of the two main characters in this book is indicative of typical family court injustices. After the protective parent is removed, there is no obstacle or limit to the abuse the children will incur. Every day American children die at the hands of their abusers. The result is that over four-hundred thousand children are abused annually, and over three million children have died at the hands of an violent parent.

Laws on the books don't stop family court injustices as judges, particularly in California, ignore laws on the books and award full custody and all family assets to cold blooded killers and convicted child rapists. California judges and judges elsewhere regularly authorize abusers to terminate medical care for their victims, knowing the likely result will be the death of those victims. If a judge makes a just ruling, the abusers will keep filing requests for orders until a new judge follows the abusers' wishes. Protective parents are lousy organizers while abusers have large organizations and enormous funds ready to ensure violent abusers and rapists almost never lose. America's family injustice courts need to be reformed to protect the lives of children and the lives of protective parents. Judges advocating for abusers from the bench need to be removed.

As noted in the prequel, *Summer Heat, Education: American Gulag-Style*, it is far more dangerous for children under the care of CPS. Seventy percent of all sex trafficked victims come out of CPS and a child is ten times more likely to die under the watch of CPS than under the worst parent.

The late Debbie Lusignan (the Sane Progressive), who was an emergency room nurse and a popular online advocate for Bernie Sanders's 2016 campaign, exposed a great many lies Americans have been told by the media and our government. Before passing away, prematurely, she awakened millions of Americans, encouraging them to look beyond what they are told to believe. Her insights, inspiration and work continue to encourage a great many Americans to do their own research and are also referenced in parts of this book.

I would also like to acknowledge Peace Activist Cindy Sheehan and former representatives Dennis Kucinich, Cynthia McKinney and Ron Paul for educating the public on what is really going on with the wars and agendas our government is financing. All four of these leaders are actively working to bring about peace in the world and save lives.

Rosie de Guzman has my appreciation for editing this book.

Also, while some of the parents in this book were cold, ambitious, abusive, and worse, most parents do love their children and try to protect them. I, myself, had two wonderful parents and I'd like to acknowledge them for the values they taught me.

ALSO BY NATALIE TRIUMPHS

Best Sellers Now Available

Summer Heat: Education: American Gulag Style

Amazon #1 Best Selling Book in Young Adult Schools & Education

Amazon #1 New Release in Teen & Young Adult Politics & Government Fiction

Amazon #1 New Release in Teen & Young Adult Fiction about Parents

After a break-up with her boyfriend, fifteen-year-old Summer Tanner, a survivor of the Family Court Injustice System, finds herself kidnapped and imprisoned in one of America's Gulag Camps, part of a behavior modification system where thousands of teens are taken against their will annually to be "fixed," often returning home in body bags or psychologically damaged for life. There, Summer meets allies, including a new love interest, who, like her, wants to escape and bring an end to America's teen torture programs. But how high up does the corruption of the multi-billion-dollar industry run and how far will the forces in power go to silence Summer and her new friends to keep the truth from coming out?

Kakistocracy of the Technocrats

Amazon Best Seller #1 in Young Adult Politics & Government

Amazon Best Seller #1 in Young Adult Fiction Alternative History

As White House researcher for a non-existent department that oversees a demented robotic President, Karissa James finds herself in the middle of a string of murders, fires, earthquakes, embassy bombings, assassination attempts, bribes, wars and an Administration that can best be described as a Kakistocracy.

Everything

Amazon Best Seller #1 in Human Rights Law,

Amazon Best Seller #1 in Young Adult Adventures and Adventurers

Amazon Best Seller #1 in Young Adults Politics and Government

After the deaths of her parents, Meadow Clarkson finds herself woven into the world of child trafficking, false flags, mass disappearances, rogue government agents and secret government operations. Her primary companions are a two-hundred-and-fifty year old talking dog named Everything and Cal, a mysterious guy who keeps appearing in her life, as Meadow fights to save children from capture and slaughter, to protect her canine companion and other dogs from a dog-killing frenzy that has swept the nation and to discover what has happened to curious people who have suddenly disappeared.

Coming Soon:

Everything II: Meadow, her talking Papillion Everything, Cal and their friends continue their adventure as they work to save the lives of dogs and other animals in a world that will forever be changed by judicial corruption, murders, dognappings and trans-species experimentation. Also coming, the final book in the series is

Everything III: Once again Meadow, Everything, Cal and their friends fight to expose government corruption so extreme that it threatens the future of humanity.

ABOUT THE AUTHOR

Natalie Triumphs is a criminal defense and civil rights attorney, private investigator, investigative journalist and best-selling author. She is a strong advocate for youth rights, for Constitutional rights and for eliminating the NDAA, the Espionage Act and other unconstitutional laws used to target whistleblowers, journalists and truth-tellers. She has fought for protections for domestic violence survivors, for victims of child trafficking and for vulnerable individuals falsely targeted by the criminal justice system. In view of all the deaths and permanent injuries that take place in behavior modification programs, Natalie has encouraged legislators to close down all such programs.